To Bill,

Christmas '

with much affection and
prayers for good crops!

Sarah x

The Complete Vegetable Grower

The
Complete Vegetable Grower

by

W. E. SHEWELL-COOPER

M.B.E., N.D.H., F.L.S., F.R.S.L., D.Litt. Dip.Hort. (Wye)
Fellow and Dr. of the Horticultural College, Vienna
Commandeur du Mérite Agricole (France)
Hon. Director, The Good Gardeners Association

FABER AND FABER LTD
3 Queen Square
London

First published in 1955
by Faber and Faber Limited
3 Queen Street London WC1
First published in this edition 1967
Second edition published in 1973
Reprinted 1974
Printed in Great Britain by
R. Maclehose and Company Limited,
The University Press, Glasgow
All rights reserved

ISBN 0 571 04797 1 (Faber Paper Covered Editions)

Contents

Author's Preface

There is something very exciting indeed in 'Giving Birth' to a book. Never having been a mother, I naturally know nothing about bearing children, but having written forty books on gardening now, I can truthfully say that the excitement and fascination of creating a new book never grows less. First of all the germ of an idea comes to one. Then as you gradually think round it, it starts to take shape. Then notes have to be made. As these are written down the book appears more and more interesting. New ideas come to one thick and fast until with a sigh we realize that the book will be too large if every scheme is to be included!

One's agent then takes charge. The publisher is then approached, and usually speaking, he is most helpful too. He probably has a 'mysterious' gentleman known as—a reader—who knows a great deal about the subject and takes infinite trouble in making the most intelligent suggestions. These mysterious readers are excellent fellows, full of first-class ideas which they pass on to an already enthused author very graciously.

Then comes the great day when the contents pages are typewritten, the chapter headings are set down, and the author's preface duly takes shape. The book is starting to emerge. Files are solemnly made to take the fair copies and the carbon copies separately, and being born an impatient type, this author can hardly wait until the book is finished. It is necessary to go on, and on, and on, until one's poor secretary cries

AUTHOR'S PREFACE

out 'Halt'! Ideas are tumbling over one another so fast, that they cannot be got down on to paper soon enough. How can one get thirty years of hard 'day to day' experience in the vegetable garden into script in a few hours? It's all so impossibly delightful and very thrilling too.

Then when the book is about half written, one finds it necessary to start to collect more materials. What about those gardens that have done some special work on this vegetable or that. What about another visit to the North, to see what is happening there. It is worth while having a conference with the No Digging experts, and to go and see what they have done in their own gardens. This person must be written to—a phone call must be made to that Head Gardener—the book must be full of facts—it must be up-to-date—it must be right.

So the visits are paid, the advice is gratuitously given, the vegetable gardens and allotments are examined in great detail; salient facts such as weights of crops per yard run are noted down. Costs are carefully considered. This must be a factual book to help thousands of men and women—not only to grow more food but to produce better food also. There must be drawings and a good artist must be commissioned who can describe in minute detail graphically what one has in one's mind.

Here indeed is, I believe, a new vegetable book. A book written with conviction. A book which has forgotten all the old wives' fables of the past. A book which has no use for 'mystery' but which is absolutely down to earth. A book which realizes that men and women have little time these days—but what time they have they want to make the utmost use of. A book which is modern in its advice *re* machinery, and yet doesn't hesitate to advise men and women to be better craftsmen. The author will be very disappointed if the book isn't liked and isn't used.

As the result of producing what originally was a 6d. handbook, *Grow Your Own Food Supply* in 1939, literally hundreds of men and women wrote in to say that this work had been invaluable to them. A Duke's daughter found the book so useful that her sister had it bound in calf for her as a Christmas present! The Army found it so useful that at least four Commands used it as the standard work to ensure that the soldiery grew the vegetables as they should. This 6d. book (which towards the end of the war sold for 1s. 6d.) had to be small, but it was the germ of an idea which has blossomed forth, first of all into *The Basic Book of Vegetable Growing*, and now *The Complete Vegetable Grower*.

I am most grateful to Mr. Michael Gibson (who years ago was Head Student at my Horticultural Training Centre), for dotting all the i's and crossing all the t's; while as usual to my efficient secretary, Miss Brenda

AUTHOR'S PREFACE

Harman, I tender my grateful thanks once again for the typing which I should imagine can be very boring!

The Horticultural Training Centre,   W. E. SHEWELL-COOPER
Thaxted.
1955

Briefly revised.
The International Horticultural Advisory Bureau, Arkley, Herts. 1964

Brought up to date.
The Horticultural Training Centre, Arkley. 1972

CHAPTER 1

Vegetables in the Modern Garden

This is the book for the amateur who wants to grow all his own vegetables and so save himself at least £100 a year. I merely quote this figure arbitrarily because this is typical of the amount spent by a family of four, with the normal greengrocer. Of course, it depends on the amount of vegetables that are eaten. My own family of four can easily spend £150 a year because we are great vegetable eaters, and always have two if not three vegetables on the table, in addition to the potatoes.

It isn't only the actual saving in L.S.D., of course, the whole question of tax comes into it as well. A man who is paying say 50p in the £1, and spends £100 a year on vegetables, is really spending £200, whereas if he grows his own he just has to face the small cost of seed, plus the amount of money he may spend on organic fertilizers and tools. The vegetables he produces at home are, of course, of far better value than those he buys. Fresh vegetables are full of vitamins, especially if they've been grown on soil properly manured with compost. Shop-bought vegetables that have been travelling for three or four days have lost much of their 'crispness' and certainly a great deal of the vitamin content.

I refuse to waste my time by saying that vegetable growing is a fascinating hobby. Everybody knows that! I have set my face against the old clichés about working with Mother Nature. There's been far too much said in other books about being 'nearer God's heart in a garden' —one can be near God anywhere—it's a matter of spiritual experience. Let's come away from sentimentalism. Let's be frank and business-like. Is this growing of vegetables really a commercial proposition? Will the family benefit? Can one say that the family budget will be easier to manage? Is vegetable growing a necessity rather than a luxury?

The answer to these questions and statements is, of course—yes—and again yes. There's no doubt about that. The great thing, however, is to get the maximum production with a minimum of effort. The whole idea

17

VEGETABLES IN THE MODERN GARDEN

of this book is to show what can be got out of the smallest plot of land by using a little intelligence, plus some ingenuity. There's going to be no heavy manual labour just for the sake of making a man sweat. The plan isn't to follow out the instructions of the early 1900's just because some old head gardener said it was necessary in those days. Why must you produce a large onion if a larger number of smaller ones are much preferred? Especially as the smaller ones are easier to produce, and don't cause so many heartaches from the point of view of pests and disease.

This then is the book for the amateur on all scales. It's for the man with a prefab garden. It's for the husband and wife with their suburban 'bottom-end'—below the trellis after the lawn finishes! It's for the allotment holder, but it's equally of value to the house owner with a larger garden. Take the man who has to be away at business all day, and is in an important executive position. It may be that he employs some odd-job man, or a chauffeur-gardener. The man may be more of a chauffeur than a gardener and here it is hoped that this book will come in and give the owner of the garden the vision of what can be done, and with this vision, the work can be satisfactorily controlled.

May it be made quite clear that this isn't the book for the commercial market gardener. There's that excellent (I hope) work *Modern Market Gardening for Profit* which I wrote some time ago, which will satisfy him. He knows the importance of keeping up the supply. He is anxious to have his vegetables and salads on the market when the prices are high. He's no fool, and so he uses the maximum of machinery which will ensure that his weeds are kept down, that his crops are sprayed, and that his vegetables are carted from one end of the field to the other at harvesting time with speed.

THOUGHTS ABOUT MECHANIZATION

Mechanization must come in the private garden. I can think as I write of the Deputy Editor of one of our big newspapers, who for years used to spend every weekend mowing his lawns by hand. I suggested and bought for him a motor mower, and as he said, it turned drudgery into a pleasure. Most men like to have a car, rather than bicycle everywhere. Even the cyclists like to have a little motor on the back wheel, because they can keep going without a lot of pedalling. It is curious the way that so many people haven't seen the wisdom of carrying these ideas into the garden. In many cases it is possible to buy the mechanical tools needed on the 'never never' plan, and those who see nothing wrong in buying

18

a motor bicycle or a vacuum cleaner on the deferred payment terms couldn't possibly be embarrassed when purchasing a mechanical hoe under a similar system.

The man who cultivates his garden in his spare time, actually has far more need of all the engineer can offer him, because he must be very economical of his hours. Not only must there be no wastage of energy, but time is so important. It may be for instance that at a particular week-end the soil is in exactly the right condition to be cultivated and pre-pared for seed sowing. He must therefore get the work done quickly. If he waits until the following weekend it may easily be pouring with rain, or at any rate there may have been a heavy rainfall during the week, with the result that the soil is sodden and sticky, and it's just impossible to get the land down to a fine tilth. The market gardener who is on the ground all day may bide his time, but the amateur should be in a position to snatch the few hours which he has in order to get done a tremendous piece of work which it may not be possible to do again for weeks!

Not only does the machine make it possible to do the job just when it ought to be done, but it gives the garden owner more time for the rest of the garden. If one is compelled to be in the vegetable garden every hour that God sends, then it's impossible to keep the flower garden looking well. Furthermore, the great value of mechanization is that one man can cover a greater area. It is said that with hand-work one man can prepare, manure and take care of at least an acre of vegetable garden, together with the care of a fair number of frames or Continuous Cloches, and probably a set of 6-10 Dutch light frames. Give him mechanical aids, machines with which to sow his seeds, a Vibro-hoe to keep down weeds, a rotary cultivator to prepare his ground, a plough attachment to do his digging, and he may be well able to look after an area of three acres.

The point of this argument is that employing a man to cultivate the one acre would at modern figures cost £900 a year, and the vegetables under such circumstances would be dear, even though there would be sufficient say for a family of six or eight. When, however, the garden owner is willing to spend £450 on capital expenditure, the gardener is immediately able to produce three times as much, and therefore the price of the vegetables decreases considerably. It's cheaper therefore to lay out a capital sum on which, say the depreciation will be on the basis of 10 per cent for ten years, than to pay two more gardeners to cultivate a similar acreage by hand.

This argument, of course, is based on the policy of selling locally any vegetables surplus to the requirements of the family. There is no tax levied on small sales of surplus produce and the money can be put into one's pocket with no further ado.

Those, of course, who have larger gardens still and can sell their produce are able to take advantage of rebates from Income Tax because they can convert their gardens as it were into market gardens, and so make legitimate claims against Tax from the Income Tax Commissioners. There's no need to go into further details of this scheme here, but it will be found, for those interested, in my book called *Born Gardeners* which was recently published.

Even those who don't have a market garden must remember that there is neither P.A.Y.E. nor Supertax on normal vegetable production in the garden, and though this factor, of course, varies with the man's income—during the last few years it has always varied upwards. I know a number of men whose families eat new peas at £2 lb. The wife pays 5p for the peas, and he has to pay £1.95 for taxation. In the good days of Mr. Gladstone such a man was able to buy 96p worth of peas before 4p had to go in Income Tax.

THE SIZE OF THE GARDEN

A family of four who want to produce all the vegetables and salads they need (without the luxuries) including potatoes, will need to have an area of ground amounting to 600 square yards—that is a plot of land for instance, 60 yards long and 10 yards wide, or alternatively, of course, 30 yards long and 20 yards wide. A man will have to be very busy to keep such a garden carefully cropped, and clean and free from weeds, without mechanical aids. I estimate it will take him 288 hours a year to get the work done, properly, and this means that he'll have to live near and so get back early enough, and furthermore, sometimes he'll not have to spend long on his tea!

There are two reasons why I always wonder whether it's worth while growing the main crop potatoes (which take 150 sq. yds. out of our 600 and roughly 72 hours from the 288). The first is that there are few gardens which are really large enough to make their cultivation worth while, and the second is that the extra labour needed for the tonnage of potatoes required may be difficult to find. It's preferable, in my opinion, to stick to the growing of the early varieties which are delicious, and more expensive on the whole in the shops, and then to buy the main-crop potatoes, if possible by the cwt. from some local farmer, or even from the retailer himself on a special basis, and then to clamp these 'in bulk' and thus use them as needed throughout the winter.

VEGETABLES IN THE MODERN GARDEN

It obviously pays to grow the more costly vegetables. If the amateur has tomatoes available from under cloches for instance, when they are 12p lb. in the shops, he is saving far more from his home production than if these luscious fruits come into use in the late summer when the prices drop to 3p lb. It pays hand over fist to grow lettuces when they are 5p or more each in the winter, spring, or early summer, it hardly pays to produce hundreds of them, as many do, when they are of no value at all in mid-summer. The chapter dealing with the cultivation of the vegetables makes this point clear. The whole slant is in the direction of production at the right time, plus continuity of supply.

Those who have wives who enjoy experiments in cooking and who like new flavours, and who appreciate variety in diet, will, of course, grow a number of the unusual vegetables, and thus have for the table, crops that are impossible to buy in the normal shops. Chapter 10 makes this evident. Here are delicious dishes which may be extremely expensive to buy, and so are the best value, not only from a cash point of view, but from the interest value as well.

A suggested Cropping Plan for 600 sq. yds.

The Cropping Plan has been worked out on the basis of supplying a family of four people with vegetables all the year round. This would include potatoes, green vegetables and other vegetables. The land required for the plan as it stands, would be about 600 sq. yds. or an eighth of an acre. It is very difficult to estimate, of course, the probable produce from a small plot, on which a number of different crops are being grown, as so many factors have to be taken into consideration, for example, to name but two, the condition of the ground and the local rainfall, but all in all, provided that the plot is skilfully cultivated, properly enriched with compost and that the best use is made of the ground, a family of four should live well off it.

Man Hours

Before anybody starts a job it is a good thing to have a rough idea of how long it is going to take, and basing the estimate on practical experience it is possible to say that about 288 hours would have to be put in to cultivate the plot. This may seem rather a fearsome total, but broken down it has quite a different aspect. The period from the beginning of March to the end of June is the one in which the most attention has to be paid to the vegetable garden and about ten hours a week would have to be put in, that is to say about two hours five evenings a week. If the garden is clean by the end of June, then things can be

21

taken more easily in July, August and September, with about six hours a week, followed by five hours a week in the shorter days of October and November in order to get most of the digging done. During the two months of December and January, practically no cultivation would be done, and the time spent would be about one hour every week for the picking or cutting of crops. In February with the weather getting better, perhaps two hours a week would be sufficient. Over the year this would mean an average of five and a half hours per week, which is not very much when one considers the return of about seventy-five pounds' worth of vegetables.

Looking at the matter objectively and disregarding the fact of whether you get any pleasure out of gardening or not, it certainly pays to grow your vegetables when you can do all, or the major part of the work yourself, but it is rather different when a jobbing or part-time gardener has to be employed. If it was possible to arrange that the jobbing gardener came only when you wanted him for the exact hours that you required at different times of the year, then you could say that you wanted a man for 288 hours a year at say 50p per hour. It is not as easy as that, however, as it is very likely that when a man comes for ten hours a week in the summer, he will want to be employed for about ten hours a week during the winter months as well. This would put up the cost of growing the vegetables considerably. That would be looking at the matter from the worst possible angle, however, and would not be taking into account the fact that so many of the part-time gardeners nowadays are five-day-week factory workers, who are glad of a Saturday morning's or afternoon's work in the summer months, but do not need the work or would rather go to the football match in the winter. Going back to the figure of 288 hours in the year at 50p per hour, this would mean an expenditure of £144 on labour for a return of seventy-five pounds' worth of vegetables.

Value Returned

The figure of seventy-five pounds has been given as the approximate value of the crop, which can be produced from a twenty-rod plot of ground. This figure has been arrived at by working out the estimated yield of each crop and valuing it at an average retail price. Retail prices are bound to vary from year to year and from district to district, but it is hoped that the rates used will give a fairly true picture over a number of years, without taking into account any abnormal fluctuations. In the same way, it is well-known that a high price can be asked for the first of the crop, such as the first new peas or potatoes, and that the price soon drops when the novelty has worn off, but this has been taken into consideration.

In addition to the variation of prices, there is the very large variation in personal taste with regard to vegetables; some people may only want greens and potatoes, while others may never eat cabbage and want a lot of spinach during the winter months. The aim in the plan has been to produce a reasonable variety of vegetables throughout the year, without the aid of any greenhouse, cloches or frames, so that an average family of four people can have all the vegetables they need, with sufficient quantities of Vitamin C, without getting sick of the same old thing day after day. Remember that it has been found that a plot of one-sixth of an acre can produce sufficient for a family of four. The working-out has *not* been done the other way round, i.e., could a plot of one-sixth of an acre produce enough for a family of four? Thus if any particular month is selected, let us say January, for example, a typical vegetable menu for the week would be as follows:

1st day. Midday meal. Potatoes, Brussels Sprouts, Onions.
Evening meal. Salsify.
2nd day. Midday meal. Potatoes, Carrots.
Evening meal. Celery.
3rd Day Midday meal. Potatoes, Cabbage, Onions.
Evening meal. Broccoli.
4th day. Midday meal. Potatoes, Sprouts.
Evening meal. Leeks.
5th day. Midday meal. Potatoes, Parsnips.
Evening meal. Spinach.
6th day. Midday meal. Potatoes, Broccoli.
Evening meal. Celery.
7th day. Midday meal. Potatoes, Swedes.
Evening meal. Cabbage.

In addition although potatoes have only been included for one meal a day, there should be enough for both the meals most days of the week; in the same way there is enough cabbage grown for at least four meals a week, should any family particularly like cabbage!

During the early summer months when growth in the vegetable garden is at its maximum, there will obviously be more of a choice and two vegetables besides potatoes for most meals, if required.

CHART SHOWING RETURNS IN CASH *

Crop	Quantity of Seeds and Plants required	Time of Sowing	Number of Rows 30 ft. each	Distance between Rows	Distance between Plants	Time of Harvesting	Estimated Crop Yield	Value of Crop £ p
1st Rotation. Peas and Beans								
Peas (a) 1st Early	½ pt.	Nov. or Feb.	1	In drills 6 in. wide. Seed 2 in. apart. Rows 2 ft. apart		June	8 lb. @ 7p	0·56
2nd Early	2 pts.	March–April	4	As above but seed 3 in. apart		June–July	32 lb. @ 5p	1·60
Maincrop and Late	2½ pts.	May–June	5	As above but seed 3 in. apart		Aug.–Sept.	40 lb. @ 3p	1·20
Beans								
Broad	½ pt.	Nov. or Mar. again April	2	2 ft.	6 in.	May–June, July–Aug.	36 lb. @ 2p	0·72
Dwarf French	½ pt.	May and June	2	18 in.	Double Row 8 in.	July–Oct.	75 lb. @ 3p	2·25
Runner	½ pt.	May and June	2	6 ft.	8 in.	July–Oct.	84 lb. @ 3p	2·52
2nd Rotation. Greens								
Broccoli (1)	Small pkt.	End Mar.	1	2 ft.	2 ft.	Sept.–Nov.	15 heads @ 6p	0·90
(2)	Small pkt.	Early Apr.	1	2 ft.	2 ft.	Dec.–Feb.	15 heads @ 6p	0·90
(3)	Small pkt.	Early Apr.	1	2 ft.	2 ft.	Mar.–Apr.	15 heads @ 6p	0·90
(4)	Small pkt.	Early Apr.		2 ft.	2 ft.	May–June	15 heads @ 6p	0·90
Brussels Sprouts	Medium pkt.	Mar.–Apr.	6	3 ft.	3 ft.	Sept.–Mar.	104 lb. @ 3p	3·42
Cabbage								
Summer	Small pkt.	March	½	2 ft.	2 ft.	June–Aug.	7 heads @ 3p	0·21
Autumn	Small pkt.	April	1	2 ft.	2 ft.	Oct.–Dec.	15 heads @ 3p	0·45
Winter	Small pkt.	May	½	2 ft.	2 ft.	Jan.–Feb.	7 heads @ 3p	0·21
Savoy Early	Small pkt.	May	1	2 ft.	2 ft.	Oct.–Dec.	15 heads @ 3p	0·45
Savoy Late	Small pkt.	May	1	2 ft.	2 ft.	Jan.–Mar.	15 heads @ 3p	0·45
Cauliflower	Small pkt.	Apr.–May	1	2 ft.	2 ft.	Sept.–Oct.	15 heads @ 6p	0·90

Sprouting Broccoli								
Early purple	Small pkt.	1	April	2 ft.	2 ft.	Feb.–Mar.	16 lb. @ 2p	0·32
Late purple	Small pkt.	1	May	2 ft.	2 ft.	Apr.–May	16 lb. @ 2p	0·32
Spinach								
Summer	1 oz.	½	March	1 ft.	8 ins.	May–June	18 lb. @ 3p	0·54
Winter	½ pt.	½	May	1 ft.	8 ins.	July–Aug.	48 lb. @ 6p	2·88
or		2	August	1 ft.	8 ins.	Oct.–Mar.	42 lb. @ 3p	1·26
Spinach Beet	2 oz.	1	April, July	18 in.	8 in.	July on, Winter and Spring	42 lb. @ 3p	1·26
3rd Rotation. Roots								
Beetroot Early	Med. pkt.	½	Apr.–May	1 ft.	4 in.	June and July onwards	20 lb. @ 4p	0·80
Late	1 oz.	1	May	1 ft.	6 in.	October	40 lb. @ 3p	1·20
Carrots								
Early	⅛ oz.	1	March	1 ft.	Sow thin	June–July	8 bunches @ 5p	0·40
Maincrop	¼ oz.	1	Apr.–May	1 ft.	6 in.	Sept. on	80 lb. @ 2p	1·60
Parsnips	1 pkt.	2	Feb.–Mar.	18 in.	9 in.	Sept. on	24 lb. @ 2p	0·48
Turnips								
Early	⅛ oz.	½	April	1 ft.	6 in.	June	8 lb. @ 3p	0·24
Maincrop	⅛ oz.	½	May	1 ft.	6 in.	July–Aug.	8 lb. @ 1p	0·08
Swedes	½ oz.	2	May–June	18 in.	1 ft.	Sept. on	64 lb. @ 2p	1·28
Salsify	1 pkt.	1	April	1 ft.	9 in.	Nov. on	48 roots @ 1p	0·48
4th Rotation								
Celery	Small pkt.	1	Feb. (under glass)	1 ft.	1 ft.	Nov. on	30 heads @ 6p	1·80
Celeriac	Small pkt.	1	Feb. (under glass)	1 ft.	1 ft.	Sept. on	30 roots @ 2p	0·60
Leeks	Med. pkt.	2	March	15 in.	4 in.	Sept.–May	72 lb. @ 3p	2·16
Maize (Sweet Corn)	Pkt.	1	May	3 ft.	2 ft.	Aug.–Sept.	16 cobs @ 7p	1·12
Onions (Bulb)								
Autumn sown	⅛ oz.	1	August	1 ft.	8 in.	July–Aug.	30 lb. @ 3p	0·90
Spring sown	1 oz.	6	Feb.–Mar.	1 ft.	8 in.	Aug.–Sept.	90 lb. @ 3p	2·70
Onions (Salad)	Small pkt.	½	August, Feb.–Mar.	1 ft.	Thinly	April, June–July	24 bunches @ 3p	0·72

Crop	Seed / Plants	Sowing		Rows apart	Plants apart	Harvest / Use	Crop	Value
Potatoes								
Early	14 lb.	Feb.–Mar.	4	2 ft.	1 ft.	June–July	120 lb. @ 4p	4·80
2nd Early	28 lb.	April	7	2 ft.	15 in.	August	28/280 lb. @ 12p stone	2·40
Maincrop	28 lb.	April	8	27 in.	18 in.	Sept. on	33/336 lb. @ 12p stone	2·88
Shallots	1 lb.	February	½	1 ft.	6 in.	July–Aug.	10 lb. @ 3p	0·30
Salads								
Cucumber (Ridge)	6 plants or Small pkt.	Apr. (under glass)	½	2 ft.	2 ft.	August September	24 @ 3p each	0·72
Lettuce								
Summer	¼ oz. succession	Mar.–July	8 × ½	1 ft.	10 in.	June–Sept.	120 @ 3p	3·60
Cos	Small pkt.	Apr.–May	2 × ½	1 ft.	6 in.	July–Aug.	60 @ 3p	1·80
Winter	Small pkt.	Aug.–Sept.	½	1 ft.	10 in.	May	12 @ 3p	0·36
Tomatoes	18 plants or Small pkt. seed	April (under glass)	1	2 ft.	20 in.	August October	90 lb. @ 3p	2·70
Endive	Small pkt.	July–Aug.	2 × ¼	1 ft.	15 in.	Nov.–Feb.	24 @ 6p	1·44
Radish								
Summer	1½ oz.	Mar.–Sept.	6 × ¼	1 ft.	Thinly	April–Oct.	30 bunches @ 2p	0·60
Winter	¼ oz.	August	½	1 ft.	8 in.	Winter	8 lb. @ 2p	0·16
Other Crops								
Asparagus	8 plants	End May	½	4 ft.	2 ft.	April–May	8 bunches @ 11p	0·88
Rhubarb	6 roots			4 ft.	3 ft.	March	30 lb. @ 3p	0·90
Vegetable Marrow	4 plants or Small pkt. seed			4 ft.	3 ft.	August–Oct.	24 @ 3p	0·72

* These figures are at their minimum. The crop weights could be higher and the value considerably higher.

VEGETABLES IN THE MODERN GARDEN

Detailed and exhaustive instructions for the growing of any particular crop in the plan will be found in the relevant chapter later, varieties are recommended and there should be no difficulty in finding out how to grow anything, but for the sake of convenience a rough analysis of the plan is given below.

The crops have been divided into a four-course rotation in order to get the maximum economical use of the ground and to provide for an integrated system of manuring and liming. The first rotation consists of peas and beans, which need some manure, and a little lime, the second rotation consists of brassicas or greens, which need a lot of lime and a reasonable amount of manure, the third rotation consists of roots, which need no manure and no lime, and the fourth rotation of potatoes, celery, leeks and onions, which need heavy manuring and no lime. Lettuce and radish can be grown as catch-crops, vegetable marrows and ridge cucumbers in odd corners, while rhubarb and asparagus are, of course, fixed.

Peas are always very popular so quite a quantity has been allowed for. Ten rows may seem a lot, but you don't usually get many peas off a row and there is nothing worse than not having enough to go round. One of the best ways of having a good succession of peas is by sowing a good variety such as 'Kelvedon Wonder' every two weeks from early *March* until late July.

Broad Beans are an easy crop to grow, but unluckily quite a lot of people are not very fond of them. They make a good alternative vegetable, and now that bacon is off the ration may become more popular.

Dwarf French beans and runner beans form the mainstay of the summer vegetables from late June until October. In the plan considerable quantities of each are budgeted for, but those people who unhappily like one but not the other, will just have to grow more of the one they prefer. Both can be salted for use during the winter months.

Greens. All the crops mentioned under greens, with the exception of spinach, are sown in a seed bed and transplanted to their final position.

Cauliflowers. Only late summer cauliflowers have been included, as the earlier cauliflowers have to be sown in a cold frame or in heat. The latter also mature when there are a number of other vegetables ready.

Broccoli. A good succession of broccoli has been planned in order to produce at least one head a week for most of the time from October to the following May or June.

Brussels sprouts. Most people prefer brussels sprouts to cabbage, so it is advisable to ensure a good steady supply over the winter months. If three varieties are used and sown in succession in March and April, it should be possible to have sprouts from September to February.

Cabbages and Savoys have been included in the plan as they are a never-failing supply of greenstuffs during the winter. If they are cooked well, the result should be very different from the foreigner's idea of the traditional boiled and tasteless English vegetable. Summer cabbage is entirely optional and should only be grown by those who like it, as there are other vegetables available at that season.

Spinach is very useful. For those who want an easy vegetable, cropping over most of the year, providing that it is sown twice a year, spinach beet is the answer. Summer spinach is inclined to bolt, though winter spinach is less difficult. As far as the quantities in the plan are concerned, if summer and winter spinach are grown, then spinach beet need not be and vice versa.

Beetroot. Early beet is young and tender and takes but little time to cook, but late beet stored over the winter needs a lot of boiling, and it is only fair to say that the cost of the gas or electricity should be taken into account, against buying it ready cooked from the greengrocer.

Carrots. Fresh young carrots from the garden taste twice as nice as those bought. All carrots should be sown thinly, but opinions differ as to whether the late varieties should be thinned to four or six inches.

Parsnips are a good stand-by over the winter months. They are best sown in stations, that is two or three seeds every nine inches apart.

Turnips make quite a pleasant change from time to time during the summer, while swedes are most useful over the winter, as they can be left in the ground until required.

Salsify is not commonly grown, but there is no reason why it should not be included in the cropping plan, as it is quite easy to grow and provides an alternative vegetable during the 'difficult' winter months. It is like a small parsnip and can be left in the ground until it is needed.

Celery plants will have to be bought, where facilities do not exist for sowing the seeds in warmth in February or March. Celery can be sown in the open in April, but it does not provide much of a crop. They are planted out in June.

Celeriac or turnip-rooted celery provides an alternative root vegetable in the autumn. The seed is sown in warmth in February or March and it is planted out in June. As it is not a very common vegetable it may be a bit difficult to obtain the plants, if they cannot be raised at home.

Leeks are easy to grow and, provided that the family likes them, should never be left out. They are sown in a seed bed in March and planted out in June–July. A different variety for each row would give more of a succession.

Sweet corn has been included as it is becoming quite popular in this country, and in most summers, if sown in the open about the middle of May, will mature and produce quite a good crop.

Onions. Autumn-sown onions are sown in drills in August and planted out in March. Spring-sown onions are sown in March where they are to mature and are used for winter storing, thus a greater quantity has been allowed for in the plan.

Salad onions or spring onions are sown either in August or in February–March. They are pulled when young for eating with salads.

Potatoes. Provision has been made for enough potatoes to be grown to supply an average family of four for a year, on the basis of 2 lb. per day. The question of whether it is worth while growing main crop potatoes is discussed later.

Shallots. These often do well along the edge of a path and can be used as pickling onions. They are usually grown from small seed bulbs which are bought by the pound.

Cucumbers—ridge. It is best that the seeds should be sown in April under glass for planting out at the end of May, or, of course, the plants can be bought from a nurseryman. On the other hand it is possible to sow in the open in early June, by putting three seeds under an inverted jam jar.

Lettuce usually forms a very large part of our summer vegetable diet and a lettuce a day has been allowed for from June to September, inclusive. It is important to maintain a succession by sowing the next batch as the previous one is showing through the ground. With the use of cloches it is possible to have lettuces in nearly every month of the year, except January and February. The cos lettuce have been included to provide a slight variation from the cabbage type.

Tomatoes. Where facilities are available seed should be sown in gentle heat in early April for planting out at the end of May, otherwise plants can be bought very easily from a nurseryman. The average price of a pound of tomatoes has been kept down as when tomatoes are available in the garden, the price usually comes down with a bang at the greengrocer's.

Endive is not grown to any great extent in this country, but it does provide a low calorie value green salad from the garden during the winter. If no cloches or frames are available, the endive can be blanched[1] by putting an old tile over the plant.

[1] Blanched here means turned yellow-white as the light is kept from the leaves.

29

Radishes have been included to provide a little variety and colour in the salad bowl. It is important to sow summer radishes in small quantities every fortnight or so, as they are best when grown quickly and soon become unpalateable if allowed to get old and big. Winter radishes are much larger and are more frequently grown on the Continent. They are lifted in November or December, and stored in sand until needed. They can be served sliced as a salad, or boiled like turnips.

Asparagus. A small bed is not much trouble to look after and a few bunches in April and May are always very welcome. It need not be considered a luxury crop. The plants are best bought in when two-year-olds.

Rhubarb. Not every one cares for rhubarb and it certainly has very little vitamin value, but it usually makes a welcome change in March and April. If cooked with syrup it tends to lose some of its tartness. Crowns should be planted in March.

Vegetable marrow. The seeds can be sown in pots in April for planting out at the end of May, or the plants can be bought from a nurseryman. The seed can also be sown, however, in the open ground towards the end of May, and are better if started under an inverted jam jar. Marrows are best when eaten small and there are many attractive ways of cooking them.

A standard row of 30 ft. in length has been chosen as being the most convenient, as so many allotments, gardens or strips are about 30 ft. wide. For such crops as endive, will be found the figures $2 \times \frac{1}{2}$, these figures being meant to indicate that a half-row of endive should be sown at a time for succession—one half-row in July, another half-row in August.

Main Crop Potatoes or Not

Having made a plan it is possible to argue for hours whether one should grow more of this or less of that, or less of this and more of that, and naturally personal taste and preference may necessitate a certain amount of minor alterations, such as cutting out the French beans and growing nothing but runners, or vice versa. There is one crop, however, on which it is possible to have a certain measure of agreement. Nearly every family eats quite a lot of potatoes, and for an average, the figure of $\frac{1}{4}$ lb. per head per day has been taken. Potatoes unluckily do take up rather a lot of space, and it is reckoned that a quarter of the plot, i.e. about 150 sq. yds., must be given over to them if the family are going to have sufficient for the year. In addition they do require quite a considerable amount of cultivation, what with preparing the ground, planting, hoeing, moulding-up, and harvesting. This cultivation is all done mechanically by the farmer who grows potatoes on a large scale, with the result that main crop potatoes can be bought comparatively cheaply during the winter months, the average fixed price per stone being about 15p, and, of course, they are even cheaper when bought by the cwt. The total value of all the potatoes produced in the cropping plan, including the earlies, second earlies and main crop, comes to £10, against which, in the case of a jobbing gardener, must be counted the cost of labour, and in any case the cost of the seed.

It has been estimated that the total amount of hours to be put into the complete plot in a year is 288, so something in the region of seventy-two hours may have to be put in for growing potatoes, which occupy a quarter of the plot. Seventy-two hours at 50p per hour would be £36, on to which must be added about 40p for the cost of the seed.

In this calculation all the potatoes have been lumped together, but the earlies by themselves present quite a different picture. On an average they cost about 6d. per lb. to buy and only four rows would be needed to produce a yield to the value of about £4; certainly nothing like twenty-four hours' work would have to be put in for the earlies and the cost of the seed would only be about 38p. On top of this as far as taste goes, there is not much difference between a farm potato and one from your own clamp, but there is any amount of difference between your own new potatoes and those you buy from the greengrocer.

To sum up, it would seem that if any main item is going to be dropped from the plan, owing perhaps to there not being enough ground available, or perhaps not enough labour, then second early and main crop potatoes could be omitted. Outside of late potatoes there is little that cannot without argument be best grown in the garden. Late beetroot has been mentioned, but here so much depends on the cooking medium, for instance, even an old beet can be cooked quite quickly in a pressure cooker, or if there is a continuous burning stove such as an 'Aga' then there is no extra expense in boiling your own beet.

VARIATION WITHOUT VEXATION

It has already been mentioned that the plan has been based on the average requirements for a family of four and consideration has naturally had to be taken of the very conservative ideas of the British housewife, and her husband, with regard to vegetables. It is difficult to deny that the average Briton prefers to go on eating the same old vegetables cooked in the same old way, year in year out. The menu, however, can

VEGETABLES IN THE MODERN GARDEN

SUGGESTED LAY-OUT OF CROPS IN CROPPING PLAN

On a Four-Course Rotation For A
Garden of About 600 Square Yards

			No. of 30-ft. rows	Space Required
38 ft.	PLOT A Peas and Beans	Runner Beans	2	12 ft.
		Peas in succession	10	20 ft.
		Broad Beans	2	3 ft.
		Dwarf French Beans	2	3 ft.
51 ft.	PLOT B Greens	Cabbage Summer	¼	
		Broccoli Autumn	1	2½ ft.
		Broccoli Early Spring	1	2½ ft.
		Broccoli Spring	1	2½ ft.
		Broccoli Late	1	2½ ft.
		Broccoli Sprouting Feb.–March	1	2½ ft.
		Broccoli Sprouting Late	1	2½ ft.
		Brussels Sprouts	6	18 ft.
		Cabbage Autumn	1	2 ft.
		Cabbage Winter	1	2 ft.
		Savoys Early	1	2 ft.
		Savoys Late	1	2 ft.
		Cauliflowers Summer	1	2 ft.
		Cauliflowers Autumn	1	2 ft.
	either {	Spinach Summer	1	1 ft.
		Spinach Winter	2	2 ft.
	or	Spinach Beet	2	3 ft.

VEGETABLES IN THE MODERN GARDEN

			No. of 30-ft. rows	Space Required
41 ft. 3 in.	PLOT C Roots and Main Crop Potatoes	Parsnips	2	3 ft.
		Beetroot Early	1	1 ft.
		Beetroot Late	1	1 ft.
		Carrots Early	1	1 ft.
		Carrots Main Crop	2	2 ft.
		Salsify	1	1 ft.
		Turnips Early	½	1 ft.
		Turnips Main Crop	2	2 ft.
		Swedes	2	3 ft.
		Sweet Corn	1	6 ft.
		*Potatoes Main Crop	9	20 ft. 3 in.
36 ft. 1 in.	PLOT D Early and 2nd Early Potatoes	Early Potatoes Followed by 1 row Spring Cabbage and 2 rows Leeks	4	8 ft.
		2nd Early Potatoes	7	14 ft. 7 in.
		Celery Trench	15 in. wide	3 ft.
		Celeriac	1	1 ft. 6 in.
		Onions Spring-sown	6	6 ft.
		Onions Salad Shallots	½ ⎫ ½ ⎭	1 ft.
		Onions Autumn-sown	2	2 ft.
17 ft.	Piece of Garden not in Rotation used for Fixed and Miscellaneous Crops, Compost Heap, etc.	Seed Bed	3	3 ft.
		Cucumbers Vegetable Marrows	½ ⎫ ½ ⎭	3 ft.
		Tomatoes	1	2 ft.
		Asparagus (3 ft. row and 2 ft. path)	1	5 ft.
		Rhubarb 2 Compost Heaps 6 ft. × 4 ft.	½ ⎫ ⎭	4 ft.

be varied considerably by a few, what might be termed uncommon vegetables. Salsify and celeriac have been included in the plan, as their seed is readily available and they are very easy to grow. Salsify, nick-named 'The Vegetable Oyster', is very tasty, especially when cooked in batter in the same way as sausage in Toad-in-the-Hole; celeriac has a delightful flavour of celery, but is eaten as a root vegetable. There are a number of other such vegetables, which will be dealt with in a chapter of their own, which are usually absolutely unobtainable from the local greengrocer, but which do help to vary the diet.

Without growing anything uncommon it is possible to create a varia-tion by cooking the common or ordinary vegetables in unusual ways. There are probably over 300 ways of cooking potatoes, but how often are they served as anything, but fried, roast, mashed or boiled, usually boiled! French or runner beans can be served in a number of different ways, so that there should be no remarks such as 'Didn't we have that yesterday'? It is generally the initial effort of following a new recipe which is the stumbling block, but once that effort has been made it is much easier when the recipe is used for a second time, and it is certainly more beneficial to your health and your pocket to provide a variety of different dishes from vegetables in your own garden, rather than to attempt to vary the menu by the purchase of expensive canned or im-ported produce. Canned peas for four will cost something like 1s. 6d., as against 'Chou-fleur à la polonaise', made with a broccoli grown by your-self, which will cost you nothing more than a fraction of the total effort you have put into your garden, and maybe about one-tenth of a penny for the cost of the seed.

The working of rotation schemes is mentioned in detail in Chapter 4.

It will be noticed that lettuces have not been specifically mentioned in this plan, the intention being that they are grown as catch-crops or inter-crops, and thus they do not interfere with the main scheme, the same applying to endive (if grown), or radishes. Winter radish, if grown, should be among the root crops. Use parsley as an edging-plant.

The four plots are roughly, but not exactly, the same in size; the plot for greens to carry the family over the winter being slightly larger than the others. In order to balance the plots, *main crop potatoes and sweet corn have been included with the roots. Potatoes in the same way as root crops, do not require an application of lime, but on the other hand benefit from manuring.

A small seed bed, but large enough, however, to raise the necessary brassica plants has been included in the odd piece of garden. There is no reason though why this should not be moveable, together with the

* See page 33.

tomatoes, cucumbers, vegetable marrows, though you should keep the tomatoes well away from the potatoes, which are of the same family and suffer from some of the same diseases. It is always best to have two compost heaps going at the same time—have them where it suits you best, remembering that they should always be near at hand, so that they are convenient for depositing your waste vegetable matter and also for fetching the finished compost for application to the garden.

CHAPTER 2

Soils, Tools and Mechanical Cultivations

SOILS

It is customary in books on vegetable gardening to dilate in detail on soils. After all, the average reader of this book will have to cope with the particular soil that he is blessed with in his garden. It's not much use, therefore, telling the man with the heavy clay what he ought to do with sand, or vice versa. There are, however, one or two general instructions that it will be worth while stating clearly. In the first place, all soils are greatly improved by the addition of organic matter. (See Chapter 3.) If it's the light sand then it needs the humus badly to hold the particles together and to make it less droughty. If it's the heavy clay, then it needs opening up, and it's only bulky organic matter that can do this properly. The only type of soil that doesn't need organic manuring perhaps is the peaty soil, and this needs lime, plus organic fertilizers.

In the case of the heavy clay soils, it does help greatly if some form of draining can be ensured. It's very difficult in a small garden to get the excess water away, and the only thing that can be done under such circumstances is to have what may be described as a square well in the lowest corner of the garden, and arrange for the agricultural drain pipes to feed this. The drawing opposite shows what I have in mind quite clearly. The drain pipes will be buried at about 18 in. down, or better still just above the impervious layer of soil which prevents the excess moisture from seeping through. There must be a very slight fall down to the point of exit, and the drain pipes should be covered with a 2-in. layer of clinkers to prevent the clay from sealing up the joints in between the pipes.

Unfortunately, when new houses are built, builders don't always take much notice of the agricultural drains that have been put in by farmers. The result is that these may be broken up during the excavations for the

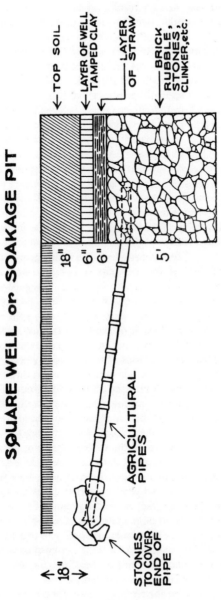

SQUARE WELL or SOAKAGE PIT

TOP SOIL

LAYER OF WELL TAMPED CLAY

LAYER OF STRAW

BRICK RUBBLE, STONES, CLINKER, etc.

18"

6"

6"

5'

18"

AGRICULTURAL PIPES

STONES TO COVER END OF PIPE

footings of the house, and the result may easily be that because the original drains had no outlet, that the garden concerned is a regular quagmire. Fortunately, this doesn't always happen. Fortunately, it isn't all gardens that need draining. Sometimes—and this is especially true in the country—it's possible to get the drain pipes running down into ditches and thus to save having to dig out the well.

Drainage is such a specialized subject that it is well worth while consulting the County Land Drainage Officer before any work is done. He is a busy man and he won't be particularly interested, naturally, in small gardens, but many of these experts are anxious to do all they can to help and at least have leaflets available which are of value. The whole point is that many is the heavy clay that has been greatly improved and made easier to work when some are kept and drainage has been carried out.

The second point about heavy clay is that it is always improved if it can be ridged up in the autumn or early winter and left rough. Frosts can pulverize heavy land far better than man, and far more cheaply too! Get the land into a really rough condition before the winter sets in and it doesn't take long to fork it down to a tilth in the spring. Make the frost and the cold winds work for you—and so save time and labour. Don't get on to a heavy clay once you've dug it, or ploughed it, and left it rough in the winter. Leave it alone for nature to do its work.

Some gardening writers have suggested that clay soils may be made more workable by the addition of sand, but it must be clearly understood that this would be quite uneconomic for the one-sixteenth of an acre plot. You would need 50 tons of sand to do any good, and it would take a very long time to work this quantity of sand into the soil, for it would roughly be a layer 8 in. deep all over the ground. Don't worry your head about trying to improve the ground with ashes or other matter. Use plenty of well-rotted compost, wool shoddy, or other similar organic material. Lime the surface of the ground, for this will help to open it up, and be sure to do the winter digging or ploughing.

Those who have sandy soils will think they are lucky because they can work them at any time of the year. Furthermore, they will warm up quickly in the spring, and so produce earlier crops than the clay soil. What a nuisance, however, they are in the summer, for they dry out very quickly indeed. They need large quantities of well-rotted compost dug or ploughed in each year. Quantities amounting to two 2-gallon bucketfuls to the sq. yd. They usually are lacking in phosphates and potash as well, and they will much appreciate, therefore, the addition of a fish fertilizer with a 10 per cent potash content.

Sandy soils haven't got the retentive power for plant food quite in the same way as clays, and so there may quite easily be a steady loss of such plant foods as potash, nitrates, and lime in the drainage water. This is why sandy soils are always described as hungry. They need to be fed far more than clays. They appreciate overhead irrigation, and mulches of sedge peat, and similar fine organic matter.

Just a word to the town and city dweller. He may have a heavy soil, but this is poisoned year after year by deposits from chimneys which are belching out fumes, hour after hour. It has been estimated that each year in London 14 lb. of extraneous matter are deposited on each sq. ft. of soil. Therefore in town gardens the liming is extremely important, for this can help to level up the sulphate deposits. Whereas in a country garden one might need 4 or 5 oz. of hydrated lime, it's a question of using $\frac{1}{2}$ lb. per sq. yd. in towns and cities.

The great bugbear, however, of the town garden are the trees. Invariably some neighbour has a towering sycamore, which causes infinite trouble. First of all it shades the land, and the plants cannot grow properly because they lack sunshine. Secondly its roots creep under the fence or wall and they rob the soil of plant foods, and of all the moisture. The more you feed the land, the more do the roots come in from round about. The more you water—the more do the roots seem to congregate in your garden.

One has got to face up to it, that very little efficient vegetable growing can possibly be done under trees. Of course, if the tree is yours it must be felled. Fortunately, there are firms to-day who can extract trees as neatly from London gardens as dentists take out teeth. If you want to produce your own vegetables, and you live in a town, get rid of the big trees immediately. If, however, the tree is next door, then all you can do is to carry out definite lopping. The law of the land allows you to cut off any branches that overhang your garden. Ask the man next door to cut off the branches first, and if he doesn't wish to do this, tell him that you are going to do so.

TOOLS AND THEIR USES

Every year there seems to be a spate of new gadgets which the inventor hopes the keen gardener will buy. Some of these gadgets are useful in the hands of intelligent men and women, and others are far too weak to be of any value. Most manufacturers should make these 'garden helps' three times as strong if they are really to do the work they are intended to. They are made, presumably, of light weight iron or steel so that they may sell more cheaply. It's never worth while wasting one's money on dud ideas. Stick to the main tools which are needed in the garden, and buy implements made of good steel, which will last, even if they do cost more.

If you buy good tools it is very important to keep them clean. Some readers will hate my saying this! I try and make all my students have what we call 'a little man' in their pockets or slung on their belts. This is a small piece of wood shaped as in the drawing, and which has a sharp chisel-like edge. This 'little man' is excellent for getting the mud off spades or forks, and other tools. It doesn't take a minute to do the job. Then if you know you are not going to use the tool the next day, it's worth while rubbing the 'working parts' over with an oily rag. Tools treated in this way last a lifetime.

'Little Man'

In the case of a spade, choose the standard pattern, treaded size 2, which at the time of writing cost 23s. The tread on the top of the blade prevents the instep of one's boots or shoes getting worn out quickly. If you dislike the weight of this spade, and you don't mind about the tread, then if you live in the South buy the Norfolk pattern non-treaded, or if you are in the North, the Yorkshire pattern non-treaded. Women who want a lighter spade can buy what is known as a Lady's Border. As for forks, a full-size 4 half-bright prong, 8 in. by 13 in. should do. Those who have heavy clay soils will find a wide-tined potato fork useful with 4 prongs, $7\frac{1}{2}$ in. by 11 in. Such a fork can often be used instead of the spade in the winter and its great advantage is that it's lighter.

A Dutch hoe is inevitable, which should be fitted with a nice long ash handle so that it's easy to use without bending low. One with a 6-in. blade is usually sufficient, but those who are energetic, or who want to do more work in the time, can have an 8-in. blade. There's a good deal of argument in horticultural circles as to whether the Norfolk swan-necked hoe or the Bury swan-neck is best. Both have their devotees and there's really not much to choose between them. Where the soil is light and one wants to get over a lot of ground, a 9-in. blade will be bought, but an 8-in. blade is very useful. For finicky work, i.e. for thinning out seedlings or hoeing in a frame, a 4-in. onion hoe handled is very useful. One would need a good garden trowel with a 6-in. blade, and a properly constructed rake. Never be tempted to buy those cheap rakes which just have the teeth cut out of a single plate. They never last. You need those with solid ends and bolstered teeth.

a single plate, They never last. You need those with solid ends and bolstered teeth.

A D-handled dibber, iron shod, is very useful indeed for planting out members of the brassica family. An Elm wheelbarrow will be invaluable, fitted with a 16 in. by 4 in. pneumatic-tyred wheel unit. For bigger gardens I can strongly recommend the Underslung Plant Truck which is 6 ft. long, 2 ft. 4 in. wide, and has removable sides. This is fitted with two pneumatic tyres and is not a bit tiring to move about.

For those with large gardens there's a lot to be said for the Bean Hand Seed Drill, which sows all seeds from the smallest up to and including peas, and French beans at a constant depth and covers and consolidates them in one operation. A tool known as the Planet Junior with two handles and two light wheels is also very useful for hoeing and cultivating in between crops. It should be used by those who don't want to purchase an Auto-Culto, and so do the work mechanically. The Tool Bar of the Planet Junior can be fitted with various hoe blades at the right distances to do the work in between different crops.

A Solo Sprayer with its double pump action will do most of the work in a small vegetable garden, though for larger gardens a Knapsack Sprayer may be necessary, though of course the real luxury is to have a mechanical spraying attachment to the Auto-Culto and this can be made an economic unit if there's a fair-sized orchard in addition to the vegetable area.

MECHANICAL CULTIVATIONS

One of the greatest mistakes that can be made is to buy a tiny machine with low horse-power that will only lead to disappointment. Again and again the author has been to people's gardens only to find in the tool shed, a rusty, unused, baby cultivator, which the owner confessed was far too much of a toy to be of any value. To cultivate ground you must have power, and it really needs for rotary cultivation or for ploughing, a minimum of 6 h.p. The great advantage of such a machine is that it cuts out the heavy digging. Take a modern Auto-Culto as an example. This costs to-day about £215[1] basic. It would do the ploughing as well as the rotary cultivation. It's just a question of taking off one tool and fitting on the other. It is very manœuvrable, and will turn round in 4 ft. of space.

The advantage of having the plough is that the land can be laid up in furrows in the autumn, and thus the frost and the cold winds can get at this 'ridged' soil, and break it down into such a condition that it's easy to work into seed beds. It isn't vitally essential, however, to have a

[1] A smaller model is available at £95 basic (1972).

plough, for the land could be left until the spring, and then with the rotary cultivators, could be pulverized down in a very short time ready for seed sowing. One would say that it's more important to have the plough in the case of heavy land than in the lighter soils. Never use the rotary tines in the autumn on a clay soil, or otherwise the earth will set down hard like cement.

Those who've never used a rotary cultivator will be surprised at the results. Angled tines whirl round at a tremendous pace, and so churn up the soil that a wonderfully loose bed for seed sowing or planting is produced in a short time. If you go over normal soil once you can prepare it say to a depth of 4 in., if you go over the same soil again you can prepare it to a depth of say 8 in. It isn't a heavy tool that can't be managed by women, because quite young girl students at The Horticultural Training Centre use an Auto-Culto[1] with the greatest of ease.

If an Auto-Culto is bought, then in the first place it will cut out all the heavy work, and there are many who find it difficult to-day to do the digging and forking. Secondly, because of the speed at which it works, it's possible to cultivate an increased area, and thus insure (a) more food, and (b) a saving in man hours. There is, of course, the capital expenditure, plus the running costs. But you are saving labour for what may be called the least capital expenditure.

It will have been seen from the very carefully prepared chart that from a plot of 600 sq. yds., you get a return of about £50. And this will easily feed four people with vegetables all the year round. Now if you put down the depreciation on the Auto-Culto at £10 a year for ten years, and the cost of running the Auto-Culto at say £20 a year, you have a figure of £30. This means that from the point of view of the Auto-Culto being a paying proposition, you ought to have a family of say six or seven. This, of course might be father and mother, a mother-in-law, two children, a maid, and a woman who has to be given her lunch during the day.

Here it's a question of an Auto-Culto really paying its way. Few of us, however, look upon a vacuum cleaner in that light. We say we must have a vacuum cleaner because it will save labour, it will be easier for one's wife, and it will be cleaner too. One can argue in the same way about the rotary cultivator. The work will be easier to carry out. It will take place more quickly, and thus a job will be able to be done at exactly the right time—a fact that cannot be over-emphasized.

The man who spends but little time in his garden, needs a rotary cultivator, far more than a man who has hours in which to do it. If you've only got an hour to spare, how wonderful to be able to cultivate quite a big strip of ground in the first half hour, and then to be able to plant it

[1] This has a reverse gear.

up in the second thirty minutes. From the point of view of time there's absolutely no comparison.

An Auto-Culto can plough a piece of ground of 400 sq. yds. in one hour. It would take a man, and a good man at that, to dig over the same area of land in 16–18 hours depending on the soil. A man to fork over a bit of ground properly, and then to rake it down to a fine tilth, would take five hours to prepare this same sized piece of ground, but the rotary cultivator would get this ground down to a fine tilth in twenty-two minutes only.

Many factors have to be borne in mind when considering the purchase of mechanical cultivators: They must have strength to withstand day-in day-out usage under the worst of conditions. Generally speaking, extra strength means extra weight, so a successful compromise has to be found. Secondly, they must have the power to dig to the maximum depth 'in as few passes' as possible. A cultivator that will dig to a 10-in. depth in two 'passes' is far more valuable than a machine that has to go over the ground three or more times to obtain the same result. Thirdly, they must be adaptable to other work.A cultivator that can be put to work, say, at log-cutting or snow-clearing in mid-winter, as does the Auto-Culto, is likely to be a better investment than a small machine with low horse power.

Those who hate hand weeding and hand hoeing should consider the purchase of one of these hoes in addition to the rotary cultivator. It is ideal for use in the spring and summer. It has to be put away for the winter, for it has no function to perform then. However, as an extra for the summer, it should be considered by amateurs who have a vegetable garden of about half an acre and more.

In fact it would seem, if our calculations are correct, that one needs about £15 a year of vegetables for every one you are going to feed, if you are a good vegetable consumer. In that case, you've only got to have two people above the normal four or five in the family, to pay for the Auto-Culto. It's not a very conclusive argument, because the quantities of vegetables used by families differ tremendously, but it is a figure which will provide a vantage point from which readers of the book can jump, in order to decide whether they really are going to mechanize their garden or no.

If on the other hand you are employing a man, then the point to bear in mind is that though a first-class gardener could look after between ¾ acre and an acre of vegetables, which ought to feed twenty people (that is including his own vegetable requisites), then with the mechanical aids that are being suggested, he would be able to look after this vegetable garden, and do the flower garden as well. Of course, under such considerations, it should be possible to sell the excess produce, and this will help greatly towards the wages of the gardener himself.

A Further Plea for Mechanical Aids

If you try and move a fat man along a level road at 15 miles per hour, you can do it with a 50 c.c. petrol engine, but if you want to get him up steep hills it will be necessary to have a 98 c.c. petrol engine coupled with a gear box. Good digging is harder work than walking, and therefore one should never make the mistake of choosing a machine with low horse-power. Buy the rotary cultivator with a 3 or 5 h.p. engine.

One wants to use a machine that really does plough to the same depth as a man when digging, or that will do the rotary digging to a depth of say 6–7 in. It never does to drive a machine full out all the time. A small-engined machine does not do the work quickly enough; it cannot operate deeply enough, and it is far too slow. (It should be made clear that this does not apply to lawn mowers, for grass cutting is relatively light work.)

The argument that some people use that a bigger machine uses more petrol and oil does not hold good, for with the larger horse-power the engine is only going, so to speak, at half its power, whereas the tiny engines are going 'flat out'. Time, to the gardener, is more important than miles per gallon. Do not say 'I have only got a tiny garden and so I only want a tiny tractor'. It is like a pedestrian saying 'I want to go a few miles so I will buy some roller skates and fit a "model engine" on them.'

A modern rotary cultivator is operated so as to leave a headland of only 3 ft. 6 in., and at the end of the work in any garden it is possible to cultivate the untouched headland by two cross passes of the machine. A good machine is governed to 2,200 revolutions per minute, whereas a two-stroke is not 'governed' at all but races away at the headlands, with the result that more petrol and oil is used.

HOW TO ROTOTILL A PLOT OF GROUND

A vegetable garden that is to be cultivated mechanically should preferably have no edging stones or tiles around it. It does not really matter if the gravel or bitumen path merges into the soil, for the old-fashioned idea of having box edges—bricks—tiles—or wooden surrounds was quite suitable when hand digging—but is just a nuisance when carrying out rototillage.

Some people imagine that because you have to have a headland at the end of a vegetable plot in order to turn round that this means that there are two wide strips of land left that have to be dug by hand. This, of course, is quite untrue. Follow the plan set out on page 46 and you will see that if you start at point A about 3 ft. inside the area concerned, you work up and down the ground until you come to point B when you start your first 'tour' round the headland. This it will be seen, is as it were, a

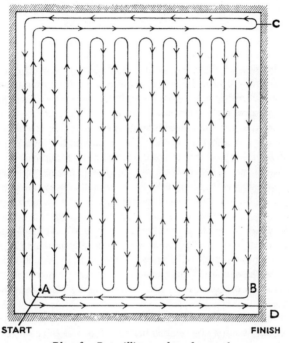

Plan for Rototilling a plot of ground

non-stop movement because at point C you turn round on your tracks to rotary cultivate the area nearest the path or hedge and thus you end at point D on the plan.

This means that the whole of the ground is rototilled and so is, as it were, dug—forked—and raked ready for seed sowing. If there is any fault with this method of cultivation it is that on light lands the land may be left in rather a 'puffy' condition, and sometimes, therefore, it is necessary to carry out a little light rolling in order to consolidate the ground. This is not necessary, however, in the case of the heavier soils.

CHAPTER 3

Feeding the Soil

The basis of all manuring must be organic matter. It's impossible to make up for the lack of dung or compost by the use of artificial fertilizers. To grow not only the heaviest yields but the best flavoured crops, and vegetables which are rich in vitamins—it is necessary to see that the soil contains sufficient humus. If the soil can be fed in the right way and kept in the right condition, the food produced in such soil will keep men and women in the right condition.

In the raising of crops, there are two complementary processes, i.e. growth and decay. If growth is to be speeded up, decay must be accelerated also. If the vegetable producer confines his attention to stimulating growth only, his gardening will become unbalanced and unstable, and he will obtain his crops at the expense of the soil's capital—which is its fertility. Every piece of work done in the vegetable garden helps to break down the humus, and every crop grown helps to reduce the organic content of the ground. Thus constant care must be exercised to ensure that humus is replaced, for where there is no capital, there can be no dividends.

Nature's plan is to try and build up the humus year after year, and this can only be done by organic matter. Humus is the complex residue of partly oxidized animal and vegetable matter, together with substances synthesized by fungi and bacteria, used to break down these wastes. It possesses biological, chemical and physical properties, to make it distinct from all other natural organic bodies. During its formation all sorts of chemical changes take place, and the soil organisms work on the proteins and the carbohydrates and break them down into simpler substances; often gases are formed which are the causes of further work.

Humus-minded gardeners believe that well-rotted dung or compost feeds the soil population; helps with the great promoting substances; encourages the earthworms to do their jobs; ensures the function of the mycorrhiza and in addition sees to it that the soil organisms complete their life cycle. Humus cannot be described as dead in the normal sense of the word. It's far fairer to describe it as in the transition stage between one form of life and another.

Actions Speak Louder than Words

I make no apology for spending some time in emphasizing the great importance of organic matter. The first thing the keen vegetable grower must promise is never to make a bonfire. The main reason why town gardens will not grow good vegetables is because they are never given sufficient organic matter and so the soil is lacking in humus. People (and jobbing gardeners are notorious at this) will burn up everything. Never burn cabbage stumps or the leaves from trees, or the tops of peas and beans. Never even allow potato haulm to be burnt, even though it has been diseased. If compost is made properly (details will be found of this in page 48) then the diseased spores will be killed because of the heat engendered in the heap. Never burn weeds. They too will rot down perfectly if the right activator is used. Don't allow the women of the household to throw away the tea leaves, the orange peel, the outside leaves of cabbages, etc. All this needs to be composted also.

Compost is a means of making rubbish into a product which can be said to be considerably richer and more lasting than farmyard manure. (Anyway dung is almost impossible to obtain these days!) A keen gardener invests work into making the compost. He invests time into the making of compost, for bulk by bulk it pays handsome dividends. It is a simple matter to make a bin with, say, wire netting, 3 yds. long by 3 yds. wide, and to fill this with the vegetable waste in the correct manner (see page 49), until it is 2 yds. high. Then after a period of three months, such a heap will have rotted down to a height of $2\frac{1}{2}$ ft., and this works out at $7\frac{1}{2}$ cu. yds. of excellent compost, or 4 tons of fully rotted organic matter, which is of more value than farmyard manure.

Looking at the aspect from the point of view of L.S.D. as we have tried to do again and again in this book, you couldn't buy 4 tons of really well rotted, properly prepared dung under £3 a ton, and I've known it in some towns to be £5 a ton delivered, and then it's only been inferior pony dung or the like. Here is a product made out of waste, which has cost time and labour, plus $\frac{1}{4}$ cwt. of a fish fertilizer, say 10s. This quantity, i.e. 4 tons of good compost is sufficient to manure an area of at least 800 sq. yds.

It is a good plan to have three open ended 'bins', each one 3 yds. wide by 3 yds. deep, so that in the first one the refuse can be rotting down;

the second one can be gradually filled as the vegetable wastes become available, and then the third one is ready and open to receive the next lot of fresh organic matter, the moment the second one has been filled. I either use no bins or have them made of wire netting, because of the cheapness. It is better, however, to have them made of wooden boards, because then the heat is kept in, and the outsides of the heaps don't dry out so quickly in consequence. Have a dustbin filled with the activator (I use the fish fertilizer with a 5 per cent potash content) close to these bins, so that it can be used the moment any vegetable waste is put in. This dustbin should have a lid, which should be wired down to the handles, so that it can never blow off.

The Making of the Compost

There are various ways of making compost, but the busy gardener has to adopt the simplest methods. It much depends on what activator he is going to use, how the work is going to be done. For instance, if poultry are kept, then when the droppings are scraped once a week, the excreta can either be put straight on to the heap and be spread evenly, or it can be put into a large dustbin where it can dry before being used. There is naturally more vegetable waste available in the summer and autumn than in the dead of winter, and therefore in practice it is convenient to use the excreta straight away when there is lots of material to compost, and to put it in the dustbin in the winter, so that plenty may be available for application the following composting season.

Excellent alternatives to poultry manure are rabbit dung, or the scrapings from pigeon lofts. Pig manure can, of course, be used, and this can be applied as the 'jam' in the 'bread and butter' sandwich, as the heap rises. Horse manure and cow manure can be used in a similar manner. Nobody can lay down hard and fast rules as to how much of this activator to use, but one would say from empirical knowledge, that you need about a 2- or 3-in. layer of dung, and then a foot layer of cabbage leaves, the tops of carrots and turnips, the potato haulm or whatever it may be.

Those who do not keep rabbits or chickens or any animals, must rely on another form of organic activator, and to them I recommend the fish fertilizer with the 6 per cent potash content in the case of those with heavy soils, and with a 10 per cent potash content in the case of those with sandy loams, or sands. Such a fertilizer must be used at 3 oz. to the sq. yd. for every 6-in. thickness of vegetable waste collected—thus you get an even layer of vegetable waste 6 in. thick, a sprinkling of the fish fertilizer, another layer of vegetable waste 6 in. thick, another sprinkling of the fish fertilizer, and so on—until the heap reaches the height of 6 or 7 ft.

It undoubtedly helps, especially in cases where the land is apt to be acid, if carbonate of lime is used every fourth layer instead of the fish fertilizer. Thus you get three 6-in. layers activated with the fish, the fourth one with the lime, another three layers activated with fish, yet another with lime, and then when the correct height is reached, it helps to keep in the heat if the top of the heap is covered with soil to a depth of 3 in. This capping of the heap is useful though it isn't imperative.

It is important to understand the use of water in the compost heap. If the material used is dry, then water must be applied. For instance, we sometimes have to buy in bales of straw in order to make more compost than can be done with the normal vegetable waste of the garden. Straw is dry, and if you buy in, say $\frac{1}{4}$ ton, you will need at least 200 gallons of water to soak the straw thoroughly as the layers go into position in the bin with the activator. It is not necessary to make vegetable wastes sodden, but the bacteria cannot work and create the necessary heat in a heap unless they have sufficient moisture. The keen vegetable grower must therefore study his compost making with interest. Any dry material that is used must be watered well. When it's a question of lettuce leaves, cabbage leaves, lawn mowings, and so on, there is, of course no need, for any water at all.

It has been said that the gardener must be very careful what he puts on to the compost heap. The author has been told never to use rhubarb leaves, laurel leaves, privet prunings, and perennial weed roots such as couch and convolvulus which such proprietory activator or lack of skill has failed to rot. One is told that all weeds must be burnt, or that crops attacked by insect pests must not go on; *there is no truth in any of these statements*. The important thing is to include the activator, and make certain that there's enough moisture. You are not making a rubbish heap, but a proper compost heap, and there's all the difference between the two.

If the vegetable matter used is bulky, for instance, cabbage, cauliflower and brussels sprouts' tops, then it is necessary to smash them up first of all on a chopping block with the back of an axe. We lay ours out on a concrete path and run over them with a baby caterpillar tractor. Those who have farms will put them through a shredder or cutting machine. Anyway the idea is to try and pulverize the stuff so that they will rot down quickly. It helps too if you always try and put soft material like lawn mowings in and amongst the more fibrous material like the brassica stumps, by intermingling the hard and the soft the best results are achieved.

There's one last important point with regard to the making of compost, and that is air. It does help if you drive into the middle of the bin, before the compost is put in position, a stout beech post, say 3 in. in diameter. The material is then piled around this post until it gets to be about 5 ft. tall. The post[1] then needs to be removed, and this leaves a circular air shaft up the centre of the heap, which is very valuable indeed. Of course, all compost heaps needn't be made in bins of the size I've mentioned. They can be about the same depth but six or seven times as long. In that case you need a post about every 4 ft. along the heap and in the centre, so that the necessary number of ventilating shafts are provided.

It usually takes about six months from the time the heap has been made until it's ready for use. Remember that soft material like lawn mowings will rot down and be ready far quicker than more fibrous matter. A compost for instance, of cabbage and lettuce leaves only can be got ready in three months. A mixture, however, as I say, normally takes six months, though all the material has been collected together and the heap is made in a day, or whether as is normally the case, the heaps take two or three months to complete. Date your timing of readiness from the time of completion and not from the time the vegetable matter was first put in the bin.

By the way, it pays for the compost heap to be on earth, so that the worms can work their way up and get on with their part of the job. It helps if the heaps can be in shade rather than in full sun—and in shelter rather than in full wind. It is useful to have water handy, so that instead of having to use a watering-can, one can apply 'artificial rain'. Make the heaps, anyway, near the garden where the compost is to be used, because then there's a minimum of carting of the waste to the bin, and of the valuable compost back on to the soil again.

Amount to Use

It's no good being foolish and advising gardeners to use large quantities of compost. This only discourages them. We must be practical about this feature, just as much as about costs. Chapter 5 talks about rotations, while in Chapter 1 there's a detailed chart showing the costs and returns from a four-course rotation. No compost will be needed for the area devoted to roots, so you can save there. Aim at giving at the rate of 40 to 50 tons to the acre to the potatoes; at a similar rate to the

---

[1] Latterly at The Good Gardeners Association Experimental Gardens at Arkley no posts are used and the results are excellent.

brassicas (i.e. the members of the cabbage family); and at about 30 tons to the acre to the plot to be devoted to the peas and beans.

Now 40 to 50 tons to the acre means 20 lb. per sq. yd., and 20 lb. is about one 2-gallon bucketful. For 30 tons to the acre it is about three-quarters of a 2-gallon bucketful. Work out, then, how much compost you will need and after the first year, if you find that you haven't been able to produce sufficient vegetable waste, then you must buy in some material and bale straw is usually the cheapest. Of course, those who live in towns can often get the road sweepers to give them the leaves from the trees. A tip goes a long way! Those who live in the country may have to rake up their own leaves, or they may be in a position as the author is, to buy in old straw far more cheaply.

I am purposely not mentioning the use of farmyard manure separately, for it is of far more value when composted with vegetable waste than when rotted down alone. No mention is made either of leaf mould alone, because again this is far better on the compost heap than when put into heaps by itself. In some districts it is possible to buy town waste properly composted and ready for use in the garden. Application for such compost should always be made in the first place to the Borough Surveyor's Department.

Sedge Peat an Additional Help

The properly prepared compost will be dug into the ground a spade's depth. The exception, of course, being in the case of the non-diggers, whose requirements are dealt with in Chapter 7. The roots of plants will go down and find the organic matter which will, of course, be in the process of being converted into humus by the soil organisms. In the top 3 or 4 in. there may be little organic matter and so it helps the young seedlings greatly if when the seed bed is being prepared, sedge peat is forked in at the rate of about half a bucketful to a sq. yd. In the case of dry, sandy soil, it pays to make this peat sodden in water first. Where it has not been possible to dig in as much compost as is desired, twice the amount of sedge peat may be added.

Sedge peat is far more valuable than any other type of peat. It may easily contain 224 lb. of immediately available humus per ton, as compared with only 45 lb. in the case of the sphagnum types. Its value from the point of view of nitrogen is equal to 140 lb. (when reckoned as sulphate of ammonia). It produces another 70 per cent of additional humus finally available, whereas with the sphagnum types of peat you get only 15 per cent of additional humus; and at most 70 lb. of nitrogen.

Some gardeners have tried to rely on sedge peat only, and this is a possibility, if coupled with the intelligent use of a fish fertilizer. It is, however, somewhat expensive to use on a large scale, and thus it is always better to make as much compost as possible, and to use the sedge peat as a valuable extra. It is, as I have said, particularly useful when worked into the top few inches, because it does give the seedlings the perfect start.

THE FERTILIZERS

Though some people dislike the terms, there is no doubt that the normal extra feeding of the soil is done either by organic fertilizers or by artificial or chemical fertilizers. The organic fertilizers may be described as hoof and horn meal, meat and bone meal, and properly prepared fish manure. The chemical fertilizers are such substances as sulphate of ammonia, nitrate of soda, superphosphate, and sulphate of potash. The organic fertilizers as a whole are slow acting, and they contain most of the plant foods necessary. Some like hoof and horn contain no potash, and this is usually added by those who are selling the fertilizer, so that the gardener may use it as a 'complete' manure.

Now there are two opposing schools of thought on this whole subject. The one will gladly use large quantities of chemical fertilizers, and cannot see that they do any harm. The other (at present it must be said in the minority) who argue that it's very dangerous to use chemicals at all, and who rely therefore entirely on compost and other organic manures. The latter group are certainly very successful, though the former group argue that the vegetables they produce cost them far more. The author's views lie perhaps midway between the two, or to be fair, perhaps much nearer the complete organic growers than those who use chemical fertilizers with them.

He occasionally finds it necessary to use a chemical fertilizer like nitro chalk as a tonic in the very early spring. Perhaps the weather has been cold or wet, and the bacteria have not been able to work as they should, and so the spring cabbage is late. Now if a little of one of these nitrogenous fertilizers is applied along the rows of plants, say at an ounce to the yard run, some extra available nitrogen is almost immediately there, the plants react well, and it is hoped the bacteria are also encouraged.

In the same way if one takes over some starved ground, it sometimes happens that celery grows rotten in the 'core' and that means that there's a shortage of Boron in the ground. Eventually, by the addition of the properly composted waste, this trace element deficiency will disappear; meanwhile, however, the celery rots. One can get over the trouble by applying Borax crystals as a tonic, along the celery trench before the plants are put out, at the rate of not more than one thirty-second of an ounce per yard run. It's necessary to mix the Borax crystals with sand first, so as to make it possible to apply this feed thinly enough.

There is always a problem with regard to potash. It is true that after regular applications of compost potash does become available. This is especially true when one can incorporate plants in the compost heap that are naturally rich in potash like bracken, and the haulm of broad beans. In the early stages, however, of starting out on compost lines, I have discovered that potash deficiencies make themselves evident. It might be necessary, therefore, to apply sulphate of potash[1] at the rate of, say, 2 oz. to the sq. yd., and there is one particular form of this fertilizer which is made from grape skins, and is at least organic in origin. This can be got from a firm in London.

Therefore, as those who are keen on compost and its use have shown, land can be got fully into a fertile condition by the use of organic manures only, and this, of course, is especially true if organic fertilizers are used in addition. On the whole the process is slower than when chemical fertilizers are applied, for the purpose of adding some special plant food at one particular time.

From the point of view of saving time and labour, there is a lot to be said these days for standardizing the type of plant food that is to be given. For this reason the author uses a fish fertilizer for all vegetables he grows. He buys one with a 5 per cent potash content for the normal crops. The analysis, incidentally, works out at 6 per cent nitrogen, 12–15 per cent available phosphates, and 5 per cent potash—while for crops that particularly need potash, like tomatoes for example, a similar fertilizer but with a 10 per cent potash content is applied.

Years ago as a young man he would make up mixtures of artificial fertilizers—for root crops for instance, 1 part of sulphate of ammonia, 5 parts of superphosphate and 1 part sulphate of potash, and for peas and beans 1 part of sulphate of ammonia, 4 parts of superphosphate and 2 parts of sulphate of potash. These separate mixings made a lot of work and furthermore, of course, they were entirely inorganic, or as the gardener has it to-day—chemical.

The fish fertilizer replaces all these. It can not only be used at the rate of 3 to 4 oz. to the sq. yd. before the seeds are sown or plants are put out, but it can be applied as has been said, on page 49, as the activator for

[1] The author eliminated all signs of potash starvation on gooseberries at Thaxted by using wood ashes at ½ lb. to the square yard.

the compost heap. There may be those who prefer to use a hoof and horn meal, to which potash has been added, or even a meat and bone meal, again with potash added. The great thing is to try and 'standardize' the fertilizer that is to be used, and to see to it that it is organic.

Experiments have shown that the action of worms are certainly discouraged by chemical fertilizers, and these creatures much prefer land that has been fed with organic manures and organic fertilizers only. We have got to think of the whole question of soil feeding from the point of view of the man consuming the vegetables, and there is no doubt that true 'life' begins with the soil. The main thing is to dig in ample organic matter each year, to use an organic fertilizer to help with the feeding, and then to give special 'tonics' according to the needs of the soil or plants if necessary.

These tonics will not be applied at more than 1 oz. to the sq. yd. as a rule, and this is especially true in the case of nitrogen.

POULTRY MANURE

A special sub-heading is made because the writer is constantly getting questions on the subject of using the excreta from hens or even pigeons. A hen produces about 12 lb. of dung a year, and a duck about 18 lb. The moisture content of the hen manure is about 63 per cent, though a duck's is as low as 53 per cent. It should not be dug into the soil when fresh or even be put along and among plants. It has, therefore, to be dried, or to be used as an activator in a compost heap.

The trouble about poultry manure is that it contains too much nitrogen. It is therefore an unbalanced fertilizer, and those who are keen on using it as a complete manure must add to each 1 cwt. of dried poultry dung, 3 lb. of sulphate of potash and 25 lb. of bone meal. The alternative is to use the dried poultry manure as a nitrogenous dressing, and apply this along the rows of brassicas and other plants that need a little extra nitrogenous food, at the rate of 2 oz. to the yard run.

It is not easy to dry poultry manure—but there are two good ways— either of which will give good results. The first is to use 2 lb. of sedge peat per bird on the dropping board, and then to scrape the peat and manure into a dustbin once a week. Put a lid on the dustbin immediately and when full leave for another three months before using. It means that you must have two dustbins in order to cope with the work during the year. Sand can be used instead of sedge peat but it doesn't absorb the ammonia fumes in the same way.

The second scheme is to spread the manure on to a perforated metal tray—as large as convenient. This tray can be placed on the shelving of the greenhouse—or on the rafters of a shed. The great thing is to get the droppings dried as quickly as possible—for the quicker the drying the less the loss of mercurial values. Pulverize the droppings if necessary by putting them in a sack and beating them with the back of a spade kept flat so as not to cut the hessian.

The interesting fact is that poultry manure is rich in plant hormones and this may be a far more important factor to vegetable gardeners than we imagine at the present time.

Soot

Soot is useful to use because it helps to darken soil and darker soils are always warmer than those which are very light in colour. Soot will contain a small percentage of nitrogen, and therefore can be described as a very mild fertilizer. It is very much liked by brussels sprout growers for putting on to the ground in the autumn and early winter, and is often used then at rates of up to $\frac{1}{2}$ lb. to the sq. yd. It is not too 'forcing' and thus can be used in the winter whereas an inorganic fertilizer like nitrate of soda is only applied in the spring.

Bone Meal

This was a very popular organic fertilizer in the good old days, but the true bone meal contains gelatine, and is therefore even slower in action than steamed bone flour, which is often applied at 2 to 3 oz. to the sq. yd. for peas and beans, which are said to need a steady supply of phosphates throughout the season. It is seldom necessary to use bone flour in addition to the fish fertilizer, which has already been described on page 49.

Wood Ashes

There is no particular virtue in the burning process and gardeners should realize that potash is *not made* by burning, all the fire does is to convert what is already present into a quickly soluble form of potash. It is far better in the usual run to compost the vegetable waste and thus add the potash to the soil with the humus. The only substances that should be burnt are those like apple prunings, which unless there's machinery available for shredding, do not compost readily.

Good quality wood ashes unleached, may contain from 4 to 6 per cent of potash, but wood ashes that have been left out in the rain and so have been leached may only contain 1 per cent of potash. The ashes from prunings often contain 15 per cent potash, I find, while the ashes from bracken may easily consist of 50 per cent of potash, especially if the bracken is cut at the beginning of the season.

Wood ashes are dangerous on clay soils because instead of opening them up, as some writers have said, they always make them more sticky. Good loams, for instance, can be converted into sticky clays by the constant use of wood ashes—because the potash present is in the form of potassium chloride and so tends to have a similar effect to muriate of potash.

Those who burn logs on the sitting-room fire could certainly save the ashes as these may contain 6 per cent of potash, and can be used either on the compost heap or for the crops that particularly require it like onions, sweet peas and tomatoes. Wood ashes, however, should always be kept perfectly dry, until applied.

LIQUID MANURE

A lot of nonsense has been written about the use of liquid manures. Old books suggested that a sack of sheep droppings or other dung might be placed into a barrel of water for an unspecified time, in order that a mysterious substance which gardeners often call 'cow tea' might be produced. No one can possibly know the value of such a liquid. It might easily be rich in nitrogen and low in phosphates. It might be fairly strong because the animals have been well fed, and the bag had been left in for six months or it might be weak because from poorly fed, creatures and because the manure had only been in the barrel for a comparatively short time.

Furthermore, there was always the problem of disease. A dirty barrel, unknown droppings gathered in a field from equally unknown animals, and with all the possibilities and probabilities of bacterial troubles. It is no wonder, therefore, that the modern gardener uses Liquinure, which is a standardized product with a definite analysis—which is made under ideal conditions, and which has as a rule, an organic base. For general use, one containing 8 per cent nitrogen, 7 per cent phosphoric acid, and $3\frac{1}{2}$ per cent potash is ideal, but where it is desired to grow crops that like more potash like the tomato for instance, Liquinure with the analysis of 4 per cent nitrogen, 7 per cent phosphoric acid, and $7\frac{1}{2}$ per cent potash is better still.

These Liquinures are dissolved in accordance with the maker's instructions. You only need $\frac{1}{8}$ oz., i.e. a teaspoon, to 160 oz., i.e. a gallon of water, and thus you have a food which contains 125 parts of nitrogen, 110 parts of phosphoric acid and 55 parts of potash per 1 million parts of water. Let not the inexperienced believe that this is too little. It is just what is needed. The great thing, however, is to supply sufficient per yard run, and I find it necessary to use about 4 gallons of diluted Liquinure per 30 ft. of row. Individual tomato plants, when they are cropping well, may have a gallon per plant once every 10 days or so during the summer.

Fortunately, there are at the present time automatic diluters which enable a keen gardener to apply his liquid manure at the same time as he does his watering with the hose. The bugbear of the diluter, however, is dirt, which can easily clog up the fine hole in the feeding tube, and so partially or completely stop the flow of the concentrated liquid manure. It is important after using to rinse the diluter thoroughly.

LIME

It is important to know about lime, because so often there are failures in gardens because of acidity, or just because of lack of calcium. It does seem important for the gardener to get it into his head that lime very quickly washes through soil, and therefore needs applying on the surface of the ground. It also means that regular applications have to be given. It's convenient to make it a rule that lime should be applied to the areas of ground that are to be occupied by peas and beans, and by the members of the cabbage family. One can give a fairly heavy dressing for the brassicas, and a lighter dressing for the pulse crops.

If a proper four-course rotation is carried out, then it will mean that no lime is applied to the potato area, and none to the parts to be occupied by roots. Thus every two years, lime will be given. See Chapter 5. And this will mean that the garden will receive just the quantity of lime it needs. After all on heavy soils lime will help to improve the texture and the workability, and it will help also to release other plant foods, and particularly potash. The lime will also assist in the decomposition of the organic matter.

Lime should never be mixed with acid artificial manures, and therefore the plan is to dig in the compost, to fork in the sedge peat and fertilizers, and then finally to apply the lime and rake this in. In the ordinary way, it should be used at 7 to 8 oz. to the square yard on the plot where the members of the cabbage family are grown, and at 3 or 4 oz. to the sq. yd. to the break occupied by the peas and beans.

There are three main types of lime, (a) Quicklime which is sometimes sold as lump lime or Buxton lime or may be ground into powder and then sold as ground lime. In the latter case it is unpleasant because it can easily blow into the eyes and burn. (b) When quicklime is slaked it turns into hydrated lime, and this is one of the most popular forms used by amateurs. It's quite safe to handle, and it's easy to store. (c) Ground limestone or ground chalk. This is also easy to store and use, but because it contains much less oxide of lime it has to be applied at a heavier rate. Therefore, if in the case of hydrated lime one uses 7 or 8 oz. with ground limestone, 9 or 10 oz. may be necessary, to get the same effect.

CHAPTER 4

The Hungry Soil and Green Manuring

Unfortunately, very little experimental work has been done on green manuring in this country. Yet the author believes that this method of feeding the soil may well be the answer to most of the problems that he meets with up and down the country. Many gardens are old and exhausted. Some, unfortunately, because of builders 'peccadillos' are largely subsoil, while there are far too many gardens which consist of poor sand. Can such gardens be built up by being given a rest under green manure crops, which after all, will largely smother weeds.

After all, this does seem to be God's plan. He made it quite clear to His people in Leviticus that the land is to be rested once every seven years. The idea undoubtedly was to allow the weeds and grasses to grow, and then to have plenty of organic matter which could be dug into the soil at the end of the season. It isn't only the importance of building the soil up from the point of view of humus content—but the author has discovered that there's something extremely valuable in soil structure.

Some years ago he made a garden in the old farmyard at the back of his offices. He had to import some 500 tons of soil to do this. It had to be levelled with a bulldozer. The result was ridiculous. The soil was there—the drainage was fair (it has now since been improved)—but because the soil had no up and down structure, the crops grown were impossibly poor. A green manure of rye grass and clovers was sown, and at the end of the year, this was dug in.

The result was (a) that the up and down structure of the soil was automatically constructed by the roots of the rye grass, and thus there was the necessary aeration and 'highways and byways' down which the rain could go. Furthermore, because during the shallow digging a fish fertilizer was applied at 3 oz. to the sq. yd., there was no de-nitrification and the ground became not only very fertile, but easily workable.

There are market gardeners to-day who because they have no stock at all, keep up the fertility of their ground by resting a certain acreage each year, and by sowing it with rye grass only. These short-term leys as they are called, have proved very effective, and thus at The Horticultural Training Centre we have made it our plan to rest one-seventh of our acreage every year, and to sow it with rye grass and clover in the early spring. Market gardeners sow the seed at the rate of 40 lb. to the acre, which works out from the gardener's point of view at 1 oz. to 7 sq. yds. It might well be a good plan to carry out such a system in the normal vegetable garden—but perhaps to sow at 1 oz. to 4 sq. yds.

Before I go into any further details on the subject of green manuring, it may be as well to discuss the principles behind green manuring or sheet composting as I believe the Americans call it. The idea, of course, is to do the composting *in situ*, that is to say, instead of carting vegetable waste to a compost heap and rotting it down there, the vegetable matter is rotted down actually on the site where the crop is grown. It does this, of course, if an activator is used all over the crops just before it is dug or ploughed in. Sometimes with a tall crop like mustard it has to be gone over first with a sickle or mechanical cultivator in order to chop it down or 'mush it up' so that it can be the more easily incorporated into the soil. Thus green manuring increases in the long run the humus content of the soil.

It also, however, smothers weeds, and so can be said to be a cleaning crop. It takes up the soluble plant foods and prevents their being lost in the drainage water, and of course, these foods are eventually passed back into the soil when the green manure is dug in. Such a crop is especially valuable during the winter to prevent leaching. In addition, however, as has already been suggested, a green manure does a great job in improving soil structure, and when the roots decay, better drainage and better aeration is assured.

One needs to look after a green manure crop in the same way as any other crop. For instance, if the weather is very dry and growth is likely to be poor, overhead irrigation must be used as suggested for all crops in Chapter 5. Such work may be especially necessary on the sandy soils which, incidentally, react wonderfully to green manures. It must be borne in mind that the younger the plant is—the more quickly it decomposes in the ground. On the other hand to dig a plant when very young means that there's less bulk, and therefore in the end less humus. It is important though to dig a crop in before it starts to seed. In fact this work should be done just before flowering. It is after flowering that the general structure of the plant becomes tougher and richer in lignin. This means that it takes longer for the bacteria to work on the plants, and it could quite easily be that the soil wouldn't be ready for cropping the following season.

Green manure should always be dug in when the soil is still warm. It is a bad plan, for instance, to wait until December, or to do the work after there's been a heavy fall of snow. The bacteria do not work when the temperature of the soil falls low. Nor can they work, either, if the soil is too dry, and therefore some artificial rain may have to be given in the case of light soils, just before the digging in takes place. If a green manure cannot be dug or ploughed in during the autumn, then it will have to be left until the spring. Fortunately, the frost-damaged stems and leaves will be very quickly attacked by the micro-organisms in the soil, but even then it will be too late to carry out spring sowings of ordinary crops satisfactorily.

DISCUSSING POSSIBLE CROPS

One naturally divides the green manures into two categories. Those which are members of the legume family, and so build up nitrogenous nodules on their roots, and those which are usually described as non-leguminous. In the latter category one can place mustard, rape, rye grass, spinach, and oats, while in the former, good crops have proved to be lupins, clovers, vetches, and field peas. Most seedsmen recommend suitable mixtures of legumes and non-legumes, because in that case you get the nitrogen augmented by the one crop and a tremendous quantity of humus-forming material produced by the other crop. Nature seems to abhor monoculture and there's always greater bulk when two crops of this character are grown together than when they are kept separate. Further, I have discovered that the organic matter from legumes has a definite action in stimulating the decaying processes in a compost heap or in soil, and therefore there tends to be an earlier liberation of the plant nutrients.

Very little work, as I have already said, has been done on the best types of green manures for the varying ranges of soils, but there is some empirical knowledge which seems to suggest that for the light sands and gravels, lupins are particularly useful, or lupins and mustard together; while for the clays—rye grass and clover have given good results, as well as oats and vetches. Of course, for a nice loam, one can almost use any green manure.

Mustard

It is important to avoid using mustard and rape in gardens where the club root disease has given trouble, see page 270. These crops are crucifers which means that they can themselves be attacked by this disease, and so they merely accentuate the trouble. As one doesn't advise brassica crops to follow one another because of the fear of this disease, it is equally important not to use mustard or rape on land which the following year is to be planted up with any member of the brassica family. One of the advantages of using mustard, however, is that it does seem to discourage wireworms, especially if sown thickly, i.e. at the rate of about an ounce to the sq. yd. at least. Mr. A. A. Clucas told me that he had got rid of quite a serious population of wireworm from a field one year before the war, through sowing mustard thickly in the spring, and then cutting it down and ploughing it in some three months later. Sow the mustard thickly—bash it down with a spade after a period of eight or nine weeks; sprinkling over the mustard at the same time a fish fertilizer at 3 oz. to the sq. yd. The bashed-up mustard with the fertilizer on it, should be dug in.

Lupins

As far as I can discover no work has been done on this subject in Great Britain but I have seen the Bitter Blue lupin used with great success in Europe. This has more stem and leaf than the other types, and grows more quickly. It is an annual and its seeds can be obtained from any good firm that has a Farm Seeds department very much more cheaply than those of the familiar perennial Russell of the border. Ask for the Bitter Blue. There I am told it produces about 10 tons per acre of green manure, which is certainly more than mustard, which is dug in at the end of the eight-week period. The plan is to sow the seed early in April in rows a foot apart with the drills an inch deep. The sowing should be done thinly with the aim of spacing the seeds out about 2 in. apart. It should be dug into the soil fifteen weeks after sowing and while it is being 'mushed' up, a fish fertilizer with a 10 per cent potash content must be added at 3 to 4 oz. to the sq. yd. This smashing up of the lupin stems with a spade or fork is important.

The Temporary Ley

I am particularly interested in the sowing down of temporary leys, because the use of Italian rye grass has a particularly beneficial effect on soil structure. At The International Horticultural Advisory Bureau, Arkley we've been very successul with a mixture of 6 lb. of Indigenous perennial rye grass, 3 lb. of S.50 Timothy, and 2 lb. of Kentish Indigenous wild white clover. We use this quantity for half an acre of land and a wonderful crop is produced. Because the grass grew so tall, it was cut several times during the season and allowed to lie. At the end of the year it was all dug in after having had a good dressing of the fish manure to make certain there would be no denitrification.

I am told on good authority that an excellent mixture for the normal town or city garden consists of 80 per cent Danish Italian rye grass, and 20 per cent finest English trefoil. The aim is to sow this at about $\frac{1}{2}$ oz. to the sq. yd., while the cost (1972) works out at 15p per lb. This ley should be left down at least six months and if the plan is to rest the ground and leave the 'grass' growing longer, then it will have to be cut four or five times during the season before being dug in in the autumn.

Those who have got a rotary cultivator should consider very seriously rotovating the green manure into the ground rather than digging it in. The great advantage is that you get all the fine organic matter smashed up and worked into the top 4 or 5 in. of soil where it is so valuable. I am quite sure that this is a very much better thing than the digging in of such green manure more deeply. On every occasion, however, that the leaves and stems of plants are worked into the ground in their fresh state, it is most important to include an 'activator' so as to avoid de-nitrification on the subsequent crop. Those who don't mind using inorganics will probably apply nitro-chalk at the rate of 1 oz. to the sq. yd., others will use a fish fertilizer at 2 oz. to the sq. yd.

A system I have not tried, but which was recommended to me by one of the leading gardeners in this country is the sowing on September 1st or thereabouts of a mixture consisting of 12 lb. of Italian rye grass and 5 lb. of rape, this being for a $\frac{1}{4}$ acre plot. The idea is to allow the crops to grow until about the second week of April, when they are either dug in, having been activated first with a fish manure, or are worked into the soil with the rotary cultivator. It is said that under this scheme you can always do your green manuring on the 'catch-cropping' idea. You sow after one crop has been harvested and get the green manure worked into the ground before the next crop is to be sown or planted up. (Remember that rape like mustard is subject to club root.)

Double Green Manuring

Mr. R. L. Scarlett, C.D.A., of Edinburgh, lectured some years ago on his double green manuring system. If he took over a piece of land that was dirty, and he wanted to get it clean he ploughed it as deeply as possible in the winter, and then in the early spring he sowed tares broadcast. When these came into flowering in June he went over the land with a disc harrow, or some similar tool to smash up the crop. When it had been thoroughly bruised and cut up, calcium cyanamide was applied all over the area at 4 to 5 cwt. per acre. The ground was then left for eight days before being ploughed in.

He then prepared the surface of the ground by harrowing, perhaps disc cultivating, and then when the tilth was sufficiently fine, he sowed rye at 40 lb. to the acre about the third week of July, with the result that it grew well and was ready to plough in between the middle of October and the end of December. This system not only enriched the land with plenty of organic matter, but it did eliminate the weeds and leave the land beautifully clean. The calcium cyanamide, of course, was used to prevent de-nitrification of the crop that was to follow.

The message of this system for the private garden would be to dig in the autumn, and then to sow early in January, tares at $\frac{1}{2}$ oz. to the sq. yd., to knock this down with a spade late in June, and before digging it in or working it into the soil with an Auto-Culto, to add the fish manure at 2 oz. to the sq. yd. Then there would be some raking to do to prepare a fine tilth and the sowing of the rye grass about $\frac{1}{2}$ oz. to the sq. yd., with the idea of digging it in about the middle of October.

WEATHER AND GREEN MANURE

Readers who live in the Eastern Counties or in any part of Great Britain where the rainfall is low may not be quite so successful with green manure as those who live in districts where the rainfall is higher. It is well worth while using artificial rain for green manures during droughty periods. Sandy soils, for instance, react wonderfully to green manures, especially if plants are dug in on the young side. But you don't get quick growth on such soils, plus bulk, in dry weather.

May I stress the importance of digging in the green manure while the soil is still warm. It is a bad plan, for instance, to wait until December, or to do the work after there's been a heavy fall of snow. Dig in a crop, however, before the plants start to seed, because there is little doubt that after flowering, the general structure of the plant becomes tougher and richer in lignin. This means that it takes longer for the bacteria to convert the organic matter into humus, with the result that the soil isn't ready as soon as it should be for sowing or planting up again.

ODD CROPS

Very often a gardener has all kinds of seeds left in his cupboard in the late summer, and he wonders whether it is really worth while saving them for another year. Quite interesting results can be achieved by sowing a mixture of vegetable seeds early in September, or in the following spring, if there's any vacant land that wants enriching with humus. It has been argued already that nature abhors monoculture and that there's always better bulk when two or more crops are sown together than when they are kept separately. This random sowing of all kinds of seeds is, therefore, quite an interesting experiment.

CHAPTER 5

Modern Crop Rotations and Schemes

When lecturing to students on the subject of rotations in the vegetable garden, I invariably give about thirteen or fourteen reasons why rotational principles are so important. This at least shows how important the subject is. There is no doubt about it, the land which gets exactly the same treatment year after year, tends to deteriorate, unless that treatment happens to be ideal. One hasn't always the time or the manure, or even the desire to give the perfect treatment to the whole of the vegetable garden each season—nor is it necessary.

When thinking about the rotation of crops, it's important to bear in mind that it isn't only the vegetables that are rotating, but the manures also, the fertilizers, the lime, the cultivations, the pests and disease control, and so on. Thus it can be said that rotations save time, save labour, save money, and they do ensure that the area cultivated gets the same kind of treatment throughout over a three- or four-year period.

The very word rotation is not always understood, and one of the simplest ways of explaining it is to describe a garden I once knew very well at Tirley Garth in Cheshire, where the walled-in area was circular and where the four main beds were divided up by four main paths. Please see the drawing opposite. Plot A then had potatoes; Plot B with the members of the brassica family (the cabbages, sprouts, etc.); Plot C is cropped with peas and beans and Plot D grew the root crops. Now if that were the cropping programme in 1972 then in 1973 all the crops would move on one, the potatoes would go on to the land occupied by the brassicas; the brassicas then move on to the land occupied by the peas and beans; and the latter go on to the plot that was occupied the previous year by the roots. Each year the crops move on one in this way, until the fourth year the potatoes come back to the spot from which they started.

Let's examine this scheme in some detail. The potatoes are what are called a cleaning crop—they are well manured—regularly cultivated—

and so they leave the land in excellent condition. The roots follow on afterwards, and you don't want to manure for these crops, or else forking takes place, but roots naturally want clean land—and land that's been enriched the precious year, and they find this as a result of the work done on the potatoes. So the spot where the roots are growing doesn't get a dressing of dung or compost, and the plot where the potatoes are growing is manured liberally.

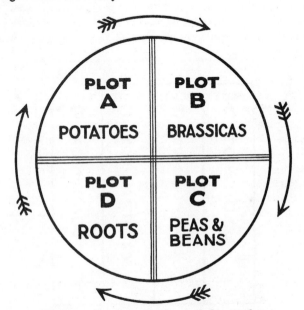

Rotation of crops in circular walled-in garden

Then the brassicas move on one and follow the peas and beans. Now the latter have a capacity of building up on their roots little nodules caused by nitrogenous bacteria, which live quite happily in symbiosis. The result is that the nitrogen which is built up in these nodules is left behind when the peas and beans are harvested, and so the gardener saves money because he gets his plot enriched for nothing with the very 'fertilizer' that the brassicas require. The cabbages, cauliflowers, and the like, grow therefore very happily.

To give but another example, the question of liming. It is important to see that the ground never gets too acid, and it helps greatly if lime can be applied as a routine. Now in this rotation which we've envisaged, the area occupied by the brassicas would receive a heavy dressing of lime—the plot where the peas and beans are growing, a light dressing—and no lime at all will be given to the potatoes or roots. The gardener, therefore, saves his money. He hasn't got to lime the whole of his vegetable garden, and yet he does ensure that the ground never gets too acid. It's a saving of money, therefore, as well as a useful reminder.

One of the greatest troubles that we have to face all over England is the club root disease (see page 270). This is always at its worst when brassicas are grown on the same piece of ground year after year. Allotment holders are notorious at planting out green crops galore with the

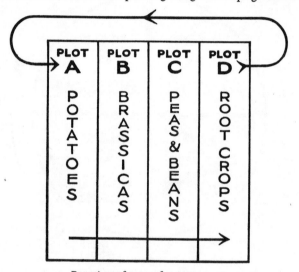

PLOT A — POTATOES

PLOT B — BRASSICAS

PLOT C — PEAS & BEANS

PLOT D — ROOT CROPS

Rotation of crops for square area

result that all over the country, our allotments are full of this club root trouble. By carrying out a system of crop rotation, the disease never gets the chance of really getting a hold on the land, and first-class crops can be grown.

One can say the same with regard to insect pests. Look what difficulties some gardeners have in growing carrots because of the maggots of the root flies. Now it's patently absurd to sow this root crop in the same piece of ground year after year, with the sure knowledge that the pupae of this pest are in the ground, right among the very seeds so to speak, with the result that the flies that emerge will have no distance to go to lay their eggs on the new crop. There is a chance of controlling this pest if the new rows of carrots are some distance away, but it's pretty hopeless when you actually sow the seed where the insect is already lurking. Rotations, therefore, do help in the controlling of pests and diseases in a way that cannot be over-emphasized.

Of course, it isn't every one who can have a round garden, but it's a simple matter to extend the lines as the drawing opposite shows and thus produce a square garden, and yet go on rotating, and one can then carry the illustrations still further, by elongating the garden, and there's still a rotation, so it doesn't really matter what the shape of the garden is, as long as some system of moving the crops on is practised.

In the same way you can often vary your rotation, for instance, in Chapter 1, I have made the roots come before the potatoes, although the brassicas still follow the peas and beans.

FITTING THE CROPS IN

It's all very well to make the four arbitrary divisions with regard to the vegetables that are to be grown, but if one examines them closely, it is soon discovered that there are a number of crops that don't fit into the picture quite so easily. Where, for instance, is the celery to go, or the leeks, lettuce or spinach? Does one rotate the permanent crops like rhubarb, and asparagus? What happens to the Jerusalem artichokes, and the parsley? These are the kind of thoughts that may be flitting through the minds of those who've read thus far. It will be necessary, of course, to have a bed somewhere for the permanent crops. They can't rotate. The asparagus row will be down many years. The rhubarb won't want to be disturbed for three or four years, and so on. The parsley is one of the herbs and should therefore go in the narrow strip as near the kitchen as possible, as suggested in Chapter 11. The celery and leeks, as they are well manured, and are cleaning crops, should really go into the potato break. It only pays, as we've said in Chapter 1, to grow earliest, and therefore there's invariably the room in this area for these two extras.

The onions should really go in with the potatoes also because they need to be heavily manured and are a good cleaning crop. They don't go well with the root crops because this plot of land is not manured, but they can be fitted in with the peas and beans, and as a matter of fact they quite like to grow near rows of French beans. The mingling of the roots of the one crop with the other seems to cause benefit to both. (This is a long story of plant affinities and mycorrhiza which one day I must write a book about.)

The lettuce and spinach can go almost anywhere. They can be looked upon as catch-crops, and they can be sown between the rows of other plants, or on land where it is going to be occupied by another crop later. The outdoor tomatoes fit happily in at the end of the plot where they get the maximum sun and should be kept as far away from the potatoes as possible, because otherwise they will be very easily affected by the potato blight.

The Three-Course Rotation

Some gardeners cannot be bothered with a four-course rotation. They say their gardens are too small to divide up into four—or else that the quantities of the various crops they grow, do not fit easily into a rotation of this kind. They therefore make for themselves a three-course rotation which may consist of: (A) potatoes; (B) members of the brassicas; and (C) all the other crops. No one could possibly say the scheme is as good as a four-course, but it's certainly better than nothing. Here one aims to manure heavily for the potatoes, a lighter composting or dunging is carried out for the brassicas, and the third portion of the ground gets no manure at all. (This, incidentally, is a bit hard on the onions.) Once again to get the picture right, the celery and leeks have to go in with the spuds, but that doesn't matter seriously.

Incidentally, note that lime here is only given once every three years when it is applied as quite a heavy top dressing for the brassica crop—it cannot be given just before potato planting, because it tends to encourage scab, and it isn't needed by the roots. The scheme then becomes dung plus organic fertilizer for the potatoes; dung plus a little organic fertilizer and a fairly heavy top dressing of lime for the brassicas; and organic fertilizers alone for plot No. 3.

'The Exception Proves the Rule'

There are a number of crops that are not sown at the same time as their friends and neighbours, and they turn in for use when other crops may be scarce. The spring cabbage is a typical example. The seed is sown about the middle of July; the plants are put out about the middle of September, and good-hearted specimens are cut, we hope, in April and May. Therefore, here you have a crop which occupies the ground between the September of one year and say the middle of May the next. It's a member of the brassica family. Can it be followed by brassicas? The answer is, yes. A crop of this kind can be regarded as a 'catch-crop' —sometimes rudely called snatch-crop—because it can be planted on the ground after the main crop of the season, say peas, and can be off that bit of ground before the main crop of the following season, which might be brussels sprouts.

Don't, therefore, take any notice of crops of this character. They fit quite happily into the scheme without upsetting the main rotation at all. The leek is another that behaves in a similar manner. It needn't be planted out until, say, July, and so could follow early peas, or even early potatoes. It's off the ground again by March at the latest, and thus it provides food. It brings in money, and yet it needn't be allowed to interfere with any rotation at all. Let's make the rotations fit into our plans—and not have them so rigid that we cannot possibly carry out the kind of crop growing that suits our pocket or taste.

I have no use, frankly, for the man who doesn't want to grow anything else but potatoes and greens. Such a fellow can only follow out a two-course rotation, and the ground is going to suffer in consequence— in the long run. Furthermore, he's not giving his family any variety at all, and therefore there's monotony at table, with little or no opportunity of ensuring a balanced or healthy diet. I have proved that if children are made to eat all the various vegetables grown when they are young, that they like them when they're older, and it's our duty as parents to see that the children have the joy of appreciating all the vegetables, because they were 'forced' to eat one or two of them that they didn't happen to fancy when they were too young to know what's good.

SUCCESSIONAL SOWINGS AND WASTE

Every year hundreds of allotments and gardens are packed with cabbages which are unwanted. You see them getting sadder and slimier as the weeks go by. Every season too, tens of thousands of lettuces go to seed, and then just as the weather is getting warmer and drier, there are no lettuces at all in the garden and they are expensive in the shops. We must all of us learn, therefore, to sow successionally, and to plan intelligently. The charts at the end of this chapter are purposely designed to help to this end.

Take lettuces to start with. It's seldom necessary to make a single sowing right the way across the plot. Far better to sow half a row one week and then complete the sowing of that row a fortnight later. Sow thinly and despite this, be prepared to thin out when the plants are an inch or so high, and transplant the thinnings to any spare bit of land that may be available 9 in. by 9 in. If the lettuces aren't needed they are first-class on the compost heap, and they do help with the ensuring of

MODERN CROP ROTATIONS AND SCHEMES

the correct rotting down of harder material like that of the cabbage stump.

Make half sowings or even quarter sowings if necessary, but do make them successional. The alternative which some gardeners have found successful is to fill a 5-in. pot with the John Innes Seed Compost and sink this into the ground up to soil level, and then to sow the surface with a sprinkling of lettuce seeds. A new part is sown every fortnight or three weeks throughout the year, say from March 1st, until August 1st. The result is there are always seedlings available for planting out. At no stage in the life of the garden hasn't one got a lettuce to cut. Once again these lettuces are used as catch-crops or snatch-crops, and they can be planted in between the rows of onions, peas and beans, or what-have-you, and so succession is ensured.

In the case of the cabbage, it's worth while trying to work out what is needed. After all, the plan which I got out so carefully in Chapter 2 has been worked out to that end. If you must grow too many greens, then for goodness' sake don't leave them in the soil to rob the ground and go to seed, pull them up when it's discovered that you do not want them, and having bashed them up, put them on the compost heap where at least they will rot down properly and produce manure for another year. See Chapter 3, page 47.

One of the things that struck me forcibly when writing the book, *The Royal Gardeners*, with the co-operation of the late King, was the way that inter-cropping was carried out to the full at Sandringham. June Giant cabbages, for instance, were planted out on the tops of the celery trenches, and, of course, were cut and therefore out of the way before the soil was needed for earthing up this crop. I have often sown spinach exactly in between the rows where the French beans were to grow. The spinach was put in about April 8th and the French beans sown about May 8th. By that time the spinach was well up and the plants gave some protection to the bean seedlings as they came through the ground. By the time the French beans needed the room, the spinach was all cut.

Suggestions for Intensive Culture on a Plot by the use of Catch-cropping and Inter-cropping

1. Hardy over-wintering lettuces can be sown in September and planted out 1ft. sq. in October. In November two broad bean seeds can be dibbled in between each lettuce in every other row.

```
        x  x  x  x  x  x  x  x  x  x  x
        x o x o x o x o x o x o x o x o x o x      Lettuce x
        x  x  x  x  x  x  x  x  x  x  x            Broad Bean o
        x o x o x o x o x o x o x o x o x o x
```

72

MODERN CROP ROTATIONS AND SCHEMES

2. Broad beans can be sown at the same time as early potatoes are planted out, putting a bean between every two potatoes. The beans will get away ahead of the potatoes and on account of their upright growth will not interfere with the potato haulm.

```
o x o x o x o x o x o x o x o x o x o      Potatoes   o

o x o x o x o x o x o x o x o x o x o      Broad Beans   x
```

3. Shallots can be planted in January 1 ft. sq. In March broad beans can be dibbled in between the shallots in every third row, so that the rows of beans will be 3 ft. apart. The shallots should be ready at the end of June and the beans a month later. Broccoli can then be planted out in rows 2 ft. 6 in. apart and 18 in. between the plants in the rows. Short-horn carrots should then be sown between the rows of broccoli, thus providing extra and tender carrots in the autumn.

```
+ o + o + o + o + o + o + o +      .:. .:. .:. .:. .:. .:. .:. .:. .:.
+   +   +   +   +   +   +          ...........................
+   +   +   +   +   +   +          .:. .:. .:. .:. .:. .:. .:. .:. .:.
+ o + o + o + o + o + o + o +      ...........................
Broad Beans  o     Broccoli  .:.   .:. .:. .:. .:. .:. .:. .:. .:. .:.
Shallots  +        Carrots  ....
```

4. Early peas can be sown in February in rows 3 ft. 6 in. apart, then in April plant a row of second early potatoes between each row of peas. After the peas have been cleared brussels sprouts can be planted where they stood. The potatoes can be lifted when ready and winter spinach and onions sown in alternate rows.

```
                                   ...........................
- - - - - - - - - - - - - - -      Y  Y  Y  Y  Y  Y  Y  Y
o  o  o  o  o  o  o  o  o  o  o     — — — — — — — — — — —
- - - - - - - - - - - - - - -      Y  Y  Y  Y  Y  Y  Y  Y
Peas- - -   Potatoes o   Brussels Sprouts Y   Onions- — -   Spinach...
```

5. Hardy cos lettuce sown in September, can be planted out in October 1 ft. sq. In February or March, early dwarf peas can be sown between every other row. After the peas are cleared broccoli can be dibbled in, with 2 ft. between the rows and 18 in. apart in the row; then parsley mixed with a little cabbage lettuce seed should be sown between each row. The parsley is gathered over the winter and spring. The ground is clear by the end of April, when it is manured and dug, after which it is planted with ridge cucumber plants. Early in August autumn cauliflowers should be planted amongst the cucumbers, 2 ft. apart each way, the cucumbers being cleared directly they start to go off.

73

MODERN CROP ROTATIONS AND SCHEMES

```
o o o o o o o o o o          *     *     *     *     *     *
- - - - - - - - - - - -
o o o o o o o o o o            c     c     c     c     c
o o o o o o o o o o          *     *     *     *     *     *
- - - - - - - - - - - -
o o o o o o o o o o
o o o o o o o o o o          *     *     *     *     *     *
                               c     c     c     c     c
Lettuce  o     Peas  - - -
                             *     *     *     *     *     *

                             Cauliflower  *     Cucumber  c
```

6. The ridges formed by digging out celery trenches can be used for a number of crops, including lettuces, French beans or June cabbage, which must be clear by the time the first earthing up is needed. Radishes will also do well.

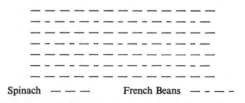

```
+ + + + + + + + + +
/ / / / / / / / /          TRENCH
/ / / / / / / / /

+ + + + + + + + + +
French Beans  + + + +
```

7. Round-seeded spinach can be sown at the end of February in rows 18 in. apart, then about April 8th rows of French beans can be sown between the rows of spinach. The spinach should give protection to the French beans, but will be cleared away, by the time the French beans need more room.

```
— — — — — — — — — — — —
— - — - — - — - — - — -
— — — — — — — — — — — —
— - — - — - — - — - — -
— — — — — — — — — — — —
— - — - — - — - — - — -
— — — — — — — — — — — —
Spinach  — — —       French Beans  — - — -
```

8. Another scheme using runner beans is as follows: sow the beans in rows 3 ft. apart with the idea of keeping the plants cut back and not of growing them up sticks. This sowing should be done in the first week of May, and then early in June brussels sprouts should be set out 3 ft. apart in a row between the beans. When the sprouts start to get tall and need more room, then the beans are cut off at soil level, and the haulm piled round the plants to act as a mulch. The bean roots have nitrogenous nodules which now become available to the brussels sprouts, considerably aiding their growth. The earlier you can sow the beans the better,

74

as you will then get the maximum out of them before they have to be 'sacrificed' to the brussels sprouts. One way of getting an early crop is to sow the beans under continuous cloches about the third week of March, but unluckily this tends to be a wasteful way of using the cloches.

```
— — — — — — — — — —
  Y    Y    Y    Y    Y    Y
— — — — — — — — — —
  Y    Y    Y    Y    Y    Y      Runner Beans  — —
— — — — — — — — — — —              Brussel Sprouts  Y
```

9. Plant second early potatoes in March after they have been sprouted. Lift the potatoes in August and plant spring cabbage and colewort (Collards) alternately, the rows 2 ft. apart and the plants 1 ft. apart in the row. In October plant out hardy winter lettuces 8 in. apart in rows between the brassica rows. The colewort will be clear by February and three broad bean seeds can be dibbled in where the colewort stood. As soon as the lettuce is cleared in April–May, the ground should be dug and manured between the cabbages and a double row of runner beans sown; these should be kept flat by cutting off the tops.

```
+ o + o + o + o + o +        Colewort  +
— — — — — — — — — — —        Spring Cabbage  o
— — — — — — — — — — —        Lettuce  — — —
+ o + o + o + o + o +

o A o A o A o A o A o        Spring Cabbage  o
— — — — — — — — — — —
— — — — — — — — — — —        Broad Beans  A
o A o A o A o A o A o
— — — — — — — — — — —        Runner Beans  — – — –
— — — — — — — — — — —                     — – — –
o A o A o A o A o A o
```

CHAPTER 6

Replacing the Watering-Can

Watering is just one of those jobs the gardener has to do in order to get the best out of his garden. Actually there are few parts of the British Isles and few seasons in which it is unnecessary to apply artificial rain to the soil, in order to help some crop or other. It must be remembered that the main growing season, i.e. when the plants require plenty of water to ensure optimum growth, is usually the one at which rainfall is at its lowest. To quote only one set of figures—the May to July rainfall in South-East England, is more than a quarter of the annual total in only one year in five, and in one year in six it is likely to be less than one-seventh of the annual total!

Vegetables and salads taste best when they are grown quickly and without a check; insufficient rainfall may lead to their becoming leathery and bitter, due to a low sugar content.

For years the watering-can was the medium of applying water to the soil, but it is highly unsatisfactory in a number of ways. It only holds a small quantity of water and constant 'toings and froings' from the tank or tap to the plants are needed. There is always the tendency also to think that as the soil looks wet you can now pass on to the next plant, when all that has happened is that the top $\frac{1}{8}$ in. has been moistened. The wind and the sun will soon dry that up, and often more harm than good has been done as the root hairs of the plants turn upwards to search for the moisture and when they are 'disappointed' they'll die. This is the reason why it has been said that 'a little water is a dangerous thing', and why water should always be given in sufficient quantities to suit the soil and the crop.

After the watering-can came the hose. Quite a lot of water can be applied from a hose in the form of a spray, by either having a nozzle fitted or by using the finger or thumb. It does mean, however, that some-one has got to be personally in attendance in order to direct the water where it is wanted, and here again one must beware for appearances are deceptive. Do not over-rate the speed of the flow of water through a hose, as a ½-in. garden hose about 60 ft. long, will only deliver water at the rate of about two gallons to the minute, which is no more than the old watering-can is able to do with a rose attached! Most people haven't the time to spare to stand at the end of a hose long enough for adequate watering. Another disadvantage in the hose method of watering, is that the spray is not as fine as it should be and so the soil gets beaten down, with the result that it's texture is impaired and the plants are unhappy. With certain soils hoeing the surface has to be done every time after a hosing, especially when a strong jet has been used.

The best method which a gardener can use nowadays for his vegetable and salad crops is the employment of a sprinkler or artificial rainer, of which there are various types. The first type to be developed was the Whirling Sprinkler, which is fixed at the end of the hose; this works on the principle of the pressure of the water spinning the upper part of the apparatus round, so that the water is forced out of the jets, which vary generally between three and four in number, in a whirling spray. All the attention they need is their removal on to the next plot, when one area has had a sufficient watering. They are fairly cheap to buy and one can get quite decent models from about £2·00 upwards—it certainly does not pay to buy types which only cost a few shillings, as they won't do the job well; the higher the water is thrown and the finer the spray the better.

Although these whirling sprinklers go a long way towards solving your watering problems, and their initial cost is low, they have one considerable disadvantage in that the area covered is always circular. Now the great majority of plots and gardens are either rectangular or square, anyhow they are usually bordered by straight lines, so with a whirling sprinkler if a minimum coverage is to be given to the whole garden, certain places will get covered twice and water will be wasted on paths, fences or walls. To circumvent this a 'Brosson Rainer' has been introduced, which will lay down artificial rain over a square area. It has an oscillating head, which throws the water well up into the air, so that it comes down in fine droplets, gently falling on to the ground. With this machine water is not wasted as it all falls just where it is needed and no ground is covered twice. Other advantages are that it can be moved without turning it off and can also be regulated by means of a trickle attachment to cover whatever area is required, taking into consideration, of course, the pressure of the water.

A square area rainer operating on a ½-in. hose, with a mains pressure of 30 lb. per sq. in., should be able to cover an area of 60 ft. sq., that is

400 sq. yds. This type of apparatus will cost you about £10, which is more than most of the whirling sprinklers cost, but it is more efficient at doing the job and saves trouble and waste.

The Crops

The next question that arises is 'Which crops are going to benefit most from irrigation?' and arising out of that 'How much water do they need?' Generally speaking shallow-rooted crops suffer more in times of drought than deep-rooting plants, and respond more quickly when irrigated. Irrigation will give improved crops of the following: lettuce, celery, cauliflowers, early potatoes, radish, spinach, onions, sprouts, rhubarb, turnips, and cabbage, and broccoli plants when young. Sea-kale is one of the few crops that does not want watering at all, as it can tolerate conditions of real drought, but while most vegetable and salad crops can be watered to their benefit when young, with little danger, they are often liable to be damaged when they are older if care isn't taken. Lettuces, which are hearting can be scorched by watering in bright sunlight, and in the same way cauliflowers showing their curds may be damaged. To avoid this, water must be applied in a very fine spray, either in the evening, night time, or early morning. Considerable damage is often done as well, by merely wetting the leaves of plants, which causes a greater transpiration of moisture, without ensuring that the ground is sufficiently moist at the roots.

In a small garden with only one or two rows of each vegetable or salad, it will be difficult to arrange all the crops so that watering on a bright, sunny day is done without harming anything, and the tip is to water in the evening or early morning. On the other hand where there is more ground and a large family, or when surplus is being sold, it would be well to have batches of young crops together, so that they can be watered at the same time. This would be difficult, for instance, if you had your rows of successional lettuce all together. By the way, because I have given a list of plants which derive special benefit from applications of water, don't go away with the idea that you can't water other crops; you certainly can, with the exception of seakale, and in a small garden you will probably have to water most things in order to water one or two, but do this as a rule in the cool of the day, or on a dull day.

The Water

Now we come to the amount of water to be applied. There are all sorts of factors to be taken into consideration, but working out the correct amount is probably best done when based on common sense and experience in your own garden with its particular conditions. It is possible, however, to give some guidance and a rough rule is that quick-growing crops, such as cauliflowers, under dry conditions will need water every ten days to a fortnight, at the equivalent of $\frac{1}{2}$ in. of rain. This amount would also apply to most growing crops, with the exception of quick-maturing crops such as lettuces, where it is better to apply the equivalent of $\frac{1}{4}$ in. of rain once a week. You may now be wondering what on earth is the equivalent of a $\frac{1}{4}$ or $\frac{1}{2}$ in. of rain! Well, most rainers and sprinklers put down about the equivalent of a $\frac{1}{3}$ in. of rain an hour, so if you want the equivalent of a $\frac{1}{4}$ in. leave the rainer on for forty-five minutes, and for $\frac{1}{2}$ in. an hour and a half—it's quite simple.

I think that a timely word of warning is due here. Don't just turn on the water tap in order to produce bounteous crops! Other conditions have to be right as well. The best is got out of artificial rain when the garden soil is rich in humus, organic matter and plant foods, especially when it is above a sub-soil which gives good drainage. The plants, if they are going to grow better and mature more quickly with the increase of available moisture, must have the necessary plant foods, and the soil must be in good heart and of good structure so that it can act as a reserve for the moisture, while the surplus is drained away. Light, sandy soil over gravel can be used profitably in conjunction with irrigation, though again it must contain organic matter, but very heavy clay soils lacking in organic matter are not usually satisfactory, as their rate of of water absorption, even with a fine spray, is very low. They are inclined to puddle and become difficult to work. This does not mean, however, that they cannot become extremely valuable in course of time, by the correct incorporation of organic matter. The judicious use of a rainer enables a gardener, in fact, to cultivate very heavy soils after they have been baked dry.

What about adding moisture to the soil, when the ground is free, i.e. before the crops are sown or planted? I have found by experience that it pays to water the soil before cultivating it, and *not* after. Spread the compost first and then put the rainer on for three hours if the soil is very dry. Do the cultivating as soon as possible afterwards and plant or sow the crop, as the case may be. Don't wait too long or the benefit of the watering will be lost.

It has been stressed that plant foods must be readily available to assist in the more vigorous growth of irrigated plants, and naturally a reader may ask 'Why can't the plants be fed and watered at the same time?' Well, this is quite feasible where quite large quantities of any one crop are grown and machinery has been developed to distribute the correct amount of plant foods and trace elements into large irrigation systems. Only very small quantities of even the major plant nutrients are needed, the dilution being something like 1 in 20,000 or 1 in 30,000, and excellent results have been obtained. Unluckily, however, at the time of writing, there is no satisfactory apparatus on the market for applying organic plant foods with artificial rain to small gardens.

One of the difficulties encountered is that there are very few cases where a number of different crops would require similar nutrients at the same time, another is that the rate of feed of any nutrient into a small irrigation system would have to be extremely slow, and a third is that a solution of plant foods in the water would tend to corrode any small rainer, and in order to offset this by the use of non-corrosive metals, the price would have to be increased. It is a pity, but I hope that the answer will be found, as certain crops can benefit immensely from the simultaneous application of water and plant foods.

I might mention that there is one fertilizer distributor available, but it only takes solid fertilizers, and its rate of application is governed purely by the time taken by the soluble fertilizers to dissolve. There is also a diluter that is affixed to the end of a hose, so that the correct quantities of Liquinure can be added to the water passing through the hose. This works on the principle of the force of the water creating a partial vacuum which draws the necessary quantity of Liquinure from the container. Although this is very useful for watering individual crops such as tomatoes or cucumbers, it does not solve the problem of artificial overhead rain, containing the necessary minute quantities of plant foods, some of which are best absorbed through the leaves.

Getting the Water

It is all very well to talk about irrigation and artificial rain, but we have got to think where the water is coming from. Those who live where the water is laid on, find there are definite charges made to cover the cost of water usage. There are some areas, luckily few and far between, where water is very short, and here only bona fide market gardeners, using water for business, can overhead irrigate in the summer months. The general rule is, however, that you pay say 50p to be allowed to have a tap in the garden from which you can fill cans, or a £1 is paid for the use of the hose. For a sprinkler a meter has to be fitted, the rent being about 40p a quarter, and the water costs anything from 30p to 40p per thousand gallons. A thousand gallons is quite a lot of water and with it can be put down the equivalent of just under a ¼ in. of rain on a plot of an ⅛ acre or 600 sq. yds. as mentioned in Chapter 1.

Taking an average price of 30p per thousand gallons, eight applications of the equivalent of ¼ in. of rain can be put down on half the plot and another eight applications of ½ in. on the other half, for about £2·40, that is using about 8,000 gallons taking it to the nearest 1,000 gallons. That should be enough to cope with any dry periods that may occur, so the actual cost of the water would be £2·40, plus £1 for the year's hire of the meter, making a total of £3·40, which would ensure a supply of vegetables *when nobody else had them* in dry periods, and would most certainly as well allow summer cauliflowers to be grown, which are a very difficult crop in a dry district—a dozen heads would be worth 60p! Runner beans must have moisture at their roots and a fine spray helps to set the flowers; in a dry year the price of runners goes up by leaps and bounds and artificial rain ensures a good supply always! Quicker growth and quicker maturing for a crop such as lettuce will mean that the crop is cleared well in time for the next successional crop, and the sowing will not be put out by the previous crop dragging on too long.

The sprinkler or rainer will also be of great value for flowers and lawns, and it can be used for soft fruit. An application of 1 to 2 in. of 'rain' at a time during dry periods will help the plants considerably especially in the case of strawberries. Where shrubs have been mulched, a gentle, steady spray will help to replace any moisture lost.

What are the disadvantages of overhead irrigation? There is one that should be mentioned, and that is if soil is over-watered, it tends to increase some diseases such as club root, which attacks brassica plants. But please notice the operative word *over-watered* and provided that the right amounts of water are applied the plants will benefit. There is much less trouble from insect pests, which thrive in dry periods. Another point is that our friend the earthworm retires deep into the ground if the top soil is dry, and as his best work is always done in the top few inches it is a good thing for us to provide the conditions he likes. On the other hand we must be careful not to douse the soil with a lot of unoxygenated water, as this will only drive worms up to the surface where they will soon die in the sun.

Weeds will be helped on by plentiful supplies of moisture in the same way as plants, so clean cultivation is as essential as is the replenishment of the used-up plant foods.

One last word to those who may have had experience overseas of overhead irrigation, where the use of brackish water in the tropics has led to the accumulation of dissolved salts in the surface layers. The same

81

troubles are not encountered here, as the most that correct overhead irrigation will do is to leach some of the lime and other plant foods out of the soil, and these can easily be replaced. There will never be any question of soil erosion, of course—if the gardener is careful to incorporate and replace the organic matter in the ground each year.

CHAPTER 7

No Digging Ideas

There has been a tremendous amount of controversy on the subject of no digging. There are a number of 'prophets' who preach and write on the subject, saying that digging is not only absolutely unnecessary—but is contrary to the laws of nature. It has been the author's privilege to travel from one end of Great Britain to the other in order to see the gardens of those who advocate this theory and to discuss the position clearly with them.

It must be said that in some cases the gardens were extremely disappointing, weeds abounded everywhere. No digging is certainly an answer to the control of weeds, especially in a wet spring and early summer. At Arkley Manor no digging is the rule in all parts of the garden. In the vegetable acreage only shallow rotavation is done, just sufficient in fact to produce a level tilth in which to sow the seeds.

Sufficient Compost Problem

If one is not to dig at all and really well-rotted compost has to be placed on the surface of the ground not only to cover the seeds but to smother weeds as well, then about 100 tons of fine compost will be needed per acre. Most of us find it very difficult indeed to make sufficient compost for our own gardens from the vegetable refuse that is available, and it is necessary to buy in straw to augment the supplies or to get hold of the leaves from trees growing at the roadside or the vegetable refuse from some greengrocer's shop. If it is difficult, and it is, to obtain one's compost needs for the digging methods, how impossible it becomes when vast quantities are needed under the no digging plans.

Is Sedge Peat the Answer?

The answer would seem to be the use of sedge peat, and it is for this reason that The Good Gardeners Association has carried out a number of experiments for some time now, in order to discover whether it is possible to use damp fine sedge peat instead of compost. It has been proved that sedge peat is the ideal substitute, but it must be used in conjunction with a fish fertilizer containing 5 per cent potash, at to 3 oz. to the sq. yd. The seed is sown on the surface of the ground without any digging at all. The damped sedge peat is then applied as a top dressing to the depth of 1 in., and the results are satisfactory. When putting out brassicas it is a simple matter to make dibble holes in the peat and insert the plants, so that the roots just get into the soil below.

Therefore it can be said with authority that those who are incapacitated in any way should not despair because they cannot dig. Vegetables can be grown on the no digging method, and one usually gets heavier yields from undug land than from the digging methods, and when the work is done on carefully controlled experimental plots, then it may be shown that crops on the dug land tend to mature quicker than the others. Some suggest that the no digging scheme is particularly suited to the north-west, especially when compost is used and where the rainfall is higher than it is in the eastern counties.

NO DIGGING AND SEDGE PEAT

The author is sometimes asked why use sedge peat in preference to any other peat? And the answer is that such peat usually contains well over 200 lb. of immediately available humus per ton as compared with only 45 lb. in the case of the ordinary sphagnum peats. Furthermore, with sedge peats there is another 70 per cent of additional humus finally available whereas with the sphagnum-type peats there is seldom more than 15 or 20 per cent. Sedge peats are not *seriously* acid, in fact their pH is usually about 5·5 whereas with most of the sphagnum peats the pH may easily be as low as 3·8. Sedge peat, therefore, is the ideal medium for using as a top dressing when growing crops under the no digging scheme.

The problem which faces the no digger is always the making of sufficiently large quantities of compost. There is never sufficient vegetable waste in the garden to produce the fine type of well-rotted compost needed to be put on to the surface of the ground as a top dressing to the depth of at least 1 in. Therefore the keen no digger has to buy in bales of straw or other similar organic materials so that he can increase his output of composted organic matter. In addition there is the labour of carting, watering, aerating and maybe turning, coupled of course with the making of the necessary bins.

To buy in farmyard manure may easily mean an expenditure of from £3 to £4 a ton in some districts and even then the manure is not fully rotted and so is usually full of weed seeds and maybe some diseases as well. If one buys in such dung and composts it, then the price may easily go up from £4 a ton to £5 a ton before it is ready to use. When it is in a fine friable condition 6 months or more later it takes about 1 ton of the original dung bought to cover about 50 sq. yds.

When buying sedge peat it comes to the gardener ready to be used. It is free from weed seeds and can be applied without any preparation at all. It costs round about £2 cwt. and this is carriage paid home in free bags anywhere in England and Wales. Those who are buying 1- and 2-ton lots find that the prices are reduced. It takes 10 cwt. to cover 100 sq. yds. about 1 in. deep. The plan is to sow the seeds in the spring on the surface of the ground and then cover with the peat. It is possible only to put the peat on the strip where the seeds are sown for a width of, say, 3 in. or so, and to leave the soil bare in between the strip and the next row of vegetables, but when that is done there are always weeds to contend with on the uncovered land. I have therefore always applied the peat evenly all over the surface of the ground, because then there is little or no weeding to carry out at all and the mulch created ensures very heavy crops even in dry weather. There is nothing better than peat for keeping the moisture in the ground.

The peat has to be replaced each spring, though in the second and third years one generally does not have to put so much on. It very much depends how much has been pulled into the ground by the worms. The plan at such a juncture is, of course, to scratch a little drill in the peat and to sow the seeds just at soil level and then to rake the peat lightly to cover, after that, say, $\frac{1}{2}$-in. layer of peat can be sprinkled all over the ground to give the perfect carpet once more. Thus after the first season one usually has only to use 4 or 5 cwt. of peat per 100 sq. yds.

Liquid manuring can be done quite easily through the peat and so, of course, can watering if necessary. There is no hoeing to do as such, but as weed seeds land on the surface of the peat there is usually a certain amount of hand weeding to do. Of course one has to start with clean land, you cannot expect to smother serious perennial weeds just by putting a coating of peat on the ground.

NO DIGGING IDEAS

There seems little doubt that the placing of fine organic matter on the surface of the ground does give tremendous encouragement to the worms. They get very busy pulling the surface material into the soil, thus they are working up and down continuously, providing the natural, perfect, almost vertical, channels down which the moisture can percolate and the air can go. The 'happiness' of the worms is quite evident for they become active, glistening, of a good colour and they breed extensively. Therefore, the worm population increases. All this results in nothing but good.

To quote but one typical example: one side of a greenhouse was dug and the compost incorporated, the other side was not dug and the compost was placed on the top. The first year there was very little difference between the tomato plants on either side of the house, either in height or weight of crop. The second year, unfortunately, through a misunderstanding, the no digging side was dug, and the compost incorporated as in the case of the dug side. The gardener who did the digging noted (though he did not know why) the wonderful friable condition and 'openness' of the last year's undug side.

Despite the fact that both sides were dug that year the tomatoes on the undug side (as we must call it) grew far better than those on the other side. They made better roots and produced heavier crops and were generally healthier in appearance. In fact so much so that the results were obvious to every visitor. There seems, therefore, a lot to be said, especially in the case of heavy soils, for attempting this no digging system for certain areas just for one year, with the idea of getting man's friend the worm to carry out the necessary soil improvement automatically.

Mr. A. Guest's Plan

It has been my privilege to discuss with Mr. A. Guest of Fairfield House, Middlecliff, the whole question of no digging and there is no doubt that he does produce wonderful crops each year on his garden and allotment. In order to get over the problem of having to use large quantities of compost Mr. Guest has devised a four-course rotation plan. On the first plot potatoes are planted on the ground in 2 in. of compost, and then over them is placed what may be described as 'sodden' straw, 1-ft. deep. Any old straw will do for this purpose. The potatoes grow extraordinarily well, and at harvesting it is a simple matter to push the straw on one side to get up the tubers. The following year the great bulk of this straw is moved over to the plot where the potatoes will be next season, while root crops are sown on plot one, in the compost that has been left behind, which is by now about 1½ in. deep. Thus it will be seen that you do not have to put any new compost on to the root crop area.

The next crops to occupy plot one, are the peas and beans. There is no problem in harvesting the root crops, they are just pulled up by hand. When it comes to sowing the seeds of the peas or beans, a very light scratching in the compost is done so that the sowing may be done on the surface of the soil. The compost is then raked over and a little more is then sown over the actual line of the drills at the rate of one 1-cwt. bag for 6 yds. of row. This added compost is raked evenly over the soil.

The fourth crop is the brassicas; after the peas and beans have been picked the haulm is cut off at soil level and is put on to the compost heap. No more compost is put on the ground but it is just raked level, and the necessary dibber holes are made through the thin layer of compost for the brussels sprouts, cauliflowers, cabbages, or what have you.

Thus the four-course rotation consists of: (1) potatoes, (2) root crops, (3) peas and beans, and (4) brassicas. By this particular scheme the minimum of compost has to be used and the quantity required works out about 40 tons to the acre. In addition, it is necessary to buy the straw which goes over plot one of the rotation, in a layer 1 ft. thick, but one only has to do this for the first year because three-quarters of it passes on to plot two the following season and about half of it to plot three the year after. Thus the replacement per year works out at only a quarter the original quantity used.

Mr. A. Guest has proved that one man can easily look after an acre of garden on the no digging method described, working only three hours a day in the spring, summer, and autumn and not more than about one hour per day in the winter. He has also proved that it is possible to start with grass land by just planting the potatoes on the grass and then putting the damp straw over the top to the depth of 1 ft. The grass rots away and provides a good organic matter and heavy, clean crops of potatoes result. I should explain that Mr. Guest, who has been doing this work now for six or seven years, is well over seventy, and it does seem that this no digging system of gardening is particularly suited to those who are of 'riper years'.

Birds and No Digging

The problem that one has to face when compost or sedge peat is used on the surface of the ground in order to make it unnecessary to dig—is that birds will come down and scratch the compost or peat in search for the worms which they know are working happily below. Sometimes they thus uncover the roots of plants as well as damaging them. It is a nuisance having to go over the ground every three days or so in order to replace the compost that has been disturbed.

Celery and Cardoons

At the moment the author has not discovered a way of growing either celery or cardoons on the no digging method. The answer might be to set the plants on the flat in 2 or 3 in. of compost, and then to use the damp straw alongside the plants for blanching purposes later. Most of the no digging experts, however, do not seem to grow celery, and so it was not possible to discuss the method of growing these two crops with them.

General Remarks

It is only fair to say that as the result of paying visits to various gardens where no digging ideas are carried out, that the author is forced to the conclusion that no digging can make for neatness, and, as some have claimed, for a disappearance of pests and diseases. The no digging gardens examined are not as full of the normal troubles experienced by gardeners as those where digging is carried out. However, in one famous no digging garden (which for obvious reasons must remain anonymous) the apples were badly disfigured with scab, capsid bugs had damaged the shoots, woolly aphides were seen, the strawberries had virus diseases, raspberry canes were troubled with virus also, there were aphides everywhere, slugs were doing damage, flea-beetles were giving trouble, and so on and so forth—but this was because the man didn't make proper compost and use it.

Some of the no diggers do fork the ground over before adding the compost. Instead of just putting the composting material on the surface of the ground they think it is not against the no digging ideas to plunge the fork into the ground for about 3 in. and just loosen it. Under certain droughty conditions no digging may pay. During dry periods in the 1960s, gardens where the compost was put on the top were looking better than similar gardens where the compost had been forked in. It is obvious that the mulching carried out by the compost does have the right effect on the soil, in that the moisture is conserved.

I am persuaded that no digging is better than digging, nobody has been able to prove otherwise to me anywhere in Great Britain; I am satisfied that it is possible to grow good plants by no digging methods and those who are infirm or who are too old to dig in the normal way should certainly consider the ideas suggested by Mr. Guest, or the use of sedge peat. To a gardener who is very keen on neatness, no digging does not appeal; it certainly is not a complete cure for weeds, and if you are a true no digger all you can do about weeds is to pull them up by hand, and that is a very tedious operation. The wife of one of the no diggers literally spent hours every day hand weeding, and she did not appreciate the work as much as her husband.

This chapter has been purposely included so that some authoritative information might be given on this subject, and it is hoped that this experience of the author and of those he has had the privilege of meeting will make for clarity on this much-discussed subject.

SAWDUST AND NO DIGGING

There are large quantities of sawdust available in the country and the author is often asked whether this may be used successfully. The gardens that the writer saw where sawdust was used in a big way were by no means eminently successful. They did not encourage the author to use sawdust! He has travelled over most counties making his enquiries and seeing gardens wherever possible.

Sawdust has far more crude cellulose in concentrated form than any green manure crop. It therefore robs the soil of nitrogen and tends to go on robbing it as soon as it is mixed in with the soil by worms or by any other method. Sedge peat may cost more, and it is entirely weed free and disease free. The trouble with sawdust is that it may contain a serious disease like *Armillaria mellea*. Even when it appears to be fully rotted and looks like 'dark peat', it may still give trouble. Far more work ought to be done on sawdust before it is used generally throughout the country.

It may be of interest to report that one market gardener in the west is having good results with sawdust. He has managed to 'tap' the local town sewer and run it into a concrete tank. The solids settle out and the liquids run back to the sewage system. He adds to the sludge that remains, a similar weight of sawdust, i.e. for each 1 ton of sludge he puts in 1 ton of sawdust and mixes these together. After a thorough mixing the product is then dug out mechanically and put into a heap.

This heap is turned three times at six-week intervals. After that period it is left for twelve months. The compost is then jet black, odourless and crumbly. Furthermore, the heaps are full of little worms. The presence of worms, incidentally, always indicates good compost! Others who have sewage available, might like to try this method.

CHAPTER 8

Sowing—Thinning—Planting and Transplanting

It is, of course, everyone's duty to buy the best seed possible. Care has been taken in Chapter 13 to recommend the varieties which the author has found to give the best results in many differing parts of the country. There is, however, all the difference between strain A and strain B within a variety. Take, for instance, seedsmen 'Methodicalist'. They take the utmost care when saving seed of the variety of onion we call 'Huge'. Only the largest bulbs are selected each season for seed production. Seedsmen 'Bartimaeus' have the variety 'Huge' but they save seed from every single bulb that's produced, whether large or small. The result is in a few years' time seedsmen 'Methodicalist' have a better strain of the onion 'Huge' than seedsmen 'Bartimaeus'.

I have been most careful to invent the names of two seedsmen so as to give no offence, and to invent the name of an onion as well. Please, however, learn the lesson. It is possible to have a variety of any vegetable you like, and for one firm to be very careful about selection, and for another firm to be very careless. In the one case less seed will be produced but seeds of a better strain, in the other case more seed will be produced, but it will be not so good. Strain, therefore, is very important indeed and all one can do is to go to a reliable seedsman and believe that it is worth his while to be extremely careful with his seed production.

Of course there are seedsmen and seedsmen. There are those who sell seeds and have their own catalogues, but who never attempt to grow or control the growing of any of the seeds themselves. They merely buy the seed they require from a wholesale seedsman in London or elsewhere. I once had a student who left me to go to one of the biggest wholesale seedsmen in London, and he told me that it was most amusing to see a particular variety of, we will say, beetroot, called fourteen or fifteen different names, as it was sold by the particular individual retail seedsmen in the various parts of the country. The author has been longing for there to be a Vegetable Synonym Committee so that all these facts could be revealed and be made public.

It is true to say that some seedsmen specialize in particular types of vegetables, thus Mr. James Unwin in Cambs. has done a great deal of work on brassicas, and is well known for his sweet corn, broccoli, peas, lettuce, and so on. Thompson & Morgan of Ipswich have gone in for having one of the most complete catalogues. Some gardeners, therefore, like to buy their runner beans from one seedsman, we'll say, their brassicas from another seedsman, their lettuces from a third firm, the roots from another source, and so on. It takes quite a long time to become a connoisseur like this and to know from whom to obtain the particular variety of vegetable required. Again and again people write to the author and say, 'We've looked at two or three catalogues and cannot find . . .' and then they mention the particular variety I've recommended. I'll be only too glad to answer queries of this sort from readers of this book.

It doesn't pay, undoubtedly, to sow old seed. It's true that there are exceptions to the rule, and old celery seed is an example. So many people, however, have disappointments from keeping seeds of one sort and another from year to year, that the best advice I can give is to just see good new seed is bought each season. It doesn't pay, either, to save one's own seed. Once again there are exceptions to every rule. Some of my friends save the seeds of runner beans from year to year, and have had very good results. On the other hand, it was only the other day that I had a complaint at a lecture in Nuneaton, to the effect that the strain of the particular variety of runner bean was deteriorating through home saving. If you're a specialist in a particular type of vegetable, maybe you'll make yourself the expert on the subject, and will save your own seed with the greatest of care. For the ordinary man in the street, however, it's better to leave the saving of seeds to the firms that should and do specialize in these crops

SOWING THE SEED

The old-fashioned way of sowing seeds was to get out a drill of the right depth, and then sprinkle the seed along this drill thinly. In order to make certain that the seed sowing is done thinly enough, some gardeners mixed with their seed quantities of sand, powdered peat, dry earth, or similar carrier material. The seed was then taken in one hand, and held

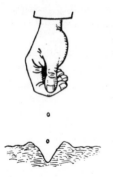

Sowing seed in drills by hand

as is shown in the drawing. It was then possible to push out the seeds on the carrier material from one side of the hand by means of the thumb. The idea was to straddle the row and to bend down and while walking forwards slowly, to push out the seed with the thumb and make certain it was easily distributed. Some people whiten the seed with lime first, and thus it will be more easily seen when it falls into the drill.

Various seed-sowing gadgets have been made and sold. Some of them fairly good and some of them not so good, and in all of them the idea is to put the seed in the container, either circular, long or square, and then the size of the hole is altered to suit the actual size of the seed to be sown, and by means of a slight shaking or tapping, the seed comes out of the hole and down a convenient little shoot into the soil. In all cases for quickness sake, one should walk forward when sowing seed, and not backwards as so many people do.

Two types of drills have invariably been recommended in the past. A V-shaped drill for the smaller seeds, which is usually scratched into the soil with the point of a draw-hoe, or with a triangular hoe, and the flat-shaped drill which was used for peas and beans. This flat-shaped drill always took a long time to prepare, and unless the soil was light and of even texture it wasn't a simple matter for the amateur to make certain that the base of the drill was level. The author has then discontinued advising the use of flat-shaped drills and there is no reason at all why peas and beans shouldn't be sown in the normal V-shaped drills, providing they are got out to the right depth.

A line should be put down where the seeds are to be sown. It should be absolutely tight. Care should be taken to see that the pegs holding the lines on either end of the row are in perfectly firmly. If a draw hoe is used, the long edge of the blade is placed against the line with the corner of the hoe pointing down to the ground. (Please see drawing.) The gardener then walks backwards slowly, scratching with the point of the hoe the drill of the right depth. He will usually have to do the work in short, jerky movements, especially if the earth is on the heavy side. The depth of the drill depends on the size of the seeds. The smaller the seed, the shallower the drill. Peas and beans should normally go in 3 in. deep in the case of the lighter soils and, say, 2 to $2\frac{1}{2}$ in. deep with the heavy clays. It is difficult to draw out a drill much shallower than $\frac{1}{2}$ in.

and it is at such a depth that small seeds like carrot, lettuce and parsley are sown; while the bigger seeds of beetroot (actually they are not seeds but capsules containing a number of seeds) go in 1 in. deep.

Most people sow their seeds far too thickly, and at the end of this section will be found a chart showing how much seed is needed for the 30-ft. row that it has been envisaged we are going to have in Chapter 1. Parsley seed is very tiny indeed. You get 1,000 seeds in ¼ oz. Each one of those seeds if they grow could produce a plant a foot across (I have grown

Making a V-shaped drill with draw line

them that way and I know it!). Therefore, if the germination was perfect, ¼ oz. of seeds should sow a row 1,000 ft. long, whereas normally, seedsmen recommend an ounce of seed for about 80 ft. only. This shows you what a tremendous amount of seed is wasted each year.

Mind you, if the germination is as high as 80 or 90 per cent in the laboratory, and there's a guarantee to that on the packet, it doesn't mean to say that you'll get that type of germination in the soil. Or even if you do, there may be early attacks of pest and diseases which will reduce the number of plants considerably. Take infinite trouble with the preparation of the soil. Be sure to produce a very fine tilth. Incorporate sedge peat into the top inch or so at one 2-gallon bucketful per yard run (this always helps whether the soil is heavy or light). Roll the soil if it tends to be puffy, or tread it, and rake down lightly afterwards. If all these things are done, the highest possible germination in the soil will be assured.

STATION SOWING

It has always seemed to me a waste of time to sow seeds in rows even if ever so thinly and then to have to spend hours thinning out the seedlings afterwards. Furthermore, of course, during the thinning operation, the plants are disturbed and this does them no good, while with a number of crops, and this is particularly true of carrots and onions, the very little damage done to the seedlings, causes a little aroma to be given off which attracts the particular pests concerned. There would be far less trouble from both carrot-and onion-fly maggot if no thinning at all was carried out.

It is obvious, therefore, that we should all of us adopt station sowing, and that is to sow the seed exactly where they're to grow. We'll say that it's desired to have the long beetroot growing 6 in. apart. Three seeds are then sown every 8 in. along the drills, and when the time comes, thinning only has to be carried out to one seedling per station, wherever this is necessary. Lettuces are going to be 10 in. apart in the rows. Three seeds are then sown every 9 in. down the drill, and the thinning carried out to one per station when the seedlings are only $\frac{1}{2}$ in. high or so.

The difference in the saving of seed, of course, is enormous. It's possible, for instance, to buy 1,500 seeds of James' Scarlet Intermediate carrot for 3p. Now if you put five seeds in every 5 in. along the drill (because you cannot be bothered to take a small enough pinch to include 3 in. or because you want to be certain about germination) then you will have 300 stations 5 in. apart, and this, if my arithmetic is right, is 125 ft. Now normally I recommend $\frac{1}{4}$ oz. of seed to sow a row 60 ft. long, and most people say 50 ft. Now $\frac{1}{4}$ oz. of this very variety, James' Scarlet Intermediate, will cost you $3\frac{1}{2}$p to 5p.

So in the one case you easily sow four rows 30 ft. long by the station method, at a cost of $2\frac{1}{2}$p; while in the other case you're sowing not more than two rows at 30 ft. long, and in all probability about $1\frac{3}{4}$ rows only for a cost of $3\frac{1}{2}$p to 5p. The whole thing is self explanatory.

The thing that people don't like about station sowing is that they hate to see the long blanks between the plants when they come up. They've got the old-fashioned idea that it's wrong somehow not to have a complete line. The answer to people like that is to tell them to sow radish seeds in between the stations, whatever they may be, and thus two things happen. One that the rows are marked very early and so can easily be hoed, and two, you get an inter-crop of radishes within the row—a useful factor. Friends of mine prefer to use lettuces occasionally as the inter-station crop, and then they use the seedlings thus produced for planting out in any odd spot that is free, so as to ensure succession of his salad crop, all the year round.

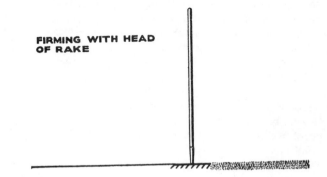

FIRMING WITH HEAD
OF RAKE

Seed Covering

Once the seeds are in the drill a light raking should be sufficient to cover them. This should *always* be followed by a firming immediately over the strip of ground where the seeds are sown. Most people do this firming with the head of the rake. They hold the handle of the rake at an angle of 90 degrees to the ground, and work up the row, pressing down as they go. (See drawing.) Seeds always germinate better if they have some firmish soil to 'push at'. After this firming, it's a good thing to give one very light raking over the surface of the ground again so as to remove the obvious depressions made by the rake head.

Seed Soaking and Chitting

When the soil is very dry indeed it is possible to help with germination by watering the seed drills through the fine rose of a can before the sowing actually takes place. The alternative is to soak the seeds in water before sowing—and this is useful with the bigger seeds like runner beans and peas. The advantage of the system is that you get quicker germination with the result that the plants are through the ground earlier, and it gives them so to speak, a flying start. Some gardeners have taken the trouble to chit the seeds of carrots. They space the seed out evenly on a plate indoors, and spray them over lightly at least once a day. The moment any sign of growth is seen, the sowing takes place. It is claimed that as a result, there are fewer losses. Chitted seed, however, is much more difficult to sow.

Treating Seed

Beans and peas are often attacked by a soil fungus which prevents successful germination. This trouble is particularly bad in the cold heavier soils, and when the seeds are sown very early in the year. This pre-emergence damping off, as it is called, can be prevented by dressing the seed before sowing with an organo-mercury dust, which is obtainable from most horticultural chemists or sundriesmen under proprietary names. Trials carried out by The Good Gardeners Association show that as the result of dressing seed it's possible to increase the natural germination of peas in the garden by 100 per cent.

Celery can be bought already treated with Formaldehyde so as to be guaranteed free from leaf spot. A gardener can sterilize his own seed by immersing it for three hours in a 2 per cent solution of Formaldehyde, and then drying it very slowly afterwards.

Compost-grown Seeds

Those who are especially keen on ensuring that the soil is properly fed, and who in consequence dig in large quantities of properly prepared compost each year believe that it is important to obtain the seeds from a source where they themselves have been grown on land that's been correctly fed with compost also. There are therefore some seedsmen to-day who guarantee to provide seeds saved from land manured with natural vegetable compost, and without recourse to the use of any chemical fertilizers at all. As far as the author knows, no trials have been carried out comparing compost-grown vegetable seeds with seeds grown in the normal way, and therefore it's impossible to do more than state the fact and express no opinion.

Thinning and the Thinnings

The operation of thinning, whether it be done in the long continuous row, or in the case of station sowings should always be carried out in the very early stages of the life of a plant. Preferably when the seedlings are not more than, say, $\frac{1}{2}$-in. high. At this stage, naturally, the least disturbance is effected. The plants that are left behind and have got to grow and produce a crop are not unduly disturbed when the thinning is carried out under such conditions. Incidentally, it helps if a row to be thinned can be given a watering through the fine rose of a can, say, in the morning of the day when the work is to take place.

Another advantage of early thinning is that the thinnings can be transplanted. Most people say that it's impossible to prick out seedlings of parsnips, beetroot or carrots and get good results. The author has transplanted all root crops with success. The secret being: (1) doing the job when the seedlings were very small, (2) ensuring that the soil was in a very fine state of division (we gardeners call this a fine tilth), (3) watering the plants thoroughly once a day afterwards for a week.

In the case where the disturbance of plants at thinning time definitely attracts the pests, it is important not to leave any of the thinnings lying about on the ground because of the odour they give off, and to firm along the row where the plants are growing, with the idea of discouraging flies from 'burrowing' down and laying their eggs on the bases or roots of the plants.

Planting and Transplanting

In the cases of the brassicas, i.e. the members of the cabbage 'family', it is usual, of course, to raise the plants in what is called a seed bed, and then at the correct time to get up these seedlings and plant them out where they are to grow. Leeks are raised in seed beds also; celery plants on the other hand are usually raised in boxes under glass or in frames; while tomatoes, marrows, cucumbers, and sweet corn which are also planted out are often raised under glass also. Fuller details, of course, of these crops will be found in Chapter 13.

The great thing with planting, or transplanting, and it's often both, is to disturb the roots as little as possible. Some brassicas, as, for instance, savoys, will put up with a good deal of bad treatment. Others, however, like cauliflowers, will refuse to produce large curds unless they are transplanted with the utmost care. As you will see on page 200, cauliflowers always have to be transplanted carefully and not too deeply or they go blind. It's also important to make certain that seedlings are absolutely saturated with moisture. Their leaves must be turgid and not flaccid. This is most important for if they are suffering from lack of moisture at planting out time, the leaves will be crying out to the roots for water, and the roots will be broken and battered so that they won't be able to do anything about it. Furthermore, of course, they are in their new position and the new root hairs will not be functioning in the new soil area.

Now this factor of moisture in the leaves of a plant is extremely important. Therefore, in addition to seeing that the seedlings are thoroughly watered the day before transplanting, it is as well to do everything possible to protect them from winds and from sunshine once they are in their new position. The methods which follow are all of them designed to this end.

First of all, there's the drawing out of a V-shaped drill 3 in. deep or so, and the setting out of the plantings in these. The result is that the leaves do get protection from the soil surface winds, in the early stages, and secondly, because the plants are in drills, it's much easier to water them if necessary. The dibber holes or the holes made with the trowel have to be done right at the base of the drills, and therefore when the plants are in position, the tops of their leaves may well be below the original level of the soil. Another advantage of this system is that if you do need to shade the plants in very hot weather, it is possible to lay some sacks across the drills without damaging the plants underneath.

A method I have adopted, and especially with cauliflowers, is to cover the plants with inverted pots, when they are in position in the open. I used to raise the autumn-sown varieties in pots, and then at planting out time if holes were made with the trowel, and the ball of soil inserted, there was a minimum of disturbance to the roots. As the pots were there, it was a simple matter to pop them over the plants so that they had complete shade in the daytime. It pays to take the pots off at night time, so that the leaves can receive the morning and evening dews. If it should prove to be a very hot day, the following morning, the pots can go back again so as to keep the plant shady and cool. In three or four days' time, once the plants are established, the pots, of course, can come off altogether.

When in the Army, acting as Command Horticultural Adviser, both in Germany and in this country, I found it impossible to use pots in this way, but in many cases effective protection was given to the newly planted brassicas by putting a large leaf over the plants for a day or two to act as a kind of parasol. Dock leaves were used, bracken, rhubarb leaves, and even on some occasions, just handfuls of long grass. The plan being to do anything that would help to prevent excessive transpiration from the foliage. In America they often use little 'caps' or 'bowls' made of paper for this purpose.

Where it isn't possible to provide shade it does help if the leaf surfaces are reduced by half. One can take a sharp knife and by holding the leaves of a cabbage or cauliflower plant together, one can cut them through as shown in the drawing. This reduction of the leaf surface has

98

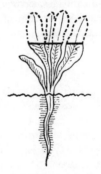

Cutting tops of leaves off brassica plants when transplanting

Shortening of leaves on transplanting

a similar effect to the shading. It merely means that less moisture has transpired because there's only half the leaf surface left. Plants, therefore, recover much more quickly from the move.

There are two ways of doing the planting. A hole can be made with a trowel, in order to receive the ball of soil, or the roots with little soil on them. Once the plant is in position, care must be taken to see that the roots are really firm in the ground, and for this reason many people turn the trowel round and use the handle to press the roots in firmly. (Please see drawing.) It's quite a good idea to leave a little depression around the stem of the plant so that what is known as ball watering may be done later if necessary. Then as the plant grows and hoeing takes place, loose soil gradually fills in the depression, and this does the plant more good than harm.

Use of trowel handle to press roots in firmly

When planting with a dibber, the plan is to make an upright hole to receive the roots of the brassica, and then a hole is made at an angle of about 45 degrees on one side of the plant, and the dibber is levered upwards so as to firm the roots as a whole, and the base of the stem. The dibber hole is then not filled in, but is left there so that water may be given as and when desired for a week or so after planting. Gradually, of course, with hoeing, this hole gets filled in. Dibber planting is more

99

suited to cabbages, savoys, kales, brussels sprouts, leeks and broccoli, but it's always better to plant out cauliflowers, tomatoes, cucumbers, and sweet corn with a trowel.

BALLS OF SOIL OR SOIL BLOCKS

It always pays to get plants up with a good ball of soil if it's at all possible. It would be nice to do this with cabbages, and savoys, and even sprouts, but it isn't really necessary. It isn't needful either with leeks or onion seedlings. Always have a good ball of soil, however, for cauliflowers if you can, and do the same with tomatoes, marrows, cucumbers, sweet corn, and egg plants. Latterly what are known as soil blocking machines have been invented, and seedlings are thus raised or pricked out into blocks of soil made with the No-Soil Compost, about the size of a 3-in. pot. These soil blocks hold together in a very curious way, even when they are watered, and plants grown in them transplant perfectly.

TABLE GIVING GENERAL INFORMATION ON
SEEDS AND THEIR GERMINATION

	Seed for One Acre lb.	Seeds Per Ounce	Average Life Years	Days to Germination	Days to Yield
Asparagus	5	1,000	3	25	3 years
Beet	12	1,600	4	10–15	60–80
Beet, Chard	12	1,500	4	6–10	60–80
Broccoli	1	9,000	4	5–10	270–450
Brussels Sprouts	1	7,000	4	5–10	100–120
Cabbage Early	1	6,000	4	5–10	70–90
Cabbage Late	1	6,000	4	5–10	90–130
Carrot	8	14,000	3	12–18	75–100
Cauliflower	1	10,000	3–4	5–10	65–120
Celeriac	1	50,000	2–3	15–20	120–150
Celery	1	50,000	3	10–20	120–150
Chicory Witloof	8	15,000	3–6	6–12	120–150
Cucumber	2	1,000	3–5	6–12	70–90
Endive	5	12,000	2–5	8–10	90–120
Kale	1	7,500	3–5	5–10	200
Kohl-rabi	4	7,000	4–6	5–9	80–100
Leek	2	8,000	2–4	7–10	100–200
Lettuce	3	16,000	4–6	5–8	60–90
Onion	10	8,000	2	7–10	130–150
Parsley	4	15,000	2–4	15–20	90–120
Parsnip	5–6	6,000	1	15–20	125–150
Peas	1½–2 cwt.	90–150	3–5	7–14	60–80
Radish	56–84	4,000	3–6	4–7	20–40
Rhubarb	6		2–3	8–16	2–3 years
Salsify	10	4,000	2–3	8–14	130–170
Spinach Round	18	2,500	3	9–12	40–50
Spinach Prickly	24		3	9–12	50–60
Spinach N.Z.	1	350	3	10–12	70–80
Swede Rutabaga	3–4	7,000	4–6	5–10	150
Tomato	2 .	12,000	3–5	7–12	100–130
Turnip	3–4	9.000	4–6	5–10	50–80

A CHART COMPARING CONTINUOUS *VERSUS* STATION SOWING AT FIXED FIGURES

Vegetable	Continuous sowing per 30 ft. row		Station Sowing per 30 ft. row						
	Quantity required	Approx. Cost	No. seeds per station	Distance between stations in inches	Total No. Seeds required	Price of Seed	Total Cost to nearest New penny	Days to Yield	Seeds per Ounce
Beans Broad	$\frac{1}{4}$ pt.	6p	1	8	45	50 × 4p	3p	90–110	(50 per $\frac{1}{4}$ pt.)
Beans Dwarf	$\frac{1}{4}$ pt.	6p	1	6	60	60 × 4p	4p	80–100	(130 per $\frac{1}{4}$ pt.)
Beans Runner	$\frac{1}{4}$ pt.	6p	1	9	40	40 × 5p	5p	90–110	(70 per $\frac{1}{4}$ pt.)
Beetroot	$\frac{1}{4}$ oz.	4p	3	6	180	200 × 2p	2p	60–80	1,600
Broccoli	*$\frac{1}{8}$ oz.	4p	4	30	48	500 × 3p	$\frac{1}{2}$p	270–450	9,000
Brussels Sprouts	*$\frac{1}{8}$ oz.	3p	4	36	40	600 × 2p	$\frac{1}{2}$p	100–120	7,000
Cabbages & Savoys	*$\frac{1}{8}$ oz.	3p	4	24	60	750 × 2p	$\frac{1}{2}$p	70–130	6,000
Cabbage Spring	*$\frac{1}{8}$ oz.	3p	4	18	80	750 × 2p	$\frac{1}{2}$p	210–270	6,000
Carrots	$\frac{1}{8}$ oz.	3p	5	6	300	1,500 × 2p	$\frac{1}{2}$p	75–100	4,000
Cauliflower	*$\frac{1}{8}$ oz.	11p	4	24	60	400 × 3p	$\frac{1}{2}$p	65–120	10,000
Cucumber Ridge			3	18	60	12 × 2p	24p	70–90	1,000
Endive	$\frac{1}{8}$ oz.	4p	6	10	216	500 × 2p	1p	90–120	12,000
Kale	*$\frac{1}{8}$ oz.	2p	4	30	48	1,250 × 2p	$\frac{1}{2}$p	200	7,500
Kohl-rabi	$\frac{1}{8}$ oz.	3p	5	9	200	500 × 2p	1p	80–100	7,500
Lettuce Cabbage	$\frac{1}{8}$ oz.	4p	6	10	216	750 × 2p	1p	60–90	16,000

Lettuce Cos	⅛ oz.	4p	6	6	360	1,000 × 2p	1p	60–90	16,000
Leeks	⅛ oz.	6p	5	6	300	300 × 2p	1p	100–120	8,000
Onions	¼ oz.	9p	5	6	300	300 × 2p	1p	130–150	8,000
Onions Salad	¼ oz.	9p							
Parsnip	⅛ oz.	2p	5	9	200	800 × 2p	½p	125–150	6,000
Parsley	¼ oz.	3p	4	12	120	800 × 2p	½p	90–120	15,000
Peas	¼ pt.	6p	1	3	120	700 × 5p	1p	60–80	90–150
Radish	¼ oz.	3p						20–40	4,000
Radish Winter	¼ oz.	3p	4	6	240	500 × 2p	1p	90–110	
Salsify	⅛ oz.	1p	3	8	135	150 × 2p	2p	130–170	4,000
Spinach	¼ oz.	2p	3	9	120	400 × 2p	½p	40–50	2,500
Spinach Beet	⅛ oz.	2p	3	8	135	300 × 2p	½p	60–80	1,600
Turnips	⅛ oz.	1p	5	8	225	2,000 × 2p	½p	50–80	9,000
Sweet Corn			2	12	60	12 × 2p	8p	110–130	
Swedes	⅛ oz.	2p	5	12	150	2,000 × 2p	½p	150	7,000
Vegetable Marrows			3	36	30	10 × 2p	5p	70–90	250

* Plants raised from the seeds sown continuously of these Brassica crops are for transplanting. In each case there should be about 250 plants from ⅛ oz. seed.

Note.—The total cost of seed needed for a 30 ft. row, when station sowing is practised, is shown to the nearest penny, fractions being disregarded. It can be seen for instance that the cost of Swede seed would be around a farthing only.

CHAPTER 9

Cloches, Dutch Lights and Frames

Agarden or allotment without any glass is only half used, for as a result home-grown vegetables are on the owner's table only when they are cheapest in the shops, and very little is actually produced between the months of November and May, and that means that the garden is not providing vegetables for something like seven months in the year.

A small glass-covered area on the other hand, gives the garden owner a good choice of vegetables during this seven-month bare period, while in addition he finds it possible to bring his asparagus crops forward a month and his broad beans are cropping really well before they are attacked by the blackfly. He is able to pick his dwarf and runner beans before they are even seen in the shops and to produce early beetroots and carrots. Furthermore, his cucumbers are early as well as being prolific. Lettuces can be had at Christmas and in the spring while they are often 6p to buy. Marrows can be had early and so can the sweetest and earliest of garden peas. It is possible to produce radishes all the year round, a crop of sweet corn in July, plus tomatoes from early July to late October.

All these delightful additions to the home larder are made possible by the use of some type of low glass. The author has been experimenting for the last twenty-five years on glass of various types, and in this chapter he purposely compares the three types of low-coverage glass which are used at The International Horticultural Advisory Bureau, Arkley. There is no doubt that glass does ensure not only that the vegetables are earlier but very much better in quality as well. From the point of view of the choice of glass the most expensive is undoubtedly the greenhouse, or glasshouse as the commercial grower calls it, but this book is not dealing with greenhouse production. Another book will have to be written on that subject. But it takes far less money to provide low-glass coverage, and comparing sq. ft. by sq. ft. it is surprising how productive the unheated glass can be.

The disadvantage of the old-fashioned frame is that it is immovable, which inevitably means sour soil in due course. Such a frame keeps out rain which means that the crops have to be given every drop of water they need. Furthermore, it keeps out fresh air, which just means another job for the gardener, for ventilation has to be done by hand. The brick-work of the frame too, keeps out a fair amount of sunlight, as is indicated by the shadows cast, while the sides keep out light too. To build a brick frame is comparatively expensive. Therefore it is advisable to turn to the cheaper forms of glass coverage, and they are: (1) the barn cloche, (2) the flat-topped cloche or sectional frame, (3) the Dutch Light with its temporary wooden frame.

CLOCHES

It will be agreed that when continuous cloches are mentioned nowa-days, in nearly every case the barn type is meant. There are other types of cloche, such as the tent, the tall tomato or the lantern, but by and large the most widely used cloches to-day are the barns, which are usually standard in length and width at 2 ft. each way, but varying in height with the width of the four sheets of glass used.

In order to determine how many cloches an amateur gardener would need, let us take again the requirements of an average family of four in those vegetable crops which can be produced out of season under cloches and which would cost a lot to buy in a greengrocer's shop. I do not mean by this any luxury vegetables, but such things as autumn lettuce or early peas and carrots, with which the housewife tries to en-liven the menu, and in addition to the out-of-season crops such things as tomatoes, which now with the introduction of dwarf varieties can be grown under cloches from the time that they are planted out until they are cleared away, and thus remain more or less independent of the vagaries of an English summer.

A large number of cloches is not needed to provide these require-ments, especially if full use is made of all of them. In the past people have often bought many more barns than they actually need and have had many of them standing idle for a great part of the year. In order to get a full return for the money spent on their purchase, they should be in full use all the year round; this is most important, especially when it is remembered that there is wasted labour in stacking away cloches when they are not in use and that, however carefully they are stacked they are probably more liable to damage then than when they are in use. About thirty barn cloches, which would make a double row 30 ft. long should be enough for average needs. The 30 ft. row has again been taken as a standard, because so many plots are about that width, but it is, of course, possible for a row of cloches to be of any length—a short row of only one or two cloches where only a small quantity of any particular crop is required, or a longer row, say for tomatoes when quite a number are consumed.

The Soil

It is well known that market gardeners taking perhaps two crops off a piece of ground in a year will have to put more back into the soil in the way of organic manures than farmers who probably only take one crop a year. The cloche strip is hardly ever left free or idle, it is cropped over and over again without ceasing, and thus it is necessary to build up first-class soil conditions and maintain them; plant foods are being used all the time and must be replenished, often they are being used up more quickly than by plants growing in the open, as the quick growth of plants under cloches demands a plentiful and immediate supply of nutrients. Thus it is no use choosing any old corner of the garden for your cloche strip and trusting to the cloches to do the rest, in that way you will never get good results.

The immediate availability of plant foods is only one part of the problem with a cloche strip, the importance of having the soil in good condition is increased by the very shape of the barn cloche itself. A good supply of moisture in the soil is all important to any vegetable crop, and soil in good heart will retain moisture much longer than a poor soil. The ground under barn cloches does tend to dry out, for when rain falls it runs down the roof of the cloche and then down the walls on to the ground at the side of the cloches—very little, if any, falls into the cloche itself.

It was always thought that this did not matter as the water would spread sideways in the soil and would thus become available to the roots of the plants growing under the cloches; experiments, however, have been carried out and it has been found that water will only travel 1 in. sideways for every foot that it sinks down vertically. Roots of plants have a very much greater spread than is usually imagined, but it will be necessary for the roots of any average plant growing under a cloche to extend beyond the side of the cloche under the ground before it can hope to benefit much from any rain. If the soil is in good condition it will remain pleasantly moist from the period that the ground was uncovered, slowly releasing the moisture to the growing crop.

Good, well-rotted compost is ideal for incorporating into the ground in order to improve the soil structure and to maintain a balanced supply of plant nutrients. Good compost contains all the major plant foods. A 2-in. layer should be incorporated into the top few inches of the soil at least once a year if good crops are to be grown—do not dig it in too deeply, but leave it where it will be readily available to the plants, it will always be pulled deeper into the ground by the worms.

In addition to any compost, an organic fertilizer such as fish manure should be used, at 2–3 oz. to the sq. yd.

Where compost is unluckily not available then sedge peat is a good alternative. It has a very beneficial effect on soils which are either too heavy or too light, tending to break up the former and provide the humus which is lacking in the latter. If it is used, however, it is advisable to apply a fish manure with a 5 per cent potash content *at the same time* at the rate of 3–4 oz. to the sq. yd. Sedge peat is also very useful when cloches have to be used on very heavy land, as it is possible to sow seed on top of the ground, covered with a layer of sedge peat, where the seedlings can get a good start in life, rather than for them to be engulfed in a heavy cold soil.

To sum up, keep the ground in your cloche strip in 'good heart' and well stored with plant foods—it will repay the trouble.·

Cloche Strips

To get the best out of your cloches it is necessary to plan ahead. You cannot use your cloches properly unless you know what crop is going to follow the one you have covered at the moment. Again your cropping plan has to be also based on the most convenient way of using the cloches, i.e. by not having to move them an inch further than necessary. Say what one will, barn cloches are inconvenient things to move any distance—you do not want to have the trouble of dismantling them as some glass is sure to get broken and they are unwieldy to carry when assembled, especially when the ground is slippery or there is a high wind.

A strip-cropping system has been devised after a number of years of experience, whereby the fullest use is made of a strip of ground and the cloches are moved a short way to an adjoining row when the time comes to move them from one crop to another. Sometimes it is only necessary to have two strips, the cloches being moved from one to the other and back again and this is usually sufficient for most vegetable cropping;

three strips are generally needed when one of the crops to be covered is a more or less permanent one such as asparagus or strawberries.

Where there is a single row of cloches 3 ft. should be reserved for each cloche strip, therefore a two-strip system would require a piece of garden 30 ft. by 6 ft., for a single row of cloches 30 ft. long, but as we have said that we would need two rows, then the ground required would be 30 ft. by 12 ft.

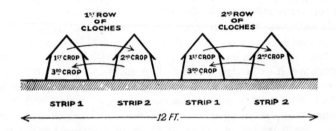

For the sake of convenience cloche crops can be divided into three or four main groups or sections; first those which are sown in the open in July–August and clocked in late September or early October, until they are cleared in November or December; these include such crops as autumn lettuce, peas, beans and endive; second are the crops which are sown in October, January or February, which will occupy the cloches over the winter, some being cleared in March, others not until June; third are the half-hardy crops sown under cloches in April and May, and including dwarf and runner beans, marrows and sweet corn, which will be clocked until late May; fourth are the dwarf tomatoes, cucumbers and melons, which are planted out in late April or May and remain under the cloches all the summer until they are cleared at the end of September.

There are a variety of combinations and successions of crops that can be adopted, and this variety is, of course, considerably increased when commercial crops are grown for market, but it should suffice here to give a few simple suggestions as to crops which will give the best value to the man with the small garden who wants to feed his family well.

First Row of Cloches

Strip No. 1. Double row lettuce 'Attractie' two sowings in August in open for cloching end September for cutting November–December.

Strip No. 2. Carrots, sown January to be clocked until April for clearing late May. 'Amsterdam Forcing', five drills 4 in. apart.

Strip No. 1. Dwarf or runner beans, sown early April, cloched until late May, the former for clearing July, the latter August–September. Dwarf bean 'Masterpiece' and runner bean 'Kelvedon Wonder'.

Strip No. 2. Melons or cucumbers, planted out late May or early June to remain under cloches until end September.

Second Row of Cloches

Strip No. 2. 'Meteor' peas sown early November in broad drill and cloched until April for clearing the end of May and early June.

Strip No. 1. 'May King' lettuce sown in small cloche nursery bed in January, planted out in open March and cloched from April until cleared in late May.

Strip No. 2. Late tomatoes, planted out late May or early June to remain cloched until cleared October.

The two cropping programmes suggested above would give a supply of autumn lettuce, early carrots, early peas, and lettuce in May and tomatoes, cucumbers and melons during the summer. All the cloches in two 30 ft. rows should not be needed to provide for the requirements of a family of four in the above-mentioned crops and thus some could be used for alternative crops to fit in with the rotations, such as:

Strip No. 1. Dwarf beans for sowing July in open, covering end September, for clearing November.

Strip No. 1. Batavian endive sown July–August in open for cloching September–October, and bleaching November–December by whitewashing cloches inside.

Strip No. 2. Radishes for sowing January and cloched until cleared in March. 'French Breakfast' is a good variety.

Strip No. 2. Lettuces 'May King' sown under cloches in October and remaining cloched until cleared in April.

Strip No. 1. Marrows planted out early April under cloches and decloched towards end of May, to be cleared early August.

Strip No. 1. Sweet corn sown mid-April under cloches and decloched late May for clearing in August.

Strip No. 1. Early dwarf tomatoes planted out under cloches April for decloching late May or keeping under cloches until end September.

Strip No. 2. Aubergines and capsicums planted out under cloches late May or early June, but adaptor wires may have to be used from July on.

It is obvious that the weather and growing conditions will have considerable effect on the timing of crops, and that in some years certain crops will not be cleared by the specified date, or perhaps the ground will not be quite right for sowing the next crop—the whole system must be reasonably elastic to allow for variations. In the same way general dates for crops have been given, but these are sure to vary in different parts of the country and the experience gained from a certain amount of trial and error in what crops you like to grow and what are the best crops for you to grow, will serve as a good guide.

Individual Crops

Detailed instructions for the growing of any particular crop will be found in Chapter 13, but where necessary a few instructions with specific regard to the growing of a crop under cloches will be found below.

Beans, Dwarf. These are usually sown in two drills 6 in. apart, with 6 in. between the beans, which should be 2 in. deep. They should not be decloched until all danger of frost has passed.

Beans, runner. These are often sown in two drills 2 in. deep and 8 in. apart, with 8–9 in. between the seeds. After decloching they can either be grown on the flat, where they will probably be earlier, or up supports.

Carrots. The seed should be sown thinly in five rows 4 in. apart.

Cucumbers. Ridge cucumbers are probably the most reliable and certainly the most prolific as a cloche crop, though they may get so rampant that they will grow out of the cloches after July. Bedfordshire Prize Ridge is a good variety. As regards frame cucumbers, most of which can be grown under cloches all the summer, Conqueror is a good variety. All cucumbers need a lot of moisture and should never be allowed to dry out. One plant for every two cloches is usually satisfactory.

Endive. Round-Leaved or Batavian is the hardy variety and makes a good cloche subject. They can be sown in two rows and thinned to 10 in. apart between the rows. It is often better to cover them early in September and October, as they are inclined to rot if covered when they are too damp. They should be cloched at intervals in order to provide a succession, in the same way they should be bleached at intervals, by whitewashing the insides of the cloches and of the end-pieces.

Lettuces. These are best grown in two rows under a cloche, most varieties being thinned to 9 in. apart in the row. Where they are sown under a cloche or two in October for transplanting January, they can best be sown in four rows.

Marrows. Seed can be sown in stations 3 ft. apart under cloches from the end of March onwards, or plants raised in greenhouses can be planted out under cloches from mid-April. It may be necessary to pollinate the earliest marrows by hand.

Melons. Plants are best raised in a greenhouse as the seed needs quite an amount of warmth for germination. In the south they can be planted out under cloches from the end of April 3 ft. apart, the soil having been well enriched with good manure. It is best for the ground to be slightly raised where the melon plants are going to stand, as although melons like plenty of moisture the stems do not want to stand in water. 'Dutch Net' is a good variety to grow and two fruits per plant can be retained.

Peas. Can either be sown in a double row 8 in. apart or in a flat-bottomed drill from 4–6 in. wide. The cloches will have to be removed when the peas start pushing against the top of the glass.

Radishes can either be sown in six drills to the cloche or broadcast thinly.

Sweet corn is sown under cloches towards the end of April in stations of two or three seeds, in two rows 9 in. apart with 9 in. between the stations. Plants should be thinned out to one per station and the cloches kept on until the end of May, or even longer if the plants have not reached the top of the glass. It is a good thing on decloching, to earth up the plants a bit to encourage adventitious rooting from the stem. This crop does not want heavy manuring, which encourages too much green growth.

Tomatoes. It is possible to start ordinary outdoor tomatoes under cloches by planting them under cloches in April, and decloching them when they get too big for the cloches towards the end of May or early June. On the other hand, with the development of such dwarf varieties as 'Puck' or 'The Amateur' it is possible to plant out under cloches from April onwards, keeping the plants under cloches all the summer until they are cleared at the end of September or October. Tomatoes can be raised from seed sown under cloches from the end of March, but these plants will, of course, be later than those raised in the greenhouse.

Aubergines and Capsicums. These have been mentioned last, as although they do provide alternative summer cloche crops, they are not particularly easy to grow, and in addition the height of the cloches will have to be increased either by the use of adaptor wires or by cloche elevators. The elevators or adaptors would only be in use during the summer months and there would be little return on the money expended for their purchase. The purple variety of aubergine should be used and the plants planted out at the end of May, 24 in. apart under the cloches. Capsicums should be planted out at the same time only 18 in. apart.

111

General

The following are a few useful hints on the use of cloches:

1. If the ground you are next going to use in winter is cold and wet, let it warm up and dry out a bit first by putting the cloches over it for a few days before sowing or planting.

2. Take care to get the ground reasonably level before putting the cloches down, so that they will set right with not too much draught through the gaps. It also pays to take the trouble to put a line down and align the cloches to it.

3. The end pieces to a row are usually fixed by pushing a cane or thin metal stake into the ground on the outside of the glass and tying the top of the cane or stake to the carrying wires of the end cloche.

4. If the glass on the cloches becomes very dirty, it should be washed with warm water containing some fungicide and a little detergent.

5. Be especially careful not to touch the side glass of the cloches with your feet in really cold weather, as a number of breakages are caused that way. Do not be frightened of the glass, however, when you are getting it on to the wire frames, you will soon be able to handle it firmly and with skill.

FLAT-TOPPED CLOCHES OR SECTIONAL FRAMES

Nowadays many choose what are described as 'flat-topped cloches' or 'Access frames' because they are: (*a*) portable, so fresh soil is offered to each crop; (*b*) they accept the rainfall and plenty of fresh air, conveying both inside to the benefit of their crops, so that watering and ventilation involve the gardener in no more work than if the crops were growing in the open. They also accept all the light which offers, and they are on the whole inexpensive.

A 30 ft. run of flat-topped cloches, 3 ft. 9 in. wide and 12 in. high, offers 112 sq. ft. of coverage. Probably the best type of section frame to choose is what is known as the 'Double 18'. This is just under 4 ft. wide but is 18 in. high and therefore covers many crops that are too tall for lower types of cloches. Another advantage it offers is that when a crop such as tomatoes reaches the top of the frame the top 'lights' can be removed, when the frost danger has passed, but the sides and ends can remain, thus keeping the soil and plants warm and providing support. These sectional frames are provided in any size starting at 6 ft. long, 2 ft. wide and 12 in. high, and they can be added to as time passes. They can be assembled in any length and any width and even one row on top of another if extra height is demanded. Access to the crops is gained by the removal of a single square of glass.

Think of the extra value of a 10 rod allotment if it were equipped with say, 30 ft. of these frames; imagine that these are in the form of three 10 ft. runs. A corner of one run will be sufficient to provide plants for the rest of the allotment—runner beans, brussels sprouts, cabbage, cauliflowers, leeks, lettuce and onions. Here are three rotations showing how they might be employed over the year.

First Frame

October to January. Lettuce—4 rows, 9 in. apart in the rows, giving a crop of more than 40 lettuces around Christmas time to January, when prices are high.

January to May. The frame now moves to a new site (or possibly to the site which originally grew the Christmas lettuces), and is planted with marrows, 2 rows with the plants 2ft. 6 in. apart. You thus have 8 marrow plants which keep you in first-class 'fruit' from June to September.

Second Frame

October to January. This frame will be over radish and should also accommodate a pinch of spring lettuce sowing; there will be 6 rows of radish yielding at a time when radish are at their most expensive in the shops.

January to April. The spring lettuce which were sown in October under the cloches will be planted out on a new site, 6 rows of them 8 in. apart in the rows, covered with the second frame and can be expected to produce more than 6 doz. lettuce in March and April when they are at least 6p in the shops.

April to September. Tomato plants, variety Amateur, will be planted either on a new plot or on the plot which originally yielded radish; 10 plants will be sufficient and a crop of 60 lb. of tomatoes between July and September can be confidently expected, or they may run into October or November under the cloches.

Third Frame

October to March. This frame will be used for September sown cauliflower plants for planting outside in March, January-sown brussels sprouts, cabbage, leek, lettuce, and onion plants for planting outside in April. Very little space will be occupied by these while they are under the sectional frames. The seedlings to be planted out later can be sown 6 or even 10 rows to the double sectional frame.

March to May. During these two months a new plot will be sown with runner beans in the centre and a line of dwarf beans on each side, all covered with the 10 ft. of sectional frames. There would be 30 plants of dwarf beans giving a very early crop, and 30 plants of runner beans giving a crop which was both early and long.

June to September. This frame would now be moved to a new site and would be used to cover 6 cucumber plants, from which a prolific crop would be gathered.

These three rotations by no means cover all the uses to which the flat-topped cloches can be put. Every crop named would be in production when prices were high and would thus be an additional output to the garden or the allotment.

The details given of the various crops for barn cloches on pages 110 and 111 apply equally well for the flat-topped cloches. Furthermore, the general strip-cropping scheme advised, of course, applies equally well to these sectional frames, in fact cloches can be moved almost as quickly as cloches, and from the writer's experiences there are far less breakages with these cloches than with the types where the wire holds the glass at a tension. It is very useful when cutting the crops under the flat-topped cloches to be able to take off pane 1, cut what crops are needed, then move pane 2 into the square recently occupied by pane 1, and harvest the crop below that, putting the lettuce or whatever it may be, on to the top of pane 2 which now acts as a glass table. Pane 3 takes pane 2's place, and in turn acts as a glass table, and so on. The vegetables are in this way kept clean.

DUTCH LIGHTS

A Dutch light by itself is a simple wooden framework with sides grooved to receive a single sheet of clear or Horticultural 24-oz. glass, size 56 in. by $28\frac{3}{4}$ in. The glass is held in place by wooden stops nailed to the end of the frame. The whole light is of the simplest construction and nowadays is usually standard in size, though there are slight variations from manufacturer to manufacturer.

The lights are not used by themselves but are supported on a framework to make up frames, or on a structure to make up what is termed a Dutch light house; it is in their use as frames that we are interested here. Dutch lights were originally developed in Holland for commercial use and they are used in very large quantities for commercial growing and market gardening in this country to-day. Dutch light frames can be used, however, by the amateur gardener to produce the same sort of crops that are produced under cloches; in this way they are not used for forcing crops, but in order to assist them to mature quickly by protecting them from adverse weather conditions.

They can protect crops from about 8 degrees of frost and save them from being buffeted about by high winds or excessive rain. As against the production of cloche crops, they can also be used for what is termed French gardening, but this means the employment of hot beds made out of fermenting manure. Soil warming units can be used to heat up Dutch light frames by electricity in order to produce quicker maturing crops, but such installations and the cost of running them must be very carefully scrutinized in the light of the requirements of the average family. It has been proved elsewhere in this book that it pays to grow your own vegetables, and it can be said that on top of that, that if you like to have lettuce in the autumn and early peas and carrots, it will pay you to have just the right number of cloches or Dutch lights

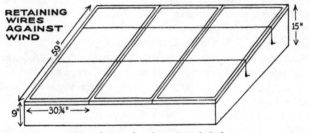

Box frame for three Dutch lights

to produce them and be fully occupied throughout the year. There comes a time, however, when one must cry halt because the additional money spent is not producing the same return in vegetables and there is a limit to what the average family is going to spend on vegetables.

If you are as a family accustomed to buying lettuce at high prices from mid-February to mid-March, then it will pay you to have the soil in your Dutch light frames heated electrically at the cost of about 1p per lettuce, together with say another 1½p per lettuce as share of the depreciation on the transformer and wiring, and exclusive of the depreciation on the Dutch light frame, which would without heating produce lettuces from April on.

Framework. For the home gardener, who would like to have, say, two small frames, each holding three lights, it would be best to have two fairly rigid wooden 'boxes' made, without top or bottom, for supporting

115

the lights; they could be 9 in. deep at the front and 15 in. at the back. These frames would be light enough to move conveniently from one place to another and would also be large enough to grow summer crops such as dwarf tomatoes, cucumbers and melons. Provided that the wood, both on the Dutch lights and on the framework, is treated with a good horticultural wood preservative such as Rentokil (do not use creosote as the fumes affect the crops), the frame should last anything from ten to twenty years. Each frame would cover about 36 sq. ft.

Soil. It is most important that the soil under Dutch lights should contain plenty of organic matter and that plant foods should be readily available. The soil should be enriched annually by the digging-in of well-rotted farmyard manure or compost, but in the case where neither is available when starting, sedge peat can be dug in at six bucketfuls to each frame, together with an application of 1 lb. of fish manure per frame. As the framework containing three Dutch lights is easily moveable, it is not necessary to crop the same piece of ground all the year round; this is a great advantage as the ground not actually covered by the lights gets weathered in the open and there is much less danger from fungus diseases. When it is necessary to apply plant foods a well-balanced organic fertilizer such as fish manure should be used; this can be obtained with a high potash content for such crops as tomatoes.

It is advisable to have the soil warm before sowing or planting winter and spring crops, so the ground should be covered with frames for a week or two before the crops are due to go in.

Water. In the same way as with cloches it is most necessary for the soil to hold a sufficient reserve of water, so that watering does not have to be resorted to in seasons such as spring and autumn, when it has to be done most carefully and only on fine days. If the soil is in good condition and full of organic matter it will hold water well, releasing it as necessary, and it must be ensured that the soil is sufficiently moist, but not over-moist, when the crops are planted.

During the summer months quite a lot of watering will have to be done and it is best to do this as early as possible in the morning, so that the foliage will have a chance to get dry by the evening.

Position. Always have your Dutch light frames where they can get the most unobstructed light. It is no use having them where they are in the shade for most of the day. If you can find a warm spot, sheltered from the winds, so much the better, but do not choose a low-lying frost pocket.

Air. Unlike cloches, Access or Dutch lights are not automatically ventilated. Ventilation is usually carried out by means of inserting small wooden blocks under the ends of the lights. Blocks about 6 in. by 3 in. by

2 in. will do very well. If you only want a little ventilation put the block on its side, or if you want more stand it on end.

During the time that seeds are germinating the lights should be kept tightly closed until germination takes place, but from then on air should be given when the conditions are favourable, especially with slow-growing over-wintering crops. After planting, a crop need not be given air until established.

A good guide is that you should let enough air into the frames without allowing the evaporation of the condensed moisture on the underneath of the glass. Lights should be shut when the sun starts going down and the day starts to cool, so that the heat from the sun should be conserved as much as possible. In the winter months of the year it is best to open the frames at the bottom only. When there has been a sharp frost overnight, it is a good thing to open the lights slightly at the bottom, so that a little air may be given before the sun's rays hit the lights and cause a sudden thaw, which often causes damage to the plants. Do not open the lights when rain might drive in, or during frosty weather, or when there is fog about.

GENERAL MANAGEMENT

The frames should be kept as free of weeds as possible and the weeds will have to be hand-pulled or hoed with a small onion hoe. The vacant plots where you are next going to put your frames should also be kept clean, and the soil hoed from time to time to kill off any weeds that may be there and encourage any weed seeds to germinate, so that the seedlings can be killed before the ground is covered with a frame,

Wind. Dutch lights can be carried away quite easily in a heavy wind, so that they should be secured by some means or other. One good way with a small frame is to have a couple of wires or cords over the tops of the lights, these being tied to nails on each side of the frames (see page 115).

Frost. Dutch lights can be covered with coconut or reed matting during very frosty weather. A good thick layer of straw will also help to keep the frost out.

Whitewash. During the hot summer months it will probably be necessary to whitewash the lights, when such crops as cucumbers or melons are being grown, in order to prevent scorch and to retain a warm, moist atmosphere. There is no need to whitewash the lights when dwarf tomatoes are the crop.

Cropping. It is, of course, possible to use a Dutch light frame for nearly all the gardening jobs that a cold frame with English or French lights is used for—raising cuttings, hardening-off half-hardy plants, storing some half-hardy plants over the winter, and the like. It is our purpose here, however, to see what vegetable crops it profits us to grow in them. Let us take it therefore that we have these two Dutch light frames each holding three lights and being light enough for removal from one position to another and back again. A suggested cropping programme for the first frame would be as follows:

DUTCH LIGHT CROPPING

Crop	Covered by	Period Covered	Sowing	Planting	Recommended Variety	Time of Harvesting	Estimated Yield
Frame No. 1 *(Position A)* Lettuce	1 light	end Sept.–Dec.	Seeds sown in open 6 rows 10 in. apart and thinned to 10 in. in the rows	If planted out from seed bed then 10 in. square	'Attractie'	Nov.–Dec.	18 heads
Carrots	2 lights	Oct.–April	Seeds broadcast thinly late Oct. or January		'Amsterdam Forcing'	May	20 bunches
Radishes	1 light after Lettuce cleared	Jan.–April	Seeds broadcast thinly January–February		'French Breakfast'	Feb.–April	10 bunches
(Position B) Tomatoes Dwarf*	3 lights	Apr.–end Sept.	Seeds sown early Mar. in heat	Plant out in mid-April 8 in. square to frame	'The Amateur'	July–Sept.	32 lb.
Frame No. 2 *(Position A)* Beans Dwarf	2 lights	end Sept.–Nov.	Seeds sown late July in 3 rows 16 in. apart. Thin to 6 in.		'Masterpiece'	Oct.–Nov.	10 lb.
Lettuce intercropped with Cauliflower	2½ lights	end Dec.–April	Seeds sown thinly mid-Oct. under light not occupied by Beans	Plant out Dec.–Jan. 10 in. square	'May King'	Apr.–May	47 heads
	3 lights	Feb.–Apr.	Seeds sown thinly mid-Oct. under light not occupied by Beans	Plant out Feb.–18 in. by 18 in.	'All the Year Round'	May–June	18 heads
(Position B) Cucumbers	2 lights	May–Sept.	Seeds sown in heat mid-March	May 2 plants per light	'Conqueror'	July–Sept.	24 Cucumbers
Melons	1 light	end Apr.–Sept.	Seeds sown in heat end March	End April, 2 plants per light	'Dutch Net' or 'Tiger'	Aug.–Sept.	6 Melons

* An alternative to having the tomatoes following directly on after the lights became available from the carrots, would be to have the lights over self-blanching celery, planted 9 in. square until the end of May, and then to have them for covering a crop of late tomatoes.

Alternative crops instead of melons, cucumbers or tomatoes, could be aubergines or capsicums, both sown in heat in March and planted out in May at 18 in. square.

CHAPTER 10

Unusual Vegetables for Original Gardeners

One of the most interesting features at the author's garden at the International Horticultural Advisory Bureau, is the Unusual Vegetable Garden, because here are tried out with success numbers of unusual vegetables which are available to-day. This experimentation is coupled with some intelligent cooking, carried out by my wife (the Vice-Principal), who's *Cook What You Grow* was one of the most popular works in the 1939–45 war. It is, of course, no good growing the less-known vegetables unless one can learn how to prepare them and serve them on the table.

Many people grow unusual vegetables but unfortunately they rarely become usual because people seem to find it difficult to know how to cook them. (It was for this reason that I recently wrote the book *Cook Veg Book*.[1]) I have purposely included some cooking directions in this chapter, in the hope that readers will find some that affect both the garden and the kitchen. All these vegetables can be grown from seed, and all the seed is obtainable in this country. Readers who have any difficulty along these lines should write to the author. Most of the plants I've mentioned are species and come true from seed, but it's quite fun experimenting in seed saving.

Most of them, too, have another great advantage, that they are hardly attacked by pests and diseases—there is no salsify-fly for instance. I presume because too little has been grown for any particular pest to take to it specially!

As so many of the unusual vegetables are cultivated in a similar manner, it will be as well to deal with them under definite headings. I propose to be quite arbitrary about this, and to classify them in accordance with my own ideas. None of the crops mentioned in the chapter

[1] *Cook Veg Book* published by George Allen.

are difficult to grow, and all of them have been tried out at The Horticultural Training Centre, Arkley, and not always under the most ideal
conditions, because it's a good thing in trials to treat plants rough!

THE PEAS AND BEANS

When preparing the ground for any of this group, it does help if
really well-made compost is dug in first, at least one 2½-gallon bucketful
to the sq. yd. This work should be done, if possible, in the autumn or
early winter, and the land should then be left rough (this is especially
important in the case of heavy soils). Then in the early spring, as soon as
the ground is fit to get on, fork the ground over and add a balanced fish
fertilizer with a 5 per cent potash content at the rate of 3 to 4 oz. to the
sq. yd. If the soil is very sandy, and so lacking in organic matter, sedge
peat may be incorporated with the fish fertilizer, at the rate of one 2-
gallon bucketful to the sq. yd. Finally, lime should be applied as a top
dressing at 5 to 6 oz. to the sq. yd., unless the soil is known to be alkaline.

The seeds of the various varieties should be sown at any time in the
beginning to the end of May in accordance with the weather conditions,
and, of course, the gardeners in the north-east of England, or in the
south or south-west. The warmer the district—the earlier the sowing.
The smaller seeds should be put in about 2 in. deep, and the larger beans
can go in 3 in. deep, especially in the lighter soils. There's no need to get
out a flat-bottomed drill, the seed can be sown in the normal V-shaped
drills at the right distance apart.

It is not difficult to save your own seeds from any of the types mentioned just leave some pods on the plants to ripen towards the end of the
season.

ASPARAGUS PEA

Looks more like a vetch than a pea, does not climb but grows 18 in.
high, and bears lovely dark browny-red blossoms which are very attractive. Sow the seeds in rows 2 ft. apart with the drills ½-in. deep only.
Space them out 4 in. apart in the drills. Put twiggy sticks among the
plants to keep them up.

Pick the pods when they are young and fresh and not more than an
inch long, boil or steam the pods whole until they are tender. We find
they take ¼ hour to cook, and we serve them with a little melted butter.
If you leave the pods for more than an inch you get more for your
money, but they are then stringy, though some people say they are

better flavoured. The long stringy pods need eating with your fingers like asparagus, and you can then bite or suck off what you need, and then leave the "string" on your plate.

THE MANGE TOUT

This is sometimes called the Sugar Pea and is the kind that is always eaten pod and all. There are two secrets of really enjoying this vegetable. The first one is to pick the pods while they are on the young side, and secondly always to gather them not more than an hour before they are cooked. All you have to do is to top and tail them. We prefer steaming them to boiling them, and, of course, it improves them if you serve with a little knob of butter.

Sow the seeds in exactly the same way as ordinary peas, say in May, having the rows 4 ft. apart. You will have to stake the peas, as in wet weather they may easily grow 6 ft. in height, but in a dry season they'll be only 4 ft. 6 in. tall. Be very careful to net the peas or protect them in some way, because birds seem to go for them quicker than any other type of pea I know.

Curiously enough the flowers are steely-blue and quite pretty—they make good cut flowers!

PETIT POIS

This, of course, is the French Pea which we all eat and like when we are over there on holiday. It's a much smaller pea on the whole than the one we have in this country and is very sugary and of a delicious flavour. The plants usually grow about 3 ft. tall and it helps too to stake them.

Sow the seeds early in April, the rows 3 ft. apart, spacing the seeds out 6 in. apart in the drill, which should be about an inch of soil. Be prepared to protect the peas when they first come through with black cotton and the usual pea guards, because the birds will certainly go for them.

The French say that the best way of cooking the peas is to steam them in their pods and then shell them afterwards. The peas are certainly very delicious when cooked in this way, and except for the fact that they are apt to burn your fingers at shelling time, on the whole you do save time in the operation, because they come away from their pods far more quickly after cooking than before.

THE BLUE COCO BEAN

This grows similarly to the runner bean and when the pods are borne they are bluish in colour. Even the stems are stained with a purply-blue colour and the foliage may be similarly stained also. It's a very heavy cropping bean and one of its great advantages is that it doesn't drop its flowers like the normal runner bean in very dry weather.

Sow the seed about the first week of May in the south and about the third week of May in the north. Buy the necessary stakes or wires up which the beans may climb to a height of at least 6 ft. The rest of the treatment is similar to that of the scarlet runner, see page 178.

One of the best ways of cooking is just to pick the beans on the young side—top and tail them—and then cook them whole. They are especially delicious steamed, and it improves them if a knob of butter can be given as they are served.

GOLDEN BUTTER BEAN

This is a dwarf bean and one of the most delicious I know. It is *not*, of course, the dried butter bean of the grocer. The pods are absolutely golden in colour, and all you have to do is to top and tail them, and preferably to steam them. Some people cook them in stock with a knob of butter. Others prefer to have them with a cheese sauce, rather like cauliflower *au gratin*.

Sow the beans early in May, in rows 2 ft. apart, with the beans 6 in. apart in the rows, and about 1½ to 2 in. deep. A few twiggy pea sticks put along the rows helps to keep the plants upright when they are bearing a very heavy crop.

Always pick the pods when they are not more than 3 in. long and keep picking even if you don't want to use them, because this ensures that the plants go on cropping. As in the case of many of the other vegetables I shall mention, these beans do pay for being picked within half an hour of cooking. We like the beans when they are cold in a salad and they give a lovely golden colour to the bowl. Do try cooking half a pound of topped and tailed butter beans with a large peeled and cored Bramley Seedling apple. Put the tiniest drop of water in the bottom of the pan, slice the apple and put them in next, and then cook slowly until the apple froths. Then put in your beans and continue cooking. In with the beans should go a knob of butter about the size of a walnut.

JERSEY BEAN

This is a climber and must be grown up sticks or string just like an ordinary runner. I don't find it quite as tall, however. The pods can be used in three ways, they can be picked on the young side, and then they only have to be topped and tailed before being boiled for 20 minutes, and then served hot with a little butter; or they can be left until the beans inside turn brown, after which they are stored and used in the winter as a dry bean. They take about 40 minutes to cook under these circumstances. The third method is to pick the pods when the beans inside are swollen, but when they are still green, and then to boil these green beans or haricots as they are usually called, and serve these hot with pepper and salt and a knob of margarine, just like peas, and they are particularly delicious this way. The pods, incidentally, are sickle-shaped and the plants look most attractive when cropping.

Sow about May 10th. The rows 4 ft. apart, and the beans 9 in. apart in the rows. It pays to mulch the rows with sedge peat at about the beginning of June. Put this on either side of the rows at a width of 6 in. and an inch deep.

ROBIN BEAN

There seem to be two robins, a climber and a dwarf form. Most catalogues seem to offer the dwarf types to-day. The pods start by being a fawny colour, and then they turn the most beautiful red or are just splashed with crimson. It's a bean which prefers to be grown in the south on the whole, and seems to like a light loam rather than a heavy clay. The climbing type will easily reach 10 or 12 ft. if it's given a chance.

Sow the seeds in drills an inch deep, about May 10th or 12th. Put two seeds every 9 in. along the drills and thin down to one per station later, gapping up with the spares, any blanks that may be seen. Syringe the plants over in the evening if the weather is very dry, as they are liable to be attacked by red spiders. Pick the pods on the young side—steam or boil them for 20 minutes. Unfortunately, they don't keep their beautiful crimson colour after cooking.

This is an attractive bean to grow in a little clump in the corner of a flower border for both the flowers and the pods are beautiful. Incidentally, the seeds are very curious for they look like a little speckled bird's egg.

PEA-BEAN

Don't be misled by the American type whose seeds are white. The seeds of the British Pea-Bean are half maroon and half white. Why it was given the name of the Pea-Bean I don't know, for it certainly isn't a cross between a pea and a bean. Members of the Wine and Food Society describe this as the most delicious vegetable there is. Always pick the pods when you start to feel the peas forming. Then just top and tail and steam or boil for 20 minutes.

Sow the seed about May 12th putting two seeds every 9 in. along a drill drawn about $1\frac{1}{2}$ in. deep. Stakes or string must be provided because it's a good climber. A vegetable that's more suited to the south than the north, and that likes light soil more than heavy clay. Some people let the seeds ripen in the pods and then use them when dry in the winter in soups and stews.

PENCIL POD BLACK WAX BEAN

I grew this first of all in 1953. It's obviously a type of French bean, which crops very heavily. The pods are golden yellow, quite round and have a slight curve to them. They are delicious to eat because they are fibreless and not stringy. They should be picked when they are about 6 in. long.

All they need is topping and tailing. They may be steamed or boiled, or they may be laid out flat in a fire-proof dish in order to be almost covered with a little stock, with a knob of butter thrown in.

TINY SNAP BEAN

Those who've travelled in Italy may remember those beans with tiny rounded pods which are often served in restaurants. The French have another which is very similar called '*Cent pour Un*'. I've only grown this bean once, but it's certainly a dwarf, and seeds need sowing 6 in. apart and drills an inch deep. Don't wait for the pods to get large before picking because they never will. Just top and tail them, and boil them in a little water, serving them while very hot, with a knob of butter.

N.B.—All the beans and peas mentioned previously are species or varieties—there are no early or late kinds. If, therefore, you need succession, sow at intervals of fourteen days, say, three times.

THE BRASSICAS

There are a number of cabbages, broccoli, sprouts and kales which are quite unusual. They all of them, of course, are subject to the club root disease, and the usual necessary precautions should be taken. Grow any of the types mentioned below on land that's been enriched with compost, fed with fish manure at 3 oz. to the sq. yd., and surface limed at 6 to 7 oz. to the sq. yd. Watch out for the blue mealy aphis and for caterpillars, and spray immediately either are seen with a strong solution of liquid derris. I like this for cabbages because it's not poisonous. You must, however, give a thorough soaking, and it is necessary to get the spraying done when the pests are first seen, and not to wait until they are large, or have built up a big colony.

CALABRESE

My American friends are always amazed that we don't grow this vegetable more. My friend, Mr. Archibald Secrett of Send, grows it in a big way for market. The plants send up a central head of what may be called a bluey-green cauliflower. It may be 6 or 8 in. across. This after being cut and used has the effect of causing dozens more side shoots to be produced, each one of them with a little flowering head. These should be cut when they are 6 in. long. The housewife usually bundles three or four of them together, ties the bases with a little cotton before boiling. They are usually served in their little groups after the cotton has been cut.

Steam the heads if possible, and if this can be done, the vegetable will be ready in about $\frac{1}{4}$ hour. Some people serve the side shoots as a delicacy, laid out on strips of hot buttered toast. Another method of cooking the calabrese is by cutting it up into small pieces, and after par-boiling, put into a fire-proof dish, and then cover with white sauce and grated cheese. Bake in a very hot oven for 15 minutes.

Sow the seed about the third week of March in the south, or April 10th in the north. Choose a warm seed bed which has been enriched with a fish fertilizer at 3 oz. to the sq. yd., and hydrated lime at a similar rate. When the plants are 3 or 4 in. high, set them out 2 ft. sq. where they are to grow. Plant firmly.

NINE-STAR PERENNIAL BROCCOLI

If you are fond of small cauliflowers and you are willing to give up a

126

little strip of land for three years, then it is well worth while planting this perennial broccoli. If you do the ground well to start with, and lime it, and if you give a fish fertilizer with a 5 per cent potash content every April at 4 oz. to the sq. yd., you should see produced eight or nine cauliflower-like heads to each plant, each season.

Start by sowing the seeds early in April in a seed bed. Transplant the seedlings when they are an inch high to a further seed bed 6 in. apart, and early in September set the plants out 2½ ft. by 2½ ft. where the plants can grow undisturbed for three whole seasons. The first cauliflowers will appear late April or early May in the year after planting. Three years later the plants must be pulled up and put on to the compost heap about the end of May or early June.

COUVE TRONCHUDA

Before the war I grew this vegetable with success at The Swanley Horticultural College, but the seed isn't so easy to come by to-day. For those who can track it down, I would say that it's the *Brassica oleracea costata*. It's a kind of cabbage that has very wide white mid-ribs. These are cooked and served in a similar manner to seakale, while the green part of the leaf is cooked as cabbage.

The seed should be sown early in April, and the plants put out 2½ ft. sq. as soon as they can be handled. You only get poor results if you let the plants grow too large in the seed bed. It's a cabbage which does best on heavy land, and if the mid-ribs are to be tender, care must be taken to see that the plants never suffer from lack of moisture. This is an interesting vegetable but I would never put it as top of the list.

JERSEY CABBAGE

Until I went to advise growers in Jersey, I wouldn't believe that you could have a cabbage with an 18 ft. high stem. There isn't much point in growing this cabbage, other than as a curiosty. The stalks when dried can be used as walking sticks! The leaves which are produced in abundance at the heads of these tall plants are quite useful as greens in the spring, when other vegetables are scarce. These cabbages are usually planted out 2 ft. apart, on well manured ground.

CHINESE CABBAGES

I always look upon the Chinese cabbages as a cross between a winter lettuce and a spring cabbage. The seeds of all of them are sown in late July or early August with the idea of producing leaves and sometimes hearts which can be eaten during the winter. The rows should be 18 in. apart and the seeds sown $\frac{1}{2}$ in. deep where the plants are to grow. I put in three seeds every 6 in. along the drills and then thin down to one later.

There are three varieties I have tried, Pe-tsay—Wong Bok—and Michihli. The latter, I think, is the best of them all, as it does do its best to produce a heart something resembling the cos lettuce, say 18 in. tall and 3 or 4 in. thick. The outside leaves are best used as cabbage, and are quite good when cleaned or boiled. The Chinese cabbages never smell unpleasant when cooking. The inner leaves do best in the salad bowl.

Grow these Chinese cabbages on land that's been well manured for a previous crop, like the early potato; just lime the ground, using, say, carbonate of lime at 6 oz. to the sq. yd., and then sow the seed, after raking the surface down fine.

THE ROOT CROPS

It's a pity to stick to the three main root crops, carrots, beetroot and parsnips when there are so many others that are even more delicious. All roots should be grown on land which was well manured for a previous crop, and it's important not to dig in any dung or compost just prior to sowing the seed. It is the fresh manure in the soil that causes the roots to fork. Just prepare the strip of ground where the seed sowing is to take place by a light forking, followed by a treading or light rolling, and then a raking to produce a fine tilth. During the forking, it pays to add a fish fertilizer with a 5 per cent potash content at 3 to 4 oz. to the sq. yd.

SALSIFY

Almost not an unusual vegetable. Often called the Vegetable Oyster because of its flavour. Prefers a rather light soil, but asks for depth and moisture. Will grow quite well in heavier land providing it is properly prepared. Sow the seed about April 10th in drills 1 in. deep and 12 in. apart. Either station sow by putting three seeds at 8 in. along the drills, or just thin out to this distance later.

Start to use about the third week of October and go on lifting during the winter. Like parsnips, the roots come to no harm if left in the soil, but like beetroot, they bleed badly if they are damaged when lifted. This vegetable is certainly one of the 'musts'.

It is possible to serve salsify steamed or boiled with a white sauce. We always cook roots in their 'skins' and then rub these off with a cloth afterwards, before putting the sauce on. After cooking, you can if you prefer, bake the roots in a pie dish with white sauce, bread crumbs and grated cheese. We have had them sliced and fried in salad oil, and then served on toast.

If you like to leave one or two rows in the ground, green young shoots will be produced in March, and these can be cut when they are 6 in. long and cooked like spinach. The flavour tends to be rather like asparagus, in fact Mr. Samuel Pepys could have described asparagus which was then a new vegetable, as being 'just like salsify but a lot more bother to grow'. The roots will continue to produce green shoots until early in June.

SCORZONERA

I call this the black salsify, and on the whole it's better flavoured. The roots seldom come very large the first year, and so they are usually left in the ground for two seasons. This is the one factor I have against this vegetable. Another trouble concerns the cooking. It's most important to boil the roots before peeling, and then when they are hot, it's not easy to get off the skin. The best way of doing this is to rub the root in a cloth. and so remove the outer skin that way.

By the way, some say that this is the best root crop for those who suffer with their liver. It always pays to cook the roots as soon after lifting as possible.

HAMBURG PARSLEY

This is usually described as a dual purpose vegetable because the tops are used as parsley, and the roots like parsnips. Personally, I think they're of a much pleasanter flavour and they are in season with us from November to April. Sow the seed late in March or early in April on deeply cultivated ground in drills 18 in. apart and thin out to 9 in. apart in the drills, or, of course, sow by stations at 9 in.

The roots can either be dug up as desired in the winter, or can be got up in November for storing in sand in a shed, or in a clamp out of doors. Just wash the roots before cooking and do not scrape them, and then boil them or steam them in the same way as carrots. We often use the roots grated raw in the winter salad bowl, when they have a nutty flavour. Always try and grow the roots as large as possible, for curiously enough, with this vegetable, it's the largest roots that have the best

E   129

flavour. When this vegetable is really liked, a second sowing is often made about the middle of July, with the idea of letting the plants stand the winter, and then pulling earlier the following season.

SPANISH RADISH

The Americans are far keener on these larger radishes than we are in Great Britain. Most catalogues, however, offer the Scarlet Winter variety or China Rose. This is a round red type with roots about the size of turnips. They also offer the Black Spanish, which is the long winter radish, whose roots are like the parsnip only, of course, black.

Both these radishes can either be cooked as turnips or can be grated and served in salads. To be successful with them, it's advisable to sow in mid-July in the north, and late July or early August in the south. If you sow earlier, my experience is that the plants quickly go to seed. Have the rows a foot apart, the drills about $\frac{1}{2}$ in. deep, and thin down to 8 in. apart in the rows. Indian Army Colonels very much like the roots chopped up and curried!

CELERIAC

This really is the turnip-rooted celery. It's absolutely delicious, and wants to be more known and more grown. We have it every year and we don't know what we should do without it. The curious thing about it is that it doesn't seem to produce its root until well on in the season. Don't, therefore, attempt to dig it early, for it will start to swell up and get really large in October. During the earlier months of the year, it will concentrate on making much leaf growth.

You can either peel the roots and boil them and serve them with a white sauce, or having peeled them you can grate them and use them raw in a salad right the way throughout the winter. Even the leaf stalks are quite nice, and when the leaves have been pulled off, these can be boiled and served like seakale.

It pays to sow the seeds in the Eclipse No-Soil Compost (see appendix) early in March in boxes in the greenhouse at a temperature of 65 degrees. Those who haven't got a greenhouse could use an electrically heated propagating frame. The seedlings should be pricked out when large enough into the J.I. Potting Compost in further boxes or under Dutch lights. See Chapter 9. Here they want to be at least an inch square. After growing on for another fortnight and hardening off say for another two weeks, the seedlings may be planted out in rows 2 ft. apart with the plants a foot apart in the rows. It pays to be generous with compost when preparing the strip of ground, and a fortnight before putting out the plants, sedge peat should be added to the soil at one 2-gallon bucketful to the sq. yd., plus 3 oz. of the fish fertilizer to a similar area.

Plant the seedlings out so that they sit on the surface of the ground. Don't attempt to bury them. If any side shoots appear during the spring and early summer, remove these, as well as any suckers that may come up from the base of the plant. When hoeing, tend to draw the soil away from the plants rather than upwards. From mid-November onwards alter the scheme and earth up towards the plants to give them some protection.

You can use celeriac in all kinds of ways. The roots can be grated raw for salads in the winter, and may be served in mayonnaise sauce. After peeling, the roots can be boiled and served hot as a vegetable. It is possible to cut them up after they have been cooked, put them in a vegetable dish, and then sprinkle some grated cheese over the top, plus a knob of butter, and then brown the whole in a hot oven.

I like celeriac boiled first, then cut up into slices, and fried in salad oil or margarine. My friend, Eleanor Sinclair Rhode, used to do a fricassee. She added some flour and a knob of butter to a pint of vegetable stock. She cooked this for about 5 minutes to form a smooth paste, and then she added a little milk to thin it. She put in a pinch of mixed herbs, and then stewed in this the sliced cooked celeriac for $\frac{1}{4}$ hour. Then she fried some onions golden brown, she put this in the centre of the dish, arranged the cut up celeriac all round, and poured the sauce over it. It was an attractive dish.

KOHL RABI

It is no good attempting to grow this vegetable unless you are prepared to use the roots when they are the size of a tennis ball. It's a crop that must be grown quickly or else it becomes tough. There are green and purple varieties, but the former is undoubtedly the more tender of the two.

Though it is possible to sow in April, it's much better to wait until about the middle of July, and then you've got a root crop that will stand the winter and yet will not be too large. The drills should be 15 in. apart and one should sow three seeds every 6 in. and thin down to one per station later. *Don't go for large roots.* Don't leave the seedlings in the rows too long before thinning. Don't attempt to store the roots, for the flavour is always so poor after that. Be very careful when hoeing or the 'bulbs' will be injured.

131

The kohl rabi should be boiled or steamed as a turnip, but preferably don't peel before cooking. Some like to grate the roots raw and use them in salads. If the roots are steamed first, they can then be sliced, dipped in a little batter, and fried. These fritters are delicious.

THE SQUASHES

My wife and I have concentrated on the various types of squashes there are available since 1935 when we got to know the late Mrs. John Stiles, a Canadian. I am often asked what is meant by a squash, and I've discovered that the name comes from a Red Indian word, 'Askuta-squash' which really means 'eaten raw'. To-day all the squashes are cooked, but the name hasn't been changed.

There are two main types of squashes; the summer and the winter. The former are usually picked when they are young and tender and can be used, as their name suggests, during the summer months; and the latter, though they can be used in the summer, are better left on the plants until they grow to full size. They then will store well and can be used all through the winter months. With the summer squashes you keep harvesting as much as possible and thus the pods go on cropping, and with the winter squashes you do exactly the opposite. For those who are interested in vitamin content, they both contain B, C and G, and the winter squash, vitamin A as well.

As to texture, the flesh of the squashes is much more solid than that of a marrow. Some people have described the marrow as a bag of water. The squash might be considered as a bag of butter. Some people have said that the squash is much more like the pumpkin. There are about twenty varieties, and one has to grow them, cook them, and eat them to realize their subtle flavour. Some of them are trailers, and can be trained up walls and fences, and under such conditions they do crop very heavily indeed. Others grow just like the bush marrows.

In all cases the seed must either be sown in pots or soil blocks in the greenhouse at a temperature of 60° F. and the plants put out where they are to grow about the third week of May, or the seed must be sown *in situ* about the second week of May, the spot being covered with an up-turned jam jar, or a lantern cloche. The trailing types spread tremendously and need a space of at least 6 ft. by 6 ft. The bush varieties can be as close as 4 ft. by 4 ft. It pays to dig out a square of soil a spade's depth and a spade's width, at the spot where the squashes are to be planted or the seeds sown. The bottom of the hole should then be filled with well-rotted compost and the soil put back and firmed. Thus a little mound will be formed over the top. Into this 2 oz. of fish manure can be worked. By the way, to get the greatest weight of crop, it always pays to pinch back the growing points of the trailers from time to time.

VARIETIES OF SUMMER SQUASH

Zapallito de tronco. This is one of the bush types which can either be served hot, but we much prefer it cold with some mayonnaise sauce. It goes well with cold French beans and cos lettuce.

Caserta. A bush type. The fruits are light green in colour with darker spots. It's really very early, and of a first-class flavour.

Cocozelle. This is similar, if not the same as the Courgette which one often has in France. Pick the squashes when they are 6 in. long and cook them whole.

Noodle. Is given this name because after cooking whole for 35 to 40 minutes in boiling water, the squash should be cut in half, when the flesh will fall out in shreds. Always pick when the fruit is 8 in. long and make a hole at one end with a large knitting needle before cooking.

Golden Summer Crookneck. A bush type. This is one of our favourites. We always pick the fruits when they are 4 or 5 in. long, and steam or boil. There's no need to peel them then. If you leave them until they are 10 in. long and 3 in. thick, they then should be cut into slices and fried or be baked, with or without some sausage stuffing.

Prolific Straightneck. Another bush type. The fruits are creamy-yellow in colour and are delicious from 6 in. long. They grow larger than the summer Crookneck, and if left on for frying, they grow to 14 in. long and 4 in. thick.

VARIETIES OF WINTER SQUASHES

Hubbard. This is my favourite. Easy to grow, crops heavily, produces fruits 15 in. long, and 12 in. thick, which may easily weigh 14 lb. The flesh is orange-yellow, firm, dry and sweet. Excellent for pies, first-class as a vegetable. Will store perfectly until the spring. A trailer.

Banana. This is another good keeping squash and a trailer. The fruits with me are usually 30 in. long and 7 or 8 in. in diameter. The skin is grey-green in colour, and the flesh an orange shade. Gets its name banana from the texture of the flesh, rather than from the flavour.

Butternut. Another trailer, which bears bottle-shaped fruits. These are no more than a foot long and 5 in. in diameter. The flesh is beautifully sweet and dry and of good quality. I can strongly recommend it.

Baby Blue. This is a semi-bush and the fruits last year weighed about 5 lb. each. It is said to be a cross between the Buttercup and the Hubbard. Anyway it has the best qualities of both. The flavour of the flesh is difficult to describe, but delicious.

Buttercup. A trailer which produces peculiar shaped fruits, round and flattened, with a kind of button on the end. The flesh is smooth and dry, and orange in colour. It's a very good keeper.

N.B.—I could go on describing the different types of squashes but I have mentioned the pick. Those who want to try baking shouldn't peel first, but should wrap the squashes in greased paper and put in the oven. When tender the seeds should be taken out and the pulp can then be put back with some other flavour if necessary. You can add cheese, a little tomato, some pimento, or those who prefer a sweet dish, can put in a handful of sultanas and some sugar, and having covered with a little custard, some pastry can be put on the top. We have served baked squash with a purée of cooked pears and apples. It is rather fun to serve the dish in the shell of the fruit, but if you are going to cover with pastry, it's better to use a pie dish.

THE ONION FAMILY

The great advantage of these onions is that they are much 'tougher' than the ordinary kinds. They are less greedy too. Those who find it difficult for one reason or another to grow the usual types should certainly try these.

Welsh Onion. Is really a herbaceous perennial and is extremely hardy. It never forms a bulb and the onions, when the plants are growing, look like a mass of spring onions. Some people sow the seed in early March, but we prefer to sow about the middle of July, and then you get a mass of little onions available in the spring.

Once you've got the plants established, propagation may be carried out by division. Each onion plant put out in the spring will produce, say, thirty onion plants around it by the end of the season. It's very useful in the garden, because it ensures that the housewife has the onion flavour available every month of the year.

The Tree Onion. A most interesting onion to grow. Little onions are produced on the tips of the stems, and then further growth may take place with another cluster of onions higher up. I have seen over a dozen small onions on the tops of the stems of one plant. The stems need support the moment the little onions begin to form. Bamboo canes can be used. The bulbs formed in the soil or those formed on the stem may be saved for planting out early in April the following year. The rows should be 18 in. apart and the bulbs just pushed into the ground 6 in. apart in the rows.

The Potato Onion. This is more difficult to get hold of to-day. It's sometimes called the Underground Onion, and is grown similarly to the shallot. Have the rows 18 in. apart and press the bulbs into the soil 9 in. apart, making them firm. These bulbs will form clusters of young bulbs around them, and the size of them to a certain extent depends on whether they are liberally fed, with a fish fertilizer at a 10 per cent potash content.

It pays to earth up the plants slightly, and to make certain that there's no lack of moisture, overhead waterings may be given during a dry year. Mulching with sedge peat is also useful. Fork the onions up in August, leave them on the surface of the ground to ripen, and when quite dry store them in a cool place and use them as desired.

Save the off-sets or little bulbs each year, and it must be known that these cannot revert back to less desirable forms. These should be spread out to dry in the sun before being stored in a dry airy shed. It's possible to dig between 5 and 6 lb. to the sq. yd., and the onions thus harvested from the beginning of August to the following May. When buying the off-sets, bulbs, or 'seeds' as they are sometimes called, you want to allow 1 lb. to 4 sq. yds.

Japanese Bunching Onion. Useful because it's absolutely hardy. Does quite well in the north. Produces what are called masses of scallions in its second season. It will increase in size from year to year and go on producing scallions almost *ad lib*. The seed should be sown early in April in rows 18 inches apart, and the pods thinned out to 18 in. apart in the rows. It is a perennial.

Chives. The plants make a very nice edging to a border, and fortunately grow well under dry conditions. They grow no higher than about 6 or 7 in. and produce masses of tiny little onion-like stems. Once established the plants can be propagated by division in the spring, and the planting done at a foot apart. Do not let them go to seed in the summer; thus the moment the flowers appear, cut them off. Chives have a very subtle onion flavouring, and are invaluable in the garden.

THE LETTUCES

The ordinary lettuces, of course, are dealt with in Chapter 12, but there are one or two unusual types that are worth while mentioning here, in case readers would like a change of flavour.

Bibb. The seed should be sown about the middle of August in rows a foot apart. The plants are thinned out to 8 in. apart in the rows later. It pays to fork in sedge peat along the strip where the seeds are to be sown at one 2-gallon bucketful to the yard run. It doesn't heart up like the British varieties of lettuce, but the heads are loosely folded and of a waxy-green colour. Sometimes they are tinged with brown. The flavour is certainly different from that of ordinary lettuce, and that makes the variety worth while trying.

Salad Bowl. For those who like a lettuce that resembles the Stags Horn endive, this is a variety to try. The seed should be sown in drills ½ in. deep from the beginning of April onwards—say once a fortnight. The plants produce a rosette of notched green leaves of good flavour. These may be picked as required and used as the name suggests in the salad bowl. Grow the plants 9 in. apart.

Gem. There is a lettuce I'm very fond of which I've seen in seed trial grounds labelled Gem and which I've bought as Little Gem. It seems to be a cross between a cabbage and a cos lettuce, and is of the Density type. It's very delicious indeed. It can be grown in rows 6 in. apart on soil that's been enriched with plenty of compost. Make successional sowings from the middle of April once a fortnight until the beginning of August, if you want a continuous supply. It's worth while seeking seeds of this variety because it's so nice.

THE TOMATOES

There are a number of unusual tomatoes that are worth trying for the sake of variety. I would say quite frankly that I don't think that any of them are better than a good outdoor variety like Ibbett's Seedling, but they are fun to grow and they look most attractive in the salad bowl. There's no need to say anything special about them because they are grown in exactly the same manner as any other tomato, and unfortunately they are subject to the same disease.

Italian Plum. This produces an enormous bottom truss, with tomatoes the shape of plums, 2 in. long and 1½ in. across. I usually stop the plants at one truss, and then surround the plants with sedge peat so as to keep the fruits off the ground.

Pear. This doesn't grow taller than 2 or 3 ft., produces quite small pear-shaped fruits, which are particularly sweet.

Cherry. Fruits are borne about the size of cherries in large clusters. The plants don't grow much higher than 2½ ft.

Currant. As the name suggests, the fruits are borne very much like red currants, only slightly larger. This variety can be grown in the open, but always does better with me in pots under glass.

Grape. Long clusters of red fruits about the size of grapes are borne. The flavour is good and the crop very heavy.

For instructions on the preparation of the ground, the raising of the plants, the planting and so on, please see tomatoes in Chapter 13.

THE KALES

Most of the kales have been dealt with in Chapter 13, but there are some unusual varieties which cannot be said to be profitable, but which are interesting and decorative. Mrs. Constance Spry often used the variegated kales, for instance, in bowls and vases for winter decoration.

Most of them want to be grown on well-manured land in a similar manner to cabbages. But the variegated kales produce their best colours when grown on rather poor ground.

Variegated Purple. Brilliantly coloured in mid-winter, useful for garnishing, for winter saladings, or for decorations.

Variegated Silver. The silvery white and green leaves are most attractive and they are just as useful as the purple variety.

Chou de Russie. Produces anther-like foliage, is pretty and attractive, and being, I am told, a Siberian variety, it is very hardy indeed. After the first cut it produces tender young shoots to eat in the spring. We sow the seed about the middle of April.

Jerusalem or Asparagus. Very hardy indeed and so first-class in severe winters. Produces delicious long shoots in the spring in abundance. We usually sow the seeds of this variety where the plants are to grow in June, because it doesn't like the normal transplanting.

Labrador. Another very hardy type, cushions of thickish succulent leaves are produced for use in the early spring, and after these are cut, you get tender young shoots available in June.

Frost Proof. A closely curled type of kale, interesting and handsome. Never grows too tall. Can be planted about 2 ft. sq., whereas most of the others want to be about 3 ft. sq.

N.B.—Kales are often listed in catalogues under the name Borecole.

SEAKALE SPINACH

This is sometimes called Seakale Beet and sometimes Silver Beet. It's a plant which produces large dark-green leaves on equally large long ivory-white stems. These stems which may be a foot long, are very delicious when cooked as seakale, while the large leaves are, of course, boiled and eaten as spinach.

The seed should be sown about the middle of April, and a second sowing about the beginning of August, and in this way succession is assured. The rows should be 15 in. apart, and two or three seeds should be sown every 8 in. with the idea of thinning down to one per station later. Always harvest the leaves and stems together. If you just pick off the leaves and leave the stems on, the plants cease to continue cropping. Grow on a well-manured strip of ground because the plants are going to go on being productive for nearly a year.

CHINESE ARTICHOKE

This is grown for the ivory-white tubers which are produced in abundance. These can either be eaten raw or may be steamed, boiled or fried. Plant medium-sized tubers about the middle of April in drills 6 in. deep. Have the rows 18 in. apart, and the tubers 9 in. apart in the rows. A sunny open situation is best. Fork in plenty of fine compost or sedge peat before planting.

Lift the tubers about the middle of October and store in sand in a shed. Be sure to get up all the 'roots' or else you may have trouble with 'self sets' appearing next year.

CARDOON

The author used to grow this vegetable well when he used to live at Queenstown in the south of Ireland. It seems to love the climate of that country. It looks rather like the globe artichoke as it grows, but it should be treated like celery, and the stems must be earthed up. When blanched white, the mid-ribs are crisp and tender, and can be boiled as celery or even eaten raw in a salad.

The seeds should be sown in the greenhouse at a temperature of 55° F. late in March. The seedlings should then be pricked out into 3-in. pots or soil blocks, and these should be planted out in trenches about the end of May. These trenches should be 12 in. deep, and 8 in. wide. Plenty of well-rotted dung or compost should be forked into the bottom, and after a good prodding, the plants are set out 18 in. apart.

Some people have had good results by sowing three seeds in the trenches where the plants are to grow about the third week of April. Thinning must, of course, be done to one per station later. In both cases the plants should be fed with Liquinure, once every ten days from the end of June until the end of September. Early in October the first earthing up should be carried out after the stems have been tied up together loosely. Remove the lower yellow leaves if any. Earth up with a fairly steep bank, and six weeks later the stems should be ready to use. Lift as desired.

Spanish Cardoon. We like this variety because it has spineless leaves but, unfortunately, we find that it quickly runs to seed.

French Cardoon. This is usually the variety Tours which is rather prickly but some people never find it difficult to work amongst. It is a much superior variety to the Spanish, both in length of stem and in flavour. It's very hardy too.

Aubergine or Egg Plant

The fruits of the egg plant may be baked and stuffed or they can be cut up into slices and fried, or they can even be boiled and served as a vegetable. I like it fried with bacon, but we often have the fruits stuffed for lunch. Any good force-meat stuffing will do, or use pork sausage meat if you prefer.

Sow the seed in February in the John Innes Seed Compost (see appendix) in boxes at a temperature of 60 ° F. After three weeks, pot up the seedlings individually into 3-in. pots, or into soil blocks. Plant out in the open about the middle of May. We always grow ours under glass cloches, 18 in. apart. The soil is enriched with plenty of compost beforehand, and sedge peat is forked into the top 2 in., at a 2-gallon bucketful to the yard run.

Pinch out the growing points of the plants when you put them out so as to make them branch. Allow no more than six fruits to form per plant. The leaves can be very badly attacked by red spider. It pays, therefore, to syringe the underneath sides of the foliage regularly with water. It helps, too, if the surface of the ground is mulched to the depth of an inch.

It is possible to raise plants by sowing seeds under cloches or Access frames about the middle of April. The cropping will, of course, be later than when the plants are raised in heat.

Blanche longue de la chine. This is the long white aubergine which we used to grow before the war with such success. It's much more 'meaty' than other kinds.

Noire de Pekin. Produces dark-violet fruits, similar in size and shape to the white variety mentioned above.

In both cases the fruits should be picked off as desired.

N.B.—Most catalogues to-day only offer a white or purple variety, but it's still possible to obtain the best kinds from seedsmen in France.

GOOD KING HENRY

This is the Mercury or Marcory whose Latin name is *Chenopodium Bonus Henricus.* It's a perennial plant which some people consider a weed, but which is grown as a delicacy for the spring in Lincolnshire. Here it is known as the Lincolnshire asparagus.

If seeds are bought, they should be sown about the middle of May in rows 2 ft. apart, three seeds being popped in every 18 in. It's possible to buy plants, and these are usually put in the soil about the middle of October. For the best results though, one can leave it till mid-February. It pays to grow on well-manured land for the plants are to last many years. Each season a dressing of fish manure with a 10 per cent potash content will be applied at 3 oz. to the yard run about mid-April.

The idea is to try and produce two types of vegetable. First of all the shoots in the very early spring, which are similar to asparagus in flavour. It's usual to earth up the plants to keep the shoots ripe. After this first crop, the leaves are produced in abundance, and these are picked and cooked as spinach. Their flavour is distinctive, though some people consider them rather coarse.

THE CUCUMBERS

There are a number of unusual cucumbers which can be grown out of doors like the ridge types. You either have to raise the seeds in heat under glass by sowings made in April in soil blocks or pots, or the seed must be sown about mid-May where the plants are to grow in the open. In this case prepare the stations by digging out holes, a spade's depth and a spade's width, and filling these up halfway with well-rotted dung or compost. The soil should then be put back, mixed with two handfuls of sedge peat, and an ounce of the fish fertilizer.

These stations should be at least 3 ft. apart. The cucumber plants can then be allowed to scramble over the ground, or better still, can be trained up a fence or up posts.

Apple. This produces cucumbers about the size of a large round apple. The fruits are non-acid, and so are loved by those who get indigestion through eating the ordinary varieties.

Serpent. Produces fruits which curl round and round like a serpent, and may be as much as 4 ft. long. It's just a curiosity, I always think there seems to be a little melon taste to the flesh.

Japanese Climbing. This we've tried out of doors but it does better under glass. Will produce fruits 3 in. thick and about a foot long when well done.

Gherkin. Try and get the true West Indian Gherkin which produces its fruits about an inch long, oval and prickly. These are delicious for pickling, and are well worth space in any garden.

CHAPTER 11

Herbs and Herb Growing

A small herb garden or herb border proves itself very useful to all housewives. Not only is it possible to use herbs for such well-known purposes as making up stuffings or sauces, but the addition of a few well-chosen 'leaves' can alter and improve the taste of most dishes. The 'sameness' can be taken out of the daily diet without having recourse to the purchase of expensive foodstuffs.

It is most important, however, for the herbs to be within easy reach of the kitchen, as no cook, in the middle of making a stew, is going down to the very end of the garden to find the plant she wants. In the same way when herbs have to be dried, it is often easier to do the drying bit by bit as the different herbs become fully ripe, so that if they are handy and by the kitchen door—they can be cut at the right moment and their optimum taste preserved.

The best position is undoubtedly near the kitchen door; a narrow border, say 2 ft. wide. Most herbs prefer a sunny position, though they can *tolerate* partial shade; deep shade should be avoided. Two or three plants of each herb are usually quite sufficient for the requirements of an average family and there is no need to have long rows or large beds. In fact it will probably be found necessary to keep the more rampant growers within bounds. The length of the border would naturally depend on the numbers of the different herbs grown, being quite small to include only the more common herbs, but up to 40 ft. to include the more uncommon ones. It is, of course, difficult to cater for all the individual tastes of the differing plants in a small border, so it usually pays to suit the herb to the existing soil, that is choose what herbs will do well on your particular type of soil.

If you do have a good medium loam then most herbs should do well on it, but there are a number which do not like a heavy clay, while others need more moisture than is offered by a light sandy soil. The majority of herbs prefer alkaline conditions, so where the soil is acid lime should be applied every three years or so.

HERBS AND HERB GROWING

There are numerous herbs which have been grown in the past, either for their medicinal purposes, for cooking or to make up salads. In this chapter only those herbs, which are quite commonly used for cooking, have been included, and instructions for growing them will be found below.

Angelica (Angelica archangelica). This plant does well under most conditions, though it does prefer a rich moist soil and partial shade. It can grow up to 8 ft. in height at the time of flowering, so the plants want to be at least 2 ft. apart. Propagation in the first place is carried out by sowing seeds when they are as ripe as possible, that is immediately after collection in late summer; the plants are then best left to seed themselves. It is only possible to move the plants when young, and they usually die after flowering which is generally when they are three years old. If the flowering stalks are kept cut down regularly, the plants can be made to last for five or six years, but it is hardly worth while.

The young stems are used for making candied Angelica and are cut for this purpose in May and June, with perhaps a second crop in August. It is possible to use the young stems in the same way as celery, or to mix them with rhubarb for tarts and jams.

Anise (Pimpinella anisum). This is a small and dainty annual, growing only to about 1 ft. high. The seed only ripens in milder districts, when the plant is growing in a warm soil, so a warm sheltered position should be chosen. The seed can either be sown thinly in April in drills 1 ft. apart, thinning the plants later to 1 ft. square, or it can be sown in April in slight warmth under glass and transplanted into the open after the middle of May. Care should be taken when transplanting as Anise does not like to be moved. Aniseed is a much more popular flavouring on the Continent than in this country, but the addition of a few seeds to a number of dishes as an experiment is worth trying. The seed should ripen in July in a good summer, and the leaves can be used chopped up in small quantities in salads.

Balm (Melissa officinalis). This plant has scented leaves and small white flowers, growing to about 2½ ft. in height. Balm does well in most conditions, but prefers a rich moist soil, so where the soil is very light it pays to incorporate some organic matter such as well-rotted compost or moist sedge peat. Propagation is most easily carried out by division of the roots in the autumn and roots are usually easily available. Seeds can be sown in May in drills 6 in. apart, the seedlings being thinned to 3 in. apart—the following season when the plants are 6 in. high, they should be moved to their permanent positions 2 ft. apart. The established plants should be cut down to ground level in the autumn, as the plants will spring up even more strongly in the spring. The leaves are cut as the plant starts to bloom and can be used as flavouring for soups and stews, or can be cut up finely for salads. Leaves when dried can be added to stuffing for poultry; Balm tea, however, is best when made from green leaves.

Basil—Bush Basil (Ocymum minimum); Sweet Basil (Ocymum basilicum). The Bush Basil is perhaps slightly more hardy than the other variety, but both are usually treated as annuals and have more or less the same flavour, which is hot and like that of cloves. The sweet Basil grows to about 18 in. and the bush to 8 in. They can be sown outside in mid-May in drills 1 ft. apart, thinning the seedlings to 8 in. apart, but it is probably better to sow the seeds in gentle heat in March or in a cold frame in April, transplanting the plants outdoors in May. The Basil is probably the strongest-flavoured herb that can be grown outside in this country and both varieties are very good for flavouring soups and stews, and sausage stuffing. The leaves can be used either dried or when fresh, and in a good summer there are often two 'cuttings'. A very few finely cut fresh leaves can be added to a salad—a delicious idea.

Borage (Borago officinalis). This is one of the more decorative herbs and should be planted so that the flowers can be seen to advantage. It is easily raised from seed and should be grown as an annual, the seed being sown in the open in rows 1 ft. apart in March or April, or in September for flowering early. The plants should later be thinned out to a foot apart in the row. The seeds can also be raised in a box for transplanting, but it will be found that in most years it seeds itself with no difficulty. The leaves have a cooling quality and are mostly used for summer drinks such as cider cup; the blue flowers are also edible and add a dash of colour to a salad. Borage tea, an infusion of the leaves, is not made much now but is a very useful cooling drink.

Caraway (Carum carvi). A plant closely related to parsley, the seeds being used in this country mostly for cakes and buns, though in other countries, especially Germany, it is used in cheeses and many forms of cooking, as well as in the flavouring of the liqueur 'Kümmel'. It is certainly not worth growing Caraway if all the members of the family cannot abide the taste of the seeds, but if they are appreciated then it is very useful to have your own supply.

The plants are easily grown from seed, which can be sown in the autumn soon after it has been collected, the plants then flowering the following summer. If the seed is sown in the spring the plants will flower the following year, the plants dying down after flowering in both cases. The seed should be sown in rows 2 ft. apart, thinning out the plants later to 18 in. apart in the rows. The seeds are harvested by cutting down the plants as the seeds start to ripen and before they have been blown away by the wind, laying the plants down on old newspapers or on a dust sheet, preferably in some warm place indoors. It is quite easy to thresh the seeds out as they become loose, and after collection they should be dried either in trays in the sun, or in a greenhouse or room indoors, though the temperature should not rise above 70° F. They should be stored in an air-tight jar.

Chervil (Anthriscus cerefolium). This is an annual and can easily be raised from seed, but hates being transplanted. The seed should be sown in spring and again in July, in rows about 1 ft. apart, thinning the plants to 8 in. apart—the plants grow to about 1 ft. high. Chervil should seed itself once it has been established. The seed is best sown when absolutely ripe, so if there is any trouble in getting seed to germinate, a couple of seeding plants should be obtained and laid on the ground—and hey presto, all is well. In order to have a supply of chervil during the winter months seed can be sown in boxes which are kept in the greenhouse, or as the plant is hardy and will grow well under cloches, seed can be sown at the end of August, being cloched at the end of September, the plants being quite happy under the cloches over the winter.

This herb is very much used by the French, the flavour being aromatic and pleasant, for sauces and stews, etc., as well as in small quantities in salads. The leaves on fading turn a pleasant shade of pink and add colour to a mixed salad. It is also possible to dry the leaves.

Coriander (Coriandrum sativum). An attractive annual, growing 2 to 3 ft. high, with mauve flowers in umbels. The seed is best sown outdoors in April in drills 1 ft. apart, thinning the plants later to 6 in. apart; the seeds take a long time to germinate.

The seeds are harvested in the same way as caraway seeds, the plants being cut down as the seeds start to ripen. The plant has an unpleasant smell until the seeds have started to ripen and in the same way the seeds have a disagreeable taste and smell until they are ripe. The seeds which are ready in August, become more fragrant the longer they are kept. They can be used in cooking or in sweets, while the leaves are useful for flavouring soups and stews, having rather a peculiar but pleasant taste.

Dill (Pencedamon graveolens). This is grown as an annual and does best on a light soil in a sunny position. The seed should be sown in April in drills 1 ft. apart and the plants thinned later to 9 in. apart in the row. It is a very quick grower and reaches about 3 ft. in height, looking something like a small fennel plant, but more compact-looking, with yellow flowers in umbels. The seeds, which are actually fruits, are harvested in the same way as caraway or coriander seeds.

Dill-water, made from dill seeds, was always regarded as one of the staple remedies for soothing children off to sleep, but a more household use is the making of dill vinegar, by the steeping of the seeds in vinegar for a week, or some people steep the green tips of the leaves before flowering for three weeks in vinegar. It is very often used for pickling cucumbers and gherkins, by adding a quantity of seeds to the pickling brine. The leaves can be used in salads or for flavouring sauces, while in Scandinavia they are used with new potatoes instead of mint. There is no aniseed flavour with dill and the dried leaves cannot be used.

Fennel—Garden Fennel (Foeniculum officinale), Common Fennel (Foeniculum vulgare), Sweet Fennel (Foeniculum dulce) synonyms Finocchio or Florence Fennel. Fennel is a tall graceful plant and the Garden Fennel, which has leaf-stalks forming a sheath around its base, often grows to 6 ft. The flowers are yellow in umbels and the leaves are fine and feathery. The Garden Fennel and Common Fennel once they have been raised from seed will go on for a number of years. They seed themselves very easily and the unwanted seedlings should be taken out before they have time to form long tap-roots. In the first place the seeds should be sown in April in drills 3 ft. apart, finally thinning out the plants to 2 ft. apart. For household purposes the plants should not be allowed to flower, keeping them cut back to within a foot or two of the ground; the stems can be peeled and used for salads, while the leaves can be chopped and used in a white sauce for mackerel, salmon and 'oily' fishes. The leaves are not often used dried.

Sweet Fennel on the other hand is a much smaller plant grown as an annual. It is popular in Italy, but is rather difficult to grow in this country, as often the bases of the leaf stalks fail to 'bulb' or swell as they should. When the swelling does occur they should be half-earthed up. The bulb is about the size of a hen's egg when ready for use and should be stewed with stock before serving with a cream or rich sauce.

Garlic (Allium sativum). It is used to a very large extent in Continental cooking and providing that it is not overdone—a very little garlic in a soup or stew does help to improve the general flavour and should be appreciated by the British palate. The plant itself is a sort of compound 'bulb' made up of bulblets or cloves, separated by papery scales, and all held together by a thick white skin. The cloves should be separated and planted in drills 1 ft. apart, 6 in. apart in the drill and 2 in. deep; a good sunny position is essential and they do best in a light rich loam. When the leaves die down at the end of July or August, the bulbs should be lifted to dry in the sun for a few days, before they are bunched for storage in a dry frost-free shed. Given the right conditions the plants are no trouble to grow and need no attention except that they should be kept free of weeds.

The best way to use garlic in a salad is to rub the inside of the bowl before use with a clove, so that only a slight flavour is imparted.

Horse-radish (Armoracia lapathifolia). Made up into a sauce it is used in considerable quantities with roast beef, and as the ready-made sauce when bought from the grocer is quite expensive, it pays to grow your own. Horse-radish is worth cultivating properly in order to get the best flavour and in such a manner that it does not spread like a weed. The best way to grow it is by making a little mound in December, about 2 ft. high and 2 ft. wide and as long as you want. It is preferable to make the mound itself out of good soil, seeing that it is on firm soil, a path or even concrete. Young roots bought early in the year, should be cut to 9 in. in length and laid in sand until March, by which time most of them should have sprouted. The best should be selected and planted in the side of the mound 12 in. apart and 18 in. above the normal level of the soil, the thongs being inserted so as to point downwards.

Keep the mound weeded and the crowns disbudded, and then if the soil is good you should have nice long, straight roots for winter storage.

In the autumn the mound can be razed to the ground and the roots will thus be exposed. As the roots are in the mound and not in the soil proper, there is no chance of their spreading. They are best stored in sand or ashes so that they can be used as required, but they can be grated up and stored in air-tight jars, though much of the flavour is usually lost.

Marjoram—Pot or Perennial Marjoram (Origanum onites), and Sweet Marjoram (Origanum Marjorana). Wild Marjoram has not the good flavour of the two cultivated species, but can be used as a pot-herb. Its flower spikes are looser than those of Pot Marjoram and it has reddish branching stems.

Pot Marjoram is propagated by taking rooted shoots from an old plant and setting them out 1 ft. apart. It is best when grown in a position where there is sufficient supply of moisture during the summer months, as it suffers in a drought, the symptoms being the yellowing of the leaves, sometimes with black spots. The harvesting should be done before the plant flowers in July, and it is only in a very good season that you can have a second cutting.

Sweet or Knotted Marjoram, the second name comes from its tight small bracts, is usually treated as a half-hardy annual, the seeds not being sown until the middle of May, in rows 1 ft. apart, thinning the seedlings later to 9 in. apart. The leaves are greyish and the plant is cut right at its base just before the flowers are fully open, for drying when it is hung up or laid on racks.

The leaves of the two marjorams can be used together, with savory and thyme for stuffing poultry, or used by themselves to flavour a number of dishes. Many cooks recommend their use in egg dishes, such as omelettes.

Mint—Lamb Mint (Mentha viridis [spicata]), Round-Leaved or Apple Mint (Mentha rotundifolia), Hairy Mint or Horse Mint (Mentha sylvestris), Bergamot Mint (Mentha citrata), and Middlesex Mint (Mentha villosa nervata). There are many species and hybrids of mints, as can be seen from the list above, which only includes some of those used in cooking.

The Lamb Mint is most commonly used in this country for making mint sauce, though people who know their mints often say that mint sauce made out of Apple Mint has a much more delicate and *recherché* flavour. The latter mint has round leaves and pinkish flowers, making a strong plant often 4 ft. high in good soil and hardy enough to go on well into the autumn. It does need plenty of room and to be kept well in bounds. It dries well, but is more hairy than the Lamb Mint, which prejudices it in the eyes of some people. The Hairy or Horse Mint has a good flavour, but does not look so well when it is dried. The best results, however, can probably be got from a dried mixture of all the three mints. Bergamot Mint has a very delicate flavour, while Middlesex Mint is a hybrid between Hairy Mint and Lamb Mint, and has reddish stems and short broad leaves. One of the main troubles encountered with mints is mint rust, to which the Lamb Mint, with its smooth narrow leaves is very susceptible; the mints with hairy leaves are more resistant.

Whatever mint or mints you choose to have in your herb border, it is always preferable, if possible, to taste a leaf from the stock you are thinking of planting. Many mints have become hybridized with wild or scented strains and even though they may look right, do not always taste right.

Many people think that as mint usually prefers a moist rich soil, that it should also be in the shade. This is not true and mints are better for being grown in the open, provided that they have enough moisture. The plants will be sturdier and produce more leaves. Before planting mint dig in a good quantity of well-rotted manure or good vegetable compost, say one bucketful to the sq. yd. Do not keep the bed for more than three years, as mint tends to exhaust the soil and it is very simple to make a new bed. Small pieces of the roots, 2 in. long, can be planted 2 in. deep in drills 2 ft. apart, either in the spring or autumn, though preferably the latter.

Mint rust has already been mentioned and if it is prevalent, one way to keep it down is burning off the tops in late September or early October, using dry straw amongst the stems for the purpose. The fire should be a quick one in order to burn the stems and the rust spores without damaging the roots. Another method is by cutting the tops down in October and removing for burning; the ground can then be watered with a 5 per cent solution of a neutral high-boiling tar wash, which can be easily obtained from a horticultural chemist or sundriesman.

Mint is probably the most used of any culinary herb in Britain, either as mint sauce, or with new potatoes or peas. A few other suggestions, however, are mint chutney, mint jelly, mint-flavoured carrots and mint vinegar.

Parsley (Petroselinum crispum). Parsley in this country is divided up into two main types, the plain or fern-leaved and the moss curled. The latter is not quite so hardy and is more suitable for growing in the warmer south; it is probably slightly more tasty. The plain-leaved can put up with more wet and cold and is therefore more suitable for the north.

Parsley seed is very slow in germination and it is often two months before the seedlings show through, so sow early in the year and then thin to 6 in. between the plants as soon as possible in order to allow room for development. Parsley is best used as an edging plant to the herb border or to the vegetable garden. It prefers a moist position and partial shade.

It is advisable to prepare the ground well before sowing parsley in order to get the best results. Good well-rotted compost can be dug in at the rate of a bucketful to the sq. yd. and where the soil is either very light and sandy or thick heavy clay, sedge peat can be forked into the top 2 or 3 in., but when this is done fish meal with a 10 per cent potash content should be applied at the same time at 4 oz. to the sq. yd. Sow the seed in April and again in August, the drills being 15 in. apart and $\frac{1}{2}$ in. deep. Sow thinly and thin out the seedlings to 6 in. apart, never allowing the young plants to touch each other.

It is possible to keep parsley going right through the winter, merely by covering the August-sown rows with cloches at the end of September; another way is to put up some plants in September in No-Soil Potting Compost, placing them in a cold frame or cool greenhouse. If you want to, you can always keep a pot of parsley in the kitchen over the winter.

Sage. This is usually a 'must' as an ingredient for stuffing the Christmas turkey or goose, but it may not be realized that very large quantities are used every year in sausage making. There are many forms of sage in gardens, as it 'sports' very readily—broad-leaved sages, variegated sages, sages with pink, blue or white flowers, and sages with narrow leaves, which used to be thought the best for culinary purposes. Broadly speaking they all have a good flavour and can be grown in the herb border.

Sages prefer an open sunny position and a light, well-drained soil and do not usually do well in colder districts. Propagation is mostly done by means of cuttings and a rooted piece from an old plant will do very well. If you want a lot of young plants earth up the centre of an old plant, so that in time the branches will root and can then be separated. The earthing up should be done in the autumn or March and the separating in May or June. Try to propagate plants that do not tend to flower and choose a broad-leaved type.

Plants can also be raised from seed sown in May in drills 9 in. apart and $\frac{3}{4}$ in. deep, sowing thinly, and thinning out the seedlings later to 9 in. apart. In their final positions they are best set out 18 in. sq. Beds are best renewed every three or four years.

Sage for drying is harvested in June and then again in August or September, this double-cutting tends to stop an unduly woody growth. After the first cutting it is a good thing to help the plants by a dressing of fish manure at 4 oz. to the sq. yd.; the second cutting should not be done after September in order that the bushes are not too weak to survive the winter.

Sage leaves are usually dried for use, but a hot tea can be made either from the green or dried leaves, being sweetened with honey. The green leaves can also be used in small quantities in salads and sandwiches.

Savory—Summer Savory (Satureia hortensis) and Winter Savory (Satureia montana). The Winter Savory is a perennial plant and is fairly hardy, especially in light soils, while the Summer Savory is an annual, making little bushes about 12 in. in height.

Propagation of the Summer Savory is by seeds sown in April, sowing very thinly in drills 1 ft. apart, thinning out the plants later to 9 in. apart in the rows. It does best in a light rich soil, but is tolerant of most conditions. The harvesting is carried out by cutting the whole plant for drying when it is in flower, usually in August.

Winter Savory is often propagated by cuttings in the spring, struck in sandy soil in a frame or under a cloche. If a rooted portion of the old plant can be severed, then it can be planted out. It can also be grown from seed, the plants flowering in their second year; the rows should be 2 ft. apart with the plants 18 in. apart in the rows.

If the cutting is done twice a year then woody growth is prevented and it is possible to keep the plants for about six years, though it is advisable to raise new plants every four years.

Dried leaves of both the Winter and Summer Savory are used in 'mixed herbs' and also very good for flavouring in stuffing for poultry and veal. Fresh leaves make a pleasant flavouring for broad beans when boiled in the same water, and it is said that they give relief when rubbed on a bee sting.

Tarragon (Artemisia dracunculus). This is a perennial plant which does well in a light sandy soil and a well-drained sunny position. Its growth becomes too lank in a rich soil and it gets killed off over the winter. It is a shrub-like plant with woody main stems.

There are two kinds of tarragon—the French and the Russian—the former should be grown, the latter not being worth the trouble.

Propagation is done by division of the roots in the spring or autumn, or by heel cuttings of side growths which have not flowered—they root quite easily. Harvesting is usually done early in July before flowering and in early September, when the leaves are required for drying. When the leaves have been dried they should be sifted well to remove the stalks.

Tarragon is probably growing in popularity in this country, the fresh leaves being used for making Tarragon vinegar, for fish cooking and fish sauces, as well as for salads. The vinegar is made by steeping the fresh leaves for three weeks in white vinegar. Dried powdered tarragon is useful for soups, salads, sandwich fillings, and also on vegetables.

Thyme (Thymus vulgaris). This is a small bushy perennial plant, with white or pinkish flowers, and green or greyish-green foliage. The cultivated thymes used for cooking are usually improved forms of the wild thymes, the three forms principally used being the broad-leaved English Thyme and the narrow-leaved French Thyme, which has rather a smell of camphor, both of these being Black Thymes, and the Lemon Thyme, which is very like the English Thyme except for its smell. There are, of course, many other thymes, some of which are used in the rock garden and others being suitable for the cracks in crazy paving.

Thymes appreciate a well-drained sunny position and prefer a light soil, as they originally come from the countries bordering the Mediterranean. They can much more easily tolerate a drought than they can an excess of moisture, and as they are lime-lovers the soil should be well limed before planting, an application of 6 to 7 oz. to the sq. yd. should be given if the soil is acid. If you can test the soil with a B.D.H. indicator to find out the exact application, so much the better.

Propagation is easiest by division or by cuttings. Cuttings from the new growth taken in May or June, just before the plant flowers, are very easy to root. The plants should be set out with 2 ft. between the rows and 18 in. between the plants in the rows. If propagation is carried out by division of the old plants, then it is a good idea to plant very deeply, only just leaving the top tufts of green showing, this does not seem to set them back seriously and does tend to counteract leggy, woody, growth. The bushes, from which you wish to propagate, can be earthed up in the same way as sage.

Harvesting can be done twice in the season, by cutting the first time towards the end of May or early June and then for the second time in late August. If the cutting is only done once a year the bushes will get very leggy and lanky, but with two cuttings the bushes should last well up to six years, especially if they are given the assistance of an application of fish manure in the autumn at 4 oz. to the sq. yd.

Thyme is one of those herbs which are usually dried before being used. This is easy to do, and when it is dry it is generally sieved twice so that there shall be no sand left in. Dried thyme keeps well and can be used as required. Lemon Thyme is said to have a better flavour than the Black Thyme, but care should be taken to see that the stock from which you are going to propagate is a good one, and as seed does not come true, you will have to propagate by division or by cuttings. If you grow both varieties of Black Thyme, they are best when mixed together.

HERB DRYING

Most herbs are reasonably easy to dry and supplies of mint, thyme, sage, parsley, marjoram, etc., are well-worth preparing. The general rule is to gather the leaves as the plants are about to come into flower, as at that time they are at their best. The cutting or picking should be done in the early morning on a fine day, just after the dew has gone, but before the sun has got too hot.

Herbs, like thyme, which are small-leaved, should be washed while the leaves are still on the stems, and then tied up in bunches for hanging up in the kitchen to dry. In order to prevent them from becoming dusty it is a good idea to put them in a butter-muslin bag. When the leaves are dry and crisp it is quite easy to strip them from the stems, after which they should be rolled with a rolling pin or sieved through a wire sieve.

The method with herbs with larger leaves, such as parsley and mint, is to pick the leaves off the stalks before they are washed. Tie them up then in a length of butter-muslin and dip them in a solution of boiling bicarbonate of soda ($\frac{1}{4}$ oz. to 2 quarts of water). The leaves retain their colour by this dipping process.

After dipping they should be drained for a few minutes, then spread on a muslin covered tray, which should be placed in a cool oven, or in a temperature of 120° F., say in front of the kitchen stove. If this temperature is maintained they should be ready in about an hour, though if they are placed above a kitchen stove they often take three or four hours.

When dry and crisp they should be dealt with in the same way as thyme, after which they can be stored, either by wrapping them in grease-proof paper, which is in turn wrapped in brown paper so as to exclude the light, or in an opaque air-tight jar.

One or two general points well worth noting are as follows: Don't try to do too much drying all at one go, it is much easier to do a bunch or two each time; don't try to dry in the sun or in a wind, as the leaves will then lose a large quantity of their essential oils; tie the herbs up in small loose bunches, so that the air can circulate freely amongst the leaves, large bunches dry more slowly and thus the flavour is impaired; for household use most herbs can be dried together with the exception of basil, which is very strong flavoured.

It is possible to store and use the herbs individually, though some cooks prefer to have a mixture. A good recipe for 'mixed herbs' for kitchen use, consists of two parts parsley, one part Sweet Marjoram, one part Winter Savory and one part thyme, the parts being by weight.

CHAPTER 12

Salads

THE SALAD BOWL

Most people who cultivate a vegetable garden will want to grow some salads in order to arrive at a balanced diet; they should therefore include salad crops in the normal rotation of their plot as shown in Chapter 1. There may be some reading this book, however, who are saying, 'It's all very well for the author to talk about big gardens, or largish allotments, but we've just got a small garden in the town. It's only about 28 ft. long and 12 ft. wide. Is there anything that we could do with that?'

I think that such a garden should concentrate on salads and should use Ganwicks or cloches in order that the maximum output can be obtained, especially at seasons when prices are dear. I have therefore planned out a little garden, which shows both the summer and winter plan. I call it my 'Salad Bowl Garden' and I know that it could be successful wherever a keen gardener has a small strip, let it be in Chelsea, or in Liverpool's Waterloo, or Manchester's Didsbury. It will be seen that the estimated value of the produce from such a garden works out at over £25, and that the value from the cloches alone is over £11. It does pay, therefore, to cultivate such a garden, and the better you cultivate it, the more it pays.

Please remember my remarks about cutting down trees (see page 39), because if this Salad Bowl Garden is to be effective, there must be as much light as possible. It does help in the case of walled gardens, for the walls to be whitewashed thoroughly so that the plants get the reflected light. Some people think that whitewashed walls are very hideous, and it is just a question of whether the garden owner will put up with the 'staringness' of the white walls in order to have all the advantages of the extra light and cleanliness.

Detailed instructions for growing most of the crops in the Salad Bowl will be found in Chapter 13, but a few special instructions with particular reference to the growing of the crop in the Salad Bowl will be found in this chapter. Those who have larger plots might like to grow one or two other salad crops, which have not been included in the Salad Bowl, instructions for growing these will be found at the end of the chapter, when they are not mentioned in Chapter 13.

By the way, you will see that I have specially orientated the Salad Bowl in order to get the most sun for the crops which need it. I expect that in a great number of cases you will not be able to do this; if you can't, do anyhow try and keep the herbs and the cloches in the sun.

CROPS IN THE SALAD BOWL

Beetroot. Provision has only been made for the growing of early beetroot, as storage space is needed for keeping the late varieties over winter, added to which there is considerable argument over the value of growing the later varieties, which will be found elsewhere in the book. One row of early beet should be sown in mid-April and a second in mid-May—the rows should be 1 ft. apart, the seed being sown thinly and the seedlings thinned to 4 in. apart. A good variety of Globe Beet should be used, or for poor or light soils Egyptian Flat-topped Early Beet is often very successful—one small packet should be enough for both rows.

Cabbages or Savoys. Twelve plants have been included in the plan for cutting January–February, the two months when it is very difficult to produce lettuce without the aid of a greenhouse. If you can get these few plants from a friend in June–July for planting out, or buy them, it will save you the trouble of sowing such a small quantity. They should be sown, however, in May, and planted out June–July 2 ft. apart each way. For cabbages January King would be a good variety and for savoys Ormskirk Late. Used as a salad the hearts should be shredded.

Carrots. Two batches of early carrots should be sown under Ganwicks, the first in late October and the second in January. The seed should be broadcast and a recommended variety is Amsterdam Forcing. Two rows should also be sown in the open, one in March and one in April, the recommended variety being Early Nantes. Sow thinly in drills 1 ft. apart.

Chives. These are very useful when chopped for flavouring a salad. In the first place they can be sown and will soon form clumps, which can be divided if further propagation is needed. Keep them well cut and remove any flowers as soon as they appear. Space has been left for them at one end of the plot where they can be left year in year out.

Corn Salad. This is also called Lamb's Lettuce and is a very useful winter salad crop. Sow it in drills 6 in. apart and thin later to 6 in. apart in the rows. It is best to make small successional sowings every two weeks from mid-August to the end of September, covering with Ganwicks at the latter date. You can use the thinnings first and then gather the plants as soon as they have made three or four leaves.

Cress—American. This is one of the few salad crops which can be cut in the open during the winter months. Sow in drills 1 ft. apart in early September and cut before it gets too tall and lanky. A small packet of seed should be sufficient.

Cucumbers. Ridge cucumbers are probably the easiest to grow under Ganwicks, as they are fairly hardy and need little attention except the pinching off of the growing points from time to time, which can be done at the same time as cutting. The seed can be sown in slight warmth in April for planting out May, 2 ft. apart in the row, or can be sown *in situ* in late April, the latter being best done by sowing three seeds to a station every 2 ft. apart. Bedfordshire Prize Ridge is a good variety and a small packet of seed would be sufficient. This crop needs plenty of water and benefits from a good soaking in dry weather.

Endive is not much grown in this country, but with very little trouble it can provide a supply of leafy salads in the winter months. Batavian Endive is the hardiest and two half-rows 1 ft. apart should be sown in July, sowing the remaining halves in August. As the cloches become available after the clearing of the autumn lettuce they can be white-washed or muddied inside and put over the endives in order to blanch them, the latter being eaten as soon as they become white. A small packet of seed would be ample.

Garlic. A suspicion of garlic helps to make a good salad and it is quite expensive to buy. The cloves should be planted 2 in. deep 8 in. apart in rows 1 ft. apart in March. When the leaves have died down in July or August the bulbs can be lifted, left to dry in the sun for a few days, and then hung in a dry shed. Also see the chapter on herbs.

Lettuce forms the major part of our salad diet for most of the year, and provision has been made in the plan for a good supply. First the summer lettuces which should be sown in succession, one row every three weeks from March to July, 1 ft. between the rows, the plants being thinned to 8 in. Trocadero Improved is a good variety and a $\frac{1}{4}$ oz. of seed would be sufficient. Second the lettuces for cutting in the autumn from under cloches; two half-rows 1 ft. apart should be sown in early

August, the rows being completed in late August. The plants should be thinned to 8 in. apart and covered with the cloches at the end of September, for cutting November–December. The variety Attractie is recommended and a small packet should be ample. Third the lettuce sown under cloches early October for cutting March–April. These should be sown in two rows 1 ft. apart and thinned to 8 in. apart. May King Improved is a good variety for this purpose and a small packet of seed should be ample. Fourth come the cos lettuces which often make a welcome change from the cabbage-type lettuces during the summer months; a row could be sown in May after the May King lettuces have been cut for maturing in July. They should be sown in rows 1 ft. apart and thinned to 6 in. apart. Paris White is a good variety and only a very small packet of seed would be enough.

Mustard and Cress. These two crops can, of course, be grown separately, but if grown together the cress should be sown three days before the mustard. They both germinate best in the dark, so the seed can be covered with brown paper, or if sown under cloches, the glass could be covered with a sack, until germination had taken place. If rape is used instead of mustard then it should be sown at the same time as the cress. Half a pint of the seed of each should ensure quite a good supply.

Onions. Provision has been made for sowing one row of salad or spring onions in August–September for pulling in April–May, and another row in March–April for pulling in June. A small packet of seed should be ample, this being sown thinly in rows 1 ft. apart. There is no thinning, of course, as the thinnings are what one eats. White Lisbon is the usual variety grown.

Welch Onions are a sort of hardy herbaceous perennial and look like a mass of spring onions growing together. They can be pulled at almost any time of the year and propagation is by dividing up of the clumps or sowing seed in July or August. They can remain undisturbed at the edge of a plot and are a useful standby for salads.

Parsley. It is always very useful to have a little parsley on the edge of a plot and a little seed should be sown both in April and August to ensure a continuity of supply, the seeds being put about 1 in. apart. If any flower stalks develop they should be cut down to ground level. A small packet of seed will go a long way. Also see the chapter on herbs.

Radishes. Radishes can be sown under cloches from December to April, and in the open during the late spring and summer, though it may be found that late sowings will bolt in hot dry weather. They should be broadcast thinly under cloches, and can either be broadcast or sown in drills 1 ft. apart in the open. They should always be eaten as soon as they are ripe and never allowed to get old, tough and hot, thus sowing a few at a time is the best policy. French Breakfast is a well-known variety and 2 oz. of seed should be enough.

Winter radishes are much larger in size than summer radishes and are not very well known in this country, but they are very pleasant when grated or cut into thin slices in salads. One great advantage they possess is that they can be left in the ground until they are required and do not have to be lifted for storage. They should be sown July–August in drills 1 ft. apart and be thinned later on to 6 in. apart. Black Spanish and China Rose are two varieties and a small packet of the seed of either would be sufficient.

Tomatoes. A dwarf tomato is probably the most satisfactory type to grow in a small plot under cloches. The variety Amateur needs no attention except for some sedge peat being put on the ground to keep the trusses clean—no side-shooting, no stopping, no supporting. If facilities exist, seed should be sown in March for planting under the glass in mid-April, otherwise plants will have to be bought. Two single rows of cloches can be put together to form a double row so that the tomatoes can be in a double row 2 ft. apart with 18 in. between each plant in the row. The plants are allowed to sprawl about as they please and remain under the glass until they have finished their cropping and are cleared at the end of September.

SALAD CROPS
(not included in Chapter 13)

Corn Salad or Lamb's Lettuce (Valerianella olitoria). This is extensively grown in France where three or four varieties are usually offered by seedsmen. It is in appearance something like a forget-me-not without the blue flowers and is very valuable as a winter salad, especially if grown under cloches. It can be eaten either raw or cooked.

Corn Salad can be grown on almost any soil, but it does best on a good rich loam containing plenty of organic matter. It is well to dig in either well-composted vegetable matter or farmyard manure at the rate of a barrowload to 12 sq. yds., and fork in to the top 3 or 4 in. 4 oz. fish manure to the sq. yd. The surface of the soil should then be dusted with hydrated lime. A sunny position is preferable.

A good tilth should be obtained before sowing and the seeds sown in drills 1 ft. apart and ¾ in. deep. This would give two rows under continuous cloches. Seed can be sown in stations 9 in. apart along the drills, thinning down the seedlings later to one per station.

The thinnings can be transplanted to form other rows if required. Successional sowings should be made from mid-August every fortnight up till the end of September, the rows being covered with continuous cloches or Access frames from the end of September, so that a crop can be assured even in northern districts.

Keep the rows well-weeded by hoeing before they are covered, and if the weather is dry in the late summer they should be kept well watered.

For harvesting the leaves can be cut singly or the whole plant can be pulled up and used. The thinnings can be used first and then the plants can be gathered after they have made three or four leaves, though it is usually best to let them develop into little bushy plants first.

The hardiest variety is probably the French Cabbaging with erect, dark green leaves growing in rosettes. This is recommended especially if you try to grow the salad in the open in milder districts.

The other varieties in order of decreasing hardiness are the Dutch or large-seeded, which has large greyish-green leaves, the Italian Regence and the Italian Lettuce-leaved, the last being suitable for the warmest districts only.

Cress—American or Land Cress (Barbarea praecox). This is one of the few salad plants which can be grown in the open in the winter. It was quite popular during the earlier part of the last century and should be more widely used nowadays. In appearance it is something like watercress, though in taste it is rather similar to ordinary cress.

It can be grown in any sort of soil but it is preferable to have the top few inches full of organic matter, which will retain enough moisture for the plant's requirements, as well as ensure that the ground is in good heart. It is best grown in a cool shady position.

The seed can be sown at any time provided that the weather is reasonable, from the end of March in the south, or the end of April in the north, making the last sowing in the north about the middle of August, and in the south early September.

The soil should be firm, but with a good tilth, when the seed is sown in drills $\frac{1}{2}$ in. deep and 9 in. apart. If the seed is sown thinly enough, there should be no need to thin out. Successional sowing should be made every three weeks to keep up a good supply.

The crop should be kept clear of weeds by hoeing through the rows, and the ground should be flooded from time to time should the weather be at all dry.

Don't let the crop get too lanky. It is better to cut it on the young side, cutting it as required.

Endive (Cichorium endivia). This is a very good salad plant, especially for the winter months, and should be grown much more than it is. It is very popular on the Continent where a large amount is grown and eaten. When it is blanched it loses most of its bitter taste and is very pleasant.

It prefers a good rich soil to grow in, containing plenty of finely divided organic matter. Sedge peat can be forked into the top 3 or 4 in. at the rate of a bucketful to the sq. yd. together with an application of 4 oz. fish manure to the sq. yd. To keep the ground in good heart it is well to dig in well-rotted compost or farmyard manure at the rate of a barrowload to 12 sq. yds.

The surface of the soil should be worked down to a fine tilth before sowing by alternate raking and treading. The seed can be sown in a seed-bed in drills 6 in. apart and $\frac{1}{2}$ in. deep, sowing very thinly, the seedlings are then transplanted when they are 1 in. high, being pricked out 6 in. by 3 in., and then transplanted again a month later to their permanent positions 1 ft. sq. It is also possible, in order to avoid transplanting, to sow in stations 1 ft. apart, the rows also being 1 ft. apart, thinning the seedlings later to one per station. Whatever way they are sown the plants should never lack water and a sunny position should be chosen. Mid-June is a good time for sowing.

The rows should be kept free of weeds and hoed regularly. A good watering is necessary once a week should the weather be dry.

It is essential to blanch the plants when they are fully grown, which is usually three or four months after sowing. There are a number of methods for doing this, three of which are mentioned below. The first is to cover the endive plant with an upside-down flowerpot, seeing also that the drainage hole is blocked up so that all the light is excluded. The second is to whitewash or coat with mud the inside of the usual continuous cloches and then placing them over the plants, taking care that the ends are also light-tight, by either using wooden ends or coating the glass in the same manner. The third method is to lift the plants in succession, planting them in a cellar or dark shed, or in a frame with closed lights, covered with straw or sacking.

Whatever method of blanching is adopted, it is important that the plants are dry at the time they are covered up or there is a tendency for them to rot. It is also better to cover them up in succession as they should be eaten directly they are blanched, that is when the foliage has turned yellowy-white.

By using a number of continuous cloches a good winter supply can be assured, and where continuous cloches are available at the end of

September it is better to cover up the plants then as they will thus be fairly dry when the blanching starts in November and December. Again in order to have a succession the clear glass cloches should only be exchanged for whitewashed or muddied ones, one or two at a time, and instead of one sowing in mid-June, four sowings can be made, the first in mid-June and then one per month until mid-September.

There are two main types of endive; (1) The Curled Endive, amongst which are the green curled Ruffec, the green curled Meaux, the white curled and the moss green curled; (2) the Batavian Endive, three varieties being Super Giant, Broad-Leaved Parisian and Improved Deep Heart. The Batavian Endive is best for winter work being more hardy, while the Curled Endive can be sown in April and May, should endive be required in the late summer or early autumn, the leaves being probably slightly more tender than with the other type. Endive seed is readily obtainable, but not all seedsmen may offer all the varieties mentioned above.

Mustard (Brassica nigra) and *Cress* (Lepidium sativum); *Rape* (Brassica napus). Mustard and Cress are usually coupled together, although there is no reason why they should not be grown separately. Rape has been mentioned as it is grown extensively by commercial growers instead of mustard. Mustard should be sown three days after cress in order that they should mature at the same time, on the other hand rape should be sown at the same time as cress.

The seed of both mustard and cress germinates best in the dark, so wherever they are sown it is best to keep them in the dark for the first few days. Supplies of these saladings can be maintained over the winter months, by sowing in boxes under glass or in the house; a temperature of 50° F. is quite sufficient. One of the troubles often encountered with this crop is that the seedlings often tend to damp off when young and it is thus a good thing to use sterilized soil when possible. Sterilization can be carried out by heating the soil up to 210 ° F., or it is probably sufficient for the purpose required to water the soil well with boiling water some time before using.

In the spring and summer mustard and cress can be sown out of doors. In order to prevent grittiness the seeds should never be covered with soil; the soil should be firmed before sowing and the seeds lightly pressed in. Some gardeners in order to avoid this trouble sow their seed in a layer of leaf mould or on a damp piece of sacking spread on top of the soil. When growing mustard and cress in the open it is sometimes convenient to raise the level of the bed in order to facilitate cutting; the bed, for instance, can be made 16 in. wide, so if the soil is scooped out to a width of 8 in. and a depth of 3 in. on each side of the bed, the bed is thus raised 6 in. above the adjacent ground. These crops can also be grown in the spring under cloches, the cloches being covered with sacking to start with in order to assist germination, or it may be preferable to sow in the dark indoors in boxes, and then when the seed has germinated bring the boxes outside and put them under cloches for finishing off. Even during the summer months it is quite a good idea to finish off the crops under cloches, as they are then protected from any heavy rainstorms.

To sow 2 sq. yds. about 1 lb. of mustard seed is needed, or $\frac{3}{4}$ lb. of either cress or rape seed. It is preferable perhaps to use rape in hot weather, as being a quicker growing crop than mustard, it is not so likely to go soft.

Watercress. As this is an extremely useful salad, it may be wondered why it has not been included in the Salad Bowl. The sole reason for this is the difficulty of raising plants without facilities, and anyone who has either a greenhouse or a small propagator, or who can obtain the cuttings or plants, is well advised to grow watercress as one of the salads. There is no need to have running water, but it is essential to have enough water so as to be able to use a hose or plenty of canfuls from time to time.

As far as position is concerned it is much better to grow watercress in a shady spot, as then, less watering will have to be done. The soil should contain plenty of organic matter and thus be capable of retaining sufficient moisture for the crop. If the soil is on the light side, it will help to fork into the strip where you are going to grow the watercress, some sedge peat at the rate of two bucketfuls to the sq. yd. It is best to grow the crop in a trench, which need only be a spade's depth and a spade's width, though it is usually better to have it a little wider, anything up to 2 ft. Having taken out the trench it should be filled to a depth of 6 in. with well-composted vegetable refuse after which some of the top-soil you have taken out should be put back, so that the top of the trench comes to about 4 in. below the level of the surrounding soil.

Seeds should be sown either in late March or early April. They are tiny and should be sown in No-Soil Compost in boxes; a little sand should be sifted over the top to cover the seeds, watering should then be done using the fine rose. The box should be put on the greenhouse staging at a temperature of 55° F. The seed usually germinates quickly and when the seedlings can be handled, they should be pricked out 3 in. apart in boxes containing John Innes Potting Compost No. 1. Both the boxes should be well drained, as the young seedlings need regular watering and should not be allowed to become dry—the good drainage will ensure that excess moisture can get away quickly. Of course, if you have an indoor, miniature propagator, you can use that instead of a greenhouse for germinating the seed.

When the plants are established, the boxes can be put out in a cold frame, so that the plants can be hardened off. Until the plants are fully hardened off, however, keep them out of the direct sunlight. The first week in June is about the right time for setting the plants out in the trenches, when they should be planted zigzag fashion 6 in. apart. See that the trench is really moist when the watercress is planted, give a good watering after planting, and from then on watering should be done at least once a week, either by letting the water run into one end of the trench by means of a hose, or by using a Brosson rainer to give artificial rain for half an hour.

During the growing season the plants can be fed once a week with diluted Liquinure, which will bring them on considerably. The plants should not be allowed to flower, and the tops should be pinched out if there is any sign of their wanting to do so. Keep your eyes open for slugs, which are very fond of watercress. They can be killed by using one of the slug baits or liquid destroyers containing metaldehyde. If you do happen to have some old soot, apply this all over the ground at about two handfuls to the sq. yd.; in addition to keeping the slugs away it will slowly add nitrogen to the soil and be much appreciated by the watercress.

These watercress beds do not last satisfactorily for more than one season, so a fresh one should be taken out every year. If you cannot raise your own plants from seed, perhaps if you buy some watercress from the greengrocer you will find some plants that have roots on them, these can be used as cuttings. Plant them in your prepared trench in the same way as you would plants that you had raised yourself. I am afraid that you are not likely to be lucky in raising plants this way, as growers are usually careful to see that there are no roots in the bundles they send to market.

THE SALAD BOWL
WINTER PLAN

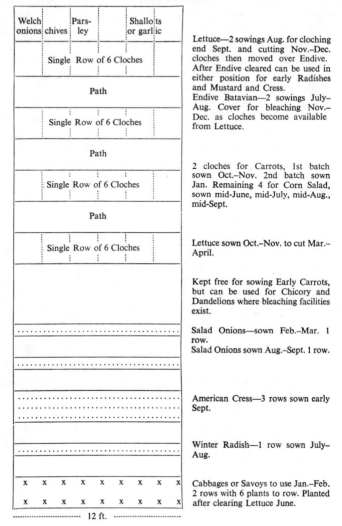

Welch onions	chives	Pars- ley		Shallots or garlic	
		Single Row of 6 Cloches			
		Path			
		Single Row of 6 Cloches			
		Path			
		Single Row of 6 Cloches			
		Path			
		Single Row of 6 Cloches			

Lettuce—2 sowings Aug. for cloching end Sept. and cutting Nov.–Dec. cloches then moved over Endive. After Endive cleared can be used in either position for early Radishes and Mustard and Cress.
Endive Batavian—2 sowings July–Aug. Cover for bleaching Nov.–Dec. as cloches become available from Lettuce.

2 cloches for Carrots, 1st batch sown Oct.–Nov. 2nd batch sown Jan. Remaining 4 for Corn Salad, sown mid-June, mid-July, mid-Aug., mid-Sept.

Lettuce sown Oct.–Nov. to cut Mar.–April.

Kept free for sowing Early Carrots, but can be used for Chicory and Dandelions where bleaching facilities exist.

Salad Onions—sown Feb.–Mar. 1 row.
Salad Onions sown Aug.–Sept. 1 row.

American Cress—3 rows sown early Sept.

Winter Radish—1 row sown July–Aug.

Cabbages or Savoys to use Jan.–Feb. 2 rows with 6 plants to row. Planted after clearing Lettuce June.

```
x   x   x   x   x   x   x   x   x
x   x   x   x   x   x   x   x   x
------------------- 12 ft. -------------------
```

The above plan has been worked out for producing as many salads as possible over the winter months, with the aid of 3 single rows of cloches, and taking into account that these crops will be followed by spring sowings and summer crops.

THE SALAD BOWL
SUMMER PLAN

Welch onions	Chives	Pars- ley		Shallots or garlic	
Double Row of 6 Cloches					

Dwarf Tomatoes plant out mid-Apr., clear end of September. 18 plants.

Lettuce sow here Aug.–Sept. for covering end September.

Single Row of 6 Cloches

Ridge Cucumbers plant out **May**, clear end of September. 6 plants.

Batavian Endive sown here July–Aug. for bleaching winter. Catch-crop piece with Mustard and Cress before Endive sown.

Cos Lettuce, one row, sown April–May and cut July. Early Carrots sown April.

Early Carrots sown March followed by Radishes.

Spring-sown Salad Onions followed by Beet.

Autumn-sown Salad Onions followed by Beet.

Lettuce 7 rows. One row sown every three weeks from March to July.

N
↑

W———|———E

S

.... 12 ft. ....

Two single rows of cloches have been combined to form a double row for covering Dwarf tomatoes, while the remaining single row is over ridge cucumbers.

It must be taken into consideration that even in the most intensively cultivated piece of ground there may be empty gaps from time to time, as allowance has to be made for one crop finishing before it is time to sow the next, and it is not always possible to have a quick catch-crop in the intervening period.

THE SALAD BOWL RETURNS
FOR TOWN AND CITY GARDENS

Crop	Estimated Yield	Retail Price per, unit	Estimated Value of Produce	Estimated Value of Cloche crops alone
		£ p	£ p	£ p
Beetroot				
Early *	4 lb.	0·06	0·24	1·52
Early	32 lb.	0·04	1·28	
Cabbage				
(Jan.–Feb.)	12 heads	0·03	0·36	
Carrots				
Early*	4 lb.	0·08	0·32	0·40
Early*	4 lb.	0·06	0·24	0·24
Early	10 lb.	0·05	0·50	
Chives	12 bunches	0·06	0·06	
Corn Salad	26 bunches	0·04	1·04	1·04
Cress				
American	24 bunches	0·03	0·72	
	26 bunches	0·03	0·78	
Cucumbers				
Ridge				
Early*	6	0·05	0·30	0·30
Others	18	0·05	0·90	0·90
Endive*	24	0·06	1·44	1·44
Garlic	8 bunches	0·12	0·96	
Mustard & Cress				
Early*	12 punnets	0·06	0·72	0·72
Summer	12 punnets	0·04	0·48	
Onions				
Salad	32 bunches	0·04	1·28	
Welch	6 bunches	0·06	0·36	
Parsley	12 bunches	0·03	0·36	
Radish				
Early*	5 bunches	0·06	0·36	0·30
Summer	20 bunches	0·03	0·60	
Winter	9 lb.	0·04	0·36	
Tomatoes				
Early*	12 lb.	0·09	1·08	1·08
Others	72 lb.	0·05	3·60	
Lettuce				
Oct.–Dec.*	24	0·07	1·68	1·68
Mar.–April*	16	0·07	1·32	1·32
May*	12	0·04	0·48	0·48
Summer	120	0·03	3·60	
			£25·36	£11·42

The value of the home grown produce will be considerably higher if and when we go into the Common Market.

* Crops grown under the cloches have been marked with an asterisk, with the exception of the main bulk of the tomatoes and ridge cucumbers, which although grown under cloches, cannot in all fairness be credited to the cloches, as in good years a mid-season crop can be got outdoors.

CHAPTER 13

The Culture of Vegetables Alphabetically

ARTICHOKE GLOBE

There are many people in this country who like Globe Artichokes, and as they are not grown in a big way by market gardeners, it is worth while having, say, half a dozen plants for the normal household. This artichoke is a perennial and is the one which produces large thistle-like heads. It is these heads which are cut off before they are open and which are cooked.

Soils and Manuring

This crop does best in a good, well-manured, well-drained soil. Good drainage is essential for although the plants want plenty of moisture in the summer, they will not tolerate sodden ground during the winter months. Before planting, the texture of heavy soils and the moisture-holding qualities of light soils should be improved by the digging-in of well-rotted compost at the rate of at least one bucketful to the sq. yd.; at the same time a fish manure with a 6 per cent potash content at 3 oz. to the sq. yd., should be worked into the top 2 or 3 in. With really heavy soils it is advisable to do the digging in the early autumn and leave the surface rough so that the soil can 'weather' over the winter. A dressing of fish manure at 3 oz. to the sq. yd. should be given every April and hoed in, and if it is thought that the plants aren't growing well, then dried blood can be applied at 2 oz. to the yard run in June. A sunny position is essential and some shelter from winds is appreciated.

Plants and Planting

It is possible to raise plants from seed but this is not a good method as they do not usually come true to type. The best way of propagation is by use of the suckers taken from established plants in the spring. These should be about 9 in. long, with a piece of root or 'heel' of the old stool attached. Set the plants out 3 ft. apart in a row, and if there is more than one row, the next should be 3 ft. away. Plant firmly 4 in. deep and the ground should be watered if dry. Planting is best done in April. It is possible, however, instead of taking the suckers at that time—to cut them in November, pot them up and keep them in a cool frame over the winter, until the actual time for planting out in the spring.

Growing Tips

Hoe in the summer to keep down weeds. The plants should be protected, in the winter by covering them with a layer of loose straw or bracken, which should be removed in the spring, and even replaced in the winter if it gets sodden. Aim at making a new bed every five or six years. The best plan is to replace the rows one at a time so that no row is more than five years old. This method has the advantage of avoiding a completely blank year with no artichokes to eat.

Harvesting and Using

There is nothing to cut until the second year. The main heads or 'King Heads' should be cut in the second and subsequent years when ready. This is when they are young and tender and before they are too fully developed. Side-shoots then develop with smaller heads, which should be removed, though they can be left until they are the size of hens' eggs, when they can be, say, fried whole. The main heads, are however, the more tasty and if the laterals are not removed in the early stages, a second crop will be produced. Harvest, if possible, only an hour before the heads are to be cooked.

The heads are either boiled or steamed, and when served, individual scales are pulled off, the fleshy parts being eaten after being dipped in melted butter, though some people prefer to use vinegar and olive oil. After all the scales have been eaten, the best part which is the heart or 'fond' is still left. This is under some unedible pith which should be removed first. If it is too much bother to eat the fleshy part of all the scales, you can just eat the heart as the French sometimes do.

Varieties

There are only two varieties, which are offered in this country—Purple Globe and Green Globe. My favourite is Grand Camus de Bretagne, but I got this from Brittany.

CULTURE OF VEGETABLES ALPHABETICALLY

ARTICHOKE JERUSALEM

This is not a very popular vegetable, but is quite useful for soups and stews. Nobody really knows the why and wherefore of 'Jerusalem', though it is thought that it is a corruption of the Italian word for a sunflower, 'Girasole', as this artichoke is a member of the sunflower tribe. It is a hardy herbaceous perennial, and as it grows to 6 or 7 ft. high it is often used as a windbreak for tender crops, but it is best replanted every year if good-sized round tubers are required.

Soils and Manuring

The Jerusalem Artichoke will grow happily in almost any soil and can even be tried where other crops have failed, but it does best when the land is fed, by digging in well-rotted compost at the rate of one 2-gallon bucketful to the sq. yd. Potash seems an essential requirement for this crop and I have had the heaviest weights when a fish manure with a 10 per cent potash content has been used along the row at 2 oz. to the yard run at planting time. It does not like an excess of moisture and it is best to choose if possible a dryish or well-drained position in the open.

Plants and Planting

Tubers are used for planting in a similar manner to potatoes. The work should take place in March or April, though I have had very good results from January or February planting. The tubers used should be as smooth as possible and about the size of a pullet's egg. Larger ones can be cut, but the nicest, least nobbly tubers result (which are, therefore, easier to peel) when the smoothest sets are planted.

For planting take out a furrow 4 in. deep, put in the manure or compost, place a tuber every 12 in. and then earth over. Next apply the fish manure which should be hoed in. If more than one row is needed the next should be 3 ft. away.

Growing Tips

When the plants are through the ground, start hoeing, tending to draw the soil up to the plants rather than away from them, so that they are earthed up more or less in the same way as potatoes. If the artichokes are to be grown in a windy place, it is advisable to put in a stake at each end of the row, and then to run a wire or thick string on either side of the stems to keep them upright. After the bulk of the tubers have been produced, say late in October, it's possible to cut the tops down to within a foot of the ground level. These tops can then be chopped up and put on the compost heap.

Harvesting and Using

It's possible to leave the Jerusalem Artichokes in the ground until they are required, or to lift them at the end of November and store them in a dry cool place in sand. Freshly dug tubers, however, are always far better flavoured than those that have been stored. Be careful when lifting to make certain that all the tubers have been removed, because 'volunteers' can be a nuisance the following season.

Some people make a point of not cutting the stems down, but they strip off the leaves early in November, cut the stems as low as possible, and then store them carefully in an upright position in a dry shed. They then use the stems as poles for runner beans the next season.

These artichokes are composed of a very digestible form of starch, but they should always be boiled or steamed in their skins and only peeled just before serving as otherwise they will lose a lot of their goodness. After cooking they are nice when served cold in a salad with a mayonnaise sauce.

Varieties

New White has a more delicate flavour than the old-fashioned purple kind. Fuseau, this is the variety with smooth tubers like those of a Dahlia. Very popular with housewives, because it is free from 'knobliness'. The tubes are rather small however.

ASPARAGUS

This is becoming more and more popular now that it is realized that it needn't be grown in special beds with extra special treatment, and that once the plants have been established they can easily last twenty years, and so are a good investment. We can be grateful to Mr. A. W. Kidner for applying the principles of genetical breeding to the raising of 'super' asparagus crowns. A strain of his K.B. asparagus has now been developed which does ensure extra heavy crops.

Soils and Manuring

It's possible to grow asparagus in a very wide range of soils, but it seems to do particularly well on the sands and sandy loams, which warm up more quickly in the spring and so stimulate the crowns into growth. It is important to give protection from the cold winds of the north and east, as otherwise the sticks of asparagus tend to grow in a crooked, twisted manner. The land where the asparagus is to be grown should be dug over in the autumn and really well-rotted dung or compost incorporated at the rate of at least one 2½-gallon bucketful to the sq. yd. The aim is to bury this at a spade's depth. The land should be then left rough until the third week in March when it should be forked over, and a fish fertilizer with an analysis of about 6 per cent nitrogen, 6 per cent phosphates, and 6 per cent potash should be applied at about 3 oz. to the sq. yd.

Every late autumn after this, well-rotted compost or fully decomposed farmyard manure should be applied down the rows at the rate of a 2-gallon bucketful to the yard run, and each March a further dressing of fish manure should be applied.

Plants and Planting

Never attempt to do any planting until the soil is free from perennial weeds. It is most important to eliminate perennial weeds, and on dirty ground it might be possible to adopt a double green manuring system as advised on page 63.

Don't attempt to raise the plants by seed, but buy in pedigree crowns. Many of the failures with asparagus in the past have been due to the plants being of poor stock and not to bad cultivation or the wrong type of soil. One-year-old crowns are the best as they can be moved without any damage being done to the roots and in the end will be better plants. Two- and three-year-old crowns do not move as well and two years should also be left before any cutting of the buds is done in the same way as for the yearlings. One year is needed for the roots to get established and a second year is needed for the plant to build itself up to produce good buds the following year.

Planting is best done in the third week of March or early in April, provided that the soil is in a suitable condition. It is necessary first to get a good tilth and apply the fish manure. A trench is opened up 4 in. deep and 6 in. wide at the bottom. The crowns are put in the bottom, spreading out the roots carefully, covering with about 3 in. of soil which was taken out when making the trench. The remaining covering-up will be done as the hoeing is carried out during the summer and it will be found that the land will be level by the autumn. The crowns should be 2 ft. apart in the row and if there is more than one row the next should be at least 4 ft. away. This spacing, using pedigree plants, will give a very much better crop than the old way of having double rows and the plants all 'jumbled up' together.

It is most important not to allow the plants to dry out between lifting and planting, so when they arrive from the raiser, cover them with damp sacks, and keep these in position over the containers in which the crowns are carried to the garden. It is a good idea to open up the trench or trenches *shortly* before you expect the arrival of the crown, so that they can be planted as soon as possible after delivery.

Growing Tips

There's nothing much else to do in the next two years than to keep the rows clean and to give the manures and fertilizers advised. The ferns can be cut with a hook when they are ripe and dead. In the third year, however, when the aim will be to make the first serious cut of asparagus, it is a good plan to earth up the rows to a height of about 5 in. This work is done with a 2- or 3-pronged Canterbury hoe, or with an ordinary draw hoe. Sometimes it's necessary to fork a little between the rows, so as to produce enough soil for earthing up. This work should be done as early as possible in March, that is as soon as the soil is fit to get on.

After all the asparagus needed is cut, and cutting must cease about the end of May or the beginning of June—carry on with the surface cultivations, so as to prevent the weeds from taking charge. Then just before the berries ripen on the asparagus fern, cut this down to within 6 in. of soil level. Don't allow the seeds to drop because seedlings, once they are established in a bed, are very difficult to eradicate. Take the cut fern to the compost heap, and rot it down. Don't burn it as some books say—it is valuable organic matter.

As a final tip don't worry about any old fashioned growing instructions, dosings of salt, etc. Good pedigree asparagus crowns, with manuring as I have advised, will give an excellent crop each season.

Harvesting and Using

The great thing with cutting asparagus is to use a narrow knife so that the actual shoot needed is cut without damaging the adjacent buds, and so preventing them from giving a further feed. Aim to make the cut at 4 in. below the surface of the soil. Special asparagus knives can be bought for the purpose and they are very useful. Early in the season go over the rows every two days, but when the weather gets warmer cut every day. In frosty weather, one often has to cut when the sticks are only 3 in. above the soil level.

Always try to cook and serve asparagus within two hours of cutting. It's possible with tender sticks to have them boiled and ready for table within twenty minutes, steaming takes about half an hour. I personally prefer asparagus served with melted butter, as stronger sauces disguise the delicate flavour. Any poorer sticks can be used for the delicious *Omelette aux points d'asperges*—just a lovely omelette with the delicious cooked asparagus tips 'wrapped' inside.

Varieties

K.B.F. This is the strain bred by A. W. Kidner, and has given me particularly good results.

Connover's Colossal. An old variety much grown. Has slender pointed buds.

Giant White Cap. Has pale green heads.

BEANS—BROAD

This vegetable has been cultivated for centuries and as it is one of the easiest to grow it should be included in any cropping scheme.

Soils and Manures

Broad beans are not particular as to soil and will grow easily on both heavy and light land.

They require the same manuring as other members of the pea and bean family and come in the same rotation. Autumn-sown beans which follow after a well-manured crop need have no special manuring of their own, except for an application of fish manure with a 10 per cent potash content just before they are sown. When the beans are sown in the spring well-rotted compost or farmyard manure should be dug into the ground at least three weeks before sowing at the rate of one 2-gallon bucketful to the sq. yd., together with an application of fish manure with a 10 per cent potash content at the rate of 3 oz. to the sq. yd., forked into the top 2 or 3 in.

Sowing the Seed

Seeds can be sown outside either in November, or from mid-February to mid-April. It is possible (but hardly worth while), to sow the seeds in frames in December and January, and then to put the plants out in their permanent positions about the middle of March.

Choose a dry day for sowing when the soil is in a favourable condition. It is best to sow the seeds in a double row with 8 in. between the drills and 2 ft. 6 in. between the rows—if there is to be more than one such row. The seed should be 8 in. apart in the drill, and staggered—or zig-zagged with those in the next drill. Where dwarf varieties are used the double rows need only be 2 ft. apart, the drills 6 in. apart and the seeds 6 in. apart in the drills.

Although the germination of broad bean seeds is very good and they are nearly all sure to come up, it is a good plan to sow a dozen or so seeds at the end of the row in a group. The resulting seedlings can be planted out when they are 3 or 4 in. high, should there be any gaps.

Another method of sowing is by dibbling the seed in, at the required distances, instead of drawing out drills.

The Longpod types, which are the hardier, are generally used for autumn sowing, while the Windsor types are mostly used for the spring sowings. The latter are more delicious to eat. Autumn and early spring sowings succeed more often on light soils and in warmer districts. In colder parts of the country it is best to wait until March.

Broad beans are sometimes grown under continuous cloches, the seed being sown in January in a double row. They are usually uncovered in April by which time the plants should have reached the top of the glass.

Growing Tips

Keep the soil clean between the rows with regular hoeing. Watch carefully for the appearance of any black aphis (blackfly) and deal with them immediately by spraying with liquid Derris. When the plants are in full bloom, the tops can be pinched out, this will encourage the production of the beans and will also discourage the black aphis, who like to feed on the tender, young growing tops. From time to time remove any side-shoots that are found growing.

Cut the stems down directly the crop is finished and put them on the compost heap for rotting down, so that full use is made of their potash content. The roots can be left in the ground and dug in. Don't leave the plants standing in the ground after they have cropped, as they will only exhaust the soil in trying to produce another crop.

Harvesting and Using

Broad beans are rich in food value and have a high protein content. They should be freshly picked before cooking, some people preferring them when they are young and tender, though there are others who like them really 'floury'. Don't eat them when they are very young, however, as they are not then wholesome.

Varieties

These are usually divided into two main groups, the Longpods and the Windsors, though these groups can be sub-divided into the white seeded and the green-seeded varieties.

Longpods

Claudia Aquadulce, perhaps the earliest and much used for autumn sowing. Medium height and good flavour. (White-seeded)

Johnson's Wonderful, medium-sized pods. (White-seeded)

Sussex Wonder White Longpod has long, broad pods and is prolific and early.

Green Giant Longpod, hardy but with green seeds.

Windsors

Harlington Green and Harlington White are good varieties.

Dwarf varieties:

The Sutton is a dwarf broad bean, only growing to 9 or 12 in., and branching freely. (White-seeded)

Dwarf White Fan, is green-seeded, with small pods and clustered head.

BEANS—DWARF, FRENCH OR KIDNEY

French beans and runner beans each have their partisans. There are many people who only eat French beans in the short time that they are available before the runners start cropping, but there are others who consider that French beans have a much better flavour, in addition to not being so coarse, and grow them exclusively. Very few runner beans are grown in France. It is possible by judicious sowing to have French beans over a very long period.

Soils and Manuring

This bean seems to prefer a light soil to a heavy one and can often withstand conditions of drought where most other vegetable crops would fail. Provided that the land has been well prepared it will produce a good crop even on poor soil, which it will help to enrich by means of the bacteria-produced nitrogen in the nodules on its roots.

It is a good thing to get the digging of the ground done in the autumn, incorporating well-rotted farmyard manure or compost at the rate of one 2-gallon bucketful to the sq. yd. Before sowing an application of fish manure with a 15 per cent potash content should be forked into the top few inches at 3 ozs. to the sq. yd., and afterwards carbonate of lime should be applied to the surface at from 4 to 7 oz. to the sq. yd., depending on the acidity of the soil.

Sowing the Seed

The first safe date for sowing French beans in the open in warmer districts is generally the last week in April, though this depends very much on the condition of the soil, and on the temperature. The enemy of the French bean seed is not the cold, but the wet, and it is no use sowing French beans if the soil is heavy, and still wet and cold. V shaped drills should be made 4 in. wide and 2 in. deep, and 2½ ft. apart. Sow a double 'staggered' row in the drill, so that the beans are 6 in. one from the other. It pays to sow a little group of a dozen or so at the end of the row in case there are any gaps to fill. In order to ensure a succession it is much better to sow a row every three weeks until the middle of July, rather than sow all your beans in one fell swoop at the end of April or in early May.

Early French beans can be raised very successfully under continuous cloches. The seed may be sown in two rows 8 in. apart and 3 in. between the seed in Mid-March and can remain covered until the end of May. It may be necessary to water if the soil dries out under continuous cloches. Glass or cloches can also be used to cover a mid-July sowing from the end of September onwards, so that beans are available during October in spite of early frosts. When this sowing is made it should be taken into consideration that the plants will be covered at a later stage, so sow in two drills 8 in. apart the beans being spaced to 10 in. apart. This is best done by sowing three times as thickly as required and thinning the plants to the right distance when the rough leaves appear.

Growing Tips

Hoe regularly between the rows and keep the soil drawn up to the plants rather than away from them. In an exposed situation some of the taller varieties may need supporting to keep the beans off the ground, where they become dirty and liable to attack by slugs. Bushy twigs can be used or a cane placed at each end of the row and a string run down either side. Slugs can do a lot of damage to this crop unless kept down with the metaldehyde form of slug bait.

Harvesting and Using

Never let French beans get old and coarse, but pick them when they are young and tender. Pick regularly and see that there are no old pods with swelling seeds left on the plants; this will ensure that the plants go on cropping.

If possible pick only a short time before required for cooking. They should just be topped and tailed. Don't boil all the taste out of them, but steam them if possible in a bowl with a little butter. A very good Belgian dish is *Haricots verts à la Liégeoise*, where the beans are served with a flavouring of onion and a little potato.

French beans can be preserved in salt in opaque jars and make quite a change during the winter months. After taking them out of the salt they should be soaked in at least three changes of water before being cooked.

Varieties

French beans are usually divided into two types, the dwarf and the climbing.

Dwarfs:

Black Prince, is a medium dwarf, with fairly straight pods, about 6½ in. in length.

Canadian Wonder, an old variety, large and upright with stringless pods about 6½ in. in length. Selected seed of this variety should be bought.

Masterpiece, fairly tall, slightly stringy with good flavour. Recommended for cloche growing.

Feltham Prolific, slender, straight pods about 4 in. in length. Recommended for cloches.

Tendergreen (Stringless Greenpod), a sturdy plant, with a stringless bean of delicious flavour, about 6 in. in length.

The Prince, dwarf with long pods 7–8 in. in length, prolific.

Mont d'Or, a dwarf leafy plant, with fleshy stringless beans. This is a Wax or Golden Podded variety—a golden French bean and should not be confused with a dried butter bean.

Climbing Varieties:

These are climbing French beans which are grown in the same way as runner beans, so their culture has been included with that of the latter. They are, however, largely used for winter and early spring work in the greenhouse.

Tender and True is an early bearer, with narrow long, fleshy pods of a delicate flavour.

Veitch's Climbing, a semi-climber with flat pods about 6 in. in length.

BEANS—RUNNER

These beans were first used in this country for their decorative effect as flowers, and it is only in the last hundred years or so that they have been used for the table. The flavour is stronger and coarser than that of the French bean, and they are therefore often preferred for that reason.

Soils and Manuring

Runner beans can be made to grow in most soils, but they do best in a deep soil where they can have a good root run. The ground needs more preparation for this crop than for the other legumes. It pays to double-dig the ground, where the beans are to grow, in late March or early April, incorporating a 2-gallon bucketful of well-rotted compost or old farm-yard manure to every sq. yd. Even if the ground is only single dug it is important to dig in plenty of manure or compost. A short time before the seed is sown fish manure with a 10 per cent potash content should be forked into the top few inches of the soil, followed by an application of carbonate of lime to the surface at 4 oz. to the sq. yd.

Runner beans must have plenty of food and moisture at their roots when growing and a good 'dose' of diluted Liquinure every fourteen days after they have started flowering is a great help.

Sowing the Seed

Runner beans will not germinate in a cold soil, so it is not possible to sow them outside until the first or second week of May, even in the south. They can be sown under continuous cloches from the middle of March, but it is necessary to combine them with some other crop in order to avoid wasteful use of this type of glass. After the first outside sowing in May, another sowing can be made in early June.

The way in which the seed is sown depends on which of the two main methods of growing runner beans is adopted. They can either be grown up sticks or poles as stick beans, or grown on the flat with the growing points being pinched out as pinched beans.

The rows for stick beans should be 5 to 6 ft. apart, double rows being recommended 9 in. apart. The seed should be sown 2 in. deep, either in drills or by dibbling in, and 9 in. apart using the staggered method so that no thinning will have to be done later.

For pinched beans the seeds should be sown in rows $3\frac{1}{2}$ to 4 ft. apart, again using a double row, the seeds being put in 9 in. apart in a staggered fashion.

In cases where beans are sown thickly, they will have to be thinned out when 2 in. high to 9 in. apart. On the other hand where beans are spaced out 9 in. apart at sowing, it is advisable to sow a dozen extra beans at the end of the row for gapping up.

Where coolhouse or cold frame facilities are available, seeds can be sown in boxes towards the end of April. The boxes should be at least 4½ in. deep, and a good size being 2 ft. long and 1 ft. wide. Fifty seeds can be sown in such a box, the plants being planted out early in June.

Growing Tips

Where stick beans are grown it is best to choose a position at the end of the plot or alongside a path, where they will not shade or interfere with other crops. There are a number of ways of sticking beans, one of the most used being that employing poles, where they are available. The poles are put into position either before sowing or soon afterwards, 9 in. apart in a double row each side of the double row of beans. The poles are generally crossed near to the top and another pole is laid horizontally in the V's thus formed. The poles are all lashed together at the joints, so that a *very firm* framework is made. This is important. Where there are not enough poles available to make such a framework, strong poles can be driven in every 8 ft. or so, and two wires run the length of the row, one near the tops of the poles and the other near the bottom. Cheap string or binder twine can be run from one wire to the other, so that there is an upright every 4½ in. Mesh wire or cheap netting can also be used instead of the string. Wobbly structures are not liked by runner beans and cropping is adversely affected.

Many people use good stout, bushy pea sticks quite successfully, taking care that the sticks are pushed in at an angle so that they meet at the top for extra support.

One old-fashioned method which can be adopted in small gardens, where a round piece of ground is available, is to have a group of poles in a circle meeting at the top like a 'tepee', where they are secured. The beans will grow up the poles very happily and the pods can also be picked on the inside.

When runner beans are grown on the flat the growing points must be pinched out from time to time. With a small row this can be done by hand, but with a long row it is easier to go along with a sickle or pair of shears. The first pinching should take place when the plants are between a foot and 18 in. high, and then the plants should be kept to about the same height.

The ground should be kept clean by regular hoeing and in late June or early July, a mulch of lawn mowings or rotted leaves is much appreciated, especially on light dry soils, as runner beans must have moisture at their roots.

Runner beans benefit considerably in dry weather from overhead irrigation, as the fine spray helps to set the flowers, as well as provide moisture at the roots.

Beware of slugs with this crop, especially when it is grown on the flat. Take preventative measures by the use of slug bait containing metaldehyde.

Harvesting and Using

If the beans are picked regularly they will go on cropping. Don't let old pods remain on the plants with seeds swelling inside them. Young beans are always nicer to eat and the great big ones are for show purposes only.

After boiling or steaming, finish off by heating them in an earthenware dish for a few minutes with a knob or two of margarine before serving.

Varieties

Princeps and Kelvedon Wonder and The Hammond are very good early varieties. They are prolific and very suitable for growing 'on the flat', particularly The Hammond.

Goliath and Streamline are both very long-podded varieties. They are much used for exhibition purposes.

Scarlet Emperor Improved is a good late variety and if sown in early June will go on cropping into October.

Painted Lady is often grown for its pretty red and white flowers, but it is not a very heavy cropper.

BEANS—HARICOT

Haricot beans are closely related to the French bean and in fact have the same Latin name. They are grown, however, for their seed which is eaten and not for their green pods. They are not very popular in this country and are not a good crop where only limited space is available, as a lot of plants are needed to produce any quantity of seed.

Soil, Manuring and Sowing the Seed

The same soil conditions, manuring needs and methods of sowing apply as for French beans (see page 175).

Growing Tips

If cloches are available the seed should be sown early at the beginning of April. The rows can be decloched at the end of May and cloched again at the end of August or early September for ripening the seed. When there are no continuous cloches the seed will have to be sown towards the end of April.

Harvesting and Using

The complete plant is uprooted and dried, after which it is put in a sack and beaten with a stick, so that the beans are threshed out.

Varieties

Comtesse de Chambord. Low, spreading and a strong grower. Probably the finest haricot bean. White seed—used in the winter after storing dry.

Brown Dutch. Coarse-growing and vigorous. Ripens well and easy to shell. Yellowy-brown seed.

BEANS—FLAGEOLET

The seeds of these are eaten when green in the same way as peas. Although they are much liked and grown in France, they are little known in this country. They are really 'varieties' of dwarf French beans and their sowing and cultivation is the same.

Harvesting and Using

Flageolets are harvested in the same way as green peas and are cooked and eaten in the same manner. A good recipe is *Flageolets à la Poulette*, where the flageolets after having been boiled, and the water poured off, are heated with butter in a saucepan for a few minutes, then white sauce, chopped parsley and cream are stirred in. Season with pepper and salt, and serve hot.

Varieties

Granda. Medium-sized, bushy and strong-growing plant.
White Leviathan. Dwarf and leafy plant. Very fine flavour.

BEETROOT

Beetroot has been grown in this country for many centuries, although it originally came from southern Europe. It is mainly used as a salad, though when it is served hot, it makes a very good vegetable. Young beet are always tastier than roots which have been allowed to get old and coarse.

Soil and Manuring

A light and deep loam is the best soil for this crop, although other soils will serve well if they are properly prepared. Beetroot, like other root crops, tends to fork if grown in freshly and richly manured ground, and does best when following a crop for which the ground has been well manured. The land is best dug over in the autumn after the other crop has been cleared and left rough until a good tilth is required for sowing the seed.

If the soil is very poor, then well-rotted compost can be dug in at the rate of one bucketful to every 3 sq. yds. Before sowing, fish manure with a 6 per cent potash content should be applied at the rate of 2 to 4 oz. per sq. yd., depending on the fertility of the soil, and forked into the top few inches.

Sowing the Seed

Every beet 'seed' is really a capsule and is actually made up of a number of seeds, so even with continuous sowing the seed need only be dropped very thinly. Station sowing of two seeds at every 6 in. answers very successfully with beet, the seedlings being thinned out later to one per station. It is possible to gap up beet by transplanting but rainy weather should be chosen for doing this if possible, and the plants should be kept watered regularly until established. The rows should be 1 ft. apart and the seed sown 1 in. deep.

First sowings outside of globe or Egyptian turnip-rooted and flat-topped beetroot are made about the middle of April, with perhaps a second sowing in a month's time. Another sowing of globe beet can be made in July to provide tender young roots in autumn and winter.

Main crop globe varieties are sown about the middle of May, while main crop long varieties are usually sown in June. With main crop varieties where the soil is fertile and the roots are allowed to reach a good size before being pulled for storage, it is best to space the rows 18 in. apart.

Growing Tips

Hoe regularly to keep the weeds down and aerate the soil, but be careful when doing this. Never damage the roots with a hoe as bleeding causes loss of colour and the roots may become deformed. If the seed has been sown continuously the seedlings will have to be thinned when they are 3 in. high to about 3 in. apart and then again when they are about the size of golf balls to 6 in. apart. It is possible to use the second thinnings for the table—served hot with a white sauce they are delicious.

Harvesting and Using

Leave the main crop beet in the ground in the winter until it is needed, if necessary, provided that some covering of straw or bracken is given, or the rows are covered with a number of continuous cloches during very cold weather. It is usually safer, however, to lift the roots and to store them in a clamp, in the same way as potatoes. The tops should be cut off, but not too near the crown, or bleeding will result and the root will not keep. Another way of storing them is in sand in a box or in a shed, but for this the roots should be lifted by late October—they will keep well this way for over six months.

Freshly pulled young globe beet are the tastiest to eat, either cold as a salad or hot as a vegetable. They take only about half an hour to cook, as against the much longer boiling of old stored beet. The long beet are always considered to have the better flavour in the north. When using beet as a salad, some salad oil with the vinegar helps to smooth the taste. As a hot vegetable beet can either be served with melted butter or with a white sauce.

Varieties

Globe beet is generally used for the earlier sowings, though it is sometimes used for main crop work. Long beet is invariably used for the main crop.

Globe or Round:

Detroit Select Globe. A popular early globe variety without rings.

Empire Globe. Globular roots with deep crimson flesh and no white rings.

Early Model Red Globe. An early variety with good quality tender roots.

Long or Half-long:

Cheltenham Greentop Selected. Bright red flesh with bronze-green foliage. Stores well.

Dobbie's Purple. Tapered roots with deep purple flesh and smooth skin. Good for showing.

Bell's Non-Bleeding. Medium-sized, blood-red root. Seldom bleeds when bruised—hence its name.

Turnip-rooted and Flat-topped:

Egyptian, Crosby's. Very early, turnip-rooted with bright crimson flesh.

Early Egyptian Flat. Very early and recommended for poor, sandy soils.

Intermediate:

Obelisk. A half-long beet—oval in shape. Excellent for those who prefer long beets—but haven't got large saucepans to cook them in.

Special Methods

Globe varieties can be sown under a number of continuous cloches from the middle of February on. The seed should be sown in rows 9 in. apart, either in stations 6 in. apart or by continuous sowing, later thinning to 6 in. apart.

BEET—SEAKALE OR SEAKALE SPINACH

This is chiefly grown for the thick ivory-white mid-ribs to the leaves, which form an excellent substitute for seakale. The remainder of the leaves can be used as spinach.

Soils and Manuring

This vegetable will grow on almost any soil. The best crops, however, are obtained by good cultivation of the ground and by liberal manuring, in which it differs from the common beet. If possible the ground should be dug in the autumn and well-rotted compost or farmyard manure incorporated at the rate of one bucketful to the sq. yd. Before sowing an application of fish manure with a 5 per cent potash content should be forked into the top few inches, and when the plants are in full growth they will appreciate an occasional watering with diluted Liquinure.

Sowing the Seed

Sow the seed in late April or early May, in rows 15 in. apart, either at stations 1 ft. apart or continuously in drills 1 in. deep. A second sowing may be made in June.

Growing Tips

Hoe regularly and feed with Liquinure as advised.

Harvesting and Using

Don't cut off the leaves separately from the stems, but pull off the stem and leaf in one piece. Cutting the leaves off only and leaving the stems on tends to discourage the plant from further production. The pulling may be done as required in the summer and well on into the autumn and winter.

A teaspoonful of lemon juice in the water in which the stalks are being boiled, helps to keep the bright white colour of the mid-ribs. The dark green leaves are boiled as spinach.

Varieties

New Giant Seakale. Broad, dark green leaves, with 2-in. wide prominent white ribs.

Silver Seakale. Bushy plant, producing many large leaves.

BROCCOLI

For the sake of convenience broccoli can be divided into two main types, first the group which produces a large white head like a cauliflower, and is in fact often known as the winter cauliflower, and second the group which produces a number of small sprouts, which may be either purple or white and is known as Sprouting Broccoli.

BROCCOLI—WINTER CAULIFLOWER

In olden times it was easy to distinguish between broccoli and cauliflower, as the broccoli heads were often coarse in texture and quality, but nowadays with the introduction of new varieties and 'crosses' it is very difficult to draw a dividing line.

As far as a seedsman's catalogue is concerned, hearting broccoli are usually divided into four divisions. The first the varieties for autumn use, the second for winter and early spring, the third for spring use and the fourth the late varieties for use from April to June. If sowing and plantings are planned carefully it is possible to have a supply of broccoli heads from late September until the following June.

Soil and Manuring

Broccoli do best on a rather heavy fertile soil, though they will grow

185

on most soils provided that they are properly manured. A sunny sheltered position is preferable with protection from the north and east. They like to grow in firm ground and often do well when following a crop such as peas, beans or potatoes—for which the ground has been well dug and manured, and thus does not have to be disturbed much again. Before sowing, fish manure with a 10 per cent potash content should be forked into the top few inches of soil. Carbonate of lime is applied to the surface of the soil at 3–6 oz. to the sq. yd. if the test with the B.D.H. Soil Indicator shows this to be necessary.*

Sowing the Seed

The seed of broccoli, in the same way as most other brassica plants, is usually sown in a prepared seed bed, the first sowings of most varieties being made about the middle of April in the north and later in the south. Sowings of the very late varieties are not usually made until the middle of May. It may be said, however, that succession in broccoli cropping depends on the varieties used and not upon succession in sowing. The seed bed need not be large as only a short row will provide a number of plants. The rows need only be 6 in. apart, but it will be found that if the distance is under 9 in., hoeing is difficult and weeding may have to be done by hand.

Plants and Planting

Don't leave the plants too long in the seed bed so that they get lanky, but plant them out as soon as the ground is ready.

The larger varieties are best planted out in rows 2 ft. 6 in. apart, with 2 ft. between the plants in the row. The smaller varieties can be planted in rows 2 ft. apart with the plants 18 in. apart. More protection is afforded when the plants are closer together, but they are more liable to disease and do not grow as large as when they are given wider spacing.

Plant firmly keeping a few plants in reserve for gapping up in a fortnight's time if necessary.

Growing Tips

In milder districts broccoli are not likely to be damaged by frost during the winter months, but in colder parts there is often a danger of damage caused by the early morning sun after a hard night-frost. To prevent this the plants should be heeled over in November, so that their heads face north. Do this by taking away a little soil on that side and then after the plant has been pushed over, place the soil on the other side.

* Fellows of The Good Gardeners Association can get their soil tested free.

The ground should, of course, be hoed regularly during the summer months and until the weeds have stopped growing or the soil is un-workable in the autumn.

Harvesting and Using

It is important to cut the curds as soon as they are ready, but when a number mature at the same time, a leaf or two may be broken over the heads to hold them back. Another method is to pull the plants up and hang them upside down in a shed.

Hearting broccoli lose much of their flavour on boiling and should always be steamed in preference, the average time needed being about half an hour. They can also be baked, or after par-boiling may be sprinkled heavily with cheese and a white sauce, the whole browned thoroughly in the oven.

Varieties

Autumn, for cutting September, October and November:

Veitch's Self-Protecting. Large, pure-white, close heads, which are well protected. October-November.

Extra Early Roscoff. Especially suitable for growing in south-west and south with large white heads in November–December.

Walcheren. Fine white heads for cutting August–September.

Winter and Early Spring:

Roscoff No. 1. Follows Extra Early Roscoff and heads December–January.

Early Feltham. Large, snow-white heads in January and early February, suitable for most districts.

Roscoff No. 2. Heads January–February.

Snow White. Large creamy-white heads of uniform size and shape. February–March.

Morse's February. Excellent heads ready for cutting February–March.

Roscoff No. 3. Heads March.

Spring:

Roscoff No. 4. Heading about March. Beautiful pure-white heads.

Leamington. Heads, white, close and well-protected in March–April.

Knight's Protecting. Well-protected firm heads in April.

Late Spring and Early Summer

Cambridge Hardy Late. Strong-growing and well protected. Very hardy. April–mid-May.

Roscoff No. 5. April–early May, especially suited for southern districts.

Late Queen. Good heads in May.

Mid-Summer. Good late variety for cutting May–June.

Rearguard. Excellent heads in May and June, sometimes until first week in July.

BROCCOLI—SPROUTING

This is a very useful crop in the late winter as it is very hardy and the small flower heads or 'sprouts' are pleasantly flavoured. It is well worth including in any cropping scheme.

The seeds should be sown in a seed bed in April or early May in the same way as hearting broccoli.

Sprouting broccoli requires the same soil conditions, manuring and cultivation as hearting broccoli, but needs no protection over the winter.

Harvesting and Using

Sprouting broccoli is cut when the flower shoots are growing out from the axils of the leaves. Cut them back to two-thirds of their length so that more shoots will be thrown out from the little stem. The main leaves, which give some protection to the 'sprouts' should not be removed until most of the latter have been cut. It is possible to eat almost all the plant by the end of the season.

Broccoli 'sprouts' are best cooked by steaming or by boiling in a little water. Don't boil in the ordinary way or the flavour will be lost. Drain and serve with melted butter poured over them.

Varieties

Purple Sprouting, Early. For use in March.

Purple Sprouting, Late. This is perhaps the best to grow if only one variety is being grown, as it is very hardy and very prolific. April–May.

White Sprouting, Early. February–March.

White Sprouting, Late. March–April.

Green Sprouting or Calabrese. Green head, which is a large cluster of buds, as well as side-shoots, in late summer and autumn. This type is best sown in late May, otherwise it comes in when many other vegetables are available.

CULTURE OF VEGETABLES ALPHABETICALLY

BROCCOLI—NINE STAR

Mention has not been previously made of this broccoli, which is a perennial, but which is sown and planted out in the first place in the same way as sprouting broccoli.

Each plant will produce about fifteen small, creamy-white heads every year for about five years. It is supposedly a cross between a sprouting broccoli and a hearting variety. Also see chapter 10.

Variety

Nine Star Perennial.

BRUSSELS SPROUTS

This vegetable was only introduced into this country during the last century, but it has now become one of the most popular of the winter greens, and is nearly always preferred to cabbages or savoys.

Soils and Manuring

It will grow on most soils, but it prefers a deeply worked fertile, but not over-rich loam. There is, however, one 'must' with regard to soil preparation for brussels sprouts and that is the soil must be firm or the sprouts will blow. If the soil is not worked deeply enough then there will not be enough root growth and the plants will be sickly and starved.

Sprouts often do best when following a well-manured and deeply cultivated crop. Because they like firm land, there is no need to do any deep cultivation immediately prior to planting. In fact very good crops often result when the planting holes have to be made with a crow-bar!— because the land is so hard.

Well-rotted compost or farmyard manure should be dug into the ground in the autumn at the rate of one bucketful to the sq. yd., and immediately prior to planting, fish manure should be applied and lightly forked into the top few inches of soil at the rate of 4 oz. to the sq. yd. Lime should also be applied to the surface before planting, where the soil is acid, and be allowed to work its way in.

In fact, to 'recap', one may say that the five main requirements of brussels sprouts are: (1) Heavy manuring, (2) Deep cultivation, (3) Plenty of room, (4) Firm soil, (5) Long season of growth.

Plants and Planting

Brussels plants are raised from seed sown in a seed bed and are then planted out into their permanent quarters. For all normal purposes seed can be sown in the open in a seed bed in February or March, depending on the locality, making a further sowing in April for succession. It is also possible to increase the succession from one sowing, by transplanting the largest plants only the first time, and waiting a fortnight before transplanting the remainder.

Where very early sprouts are required or where climatic conditions render early (New Year) sowing difficult, the seed can be sown in the open in the autumn, i.e. late August or early September, or in January in cold frames. The first method was more popular than it is now, though it is still often used in the north.

Whatever method of sowing is adopted, it should be remembered that this crop is all the better for a long steady period of growth. (See the five main requirements.)

The plants are best put out in May or early June, and if possible plant at least 3 ft. sq., especially with the larger varieties. Choose a showery period for the job if possible, or be prepared to water the plants in. Mercuric Chloride, as recommended on page 271, should be used to control club root where necessary. The ground must be firm and the plants well firmed in. The best plants are those which are sturdy and short-jointed, and should be 4 to 6 in. high. Don't plant any weaklings or those with no growing points.

Growing Tips

As brussels are planted out 3 ft. sq., it is usually possible to have a quick-maturing inter-crop, such as lettuce, between the rows.

Hoe regularly to kill the weeds and aerate the soil. Try not to damage the leaves, as they should only be removed when yellow and decaying. The head of the plant is best not cut until the end of February, as it helps to protect the rest of the plant as well as manufacture plant foods to assist in the growth of the sprouts.

Harvesting and Using

Yellowing of the lower leaves is a guide that the first sprouts are ready. It is best to pick them by pushing downward quickly with the thumb, and also to remove at the same time the lower leaves in order to assist the development of the remaining sprouts. Pick regularly to ensure that the sprouts are gathered when they are just right. The first sprouts are usually ready in early September, but there won't be much of a heavy crop until late October or November, and provided that different varieties are used and successional sowing is practised, harvesting should go on until the end of March.

If early sprouts are cut instead of picked, a second crop may be harvested. This is useful to the man with little space in his garden.

The best sprouts to eat are undoubtedly those that are small and hard when picked, though most of the modern varieties which have been largely raised for market growers, produce larger-sized specimens. Anyhow the sprouts must be firm. Sprouts are probably best cooked by boiling in a small quantity of water for about twenty minutes—do not overcook or the flavour will be lost and the sprouts become mushy. One way of serving after boiling is *Sautés au Beurre*. Let them cool a little and then melt some butter in a frying pan, put in the sprouts, season with pepper or a little grated nutmeg, and keep them moving over a fairly hot plate or fire for about ten minutes, dish up, sprinkle over a little chopped parsley and serve.

Varieties

With brussels sprouts strain seems more important than variety. For a start it is often better to choose a variety which has already proved itself in the district, though the new Cambridge varieties produced by the Horticultural Research Station at Cambridge, are well worth while growing in most places.

Early Types:

Cambridge No. 1. Large firm sprouts of good quality, suitable for autumn or spring sowing.

Rous Lench. Solid dark-green sprouts and much favoured by gardeners in Worcestershire district. Medium height.

Lyons. A new early dwarf French variety, with small firm sprouts. Should be grown by those who prefer 'tiny' sprouts.

Darlington. An early dwarf variety doing well on light sandy soils.

Mid-Season Types:

Cambridge No. 3. Large sprouts. The main crop selection of this series.

Forex. A good variety, with medium-sized sprouts on sturdy plants.

Cambridge Special. Small compact-grown sprouts. Should be grown by anyone preferring the small button sprouts.

Late Types:

Timperley Champion. Medium height, producing good size hard sprouts. Has proved its worth in the north.

Cambridge No. 5. The late selection of the series.

CULTURE OF VEGETABLES ALPHABETICALLY

CABBAGE

Cabbages have been cultivated for hundreds of years in this country, and are originally descended from the sea cabbage, which grows wild in the southern coastal regions, as well as in southern Europe. There is no need for cabbage to form a large part of the vegetable supply, but it is always useful to have some in the garden.

There are a number of different types, some of which will be dealt with under separate headings, but the three main categories, however, are: (1) The spring cabbage and spring greens, (2) The summer and autumn cabbage, (3) The winter cabbage. Their cultivation is given below.

Soils and Manuring

Cabbages are not very particular as to soil, though they prefer a good loam. Spring cabbages require a lighter soil than the other two categories, one which warms up quickly in the spring so that they can soon get away.

Where they follow on after a well-manured crop, such as peas or beans, no bulky manures or compost may be needed, except in the case of less fertile ground, where well-rotted compost or farmyard manure can be incorporated at half a 2-gallon bucketful to the sq. yd. There is a danger, however, of too much sappy growth with cabbages when such compost or manure has been recently dug in, so it is best to use a balanced fish manure with a 10 per cent potash content, which should be forked into the top few inches before planting. As with other brassica crops, carbonate of lime must be applied to the surface soil, if the soil is at all acid. Use a B.D.H. Soil Indicator to discover the quantity to use. (See also footnote on p. 186.)

Spring cabbage will probably need a 'fillip' in the spring to help them on after the winter, and nitro-chalk is excellent for the purpose, at the rate of 1 to 2 oz. to the sq. yd. If the gardener disapproves of 'inorganics' then dried blood should be applied at 3 oz. to the yard run, but this is considerably more expensive.

SPRING CABBAGE. These cabbages should not be confused with spring-sown cabbage, as these are sown in the summer, planted out in the autumn, and mature in the late spring and early summer.

As already stated they need a lighter ground than other cabbages, and it is preferable to choose a sheltered position, where there is no danger of waterlogging.

CULTURE OF VEGETABLES ALPHABETICALLY

Plants and Planting

Sow the seed thinly in a seed bed with a fine tilth—mid-July is the best time for the north, but late July in the south. Two small successional sowings can be made as an insurance at ten-day intervals.

This crop follows very well after early potatoes, peas, or beans, and the plants are put out in late September or October. The rows are usually 18 in. apart, and when dwarf varieties are used, the plants are put 1 ft. apart in the rows. Larger varieties, such as Flower of Spring, will want to be 18 in. apart.

Growing Tips

If the plants are looking seedy in the spring, apply nitro-chalk as advised. As soon as the cabbages are cut, the stalks should be removed and placed on the compost heap, as they will rob the land if left to grow on. Bash the stalks up with a spade, or with the back of an axe on a chopping block, and they will rot down more easily.

Harvesting and Using

This crop can either be cut before the hearts have been formed and used as spring greens, or used as hearted cabbage. It is probably better not to leave too many of them to heart up, as they are likely to come on at the same time, and won't 'stay put' as winter cabbages will.

SUMMER AND AUTUMN CABBAGE. These varieties are generally sown in March, making a successional sowing two weeks later. Not many of them are likely to be needed so they can be planted on any odd piece of ground available. It is better to have a few coming on at intervals, rather than a lot at one time, as they will soon burst, if not cut when ready.

For earlier cropping in June, the seed can be sown in January or February, in a cold frame, planting out after hardening off in rows 18 in. apart and 12 in. between the plants, in March or April. Plants raised from outside sowings are planted in their final positions in May or June in rows 2 ft. apart with 18 in. between the plants.

WINTER CABBAGE. This is the cabbage which is sown in April and May, and cut from November to February. It is not usually quite so hardy as the savoy, but is not so coarse in texture.

Heavier loams are suitable for this crop, but waterlogging must be avoided. The basic manuring is the same as for other cabbages, but they do not usually require any top dressing.

Plants and Planting

In the north the seed is often sown in March at the same time as the summer varieties. In the south, however, it is desirable to sow later in April and May, or the crop may mature too early. In addition to sowing in a seed bed for transplanting, it is possible to sow in stations *in situ*, so as to avoid the difficulties of planting out in a hot, dry period. The plants are best put out 2 ft. sq., i.e. that is the rows are 2 ft. apart with 2 ft. between the plants.

Growing Tips

Hoe regularly to keep the weeds down and to aerate the soil. This crop is often badly attacked by caterpillars, cabbage aphis, and in earlier stages by flea-beetle, which should all be dealt with immediately, as advised in Chapter 14.

Harvesting and Using

This crop is cut from November to February, and has the advantage over spring and summer cabbage, that once the cold weather starts the heads will remain a long time on the plants after maturing before bursting.

Pull up the stalks as soon as possible after cutting, so that the ground is not robbed.

Varieties

It is most important to buy a good seed and for preference choose a variety which is known to do well in the district.

Spring Cabbage:

Early Durham. Very early, with well-formed, medium-sized, pointed hearts.

Clucas First Early 218. Uniform heads, solid, and well pointed. Few outer leaves. Very early.

Enfield Market. Main crop variety, with large good quality heads.

Flower of Spring. Very popular variety, which matures early, with good pointed heads.

Harbinger. Dark green with small pointed heads. Not prone to bolt.

Summer Cabbage:

Primo. Small, round-headed and very early. Recommended for frame sowing in February and planting out in April to cut in June.

Golden Acre. Very early, ball-headed on short stems.
Greyhound. Very early, with pointed hearts and few outer leaves.

Autumn Cabbage:

Winnigstadt. Grey-green, compact cabbage, with solid pointed heads.
Autumn Queen. Follows Winnigstadt. Moderate size.

Winter Cabbage:

Christmas Drumhead. A very useful variety, with large and firm hearts.

January King. The hardiest cabbage. Can be sown from May to July to produce good solid, flattish heads, from November to January or February.

RED CABBAGE

This is usually grown for pickling, but it is eaten when stewed in some districts.

Plants and Planting

The seed is sown in a seed bed in March as for summer cabbage, and the plants should be planted out 18 in. apart, with 2 ft. between the rows if there is more than one row. For really large plants the seed can be sown in August for transplanting the following spring and cutting in the summer. For stewing, the seed may be sown in April.

Growing Tips

Treat as other cabbages.

Harvesting and Using

Some people like to let frost touch the leaves before cutting, as they find the flavour improved. A good recipe for stewing cabbage is as follows: cut the cabbage into thin shreds and place in pan with slice of ham and ½ oz. butter at the bottom. Add ½ pint stock and 1 gill vinegar. Then let it stew for three hours. Add some more stock, salt, pepper and a tablespoonful of sugar. Now mix well and boil, until all the liquor is exhausted, after which put it in a dish and serve with fried or grilled sausages.

Varieties

The Lydiate. One of the largest. A very firm heart. Late and hardy.
Ruby Red. Early. Sow in the spring. Not too large. Suits the north.

Coleworts or Collards

These are small cabbages, which were much used formerly on account of their hardiness, but which have now been largely supplanted by hardy cabbages such as Christmas Drumhead.

Plants and Planting

There are two methods of raising the plants, the first is by sowing in a seed bed and transplanting, the second is by sowing the seeds by stations *in situ*, in which case the rows should be 1 ft. apart and the stations 1 ft. apart. The sowings can be made almost any time from mid-March to mid-August, but the main crop sowing should be made in July. Plants from the later sowings are used as spring greens before they are fully mature.

The spacing on planting out should be 1 ft. apart each way. It is also possible to plant them up between cabbages, cutting them when the cabbages want more room.

General Cultivation

This is exactly the same as for cabbages, except that it is unnecessary for the ground to have been heavily manured.

Harvesting and Using

As already mentioned the earlier sowings are cut as small-hearted cabbages, while the later sowings are generally used as spring greens.

Varieties

The only two varieties normally offered by seedsmen nowadays are:
Hardy Green. This is usually sown late and cut green.
Rosette. For earlier sowings and cut when hearted.

Cabbage—Savoy
(see under Savoys, page 242)

CARROTS

Wild carrots are native to this country, but the cultivated varieties were introduced by the Flemings during the reign of Queen Elizabeth I. There is no reason why there should not be a supply of carrots all the year round, either from early carrots raised under continuous cloches or Dutch lights, or from early varieties grown in the open, or from main crop varieties lifted in the autumn and stored over the winter.

CULTURE OF VEGETABLES ALPHABETICALLY

Soils and Manuring

Carrots undoubtedly prefer a good, deep, well-cultivated sandy loam. For the early outdoor sowings the earth must be warm, and even the later main crop sowings will never succeed in heavy wet land. A heavier subsoil will be of assistance in retaining moisture during dry periods.

Good fine soil texture is essential and heavy soil should be left rough over the winter, so that it can be weathered and broken down.

Fresh bulky organic manure is not suitable for carrots, as they are liable to fork if it is incorporated fairly soon prior to the seed being sown. Carrots, in the same way as most root crops, grow best in ground which has been well cultivated and manured for a previous crop. Before sowing an application of fish manure with a 10 per cent potash content is recommended at the rate of 2 oz. to the sq. yd. for the early sowings and 4 oz. for the main crop. This is best applied and forked into the top few inches of soil a week or so before the sowing.

Sowing the Seed

Choose a south border or a warm spot for the early sowings in March, or give protection by using a number of continuous cloches. A further successional sowing three weeks later is advisable. Sow very thinly in rows 1 ft. apart and there will be no need to thin later on. Remember that it is no use sowing carrots unless the soil is warm. It is much better to wait until the soil warms up, than to be guided by an arbitrary date on the calendar. Furthermore, the seed will not germinate unless there is moisture present.

Main crop sowings are best made in April in drills 15 in. apart and $\frac{3}{4}$ in. deep. Station sowing is excellent for this crop, as it is after the heavy thinnings needed with 'ordinary sowings', that the carrot-fly are likely to attack. Make the stations every 6 in.

Late sowings can be made with early (quick-maturing) varieties in July, so that there will be a supply of tender young roots in autumn and early winter. This sowing sometimes escapes the carrot-fly, which is at its worst in June. Sow very thinly and pull for eating when the roots are young and tender.

Growing Tips

Hoe regularly throughout the season and thin the main crop, where continuous sowing has been practised. Always choose a damp evening, if possible, for thinning and draw the soil well up to the plants after the operation, then firming it down. Before thinning it is a good idea to dust in between the rows with a Derris dust, using a proprietary brand which does not taint the crop. The effect of the dust is to discourage the flies from laying their eggs. The thinning should be done in two stages, first to 3 in. and then to 6 in. apart. Latterly we have not done any thinning at all and have had good results.

If the weather is dry, it may be necessary to irrigate the rows after sowing, as carrot seed must have moisture to germinate.

Harvesting and Using

Early varieties are best used when they are young and tender. The main crop is lifted before the autumn and winter frosts, for storage in sand or dry earth, after the tops have been cut off and put on the compost heap. One good way is to have the roots in sand in a box under the larder shelf, so that they are always handy when needed. If stored in the open, they should be clamped in the same way as potatoes.

Carrots are rich in vitamin A and C, and can be eaten either raw or cooked. When eaten raw, they should be grated immediately before serving, otherwise they will lose a lot of their goodness.

Varieties

There are roughly three main classes of carrots—The Short Types, the Intermediate or Half-Long types and the Long types. In my opinion the Long types are not worth growing, as they often tend to be coarse. Anyway they require a very deep and light soil. The intermediate varieties are to be preferred for the main crop sowing.

Short Carrots:

(1) For Dutch lights or continuous cloches.
Dutch Scarlet Horn. Early. Fire colour. Delicious.
Early French Forcing Horn. Almost spherical roots, crisp and sweet.
(2) For early outdoor sowings.
Early Gem or Guerande. Short, thick and very stump-rooted. Good for hot, dry soils.
Early Market. Good deep colour, even in shape.

Intermediate or Half-Long Carrots (Stump-Rooted):

(1) For early sowings.
Early Nantes. Orange-scarlet, keeps well.
Amsterdam Forcing. Excellent for early forcing. Length about 5 in.

(2) Main crop.
Chantenay. Popular half-long stump-rooted variety.
Autumn King. Heavy with rich, deep-orange flesh.

Pointed Roots and suitable for Main Crop.
James' Scarlet Intermediate. Good colour and texture. Very popular. More grown perhaps than any other variety.
New Red Intermediate. Smooth roots of excellent colour and quality.

Long Carrots:
Altrincham Large Red. Long, main crop variety, very hardy.
Surrey Long Red. Long tapering deep-orange roots.

CAULIFLOWER

Cauliflowers are believed to be of Italian origin and were introduced into this country in the sixteenth century. They are probably the most popular of all the brassicas, but they are certainly not the easiest to grow, as they need plentiful supplies of plant foods, ample moisture and the kind of conditions which will help rapid and unchecked growth.

The cultivation of winter cauliflowers, or to give them their more usual name of broccoli, will be found under broccoli.

Soils and Manuring

This crop demands a deeply worked soil, which should be well-drained and enriched with well-rotted manure or compost. The soil, in addition to being well drained, must have an ample moisture content and reserve.

If possible, cauliflowers should follow a crop for which the ground has been well manured and cultivated, such as peas or beans. If not, well-rotted compost or farmyard manure will have to be dug in over the winter at the rate of half a 2-gallon bucketful to the sq. yd. Carbonate of lime should be applied to the surface after the digging should the soil be at all acid, usually at, say, 5 oz. to the sq. yd. Ten days or so before planting, a dressing of fish manure with a 6 per cent potash content should be applied and lightly forked into the top few inches of soil.

Sowing the Seed

A succession of cauliflowers is ensured by sowing seed at various times of the year, while with broccoli the seed sowing usually takes place in a short period of a few weeks and the variety is the most important factor.

Autumn sowing. The seed may be sown in September in cold frames. Sow thinly in raised beds, the soil being as near as possible to the No-Soil Compost. After sowing cover the seed with some more compost and firm down. Before sowing the soil should be evenly moist and there should be no need to water until after germination. Keep the frames closed before germination, but give full ventilation afterwards, giving protection only when there is a frost. Sometimes the seedlings are pricked out into other frames for overwintering, but it is usually more satisfactory to leave them where they are until they are planted out.

If continuous cloches are available, the seed can be sown under them at the end of September in three rows 8 in. apart. The seedlings should be thinned to 1 in. apart and planted out at the end of March. March.

January and February Sowings. Seed can be sown in warmth in January or February and when the young seedlings have come through they can be pricked out into cold frames, or better still, in soil blocks which are placed in cold frames.

Seed may also be sown under cloches in January for planting out in April.

Outdoor Sowings. The first outdoor sowings are made in a seed bed in early April, with successional sowings in late April or early May.

Plants and Planting

The earliest varieties from seed sown in the autumn will go out in late March, with the January sown plants following in April. Plants from the outdoor sowings will be put out in June or early July. Space the rows 2 ft. 6 in. apart and leave 20 in. to 2 ft. between the plants in the row. Plant shallowly (this is very important) but firmly. Full details of planting out are given in Chapter 8, but remember that cauliflowers need extra careful handling

Growing Tips

Hoe regularly between the plants. In dry periods it will be necessary to irrigate well. Cauliflowers are definitely not the crop for quick-drying soils with no irrigation. When the heads start to come on and the white curds begin to show, a leaf should be broken over to keep it white and clean. If weathered soot is available the plants will appreciate a dressing or two at 5 oz. to the sq. yd. during the growing period. The alternative is to use dried blood at not more than 2 oz. to the sq. yd.

Bear in mind that cauliflowers should have a steady rapid growth and that for this they should have ample moisture and supplies of plant foods.

Harvesting and Using

Cut the curds as early as possible in the morning, when they are still wet with dew.

If too many heads become ready at the same time, whole plants can be pulled up with the soil on their roots and be hung in a cool shed upside down for use when required.

It is really better never to boil a cauliflower, but steam it instead—half an hour is the average time. Instead of plain cauliflower with a white sauce, why not try cauliflower fritters. I have had them on the Continent. Divide a cooked cold cauliflower into sprigs, dip each floweret in some thick cold white sauce, which should be well seasoned. When the sauce is set dip the pieces of cauliflower into a light frying batter, and drop them into hot fat. Fry to a golden colour, take up, drain, sprinkle with salt and pinch of pepper, and serve garnished with fried parsley.

Varieties

For autumn sowing in frames or under continuous cloches.

All The Year Round. A good dwarf variety with large compact heads, suitable for autumn or spring sowing.

Pioneer. Large early variety, suitable for autumn or spring sowing.

Cambridge Early Allhead. Compact dwarf variety with large head, which also can be sown outdoors.

Early Erfurt. Compact and dwarf.

For January–February sowings under glass.

Early Snowball. Firm and uniform heads.

White King. Early with medium-large solid heads.

Feltham Forcing. Good for September, January, or spring sowing.

Cambridge Earliest No. 5. Very dwarf, with large pure-white heads.

For Outdoor Sowing.

Dwarf Mammoth. Good-sized heads, ready for cutting in August.

Early Veitch's Autumn Giant. Large firm heads, ready in September.

Veitch's Autumn Giant. Large, fine quality heads, ready late September.

Autumn Mammoth. Ready for cutting in October.

November Heading. Good even heads, ready for cutting October–November.

CELERY

Celery was originally cultivated in England for its medicinal properties, but since the end of the seventeenth century has been fairly commonly grown as a vegetable. It is a useful crop to grow, because in addition to being appreciated by most people, the cultivation needed for it leaves the land in a very good condition for the next crop.

Soils and Manuring

The best soil for this crop is a deep fertile one with a high water table. This doesn't mean that celery wants or will grow in a waterlogged soil, but that there should be an ample reserve of water, so that there is no check owing to dryness at the roots, which often causes a tendency to go to seed. Commercially celery is often grown in peaty soils, as they have a high organic content, are retentive of moisture, and are usually on the acid side. Celery does better in acid conditions than in soils which are very alkaline.

The main preparation of the soil for this crop is the taking out of trenches in which the celery is to grow; the purpose of this is not so that the plants should just be planted deeply, but to make the blanching easier. The trenches are usually made 18 in. wide and 16 in. deep, the soil being thrown out equally on each side of the trench, making ridges of the same height. If there is more than one trench, 2 ft. 6 in. is generally allowed between the trenches and this strip of ground is often used for catch-crops.

A trench 18 in. wide allows one row of celery to be planted, so some people like to have a wider trench and grow two or more rows, allowing another 6 in. for each row. With more than one row it is not so easy to do the earthing up and the beginner is therefore better advised to start with the narrow trench and the single row.

Dig the trenches in the autumn, if possible, as there will be more time for the soil to get weathered and more opportunity to take a catch-crop from the flat ridges on either side. Some people prefer to grow their catch-crops in the sides of the ridges away from the trench, as there is then less likelihood of their drying out.

Celery must have plenty to feed on and the bottom of the trench should be filled with a good 6-in. layer of well-rotted compost or old farmyard manure. On top of this layer there should be another layer of about 5 in. of good friable soil.

Before planting, an application of fish manure at the rate of 4 oz. to the sq. yd. run can be lightly forked in, and during the growing season the plants will appreciate regular doses of Liquinure every ten days or so.

One final word on soil preparation—don't dig over the ground first before the celery trench is taken out, or it will be found that the soil is too loose for taking out a really neat one.

Plants and Planting

Celery seed needs a temperature of 60 to 65° F. to germinate and so if no facilities for sowing seeds in warmth are available, the best way is to buy the plants in from a nurseryman. Details are given below of how to sow seed under a number of continuous cloches in March or April, but the plants raised in this manner are usually very late.

The earliest seed should be sown about the middle of February in seed boxes in the greenhouse at a temperature of 60 to 65° F., using a John Innes Seed Compost. When the seedlings can be handled they should be pricked out 3 in. apart in Alex No-Soil Potting Compost No. 1.

The main sowing should take place in early March in the greenhouse under the same conditions as before. All greenhouse-raised plants will have to be gradually hardened off, by putting them out in cold frames, etc., before they are planted out.

Celery is a very suitable subject for raising in a miniature propagator, because as soon as the seeds have germinated, the seed tray can be put out in a cold frame, taking care to give protection in case of frost. Warmth is necessary to germinate the seed, but the seedlings are quite happy in cool conditions.

As already mentioned, seed can be sown under a number of continuous cloches from late March until mid-April. Any plants raised this way are likely to be very hardy, but they will be late. Cover up the glass with sacks until germination has taken place, and then remove them during the day, replacing them at night for frost protection. It is no use trying to employ this method on a cold, wet soil, but it may be successful on light warm loams.

Be sure to buy good 'treated' celery seed from a reputable seedsman, as spores of the leaf spot disease are sometimes carried on the seed coat and the crop can be badly affected by the fungus, should diseased seed be used.

Planting out should be done when the plants are ready, which is often in early June. They are generally 3 or 4 in. high at the time. Greenhouse-raised plants must be thoroughly hardened off first.

Plant carefully in the trench with a trowel 1 ft. apart. Planting can be a little closer with weaker varieties. See that the soil is firm round the plants and then give the trench a good soaking with water. If the soil at the bottom of the trench pans down too much from the soaking, it should be hoed through in a day or two's time. If there is to be more than one row, the plants should be staggered, i.e. planted zigzag fashion, so that they are still 1 ft. apart, one from the other.

Growing Tips

Keep the trenches moist by regular irrigation, as the roots must never dry out. Feed with Marinure every ten days as advised, and this feeding will supply moisture as well as plant foods. Hoe along the ridges and harvest any catch-crops before the first earthing up is needed.

Remove any side-growths that come from the base of the plants, as these suckers are valueless. Spray with Bordeaux mixture or some other suitable copper fungicide two or three times during the growing season —this is for the prevention of leaf spot or blight.

During the winter months celery will probably need protection from the frost. This is done by covering the tops with straw or bracken, taking care at the last earthing up to bend the tops over slightly so that moisture does not trickle down and lodge in the tops of the crowns during a rainy spell or a thaw. Some gardeners who have cloches to spare have put these over the celery in November to protect them.

Earthing Up

In order that celery should be edible it must be blanched, and this is done by earthing up at regular intervals.

The first earthing up is done quite lightly and is usually carried out about the middle of August when the plants are approximately a foot high. The soil is brought to half way up the plant and all around it. It is most important that no soil should fall into the centre of the crown or in between the stems so it is best for it to be in a loose and friable condition, and for the hand to grasp the plant firmly during the operation. The second earthing takes place about three weeks later, and the final earthing up when the soil is brought right up the stem as high as the bottom leaves, is usually done in October. Take care to make the ridges smooth and steep on earthing up, so that the rain does not penetrate down into the plants, but runs away down the sides.

For show purposes celery plants are often wrapped round with paper or cardboard before earthing up. In this way the soil cannot reach the stems, which perhaps are whiter and cleaner as a result, but which, I think, lack something of the flavour they get from actual contact with the soil. Special cardboard collars can be employed and sometimes people make a loose tie with a rubber band, which can be slipped up the stems as earthing up progresses. For people who want to grow good, tasty celery for the table, none of these methods need be employed, though a loose tie of raffia round the plant will help beginners to earth up without getting any soil on to the crowns.

As a final tip, don't earth up after rain or when the soil and plants are wet!

Harvesting and Using

The first sticks will probably be sufficiently blanched and ready for use about two months after the first earthing up. After a stick has been dug up the soil should be replaced, so that adjacent sticks do not turn green from exposure to the light.

Celery is not rich in food value, and its popularity is entirely due to its flavour. It can either be eaten raw or cooked, but for both purposes it is much better when it is dug only just before it is needed. It is much liked by those suffering from rheumatism. Wash the celery well, so that there is no unpleasant grit on the sticks, but a long soaking is absolutely unnecessary.

Keep any coarse stems for use in soups or stews.

Varieties

These can be divided into two groups, the white and the pink or red. White varieties are usually earlier and are more popular, but the others are hardier and can put up with heavier soil conditions.

White:

Clandon White. Perhaps the best of the whites, being of medium height and reasonably immune to disease. Well worth growing if the seed can be obtained.

White Perfection. Compact growth, crisp and solid in the stalk.

Dwarf White Gem. Good dwarf variety.

Wright's Giant White. Large, strong and hardy, with good flavour.

Pink and Red:

Standard Bearer. Dark rose, tall and large. A recommended variety.

Clayworth Prize Pink. A pale pink of medium size, early.

Wright's Giant Red. Large compact heads and very resistant to frost.

CELERY—SELF-BLANCHING

This type of celery can be grown where there is not enough room for trenches or where the gardener does not want the trouble of taking them out. It can be grown on the flat, as it is self-blanching and does not not need earthing up. It is, however, an early celery and should be used in September and October.

A good rich soil is best for this crop and well-rotted compost or farmyard manure should be dug at the rate of one 2-gallon bucketful to the sq. yd. Shortly before planting, an application of fish manure with a 5 per cent potash content should be given at the rate of 4 oz. to the sq. yd. and lightly forked in. The plants, which are raised in exactly the same way as other celery, are planted out 1 ft. apart in the rows, which should be 18 in. apart, though with smaller varieties the planting may be 1 ft. sq.

Growing Tips

If the stems are to be really pure white, straw can be placed among the plants to keep out the light, or when there are only a very few plants, collars can be made out of stiff paper and put round the stems, being held in position by a rubber band.

Although this crop does not require the ample water supply that the ordinary celery must have, growth will be steadier with regular irrigation if the weather be on the dry side. Hoe regularly but take care not to damage the stems.

Harvesting and Using

The sticks are generally ready for use at the end of August, and all the crop must be cleared before the first serious frosts.

It is used in the same way as the trenched celery, though most people find that the flavour is not so delicate.

Varieties

Golden Self-Blanching. This is the variety generally offered in this country.

Golden Plume and White Plume are two French varieties, the former being disease resistant, while the latter has silver-white foliage.

American Green. A delicious green stemmed celery.

CHICORY

This crop is grown for the thick stalk and ribs of its leaves, which are eaten when blanched either as a salading or when cooked. It is very popular on the Continent, especially Belgium, where large quanities are grown. The variety used for blanching is generally the 'Witloof de Belgique' or the Belgian White Leaf. Do not confuse this type of chicory with either the wild chicory or common chicory, which is only a poor substitute, or with the Magdeburg types with thick roots, which are used for making the ground chicory, which is blended with coffee.

Soils and Manuring

The best soil for chicory is a well and deeply worked loam, liberally supplied with organic matter and a good reserve of moisture.

In the autumn well-rotted compost or farmyard manure should be dug into the ground at the rate of one 2-gallon bucketful to the sq. yd., after which the land should be left rough until the following late spring when the piece can be worked down and fish manure with a 5 per cent potash content forked into the top few inches at the rate of 3 oz. to the sq. yd.

Sowing the Seed

Late May or early June is the best time to sow the seed, having obtained a fine tilth. The rows should be 18 in. apart and the seedlings thinned later to 1 ft. apart, or the seed sown in stations 1 ft. apart in the first place. Be sure you get the right variety and a good strain.

Growing Tips

Hoe regularly during the summer months to keep down weeds. Irrigation will not be necessary unless the season is a very dry one, as chicory is deep rooting.

Lifting of the roots can take place any time between the end of September and the beginning of November. The best roots to use are those which are straight and clean and not fangy. Cut off the tops to within an inch of the crown. The roots can now be forced straight away or kept in damp soil or sand in a cool place until they are required.

One of the best ways of forcing small quantities where there is limited space available is to pot up three or four roots in a big pot and then invert a similar-sized pot on the top, the whole contraption being placed in a room, shed or greenhouse, where there is an average temperature of 45 to 50° F. The roots can also be placed in boxes of sand tightly one against the other, the boxes being placed somewhere dark, such as under a greenhouse bench or in a cellar, the optimum temperature being that mentioned above. The 'chicons' should be ready for eating in about three to four weeks. It is possible to keep up a good supply over the winter months, by potting or boxing up a few roots every week or so for forcing.

Harvesting and Using

The chicons or shoots are cut when they are about 6 to 8 in. long, with a piece of root attached, which helps to keep the leaves together. The hand used for holding the chicon at the time of cutting should be clean, as they are better when they do not have to be washed too much, especially if they are going to be used as a salad.

Don't cook all the goodness and flavour out of them by boiling them in a lot of water, but just remove the outer leaves, and then put the heads in boiling salted water for five minutes only. After this drain and then cook slowly in a closed pan for an hour and a quarter, with plenty of butter and whatever seasoning is preferred. Serve with melted butter or a little gravy sauce.

Varieties

Witloof de Belgique
Brussels Witloof } Good easy to grow varieties.

Brussels Witloof Vesta. Recommended for forcing when the outside temperatures are mild.

CUCUMBERS

It is possible to grow cucumbers, or rather ridge cucumbers, outside during the summer months, but the more attractive-looking frame varieties can also be grown if Dutch lights or continuous cloches are available.

Soils and Manuring

Cucumbers like a moist but well-drained soil, rich in organic matter. It is best to dig the ground well in the autumn or winter, and then a week or so before the plants are to be put out, a trench can be opened up and a good 4- to 5-in. layer of well-rotted compost or farmyard manure put in before the soil is put back, the top of the layer being about 6 in. below the surface. The main point is to have a good layer of compost 6 in. below the surface, so if there are only going to be a few plants, it is often sufficient to incorporate the compost in a hole, say, 15 in. sq., where each plant is to grow. When the soil is replaced on top of the compost it will form a little mound.

Plants and Planting

It is possible to raise ridge cucumber plants from seeds sown in the open in late May or under cloches earlier on, but the seed of frame cucumbers has to be sown in warmth in early April.

If there is a greenhouse or home propagator available, the seeds of both types can be sown in Eclipse No-Soil Compost No. 1 in the first week of April at a temperature of 60° F. The seeds can either be sown singly in soil blocks, two to a 60 pot (thinned down to one later), or spaced 3 in. sq. in a seed tray. This sowing applies to seedlings which will be planted out in frames, or under continuous cloches in early May, but ridge cucumbers for planting out of doors at the end of May, should not be sown before the end of April.

A simple and successful way of sowing ridge cucumbers *in situ* in late May or early June, is to sow three seeds to a station and then cover each station with an inverted 2-lb. jam-jar. Keep the jam-jar on until the plants are well through and then remove and thin to one plant per station.

Stopping

It is necessary to stop frame cucumbers one leaf beyond the forming cucumber, after which a lateral will form, which should then be stopped one leaf beyond the forming cucumber, and so on.

The stopping of ridge cucumbers is more simple in that the top or growing point should be pinched out after seven leaves have formed. Then after that it is usually convenient to combine the harvesting with pinching out growing points, especially in the case of plants growing under continuous cloches, as the glass will have to be taken off anyhow to cut the produce.

The male flowers of the frame varieties should be pinched off, as the cucumbers taste bitter if pollinated. Leave the male flowers on the ridge cucumbers, so that a good set of fruit will be ensured.

Growing Tips

It is a good idea to mulch cucumbers with a layer of sedge peat, as being surface-rooting plants, they do not care for being disturbed by hoeing. A mulch will also help to preserve the moist conditions which the plants like. Keep the plants well watered in dry weather, but do not let water collect round the stems, as stem rot may result, and don't let the roots get exposed by washing all the surface soil away.

To avoid scorching if the cucumbers are grown under glass, the lights or continuous cloches should be given a light lime wash to break up the rays of the sun.

A good feed with dilute Liquinure once a week after the first fruits are 3 to 4 in. long, is an aid to the production of good cucumbers.

Harvesting and Using

It is best never to let the cucumbers get too old. The plants will go on cropping if the cutting is regular and there are no old fruits left uncut.

Most people use cucumbers only when cold as an addition to the salad bowl, but there are a number of excellent ways of cooking them. Stuffed cucumber, when the fruit is cut into pieces 2 in. long, stuffed with sausage meat, braised and served on toast, is very tasty.

Varieties

Frame Varieties:

Conqueror. Prolific cropper with good flavour. Recommended for cold frames and continuous cloches.

Telegraph. Popular variety, even in size and shape.

Ridge varieties:

Hampshire Giant. An excellent variety, heavy cropping with large fruits. Almost a frame variety!

King of the Ridge. Dark green, hardy and vigorous.

Perfection Ridge. Long fruits.

GHERKINS

Some people like to grow gherkins for pickling, and the whole idea is to try and produce fruits 2 to 3 in. long, and to ensure this, the harvesting must be done frequently so as to ensure that the fruits do not get too large and old.

The culture of gherkins is similar to that of cucumbers, but the great thing to remember is that the sowing must always be done *in situ*. They do not transplant satisfactorily.

Sow the seed, therefore, early in June in the ground where the plants are to grow, say three seeds every 2 ft., seeing that they go in 1 in. deep. If you want more than one row the next should be 2 ft. apart.

The two varieties that are worth while growing are Boston Pickling, which produces short, bright green fruits, and Small Paris, which is even more prolific.

KALE OR BORECOLE

Kales are usually grown because they are a most useful winter vegetable. They are very hardy and usually come into use in February and March, when other greens may be very scarce. They may succeed on even the poorest soils and the plants are seldom killed even in the most severe winters. Curiously enough they are never very badly attacked by the club root disease, and I have known them grown with success on diseased land without any particular precautions taken.

Soils and Manuring

Kales will grow on almost any soil. They are not at all particular. They appreciate, of course, good drainage, and the pH should be about 7. They do well after a crop that's been treated liberally such as the potato. On very poor land well-rotted compost might be dug in at one 2-gallon bucketful to the sq. yd. There is never any need, however, to do this if the previous crop has been adequately fed. Give, however, a fish manure at 2 to 3 oz. to the sq. yd. just before planting and rake this in.

Plants and Planting

Sow the seed in late April and early May in the south, and early in April in the north. Have the drills 9 in. apart, and thin the plants out to 2 to 3 in. apart later; the thinnings may be transplanted to a further seed bed if necessary.

It is best to sow the variety Hungry Gap where it is to grow, and thin it out. This is usually done in late May, or up to the middle of June. Here the rows should normally be $2\frac{1}{2}$ ft. apart, and the thinning out should be done later to 2 ft. apart. Asparagus Kale has been sown late in June for transplanting late in July. This scheme, however, is more suited to the south than the north.

Set the plants out any time in June or July as is convenient, allowing 2 ft. 6 in. between the rows and 18 in. between the plants with the dwarf varieties, and 2 ft. with the taller kinds. Always plant while the soil is in a moist condition, or be prepared to pour some water into the holes at planting time.

Growing Tips

Kales usually follow early potatoes, early peas, or early French beans. See that the plants have plenty of water for the first few weeks and if the cabbage-root maggot abounds, sprinkle a little calomel dust around the

211

plants the moment they are in position, to keep this pest at bay. Hoe regularly in between the plants to keep down weeds, and watch out for diseases and pests like aphides, caterpillars and downy mildew. Take necessary precautions against these as detailed in chapters 14 and 15.

Harvesting and Using

Don't be tempted to cut the kales too early. There are usually plenty of other greens about in the winter so leave them until last, say January. The idea is for them to keep on until April. The leaves are usually more delicious if they've been 'touched' by the frost. Let them, therefore, grow unrestricted and make really good plants. Some gardeners make a point about the middle of January of removing the central top of each plant, so as to encourage the development of side-growths.

Varieties

There are a very large number of varieties to choose from.

Ragged Jack, a northern variety, very popular in Scotland and in Northumberland and Durham. The leaves are dark green, deeply 'cut about' as its name suggests, and at the top the foliage is very crowded.

Extra Curled Scotch, as its name suggests, the leaves are densely curled. The plants are robust and the growth is compact. This variety is both hardy and productive.

Hungry Gap. May grow 20 in. high, will survive the hardest of winters. Is sometimes available as late as May and June. The leaves are much curled and of a dark green colour, and the mid-ribs are stout and pronounced.

Russian Kale. Dense heads are produced in November, or December, and if these are cut then, delicious young shoots are produced in the spring.

Cottagers. A plant which will grow 30 in. high, with a strong, upright, main stalk. The leaves are curled and crimped along their edges, and in hard winters may have a purplish shade. Shoots will also appear of a similar colour. Usually used in February and March.

Asparagus Kale. Produces very frilly leaves from whose axils arise delicious shoots, which are often cooked as asparagus. It is usual to go on cutting shoots from the plants throughout the early spring. One of the best of the later varieties.

Thousand Headed. One of the most hardy varieties. A strong grower and branching in habit. Remarkably productive, but not particularly delicious to eat. Usually cut and used in the spring.

Ormskirk Hearting. An unusual type of kale because it produces a rather loose heart, because the leaves curl over in the centre. Is very hardy and much liked in Lancashire and Cheshire. The leaves have quite a thick mid-rib but only a very short leaf stalk.

LEEK

At one time the leek was largely a North country vegetable, for though it is the national emblem of Wales, it isn't eaten so much in that country as in Scotland! It is one of the most useful vegetables, because even the severest of winters do not harm the plants. Some claim that this vegetable has a medicinal value and Nero said that they helped to clear his voice.

If you cut off the fibrous roots at harvesting time, and let them fall to the ground, they rot down quickly and provide a wonderful medium for the growing of lettuce.

Soils and Manuring

Grow the leek in the deepest soil you can and where they can be given plenty of water. They hate acid soil, so be prepared to add lime in order that the pH stands at 8. If leeks are to be grown on light, sandy soils, heavy dressings of organic matter must be dug in, plus sedge peat at a bucketful to the sq. yd., forked into the top 6 in.

In addition to the well-rotted compost which should be dug in at one large barrowload to 8 sq. yds., an organic fertilizer such as fish manure should be applied at 2 to 3 oz. to the sq. yd.—for leeks are gross feeders and repay generous treatment. Never give raw dung to leeks as they dislike this greatly.

Plants and Planting

Prepare a strip of land by forking in sedge peat at a bucketful to the sq. yd. Rake this down fine and level. Then sow the seed in a very shallow drill, aiming to have the seeds at an inch apart. Some people whiten them first so they are more easily seen. If a sowing is made about the third week of March, good plants can be ready for putting out in June or early July, and the vegetable will thus be ready in the winter and going on as late as April.

Those who like very early leeks may take the trouble to sow the seed in the No-Soil Compost under glass towards the end of January, and when the seedlings are an inch or so high, they are pricked out an inch apart into further boxes containing the No-Soil Potting Compost. The boxes are placed on the shelf of the greenhouse at a temperature of

55° F. and the plants are hardened off in a cold frame about the end of March. The leeks are then planted out about the third week of April.

Another method of raising plants is to sow the seed under cloches about the middle of February with the drills as close as 9 in. apart. The cloches can then be removed about the third week of March, and the plants can be thinned out 4 in. apart, with the thinnings planted out into a strip of land, which has been enriched by forking in sedge peat at one 2-gallon bucketful to the sq. yd. The plants can then go on until they are about 8 in. high and they can be planted out to where they are to grow.

The simplest way of planting is to make dibble holes 6 in. deep and 5 in. apart in the case of early leeks wanted before Christmas, and 6 in. deep and 8 in. apart in the case of the late leeks. One plant is then dropped into each hole, but no firming is done. A little water should be poured into each hole after planting. This will wash down some soil to cover the roots. It is customary to trim the roots back to 2 in. and cut the leaves back to, say, a 5-in. length. They thus do not droop down when they are placed in the holes. Get the planting done in June or early July.

For the largest leeks, and for those that are to be used for show, the planting is done in trenches which are taken out a foot deep. Well-rotted compost then being placed in position, and to the depth of 4 in. before being forked in. Three inches of good soil is then put back on top of this, and the plants are set out in the trenches 1 ft. apart. If more than one trench is required, the next should be 18 in. away.

Growing Tips

Dried poultry manure has proved to be particularly useful for leeks, and may be applied along the rows three weeks after planting, at the rate of an ounce to the yard run. Fish manure may be used instead at 2 oz. to the yard run, a further dressing being given a month later. In dry weather leeks benefit from being watered thoroughly once a week. It is here that the Brosson Rainer (see page 77) proves so useful. In small gardens it pays to give Liquinure to leeks once a fortnight from, say, the middle of August till the end of September.

Regular hoeings must be carried out between the rows to keep them clean, and if any flower stems should appear, these should be cut off immediately.

Those who are growing leeks in trenches will have to start the earthing up process about a month after planting, and then once a month after this, a little more finely broken-up soil may be hoed around the plants. Some experts have tried corrugated cardboard around the white stems, before doing the earthing up. This does prevent the soil getting in between the leaves and thus they are not gritty when cooked. It is so difficult to wash the earthiness out of the overlapping leaves of leeks.

Harvesting and Using

One can start lifting the earliest leeks at the end of September or the beginning of October. If the soil is first loosened with a fork, the plants can easily be pulled up by hand. The fibrous roots should then be cut off as well as removing the outer leaves. In the case of the trenches, the soil must be put back in position so as to keep the stems of the other plants white.

Varieties

Over a period of years I've found that you can divide the leeks up into three groups, (1) the Broad Flag or London Flag, (2) the Scotch or Musselburgh, and (3) the Lyon.

The London Flag is definitely less hardy than the Musselburgh or Lyon, but it's very much liked in the south, and can be regarded as an early variety. The stems are long and thick, and the leaves are broad, green, long and softish.

The Lyon. This is sometimes called Prizetaker. Is an old variety, which is larger and thicker than the London Flag, and slower to mature too. The leaves are very wide.

The Musselburgh or Scottish leeks are grown in quantities around Edinburgh. They are very hardy and have narrower leaves than any other type. The white stems are thick and large, and stand any amount of frost.

There are one or two newer varieties which have interested me during the last few years, viz.:

Leicester Hero, which seems to be very hardy, with broad, dark green leaves. It has a long white stem, and is quite distinctive to look at.

Renton's Monarch. Produces stout, large, white stems, and dark green broad leaves. May be described as a mid-season variety of mild flavour.

Northumbrian. I am including this variety, though it got an R.H.S. Award of Merit as long ago as 1937, as I have only recently seen it. It grows almost 'hand' shaped; the leaves are very broad; the white stems very stout, but only of medium length. The flavour is mild.

Carentan. A French type with the stems only 6 in. long, and often 3 in. in diameter. Very hardy and very late.

LETTUCE

There is no more popular salad than the lettuce. For this reason, of course, it has been dealt with in the special chapter on 'The Salad Bowl'. I make no excuse, however, for dealing with it in detail here because it is such an important crop. The gardener must aim to obtain good hearts out of doors from, say, April or May until the end of October, and for the remaining months of the year he must use Dutch lights or continuous cloches to provide for his needs.

Unfortunately, I must report that the inner leaves of the lettuce which are partially blanched are of lesser importance from the protective food point of view than the green outer leaves. Further, it must be made clear that the anti-scorbutic value is much lower than in the case of water-cress, spinach or even dwarf cabbage. It can, however, be regarded as a protective food, especially as it is eaten raw. The great thing is to be sure to select the right varieties and sow them in the right way at the right time. It is of greater importance to prepare the ground by forking in plenty of organic matter than to be constantly watering in a droughty summer. Water is useful, but it cannot prevent bolting if the soil is not properly prepared. It helps too, to sow the seed *in situ*, rather than to transplant, especially in the case of summer sowing.

It is possible to classify lettuces in various ways. There are: (*a*) the cos versus the cabbage lettuce, (*b*) the summer lettuce versus the winter varieties, and (*c*) the outdoor kinds versus those that are specially suited for frame, cloche, or even greenhouse work. Even the cabbage lettuces can be divided up into two groups—the Butter-Heads, which have smooth, soft, light green leaves, and the 'Icebergs' which have large, crisp, crimped, cool leaves, so brittle that the market gardener finds it almost impossible to pack them for market. They are, however, ideal for home use.

In addition, there are special types, like the Gem, which seem to be a cross between a cos and cabbage, and are very delicious—and Tom Thumb which is a tiny Butter-Head and is often grown in small gardens because of its size.

Soils and Manuring

Here we must make a difference between the summer and winter lettuce, for the preparation in one case is quite different from the other.

WINTER LETTUCE. Choose if possible well-drained soil, the light lands and medium loams are best. There should be some shelter from northerly and eastern winds. These lettuces do best on a sunny slope! Don't dig in compost or rotted dung specially for this crop. Always follow another crop like the early cauliflower or second early potato, which was well manured. The disease Botrytis is often bad with winter lettuce when farmyard manure has been used just before seed sowing. When the land is being raked down, just prior to sowing the seeds, a fish manure with a 10 per cent potash content should be added at 3 oz. to the sq. yd. If the soil is acid, a dressing of lime should follow at 4 to 5 oz. to the sq. yd. A further dressing of a fish fertilizer may be applied early in March at 3 oz. to the sq. yd. This should be put on in between the rows and lightly hoed in the moment the soil is fit to work.

SUMMER LETTUCE. In this case well-rotted compost should be dug in when preparing the soil at the rate of $1\frac{1}{2}$ 2-gallon bucketfuls to the sq. yd. In addition sedge peat should be applied at the rate of one bucketful to the sq. yd., and this will be lightly forked in. This extra dressing is given to help the crop to grow quickly and without a check. A dressing of a concentrated organic manure such as fish can be applied with the peat at 4 oz. to the sq. yd., and lime can be given as for winter lettuce as a top dressing just prior to seed sowing.

Plants and Planting

WINTER LETTUCE. In the case of the winter lettuce, it's best to sow the seed direct into the soil where the plants are to grow, having the rows a foot apart, and thinning the plants out to 5 in. apart before the winter sets in, and giving a second thinning to 10 in. apart in the spring. These second thinnings, though not fully hearted, can be used in the salad bowl. This sowing is usually done early in September.

An alternative method is to sow the seed about the 15th of the month in a fine seed bed, in rows 9 in. apart, into which ample fine sedge peat has been raked. The seedlings thus raised are planted out about the middle of October in the north, and often as late as the middle of November in the south. Some gardeners leave the lettuces in their seed beds to over-winter with the idea of planting out early in March. The rows should be a foot apart with the plants 9 in. apart in the rows. The great secret at this time of the year is to plant firmly. Keep the land clean after planting until the hard winter makes this impossible, but start to hoe again as soon as it's feasible to get on the land early in March. It is then that the fish fertilizer can be applied at 2 oz. to the yard run for hoeing in. Such lettuces are usually ready sometime during May.

SUMMER LETTUCE. Here the idea will to be to sow the seed where the plants are to grow, starting about the middle of March in the south, and perhaps early in April in the north. The drills should be 1 ft. apart and only ½ in. deep. In order to keep up the supply, successional sowings may be made once a fortnight until the middle of July. Don't make the mistake however, in a small garden, of sowing whole rows at a time. Quarter rows will be ample, or if necessary, some of the seedlings may be transplanted at the first thinning time.

Growing Tips

There is little to be said under this heading, except to emphasize the fact that it pays to hoe regularly to keep down weeds, and to give artificial rain by means of the Brosson, see Chapter 6, whenever the weather is dry. Thinning should always be done very early so that the plants have no check. Any check to growth, either from drought or overcrowding leads to bolting.

Harvesting and Using

Always cut lettuces the moment they are fully hearted and preferably first thing in the morning. When testing for firmness, do this with the *back of the hand*. If you squeeze them with the thumb and forefinger, they are easily bruised. Cut the heads with a sharp knife just above the lowest leaves.

Varieties

Winter:

Arctic King, very hardy, one of the earliest to turn in in the spring. Its two faults are that the hearts are small, and they are not absolutely compact.

Winter Crop. A good grower. Perfectly hardy in normal seasons, produces large, solid hearts, probably the best winter variety to-day. Some say it's a bit particular as to soils.

Imperial. Reasonably winter hardy, produces light green leaves, and solid, large hearts. One of the most popular varieties to-day.

Majestic. One of the newer varieties, suitable only for the south, produces a large and fairly solid heart of excellent quality. Not so hardy as Imperial.

Summer:

Borough Wonder, is a compact grower, produces a large, solid heart with pale green, folding leaves. Very delicious and very popular. In the

218

sheltered parts of the south of England, has been grown as a winter variety.

New Market. Very similar to Borough Wonder, obviously belongs to the Trocadero family, produces a large heart with few outer leaves.

Trocadero. The original type of this group which includes Unrivalled and Market Favourite. Sometimes grown in the south as a winter hardy variety, There is a good strain known as Trocadero Improved. The hearts are large and firm, flattish round in shape, and pale green in colour.

Webb's Wonderful, perhaps the best of the Icebergs, produces large, crisp, cool, delicious hearts, with large, tender crisp leaves around. Does particularly well in hot, dry summers. A favourite variety with the author.

Cos Lettuce

Cos lettuces are less popular in Great Britain than the cabbage types. They do, however, withstand droughty conditions far better than the cabbage varieties. They are cultivated in a similar manner to cabbage lettuce, only in order to help the lettuces to heart, and to make certain that the inner leaves are properly blanched, a rubber band is put around each heart about half-way down fourteen days before cutting.

The best varieties are:

Lobjoit's Green, produces a large, self-folding and compact lettuce, usually grown as an early summer variety, but is winter hardy in the south—so may be sown in September out of doors.

Mammoth, a good, large, solid variety, often used to win prizes at shows.

St. Alban's Allheart, a compact grower of medium size, dark green and self-folding.

Winter Density, really a hybrid between the cos and cabbage, very delicious and sweet in flavour. It's compact and produces medium-sized hearts. Only winter hardy in the south.

Little Gem or Osmaston Gem is really a smaller type of plant of this variety. It is particularly useful in a small garden.

Some Special Methods

For the very early spring it is possible to sow seed in mid-October under Dutch lights, making the soil as near the No-Soil Compost as possible. Broadcast the seeds evenly and rake in lightly. Prick out the seedlings under further Dutch lights 1 in. sq., making certain that the soil runs parallel to the lights, and within 4 in. of the top of the frame.

Keep the lights closed over the lettuces until they start to grow, after this ventilate and in dry, warm weather, the lights may be removed altogether. Never remove the lights when it's raining. Early in April set the plants out 18 in. apart between the rows and 12 in. apart between the plants. Plant out, say, three batches at intervals of ten days. As the result you'll have lettuces from mid-May to mid-June. Choose the varieties May Queen, or Harrison's Gloria for this purpose.

For late autumn cutting, sow seed in late July in the open and transplant the seedlings 1 ft. sq., under Dutch lights in frames in September. The variety Improved Trocadero is grand for this purpose.

For cutting in late March and early April, sow the seed about the middle of October in aluminium seed trays or boxes under glass at a temperature of 55° F. Prick out the seedlings 1 in. sq. when the first pair of seed leaves are fully developed. Do this under Dutch lights and treat the plants as advised in the previous paragraph but one. Plant the seedlings out in late January or early February under further Dutch lights, 1 ft. sq. Give plenty of ventilation from now on, but water regularly between the plants so as to prevent the soil from becoming too dry. If it does get dry Botrytis will break out. To give succession, try the varieties May Queen and Cheshunt Early Ball.

MARROWS

The marrow didn't arrive in this country until the beginning of the nineteenth century. It is a member, of course, of what may be called the cucumber family, and has male and female flowers produced separately on each plant. The fruits are most delicious when eaten when they are half grown. Sometimes they are ripened off fully for storage, and then can be used in the winter. When other fruits are scarce, they are often made into jam, with a little ginger for flavouring. For the types of marrows of better texture and flavour, see squashes in Chapter 10.

Despite popular belief, marrows are rich in vitamin A and contain also vitamins B1, B2 and C. Though they contain 90 per cent of water, there is 7·3 per cent of carbohydrates, 2·5 per cent of sugar, and a trace of iron!

Soils and Manuring

Marrows like soil containing plenty of moisture, especially in the early summer. It is undoubtedly the heavier lands that suit them best. The only disadvantage of clays is that they warm up late; while the disadvantage of sands is that they dry out in the growing season. Try and choose a sunny situation where there's some shelter from winds in late May and early June.

Dig the soil in the winter and add well-rotted compost or old manure at the rate of $1\frac{1}{2}$ bucketfuls to the sq. yd. If the compost is in short supply dig this in at the actual spots where the marrows are to be planted. In this way a certain amount of bottom heat is generated. A good fish fertilizer should be lightly forked in before planting at 3 oz. to the sq. yd.

Plants and Planting

I have discovered that two- or even three-year-old seed can produce plants which bear a higher proportion of female flowers than those from fresh seed. The seed may either be sown where the plants are to grow about the middle of April under upturned 2-lb. glass jam jars or in 3-in. pots or soil blocks under glass at a temperature of 50° F., the compost being the usual No-Soil No. 1. In the latter case, the plants are hardened off when two rough leaves have been produced, and then put out where they are to grow the last week in May, or early in June if the weather is cold and wet. In the former case the idea is to dig out a hole a spade's width and a spade's depth so as to bury a bucketful of compost below, and then to put back the soil to cover over thus leaving a slight mound. Three seeds are sown in the centre of each mound an inch deep before the lantern cloche goes over the top.

A third method some gardeners adopt is to sow the seeds in frames about the second week of April. The soil must either be heated electrically, or should be over a hot bed of horse manure. Three-inch pots may be sunk up to their rims in the soil, filled with the Eclipse No-Soil Compost, with one seed sown in the centre of each. Such plants are gradually hardened off, and are planted out in the case of the other varieties late in May or early in June.

If no glass jam jars or frames are available, the seed must be sown about the third week of May out of doors in the centre of the little mounds already advised, and if all three seeds germinate, two of the seedlings are removed. In all cases, the plan is to have the bush types growing on the 4 ft. sq. principle, and the trailing varieties on the 6 ft. sq. principle. When planting, take care not to damage the soft, succulent stems. One can do much to protect newly planted marrows by covering them with greaseproof paper 'hats'.

Growing Tips

Hoe between the rows as regularly as necessary to keep down weeds.

About the middle of June, apply a top dressing of sedge peat for a foot or so around each plant to the depth of an inch. Use instead lawn mowings if desired, but put these on no deeper than ½ in., giving a second dressing a month later, and a third dressing a month after that. Pinch out the end of each shoot when it reaches an 18-in. length to encourage the formation of branches. Water regularly by means of the Brosson Rainer, during droughty spells. This will help to prevent the fruits from rotting off in the young stages, which often happens in a droughty season. Regular waterings, too, will help to control mildew. In the early part of the season it will be worth while pollinating the female flowers by transferring the pollen from the male blooms to the stigma of the females with a camel-hair brush.

Harvesting and Using

Cut the marrows when they are young and tender. The more you cut, the heavier the crop will get. You can easily treble the crop by regular harvesting. One can usually start in July and with care go on until the end of September. Some gardeners aver that you get better fruits when the marrows are twisted from the plants and not cut. Harvest about three times a week until the beginning of September. From that time onwards allow the fruits to remain on the plants so they may grow large and ripen, and then they can either be stored or be made into jam.

Varieties

These may be divided up into two groups, the bush types and the trailers.

Bush

Green Bush, dark green fruits, striped paler green. Can be had very early.

All Green Bush. A variety having dark green fruits with no stripes, rather delicious.

White Bush. Preferred by some people to Green Bush because the fruits are creamy white. Personally, I cannot see any advantage in this variety.

Custard. You can either have the white custard or the yellow custard. The fruits have a scalloped edge, being flat in shape, with a concave base. Very popular to-day.

Tender and True. Another flat group, but with no scallops, but with mottled green skin.

Trailers:

Long White, large, long white fruits. A heavy cropper.

Moore's Cream, smooth oval-shaped fruits of medium size. Early and prolific.

Long Green. Similar to Long White, but with large, green striped fruits. Very prolific.

Clucas' Roller. Produces a long white fruit, without any ribbing at all. A good grower particularly for the north.

ONIONS

The onion is one of the oldest vegetables known and grown. It was used by the Chaldeans about 5000 B.C. There are many types of onions, some of which are unusual, and therefore described in Chapter 10. It undoubtedly would be more cultivated in this country if it wasn't for the ravages of the onion-fly, whose maggots ruin hundreds of rows each year. However, it is possible to control this pest as will be seen on page 267. Interestingly enough, though this vegetable is so popular, it is of very little value from the food point of view. It's the flavour and smell which are so important to the housewife.

The normal bulbing onions can be divided up into three groups; the autumn-sown varieties for bulbing, the spring-sown varieties for bulbing; and the salad or spring onions. The latter must not be confused with spring-sown onions. There are also types which can be grown to produce tiny bulbs for pickling.

Soils and Manuring

Good drainage is extremely important. The best crops are perhaps produced on the medium loams, which have been deeply cultivated and enriched with plenty of compost or rotted farmyard manure. Always choose an open site away from overhanging branches, and see that there's a free circulation of air as well as exposure to the sun. Give sufficient hydrated lime to ensure that the soil is not acid. No onions can stand drought when they are growing, and overhead irrigation will be necessary in mid-summer. Don't give artificial rain, of course, when the bulbs are starting to ripen off.

Dig the ground over as early as possible so as to allow it to settle afterwards. Firm land is a real necessity for onions. The ground should also be free from all perennial weeds. Always choose a clean plot for onions, because weeds can easily become masters of the situation. Dig deeply and manure in the autumn, say October, and then fork down the land in March. When digging, add well-rotted compost or old manure at at least a bucketful and a half to the sq. yd., and three weeks before sowing or planting, rake in a fish manure with a 10 per cent potash content at 4 oz. to the sq. yd. Those who have old soot can use it at one large handful per sq. yd. in February to help warm the soil. It should be lightly forked in.

Those who are going to sow the seed in the late summer need not dig in dung or compost but can follow a well-manured crop, and then just fork the ground over, adding the fish fertilizer with a 10 per cent potash content at 3 oz. to the sq. yd. at the same time. If the soil is puffy, it may be necessary to roll or tread well.

Plants and Planting

The seeds may be sown late in the month of August in the open, and the plants thus raised are thinned out in the early spring, say during the second week of March, the thinnings being transplanted into rows 10 in. apart, giving 6 in. between the plants. The bulbs from such sowings ripen better and are ready for harvesting in mid-August. The disadvantage in the scheme is that if the weather conditions are very mild in the autumn and early winter the seedlings grow too large, and much bolting or going to seed then takes place after transplanting in the spring. If one could only know there was to be a mild winter, then the sowing could be delayed until early October. Some gardeners therefore do both sowings as a kind of insurance, using the special varieties listed at the end of this section.

The seedlings must be lifted carefully with a fork, and only such plants got up at one time that can be transplanted within an hour. Plant the seedlings shallowly so that the base of the plant sits on the ground. Use a dibber so that the roots can be buried to their full length, and then see that the seedling is planted firmly by plunging the dibber in at an angle of 45 degrees and pressing the soil towards the plant. This fastens the roots firmly, and yet leaves the base of the plant almost at ground level.

Spring Sowing

In this case the seed is sown as early as possible out of doors from the middle of February onwards. One mustn't get on the land until the soil does not stick to one's boots. It's when that happens that the seed can be put in. Always sow very shallowly and at the rate of not more than $\frac{1}{4}$ oz. of seed per 50 ft. of row. The drills should be 10 or 12 in. apart, and the plants should be thinned out later to about 4 in. apart in the drills.

Some people don't thin to more than 2 in. apart as they prefer to have smaller bulbs. Many people have discovered that parsley helps to keep away the onion-fly, and they thus have a row of this herb every fourth or fifth row of onions. Another scheme which is much liked in some districts is to sow onions and carrots in alternate rows.

Only rake very lightly along the ground the same way as the drills run to cover the seed, and then firm with the head of the rake down over the seed to firm the soil.

Under Glass Sowing

Those who have a greenhouse and who want to grow very large onions may like to sow the seed in the Eclipse No-Soil Compost in boxes during the first week of January. The soil should be put into the aluminium trays or boxes and firmed level to within $\frac{1}{2}$ in. of the top. The seed is then sown 1 in. sq. on the surface of the soil, and a little more of the compost is sifted over—this being pressed down evenly with a wooden presser. A watering is then given through the fine rose of a can, and the boxes are placed on the staging of the greenhouse at a temperature of 65° F., being covered with a sheet of glass and a piece of brown paper.

The moment the seedlings are through, the boxes or trays are placed on the shelving near the light, and the sheet of glass and piece of brown paper are removed. After another three weeks the boxes or trays are moved to a frame where they are hardened off for just over a fortnight. Then they go out into the open and are planted out where they are to grow about mid-April in a similar manner to the autumn-sown plants out of doors.

For the exhibition-sized onions, the scheme is to prick out each seedling when it's about 2 in. high into a soil block or 3-in. pot filled with the Eclipse No-Soil Compost No. 1. The pots or blocks are then put back on to the shelving of the greenhouse and are lightly watered from time to time. About the third week of March they are transferred to the cold frames for hardening off, and about the middle of April they are planted out into a well-manured plot—the rows being 15 in. apart and the plants 9 in. apart in the rows. If the plants are tall, and tend to fall over—a little bamboo stake is provided, and the tops are tied up to this. It's always necessary to give artificial rain after planting if the weather is dry.

Growing Tips

One has to fight a regular battle against weeds in the early stages. For

H   225

this reason many gardeners crawl down the rows on their hands and knees using the short, specially made onion hoes for the purpose of hoeing. One cannot do this crawling until the soil is really dry—say some time in April. By the way, the onion hoes usually have 4-in. wide blades and swan-necked handles 15 or 16 in. long.

A dressing of a fish fertilizer with a 5 per cent potash content may be given about the beginning of May. Never, however, apply any fish after the second week of June. Do not hoe between the rows after the second week of July. Up till this moment, however, keep the land absolutely free.

One of the ways of helping to prevent an attack of the onion-fly is not to do any thinning, but to sow the seeds extremely thinly and then to leave the bulbs to grow naturally. Of course, only medium-sized bulbs are produced, and on the whole they tend to ripen better, and so they keep better.

OPEN SPACE IS LEFT BETWEEN ROWS B AND C and D AND E, AFTER BENDING ONION TOPS WITH BACK OF RAKE.

Harvesting and Using

The actual time of harvesting will differ in accordance with the method and time that the plants are raised. The autumn-sown crops are usually ready in late August, and the spring-sown varieties late in September and early October. When the tops show signs of ceasing to grow, and start to turn yellow, the necks of the plants are bent over to within 1 in. above the bulbs. This is usually done with the back of the rake. Row A being bent over towards Row B and Row B towards Row A; Row C towards Row D, and Row D towards Row C. This leaves an open space between Row B and C (see drawing).

After the tops dry off and the skin of the bulbs starts to turn yellow, the bulbs should be lifted. A fork should be plunged on one side of the row, so that the onions may be easily pulled up, and then they should be laid out in rows facing the sun to dry off. In a fortnight they are usually turned over, so that both sides are ripened equally. It's usual to leave them on the ground for about a month before taking them in to store. If the weather is wet, one may have to complete the ripening off under rows of continuous cloches, or in the greenhouse.

It's convenient to store the onions by making them into ropes and hanging these up under the eaves of some building out of doors. I have hung ropes from the beams of the loft in the house with great success. Another method of storing is to lay the onions in the trays used for potato sprouting, stand these one above another and store them in a dry, airy shed. In either case great care must be taken in handling for bulbs that are bruised or damaged will not keep.

SALAD ONIONS

Here the seed is usually sown early in September, for the great demand for the salad onion is in the spring. A second sowing may take place late in February or early in March as soon as the right conditions arrive. Some people who love spring onions make further sowings once every three weeks until the end of May.

Prepare the ground as for normal autumn-sown onions, or in the case of the ones sown in the turn of the year, for the spring-sown onions. In both cases have the rows 9 in. apart, sow the seed sparsely and do not do any thinning at all. Pull the salad onions when they are large enough to use and continue to pull them as and when they are needed, until complete rows have been harvested.

PICKLING ONIONS

Choose an odd corner for growing this type of onion which prefers to have poor soil. Just rake down the land to produce a fine tilth; sow the seed broadcast and lightly rake it in. Do this work early in April. One has to hand weed to keep the plot clean, but no thinning is done. It won't be long before little pickling bulbs start to form. Allow these to grow naturally and when the tops start to die down, fork them up and leave the bulbs on the surface of the ground for ten days or so for ripening. When the seeds are sown shallowly, the bulbs are round, when they are sown an inch deep, oval shape bulbs are produced, which are preferred by some cooks.

Varieties

There are a very large number of varieties to choose from, and thus I am only including those which I've found to be (*a*) the easiest to grow, and (*b*) to give the heaviest of crops.

Autumn-Sown:

Giant Rocca, sometimes called Giant Rocco. A flattish oval type of mild flavour. Quite a good keeper.

White Tripoli. A delicious onion, but doesn't keep well.

Red Tripoli. Similar to the White Tripoli, but has a red outer skin. I have seen it sold as the Red Italian, or the Red Neapolitan. The bulbs are large and flat.

Autumn Triumph. Fairly new and good. Keeps better than the Tripoli's. Produces large, flattish-round, golden-brown bulbs.

Spring-Sown:

Bedfordshire Champion, produces moderately large, round bulbs, with brownish-orange top skins and firm white flesh beneath.

James' Keeping. As its name suggests is one of the best keepers and is really hardy. The bulbs never grow very large, but they are of a reddish-brown colour.

Up-To-Date. One of the heaviest croppers, a good keeper, with mild flavour. If I have a quarrel with it, it is because the bulbs are apt to be variable in shape. They are of a bright yellow colour and have a rounded base.

Best of All. A good keeper, with the bulbs of globe shape, and light brown in colour. The texture is firm and the quality good. One of the heaviest croppers in our trials.

For Exhibition or Show:

Crosslings' Selected. Usually wins the prizes at the shows. Probably the largest onion extant. The seed is not too easy to obtain.

Selected Ailsa Craig. Produces large bulbs, somewhat pear-shape and tapering at the neck. Is usually of a dull, pale colour. It's the strain which is so important in connection with this variety.

The Premier. May grow to an immense size if the right strain is obtained. The bulbs being flattish in shape, and of a pale, straw colour.

Salad Onions:

White Lisbon. The foliage is grass-like and on the pale side. Very delicious, but somewhat subject to disease.

New Queen. A salad type which is often grown where White Lisbon gives trouble.

White Portugal. Sometimes I think called White Spanish. Is what I would call the next best to White Lisbon.

Pickling Onions:

Paris Silver Skin. Produces a tiny bulb flattened at the base with white flesh and a silver-like outer coating.

The Pearl. Sometimes called Barletta or The Queen, and I have heard it given the name of Covent Garden Pickling. Grows a small bulb, flattish at the top and rounded at the base, the flesh is pale and the outer skin white. One of the earliest varieties to buy.

Some Special Methods

With the variety Unwin's Reliance, which has been called Okey or Isleham, the seed may be sown thinly during the second week of August on firm ground, where a shallow, tilthy surface has been prepared. The rows should be a foot apart. The seedlings should not be disturbed until early in March, when they are planted out on well manured land which has been allowed to settle, in rows 18 in. apart, giving 8 in. between the plants. The plan is to harvest the onions in August.

Onion Sets

One can buy ripened-off onion bulbs known as sets from the seedsmen and plant these out at the end of March in V-shaped drills which have been drawn out 1 in. deep and 12 in. apart. One should give 6 in. between the sets and just push them into the soil like shallots. Prepare the ground concerned as for spring-sown onions.

PARSNIP

The parsnip is certainly a native of Great Britain and has been described as one of the easiest root crops to grow. Unfortunately, it isn't very popular but I think that is this partly due to the fact that few people know how to cook the roots properly. We often steam them and cut the roots up into slices and fry them. Sometimes we bake them around a joint of meat in the beef dripping, and they are particularly delicious that way.

Some gardeners dislike this particular root crop because it occupies the ground for the best part of the year. The seed has to be sown as early as possible in the season, and the roots are not harvested very often until later on in the winter. The roots contain vitamin C in fair quantity as well as some vitamin A and B1. The analysis shows some iron and calcium present also.

Soils and Manuring

Because the roots are long it's inadvisable to attempt to grow on shallow land. Other than this, any soil will do, providing it's not too stony. Those who have such soil may bore holes 3 ft. deep and 3 in. in diameter at the top, and fill these holes up with No-Soil Potting Compost. Three seeds are then sown on the top of each hole, and the seedlings are thinned down to one if necessary later. The crop does quite well on heavier land, because this doesn't dry out in the summer-time.

Don't manure the ground specially for this crop, or the roots will be fangy and forked. Sow, therefore, on land which was well manured for a previous crop, and just apply before sowing the seed a fish fertilizer with a 10 per cent potash content at 2 to 3 oz. to the sq. yd.

Sowing

Sow the seed the moment the weather and soil conditions allow, preferably towards the end of February and certainly before the end of the third week of March. Because the seeds take a long time to germinate, mix in some radish seed and the lines of the rows will then be seen early, and so hoeing can be carried out. The drills should be 1 in. deep, and 15 in. apart. When the seedlings are an inch high they should be thinned out to 8 in. apart. The alternative method of sowing is to put three seeds in every 8 in. and then thin down to one per station later. Radish or lettuce seed can then be sprinkled in between the stations before the soil is raked to cover over. Incidentally, if the disease known as canker has given trouble in the past (see page 278) don't sow the seed until early April. I have discovered that late sowings often are free from this disease.

Growing Tips

There is little to be done except to pull the radishes or cut the lettuces that have been grown as an inter-crop in the rows. After that, it's a question of hoeing until, say, the end of July to keep the row clean.

Harvesting and Using

You can leave the roots in the ground as long as you like because they are never damaged by frost. I always think they are sweeter in fact when they have been touched by Jack Frost's fingers. The only trouble, of course, is that if the ground gets frozen hard, it's impossible to dig the roots out. The alternative is to dig up all the roots carefully, and then to leave them on the surface of the soil in a heap. There, of course, they will be sweetened by the frost and can easily be taken to the kitchen as needed.

In the north where frosts may be prolonged and more serious, some gardeners find it necessary to store some of the roots in a dry shed without any covering at all. I have never, however, found this necessary in the south.

CULTURE OF VEGETABLES ALPHABETICALLY

Varieties

Improved Hollow Crowned, similar to Elcombe's Improved, a heavy cropper, produces well-shaped roots, especially useful in the south.

Tender and True. Said to be the most delicious variety, but the roots are smaller, even though the flesh is tender.

Syston Intermediate, seems to be somewhat immune to canker, produces a shorter and thicker root, with a wide shoulder and white skin. First-class quality.

Offenham. Very suitable for shallow soil, especially if sown early in April. Very subject, however, to canker, and that's why it must be sown late.

PEAS

There must be few people who do not like fresh, sweet, tender, delicious green peas. It isn't that they know that they are very nutritious, it is just that they like them. They contain vitamins A, B and C—calcium and iron, and consist of albuminoids, carbohydrates and, of course, some mineral matter.

There are the two main groups of peas, the round-seeded and the wrinkled-seeded, usually called the Marrowfats. The latter are sweeter and are much praised by the epicure. Within these two headings there are (*a*) early varieties, (*b*) second earlies, (*c*) main crops, and (*d*) lates. In addition there are the edible podded peas which are described on pages 121–2 under the heading Unusual Vegetables.

Soils and Manuring

It is fortunate indeed that peas will grow quite well on a great variety of soils. They probably prefer a medium loam with a high water table in the summer. Those who like sowing peas in November must, of course, choose the lighter soils. In any case, there must be no acidity present, and lime must always be added. As the peas are only on the ground a short time before they start to crop, it's important to apply plant foods sufficiently early, so that the roots can take them in when required. Add well-rotted dung or good compost about 8 in. down when double digging is done.

A fish manure with a low nitrogen content and a high potash and phosphate content should be applied at 3 to 4 oz. to the sq. yd., and after this has been raked, or forked in, if the roughness of the land makes this necessary, hydrated lime should be applied as a top dressing at the rate of from 5 to 8 oz. per sq. yd., depending on the acidity. A good gardener will always take the precaution of testing the soil first with a B.D.H. Soil Indicator.

Sowing

After the soil has been forked over lightly in the spring and the surface is really friable, drills may be drawn out 3 in. deep. If the land is 'puffy' and the soil light, it may be necessary to tread the strip of ground where the peas are to be sown or to run a light roller over it. I always used to advise the use of flat-shaped drills 5 in. wide, but latterly these have been dispensed with and V-shaped drills are got out as for other seeds. The distance apart depends on the variety. For those that grow a foot high—they usually give 15 in. apart; for 2 ft. varieties—2 ft. apart; for 3 ft. varieties—3 ft. apart, and *pro rata.*

On the whole the earlier varieties are given a little wider spacing to encourage growth, but with the later kinds the drills can be closer together than their height suggests. Furthermore, the seed of the early varieties is sometimes sown at the rate of $\frac{3}{4}$ pint per 50 ft. row, while with the second early and main crops, $\frac{1}{2}$ pint per 50 ft. row is ample. In the case of seed that is sown in the autumn or in February, when the soil tends to be damp—a treatment with an organo mercury dust should be given to the seed first. This prevents the pre-emergence rot.

Protect the plants from ravages by birds just as they are coming through the ground by using wire pea-guards or by stretching black cotton in between twiggy sticks, pushed in at the ends of the rows, and as many times down the rows as necessary. Mice must be killed by putting down back-breaking traps baited with marrow seeds.

Growing Tips

The moment the peas come through the ground they may be attacked by weevils or slugs. Weevils nibble the leaf edges and scallop them. Slugs nibble the plants off at ground level. In the former case, dust with a Derris and Pyrethrum and in the latter case bait with the blue pellets of Draza. As early as possible, provide twiggy sticks up which the plants can climb. It always pays to use these, even in the case of dwarf varieties which most books say needn't be sticked. I usually push in little twiggy brushwood first when the plants are about 3 in. high, and then push in the taller pea-sticks when they've grown to a 6 in. height. This should be pushed in sloping say, to the north at an angle of 45 degrees on one side, and sloping, say, to the south an angle of 45 degrees on the other side. Where pea-sticks are not available, it is convenient to use a double line of 3-in. sq. mesh netting on either side of the row. This always 'supports' the row better than a single line, especially as modern kinds of peas don't seem to use their tendrils as they should do. Whenever netting is used, it must be really firm, for it's going to bear the weight of the haulm later. See, therefore, that the end posts are stout and make them firm by adding a little guy-rope tied to a peg driven in at the back of the post so as to help to take the strain.

A little hand weeding may be necessary among the plants in the early stages, coupled by hoeing between the rows. Such hoeing should be continued until the middle of July. Sometimes in droughty years it's necessary to use the overhead sprinkler. Mulchings of sedge peat will help if applied on either side of the rows to a width of 3 or 4 in. Lawn mowings may be used instead if desired, never any deeper than $\frac{1}{2}$ in. Before these mulches are applied, it's quite a good thing to earth up the plants a little when they are about 4 in. high, and this gives them some protection, from surface winds.

Many gardeners like to grow inter-crops between the rows of peas and lettuces, spinach and radishes are often used for this purpose. For succession, it's quite a good idea to make another sowing of peas directly the previous sowing has come through the ground. The earlier sowings should be ready to pick in late June or early July; the main crop peas are usually gathered in August, and the later-sown peas in September. Thrips can do a great deal of damage, especially in dry weather. You can tell whether they are present or not by tapping one or two of the stems above a white handkerchief, and if little black specks appear on the linen, then you know that the pest is present. (For control see page 268.) It may be necessary to use strips of special shiny metal which flash and clatter as the pods become ready to use—in order to prevent birds and particularly sparrows from robbing the pods.

Harvesting and Using

Always pick regularly and be sure to miss no pod when it's ready. If only one or two pods are left on to ripen their seeds the cropping power of the rows is reduced immediately.

Varieties

There are a very large number of varieties to choose from, and I propose to classify them under four headings.

First Earlies:

Kelvedon Triumph. A heavy cropper with fine pods. Slightly pointed and dark green in colour. Wrinkle-seeded. $1\frac{3}{4}$ ft.

Kelvedon Wonder. A Marrowfat pea, suitable for spring or June sowings. 1½ ft.

Feltham Advance. A delicious, heavy cropping variety, first-class R.H.S. 2 ft.

Feltham First. Said to be a cross between Foremost and Onward. Very early, produces well-filled pods of round peas. 1½ ft.

Kelvedon Champion. Produces large pods, well filled. 1½ ft.

Laxton's Superb. A hardy variety, sometimes sown in November. 2 ft.

Meteor. A good variety for sowing in the autumn, does well under cloches. 1½ ft.

Pilot. A good old-fashioned variety, round-seeded, often used for very early spring sowings. 3 ft.

Second Earlies:

Duplex. Produces large pods in pairs; the quality is good and the cropping is heavy. 2½ ft. (Sometimes called an early main crop.)

King Edward. Produces large, broad, blunt-ended pods of a medium colour. 2½ ft.

Miracle. Excellent for dry soils. Produces slightly curved, large pods of a dark green colour. The peas are of good flavour. 4 ft. (It is important to get the sharp strain.)

Onward. The best general-purpose pea grown. A heavy yielder; a sturdy grower with pods produced in pairs. Often has eight large peas to a pod. 2 ft. (Sometimes called an early main crop.)

Main Crop:

Lord Chancellor. A heavy cropping, strong grower. Large pods produced in pairs. 3ft.

Ormskirkian. Has been described as an Improved Alderman. Produces heavy crop of good quality pods. 5 ft.

Admiral Beatty. A Marrowfat with well-filled, curved pods. 4½ ft.

Alderman. An old variety which often produces soft growth. The quality of the peas is, however, good. The pods are large and curved. 5 ft.

Kelvedon Hurricane. Beautiful deep green foliage and grand pods. 2¼ ft.

Kelvedon Perfection. Produces large pods filled with delicious peas. 2 ft.

Late:

Autocrat. Marrowfat. Produces large pods of first-class flavour. Straight and dark green. 4 ft.

Gladstone. A favourite with exhibitors. Pods invariably well filled with peas, but of moderate size. 4 ft.

Late Gem. The best heavy cropping, dwarf late I know. First-class quality, 2½ ft.

Some Special Methods

In the south and in some very warm sheltered parts of the north-west it is possible to sow one of the round-seeded varieties like Meteor in November or early December. I draw the drills out in the morning of a warm day—let them dry out—and then sow the seeds in the afternoon. I erect little sacking screens on the windward side of the rows to protect them when they come through from the winter surface winds. It is possible to make yet another sowing in February, though in Cheshire you'll have to wait until the end of March. Such sowings, of course, are not a gamble when covered with cloches.

The earliest varieties (i.e. those that mature early) can be sown again late in June or the beginning of July, so as to have fresh peas in the month of September. Sow on land from which cauliflowers or early potatoes have recently been harvested. If the V-shaped drills are dry when they are got out, give them a good flooding.

POTATOES

In Chapter 1 we discussed fully as to whether it was worth while for the normal family to grow main crop potatoes. After all, these can be produced far more cheaply by the farmer. Earlies, of course, are quite different, for they give good value for money, and as has been said, there's all the difference between your own freshly dug new potatoes and those bought from the greengrocer. Don't try and economize when buying 'seed'. Always get the best Scotch or Irish, which have been inspected and given the appropriate Certificate. Ask for the Certificate number. This is the guarantee.

Soils and Manuring

The potato is regarded as a cleaning crop and is usually dunged well. The dung or compost is put into the drills at planting time at the rate of one bucketful to the yard run. In addition, the fish fertilizer with a 5 per cent potash content is sprinkled along the furrows at 3 oz. to the yard run. The land can be dug in the autumn and left rough. In fact in the case of heavy soil it may be left ridged, so that the frost and rain can pulverize it and make it easy to work in the spring. Ridges when made should run north and south.

The Seed

The gardener should buy seed tubers about the size of a hen's egg which should weigh from $2\frac{1}{4}$ to $2\frac{1}{2}$ oz. each. This is the most economical weight to get, and such tubers produce the heaviest crops. Those that are larger than this should always be cut as the tubers are planted, and not before. The cutting should be done from end to end of the potato, so that each portion contains several eyes.

When the tubers arrive, they should be placed in shallow trays, rose end upwards, to sprout. The rose end is the end where the majority of the eyes are seen. Potato trays are usually 2 ft. 6 in. long, 1 ft. 6 in. wide and $3\frac{1}{2}$ in. deep, but the whole point of them is that there are 1-in. sq. posts at the corners, which stand up 3 in. above the sides. Thus the trays can be stood one above the other, without injuring the tubers.

Put the trays when full of potatoes, all standing rose end upwards, in an airy shed or room, where there's no chance that the tubers may be frozen. Some gardeners have used a cool greenhouse for the purpose. It is necessary to keep an eye on the potatoes from time to time, and if as they sprout, pests like aphides appear, a dusting should be carried out with derris. If numerous eyes should grow, carry out some disbudding, leaving only two, and the strongest shoots at the rose end. The aim is to produce beautiful dark green shoots, not more than 2 in. in length.

At planting time, in order to prevent the sprouts being broken off, the trays should be taken out into the garden, where the furrows have been drawn out. The potatoes should then be taken out one at a time for placing carefully in position. If the tubers are dropped, the sprouts may break off. Sprouting or spritting as it is sometimes called, secures a few weeks' growth before planting takes place, and thus heavier and earlier crops result.

Planting

With a Canterbury hoe (a two-pronged hoe), a triangular hoe, or a draw hoe, prepare V-shaped furrows about 4 in. deep, for normal cropping. The earlier varieties need only be 3 in. deep. Arrange the rows running north and south. In the case of the earlies, these furrows may be 18 in. apart, if the idea is to dig up when the new tubers are quite small. The rows of ordinary earlies will be 1 ft. 9 in. apart; second earlies 2 ft. 3 in. apart, and main crops 2 ft. 6 in. apart. When planting, the tubers should be 1 ft. apart in the rows in the case of the earlies, and 1 ft. 3 in. apart with the second earlies, and 1 ft. 6 in. apart for the main crops.

As to the time of planting, this will take place in the south about the middle of March, and in the north perhaps as late as the second week of April. There are exceptions to this rule as the paragraph under 'Some Special Methods' shows. It is really better to plant the late potatoes first if one has a chance, and the earlies last. This gives the main crops a longer season of growth, and the tops are not usually through the ground sufficiently early to be damaged by the late spring frosts.

Growing Tips

After planting, of course, the tubers are covered in by drawing the earth over them with the hoe. This leaves a slight ridge immediately over the furrow. (Two of our students here were able to plant $\frac{1}{4}$ acre of potatoes and cover them over in two hours.) Directly the tops come through the ridges, a further hoeing up may be done to give the leaves some protection from frost. When, however, the frosty period is over, some of this soil may be drawn away again, The real earthing up takes place when the tops are half grown, that is when they are about 8 in. tall. The soil is then drawn up on either side to a depth of 6 in. Don't make this ridge too steep, or the potatoes may appear through the sides and turn green. Do another earthing up three or four weeks later, and yet another three weeks after that.

Always be on the look-out for potato blight which usually starts in June in the south and July in the north. Spraying with a Bordeaux mixture is a preventative as is dusting with a copper-lime dust (see page 279).

Harvesting and Using

Start lifting the early potatoes the moment the tubers are of a good size to use. Don't be greedy, however, because the more you have in the very early stages, the less there will be later. I have known, for instance, a row to double its weight in a fortnight's time in suitable weather. I always use a broad-tined fork for digging as this doesn't injure the tubers. Start with the earlies, and when these have finished go on to the second earlies if you are growing them. There is no need to lift the main crops until the haulm has died down. By this time the tubers will have formed their firm skins, and so should keep well.

Cut the tops off the main crops before harvesting them, especially if they have been attacked by potato blight, as then the spores from the leaves will not be able to drop on the potatoes themselves, and so cause them to rot off eventually. Main crops are usually stored in clamps, 'hogs', 'hales' or 'buries' outside. The scheme is to make a ridge-shaped heap, 4 ft. wide at the base and about 3 ft. high, and then to cover this triangular-shaped mound with clean straw put on to a depth of 6 in., and on top of this to place a 6-in. covering of soil, which should be dug up from the ground immediately surrounding the clamp, thus to form a gully which will carry the excess water away. A twisted tuft of straw is allowed to project through the soil to act as a ventilating shaft. For long clamps you need a ventilator every 6 ft.

Varieties

The difficulty about choosing varieties is that I have found that flouriness and waxiness, for instance, of the flesh of individual potatoes may differ from soil to soil, and certainly does differ in the case of soils rich in humus, and those that have been regularly fed with chemical fertilizers. There seems to be a tendency for soils which have adequate potash content to produce more flouriness in potatoes than those which are lacking in potash. The cook, of course, can sometimes be blamed when the potato is unpalatable.

The majority of varieties mentioned, however, are those that we've tried out ourselves and which we have cooked and actually tasted.

First Earlies:

Arran Pilot. This is included because if you don't want to dig it early, the tubers can be left in the ground and become a second early, without spoiling. It's a white kidney-shaped.

Home Guard. Is now widely grown and rightly so. It's a heavy-cropping oval, and has the great advantage of resisting the dry rot disease.

Stormont Dawn. A lovely floury potato of good flavour; produces tall and sturdy haulm.

Ulster Emblem. A heavy cropper, producing oval-shaped tubers; very floury. The haulm is sturdy and short.

Second Earlies:

Olympic. The haulm is short and sturdy; the flowers are mauve coloured and attractive; the tubers are delicious and of the King Edward type.

Ulster Premier. A white kidney with pinkish eyes. Excellent quality.

Ulster Chieftain. A beautifully floury potato; kidney-shaped; one of the earliest.

Ben Lomond. Oval, good-shaped tubers, but apt to be rather soapy on heavy soils.

Dunbar Rover. Produces nice, dry, floury tubers, of good size and quality.

Craig's Royal. Cropped heavily with us. Tubers slightly soapy, but shapely.

Orion. Heavy-cropping, floury, white skin, oval, lemon flesh and shallow eyes.

Main Crop:

Arran Banner. One of the heaviest croppers I know, with flattish, round tubers. Quite good quality.

Arran Peak. A very good keeper; produces even-shaped oval tubers, with 'netted' yellowy skin. First-class.

Arran Consul. Included because it's given the heaviest crops on poor land. The foliage is sparse and open.

Ulster Supreme. One of the latest keepers, well shaped tubers, with shallow eyes. Plant early as it matures slowly.

King Edward VII. The most popular potato, but not a heavy yielder, unless the soil is just right.

Majestic. The potato that gives me the most enormous crop. Very large tubers of kidney shape, but not of great culinary merit.

Kerr's Pink. Included because it's a great favourite in the north. Does well on heavy soils and where the rainfall is high.

Dr. McIntosh. Included because we find it resists potato blight better than any other variety. A white kidney, floury.

Salad Potatoes:

There are some special varieties of potatoes which are excellent for salads. They are not floury, but you don't want this particular 'trait' in the salad bowl. Furthermore, it's useful to have potatoes with colour, because they add interest.

The two varieties mentioned below have a nutty flavour and waxy flesh. They are grown in exactly the same way as the ordinary potato.

The Congo. A purple, almost black-fleshed variety of excellent flavour. The tubers should not be peeled before cooking, and after boiling or steaming the outer skin should be removed by rubbing with a cloth.

Firapple. Produces pink-skinned, knotted tubers with a lemon-flushed interior. Cook them as for The Congo.

There is a white variety which I haven't seen for some time and a large red. Plant in late April or early May in rows 18 in. apart with the tubers a foot apart in the rows. Lift in the autumn and store in sand.

Chipped Potatoes:

I am sometimes asked why the chipped and fried potatoes abroad are far more delicious than those in this country, and the reason is that they grow special varieties for the purpose. These are of the waxy type, and those who've been to Vienna will know the variety Kipfler, or in France you can have the Belle Juillet and in Germany the Eigenheimer. Before the war it was possible to get these varieties in Great Britain, but I haven't seen them advertised since.

RADISH

When discussing radishes most people think about the small roots, but there are, of course, the 'giants', or 'winter varieties'. These latter are dealt with separately. There has been a great improvement in varieties and strains recently as well as in flavour and form. The result is that the modern groups are not quite so 'hot', nor are they as indigestible.

Soil and Manuring

A light loam is best, but one can grow radishes on almost any soil, providing the top 2 or 3 in. are enriched with ample fine organic matter. In the case of the sands, the sedge peat, or whatever is used, should be soaked well first. Radishes are often grown as a catch-crop, i.e. to use up a piece of land until the main crop is to be sown—or they can be sown as an inter-crop.

There should be no need to manure the ground especially, for radishes can do well on the residues left from a previous crop. On very poor soil, however, a fish manure may be applied with the sedge peat at 2 to 3 oz. to the sq. yd. The great thing is to see that the surface soil is not left lumpy, and whatever treading and raking is necessary should be done, so as to get the surface down to a fine tilth and level.

Sowing

Start sowing as early as possible, southerners can often make a start in a sheltered spot out of doors in February. Further successional sowings should then be made, say once every three weeks until August. Don't make the mistake of sowing too much seed at a time. Very often $\frac{1}{4}$ row will do. Or if you prefer to sow broadcast, $\frac{1}{2}$ sq. yd. at a time.

Never sow too thickly or poor roots will result. Sow, however, very shallowly, and after raking to cover the seed, make the soil firm, with the back of the rake, or the back of the spade, for you can't really get firm radishes from loose soil. Some people cover their February sowings with straw, 6 in. deep, to give protection, and then when they are through the ground, the straw is raked off.

In the south-west I have sown seed in December, in a slightly raised bed, so as to make certain that the drainage was perfect. Such a bed was covered with straw also. The second sowing would then be in February; the third sowing in March; and so on. All these being in a sunny, warm spot. The moment, however, you come to the June sowing and onwards, a cool, shady position could be chosen. When in rows the seeds should be 6 in. apart, but they will fit in well in between the rows of most other crops.

Growing Tips

In dry seasons, and especially on light soils, it is necessary to use the Brosson Rainer to give artificial rain. The aim should be to have the radishes ready for pulling in a few weeks, because the quicker they grow, the more delicious they are.

Radishes can always be grown under cloches in the colder periods of the year. Plenty of fine organic matter must be forked into the top 3 or 4 in. first. They grow equally well in frames under Dutch lights, and I've had continuous supplies from these circumstances by making a small sowing early in December; a second one early in January; and a third early in February. I have sometimes done this in between rows of lettuces and even among early marrows.

Harvesting and Using

It is a good thing to pull the roots while they are still young and tender, and never to allow them to become coarse and woody and hollow inside. Therefore, gather frequently, even if the roots are not required. The surplus can always be put on the compost heap where they will make grand manure, if activated with a fish fertilizer.

It is a very good idea, incidentally, to sow mixed radishes, whites, reds, rounds, longs, red and whites, and so on, because when harvesting you get all kinds of colours, sizes and flavours for the salad bowl. Further, I've discovered that this helps the continuity of supply.

Varieties

Short Top Forcing. This is best for the frames under cloches, because it has very few leaves and bulbs quickly. It is useful, too, on very shallow soils.

Red Turnip. A beautiful bright red colour, with crisp, tender roots.

Scarlet Globe. Particularly delicious. Tender and crisp.

Sparkler 50/50. The top half of the round root is scarlet, and the bottom half pure white.

Saxa. Round little scarlet roots, much liked in the north.

Oval:

Forcing French Breakfast. The best oval variety for the frame or cloche, turns in quickly.

French Breakfast. Deep crimson-coloured oval roots with pure white flesh inside. Solid yet sweet.

Long:

Wood's Frame. A scarlet, very early variety, useful for frames or cloches.

Icicle. A crisp, long, white variety of good quality.

WINTER RADISH

Here the scheme is to sow the seeds about the middle of July in the north, and about the middle of August in the south. The drills should be 9 in. apart, and 1 in. deep. Three seeds being placed every 6 in. along the rows, and the seedlings thinned down to one per station later.

The radishes produced are most like turnips. Hoeing has to be done between the rows to keep down weeds, and dustings carried out with BHC to keep down the flea-beetle, which can be a tremendous nuisance. The roots can be dug as required in the winter, and can either be used as a cooked vegetable or can be grated up and used as a salad.

Varieties

Black Spanish Long. The skin is jet black but the flesh inside pure white and firm.

China Rose. A round pink variety with white flesh.

Black Spanish Round. Similar to the long black but with round roots.

RHUBARB
(see page 283)

SAVOY CABBAGE

Savoys are very hardy, in fact their flavour is improved by frost, and they are thus extremely useful during the winter. Although they have been supplanted to quite an extent in the milder districts by winter cabbages, such as January King, they are still the favourites in the colder northern regions. The savoy has deeply crinkled dark leaves, while the cabbage has smooth leaves.

Soils and Manuring

Savoys can be grown on pretty poor soil, but they do best on a light rich loam, which has been deeply cultivated. They do well when fitted into a rotation after early peas or potatoes, for which the soil has been well manured or cultivated. If they don't follow such crops and the ground hasn't been recently manured, then it is best to dig in well-rotted compost or farmyard manure at the rate of half a 2-gallon bucket-ful to the sq. yd., doing this in the autumn if possible. Anyhow an application of fish manure with a 5 per cent potash content should be forked in before planting. As with other brassica crops lime should be applied to the surface if the soil is acid.

Sowing the Seed

Seed is usually sown in a seed bed in three sowings, the first during March in a warm sunny position, the second in early April and the third in late April.

Plants and Planting

Planting out is generally done towards the end of June and during July. Most varieties are planted in rows 2 ft. apart with 2 ft. between the plants, but smaller varieties need only be put in rows 18 in. apart with 15 in. between the plants. Choose showery weather for the job, or otherwise it may be necessary to water the plants in, so that they will get away quickly.

Growing Tips

Hoe regularly and remove the stalks to the compost heap immediately the heads have been cut in order to avoid robbing the ground of plant foods.

Harvesting and Using

Cut and use in the same way as cabbages. The smaller varieties have a better flavour and are more suitable for a small family, than the giant types.

Varieties

Dwarf Types:

Early Dwarf Ulm. Dark green leaves and small solid round heads. Very early.

Green Curled Dwarf. Solid heads with medium green leaves.

Other Types:

Best of All. Large and early with coarsely blistered outer leaves.

Green Curled Large. Medium size heads, with dark green closely curled leaves.

For a good succession use the northern varieties:

Ormskirk Early. For cutting September–October.

Ormskirk Medium. For cutting in succession to early Ormskirk.

Ormskirk Late. Hardy, for cutting from January to the end of March.

Ormskirk Extra Late. Very hardy with dark green heads, for cutting March and April.

SEAKALE

Curiously enough seakale is one of the few vegetables which are native to this country, and is very little eaten abroad, either on the Continent or in America. It is not difficult to grow, but usually has to be dug up, so that it can be blanched or forced, though this can sometimes be done where the plants are growing.

Soils and Manuring

Seakale prefers a rich sandy loam, which is well drained and has been well cultivated and manured. The ground should be dug in the autumn and one 2-gallon bucketful of well-rotted compost or farmyard manure incorporated to every sq. yd. Before planting in the spring an application of fish manure with a 10 per cent potash content should be given and forked into the top few inches of soil. After this lime should be applied to the surface if the soil is acid. Dried blood at $\frac{1}{2}$ oz. to the sq. yd., given two or three times during the growing season is a help.

Propagation

Plants can be raised from seed and although they may be more robust by this method, it takes two years to produce a forcing crown. The usual method of propagation is by root cuttings or thongs.

Seed is sown thinly in a seed bed with a fine tilth in March or early

April, the seedlings being thinned out later to 6 in. apart when they are 2 in. high. The plants should be dug up the following February, and planted in their permanent positions, after cutting off the tops just below the crown, in order to prevent flowering.

Thongs or root cuttings are usually taken when the plants are lifted for forcing, clean straight side-shoots, about the thickness of a good pencil being selected. These are then cut into pieces about 6 in. long, and as with all root cuttings it is preferable to cut the top level and slope the bottom, so that there will be no doubt as to which way up to plant them. These cuttings should then be tied together in bundles, which can be put upright, either in cold frames, and surrounded with moist sand or fine soil, or in the open at the base of a wall in sand. It will be found that by February or March when the time comes for planting, a number of buds will have developed on the top of each cutting; these should be removed with the exception of the strongest one or two.

Planting

March is the best time for this, the rows being 18 in. apart, with 12 in. between the plants in the rows. The top of the thong should be 1 in. below the surface of the ground. Plant firmly.

Growing Tips

Hoe regularly throughout the summer and cut off at once any flowering stems that appear.

If the foliage has not died down by mid-October, it should be cut off. The roots are then lifted, the main crowns being used for forcing and the best of the side-roots for next year's thongs.

Forcing

Forcing can be done in cellars, in frames or under the staging of a greenhouse. The roots should be stood upright in soil or rotted leaves, using large pots or boxes, inverting similar pots or boxes over the top to provide complete darkness. If in rows the roots can be about $\frac{1}{2}$ in. apart in rows about 3 in. apart, and as a guide six roots can generally be put in a 9-in. pot. In the early part of the season there should be some edible stalks in about seven weeks, but later on the time taken to mature will drop to about five weeks. Throw the roots away after forcing as they are then useless. A high temperature is not required for forcing seakale, and it is best not to exceed 55° F.

In addition to forcing indoors it is possible to force in the open, by covering the crowns with forcing pots or boxes, which should be surrounded with a good 6-in. layer of farmyard manure. This should produce enough heat to make the seakale grow. Old 'rhubarb pots' or any large earthenware pots are excellent for this, but it is advisable when planting in the first place to use a triangular system of planting so that three crowns can be covered with one pot.

Natural Seakale

Seakale can also be blanched in the open by earthing up the rows to a depth of 8 or 9 in., after they have been cleaned up in the autumn. A dry period should be chosen, as the soil should be dry and friable, in fact this method is really only successful where a very light and sandy soil is available. The seakale will grow up through the ridges and the stems may be cut as soon as the tops of the shoots can be seen. The heads are cut off with a sharp knife just below the crown, and then when all the crop has been harvested, the soil from the ridge can be thrown down, leaving merely an inch or two of soil on top of the plants. If seakale is grown in this, the 'natural way', or forced in the open, the plants will last for several years, but a good top dressing of well-rotted compost or farmyard manure should be given every year.

Care should be taken not to leave any roots in the ground when clearing an old bed, otherwise even small pieces may go on sprouting over and over again.

Harvesting and Using

Generally the heads are cut down when they are 6 in. long, together with a small piece of the crown. Seakale should be harvested just before it is required for use, as it will only deteriorate if left lying about in the light. It can either be used cold in a salad (when it should be sliced thinly), or served hot after cooking. Never overcook seakale. Steaming is probably the best method and takes about three-quarters of an hour. It is very pleasant when served with a Hollandaise sauce.

Varieties

Lily White. The most popular variety. Good flavour and pure white when forced.

SHALLOTS

Shallots are now very much less commonly grown than they used to be and are largely used for pickling. They are very easy to grow, though they do not like heavy clay soils.

CULTURE OF VEGETABLES ALPHABETICALLY

Soils and Manuring

Shallots grow best on a light deep soil, similar to that required for onions, but it need not be so rich and therefore the manuring programme will not be as heavy. Half a 2-gallon bucketful of well-rotted compost or farmyard manure dug in in the autumn should be sufficient, together with an application of fish manure with a 10 per cent potash content, which should be given just before planting at the rate of 3 oz. to the sq. yd.

Planting

Shallots can be raised from seeds sown in the spring, but the usual method is to plant small bulbs.

The old rule was to plant on the shortest day and harvest on the longest, but it will usually be found that February and March are good planting times in the south, and late March for the north. Shallots are liable to bolt if bulbs grown from seed are planted, so small bulbs from the previous year's harvest are used. These are sold by seedsmen by the pound, there being about twelve bulbs to the pound, and each bulb should produce a cluster of about twelve bulbs. Before planting, any loose skins or dead tops should be removed from the bulbs, which are then just pushed into the soil to half their depth. The soil should be firm, so that the planting can be firm. The rows should be 1 ft. apart and the bulbs 4 to 6 in. apart in the rows.

Growing Tips

It is advisable to inspect the shallots a fortnight or so after they have been planted, and any that have come right out of the ground should be pushed back. Shallots, however, do not like to be buried, but prefer to grow on the surface. Care should therefore be taken when hoeing not to push the soil right up to the bulbs and not to cut them with the hoe. Hoe regularly, but do not move the soil deeply.

Harvesting and Using

They should be ready for harvesting sometime in July. Wait for a sunny day, a week or two after the leaves have started to turn yellow; they can then be lifted and left on the surface in the sun to dry. In order to be certain that they are really dry, it is a good idea after a few days to put them on a path or piece of concrete, turning them a few times. They can then be divided and hung up in a cool dry shed. They should not be left on the ground, as they keep best with a good air circulation.

In addition to their being used for pickling, they are not so strong as onions when grated in a salad.

Varieties

The Red or Common Shallot is now the only variety to be generally offered.

SPINACH

What might be termed true spinach, that is either round-seeded summer spinach or prickly winter spinach are not really easy to grow, but there are a number of substitutes including spinach beet or perpetual spinach, seakale spinach and New Zealand spinach, which are very similar in taste and not nearly so difficult to cultivate.

SUMMER AND WINTER SPINACH. ANNUALS.

Soils and Manuring

A good rich, well-worked loam is the best soil for spinach, though it can be grown on heavy soils. It is almost certainly bound to go to seed very quickly on light sandy soils, which have not been enriched with plenty of organic matter, and thus have no reserve of moisture.

The soil should be well dug and one bucketful of well-rotted compost or farmyard manure incorporated to every sq. yd. In addition, 4 oz. of balanced fish manure with a 6 per cent potash content should be applied just before sowing. Liquid manure when the plants are in growth, given at fortnightly intervals, of course, gives moisture as well as food.

Sowing the Seed

The first sowing of summer spinach can be made in early March in a warm sheltered position, and then two or three successional sowings at fortnightly intervals. Later sowings should be made in a moister, shadier position and the seed can be soaked in water for a day before sowing to assist the germination. The quicker the germination the better.

Sow the seed in drills 1 ft. apart and 1 in. deep, thinning later to 6 in. apart, or sow in stations 6 in. apart.

Winter spinach is sown from early August to mid-September in batches every two weeks. Where the soil is very heavy it is a good idea to raise the beds a little so that the excess rain can get away, but keep the beds narrow so that the crop can be picked easily.

CULTURE OF VEGETABLES ALPHABETICALLY

Growing Tips

Hoe regularly and mulch whenever possible with lawn mowings or sedge peat. Summer spinach must have moisture.

In colder districts winter spinach should be afforded some protection by putting bracken or straw in between the rows, or by covering during really cold weather with cloches.

Harvesting and Using

The leaves should be pulled when still young and tender and not too large. Summer spinach can be picked regularly and fairly hard, leaving only a few leaves on the plant.

With winter spinach only the largest leaves should be taken, taking only a few from each plant, otherwise the plant may be ruined.

Spinach should never be boiled in a lot of water. At most a cupful is necessary and if the leaves have just been washed, there will be sufficient water on them for boiling. There is less chance of losing the flavour after cooking if the spinach is chopped rather than sieved, but most recipes call for sieving. The iron in spinach is not easily assimilated by the human body, so this vegetable has not the food value it was always 'cracked up' to have, but on the other hand it is very tasty and makes a welcome change to the coarse roughage of 'greens'.

Varieties
Round or Summer Varieties:

Monstrous Viroflay. Perhaps the best-known summer spinach, with long, broad pointed, thick, fleshy leaves. Mid-green.

Bloomsdale Long Standing. Dark green and crinkled leaves. Stands well before bolting.

Victoria Improved. Heavy cropper, long standing and of good colour.

Prickly or Winter Varieties:

Long Standing. Large leaved and hardy strain.
New Giant Thick-Leaved. Broad, thick, fleshy leaves. Long standing.

SPINACH BEET OR PERPETUAL SPINACH

There is little difference in taste between this and the annual spinach. It is easy to grow and keeps up a succession of leaves for pulling all the year round, no matter whether the summers are dry and hot and the winters cold and wet.

Soils and Manuring

As for beetroot. (See page 182).

Sowing the Seed

To ensure a succession and regular cropping, seed should be sown in April, with a second sowing in August. The rows should be 15 in. apart, sowing in stations 8 in. apart, or if continuous sowing is practised, the plants must be thinned later to 8 in. apart.

Growing Tips

Hoe regularly and keep weeded. An occasional watering is appreciated, but the plants are not at all demanding.

Harvesting and Using

The leaves should be picked as soon as they are ready, and not left to grow old and large on the plant. Even if the leaves are not required they should be picked in order that the plant should go on producing fresh young ones. Plants from the autumn sowings should be allowed to build themselves up a bit more for the winter months, so that there will be good sized plants when the winter really starts and growth will be at its minimum.

Spinach beet is cooked in the same way as annual spinach—but isn't so indigestible!

NEW ZEALAND SPINACH

This plant is a half-hardy annual, rather resembling ivy as it tends to grow flat on the ground and has numerous small fleshy leaves. It succeeds in hot and dry weather, where the round-seeded spinach would go to seed, but as far as true spinach flavour is concerned it is not as good as the spinach beet.

Soil and Manuring

The same as for annual spinach, except that it will tolerate very much drier soils.

Sowing the Seed

The plants can be raised under glass by sowing seeds in boxes in late March, using Eclipse No-Soil Compost,[1] and then transplanting the seedlings when large enough to handle to soil blocks or one per 60 pot, using Eclipse No-Soil Compost No. 1. They should be kept near the

[1] See appendix.

glass until put out at the end of May. Seed can be sown in mid-April in a cold frame, putting three seeds in a 60 pot, later thinning to one seedling, or the seed can be sown under continuous cloches in early April where the plants are to grow. Sowing in the open should not be done until after the middle of May.

Plants and Planting

Planting should be done in rows 3 ft. apart, with 2 ft. between the plants in the rows. The intervening spaces will soon be covered by the growth, so regular picking and cutting back is necessary.

Growing Tips

As the ground is soon covered by the plants very little hoeing is either possible or necessary. If the weather is dry, frequent irrigation is appreciated, as although the plants will grow in much drier conditions than annual spinach, they will be much the better for ample supplies of moisture. The pinching out of the growing tips will cause further branching out and a more compact growth, as well as preventing the plants from becoming too crowded.

Harvesting and Using

The small leaves are stripped off the stems and used in the same way as ordinary spinach. The growing tips, which are pinched back, can also be used and are usually considered to be of a better flavour than the leaves. They are easily digested.

SWEDE

Swedes are hardier than winter turnips and in addition have a higher sugar content. They are probably a better winter root crop for the average gardener than turnips, their only drawback being that they require a longer time to mature.

Soils and Manuring

As for turnips. (See page 258.)

Sowing the Seed

Seed should be sown in drills 18 in. apart, either in stations 1 ft. apart, or thinning later to 1 ft. apart if continuous sowing is practised. Early May is the usual time for sowing in the north, while the seed is put in in the south in late May or early June.

Growing Tips

See turnips.

Harvesting and Using

Swedes need not be lifted for winter storage, but can be left in the ground for use as required. They are hardly ever damaged by the frost.

Varieties

It is always better to grow the farm swedes than the garden varieties.
Tipperary, which I think is the best oval-shaped kind.
Lord Derby, is a first-class globe-shape and very hardy too.
Gateacre, which I always call globe-shaped. It keeps splendidly.
Great Scott, which has bronze, shaped leaves and an oval root.

SWEET CORN

Sweet corn is, of course, a form of maize of which there are hundreds of varieties, only a few being pleasant to eat, the remainder being cultivated to provide animal foods. This vegetable is now much more popular in this country than it used to be, and it has been found that it can be grown with little difficulty provided that there is the room.

Soils and Manuring

Sweet corn grows best on a medium loam, which is well supplied with organic matter, though it will grow quite well on most soils. If it can follow a crop for which the ground has been well manured and cultivated, so much the better, otherwise it is advisable to dig in shallowly compost or farmyard manure at the rate of half a 2-gallon bucketful to the sq. yd. Anyhow, before sowing or planting, sedge peat should be forked into the top few inches of soil at the rate of half a 2-gallon bucketful to the sq. yd., together with an application of balanced fish manure with a 10 per cent potash content at 4 oz. to the sq. yd.

Sowing the Seed

It is better not to transplant sweet corn and so the ideal way of raising plants is to sow the seeds under cloches in early April in the south and late April in the north. Seed-sowing in the open is usually done in May, but on light soft soils in the south it may be possible to sow with some success in April. A number of people do raise plants in the greenhouse by sowing two seeds to a 60 pot in Eclipse No-Soil Potting Compost No. 1, later thinning the seedlings to one per pot. With pot-raised plants there is not very much root disturbance when the plants are put out. Those who can make 'soil blocks' should use these for they are very successful with sweet corn.

Seed-sowing in the open should be done in stations (two seeds per station) 9–12 in. apart depending on the variety, with 2 ft. between the rows. It is always best to aim at a small block of plants, rather than a single row, as the block system aids pollination greatly. This is so important.

Growing Tips

This crop wants all the sunshine possible, as well as an ample supply of moisture. It can be well irrigated during dry periods and will benefit from a mulch of sedge peat. If the position where the sweet corn is grown is very windy, it is a good idea to earth up the stems a little, so that the adventitious roots can give more support.

Harvesting and Using

One of the most important points in cultivating sweet corn is to know exactly when it is ready to eat; this is when the grains of the cobs are in a milky state. Earlier on the grains are too small and watery and later too hard and yellow. The browning and withering of the 'silks' is one of the signs that the cobs are ready for eating, but it is best to make sure by pulling part of the sheath back from the cob and pressing one of the grains with a thumb nail. The liquid inside the grain should burst out and look something like clotted cream. The cobs can be pulled off with a slight jerk or can be cut with a knife. They should be used as soon after harvesting as possible.

The cobs should be stripped of their husks before cooking, which is done by putting them in boiling water and simmering lightly for ten minutes. They should then be removed from the water and served with plenty of melted butter, and salt, pepper or sugar to taste.

Varieties

Canada Cross. Early and reasonably hardy.

John Innes Hybrid. Good flavour, especially developed for growing in this country.

Golden Bantam. Hardy, medium-sized, bright yellow.

Golden Standard. Prolific cropper, taller and later, not a true 'sweet corn'.

TOMATO

Although tomatoes have been known in this country for over 300 years, it is only in the last four decades that they have gained their enormous popularity. It must be remembered, however, that even though this crop can be grown in the open in the summer, the plant originally came from the tropics and whether it does well or not depends entirely on the vagaries of the climate. In cold, wet seasons it is often difficult to get the fruit to ripen out of doors and it becomes especially open to the onslaught of such diseases as potato blight, potatoes being of the same family.

Soils and Manuring

Tomatoes above all demand a well-drained soil, though they are not very particular as to whether it is heavy or light.

The preparation of heavy soils for this crop is probably best done by digging the ground into ridges in the autumn and leaving it to weather until the early spring. Well-rotted manure or compost can then be put into the furrows at the rate of one 2-gallon bucketful to the yard run, after which the ridges can be pulled down to cover the manure. The plants in time can be put out on the new shallow ridges, which will be composed of friable soil broken up over the winter and the plant foods will be immediately available from the manure or compost at their roots.

With light soils it is merely a question of incorporating a similar quantity of manure or compost by digging it in over the winter months.

In addition to any bulky organic manuring, all soils should receive an application of fish manure, which should be forked in just before the plants are put out, at the rate of 4 oz. to the yard run. This fish manure should have a 10 per cent potash content.

The best way of feeding the growing crop is by the use of the Liquinure with the high potash content. This can be given every week after the first truss of fruits has set and it is possible by following the instructions on the bottle to give exactly the right quantity of food.

Sowing the Seed

Care should be taken to select the seed of a variety which does well out of doors, and is preferably one which has been proved in the district.

Plants can be raised from seed sown in a greenhouse, in a frame or under cloches, or, of course, they can be bought in quite cheaply from nurserymen, who often specialize in the raising of outdoor tomato plants for private customers.

The end of March is quite early enough for greenhouse sowings. The seed should be sown fairly thinly in boxes, using John Innes Seed Compost and taking care to have only the lightest covering of compost over the seed. The boxes should then be covered with glass, which should in turn be covered with paper to exclude the light. The greenhouse temperature should, if possible, be about 55° F. Directly the seeds have germinated, the glass and paper should be removed and the boxes placed near the glass on a shelf. Watering should be done carefully with water at the same temperature as the greenhouse; the soil should never be overwet. When the seedlings can be handled they should be pricked out singly into soil blocks, or 60 pots, or 3 in. sq. in deep boxes, but this is not nearly as satisfactory as the plants tend to grow leggy. No-Soil Potting Compost No. 1 should be used. The plants will have to be hardened off in cold frames so that they are ready for planting out at the end of May.

Seed can be sown in cold frames in early April, one of the most successful ways of doing this is by putting three seeds in a 60 pot, using No-Soil Potting Compost No. 1. The seedlings are thinned later to one per pot. Plants raised this way will be hardy and sturdy, when the time comes for planting out.

Seed can be sown very successfully under cloches. It is best to warm up the soil by putting the glass in position a week or so before sowing, and in addition either to remove the top 2 or 3 in. of soil and replace with No-Soil Potting Compost No. 1, or to try to make the soil approximate as much as possible to the potting compost by the addition of sedge peat, sharp sand, and if necessary superphosphate and lime. The seed should be sown about the end of March in the south and mid-April in the north, spacing the seeds 1½ in. apart and ¼ in. deep. The continuous cloches should have their ends sealed, and be covered until the seeds have germinated. When they can be handled the seedlings may be potted up into 60 pots, which are then placed in a trench 3 in. deep under cloches.

Sowing *in situ* can be carried out in early May by sowing three seeds to a station, and then covering each station with an inverted 2-lb. jam-jar. The seedlings can be thinned to one per station and the jam-jar left on as long as possible. The seedlings in this way do not receive any check from transplanting.

[1] See Appendix.

Planting

Tomatoes are usually planted out at the end of May or in early June, depending on the weather. If the weather is uncertain it is much better to wait a little for more settled conditions, and it is no use planting out tomatoes if the soil is cold and wet. It is essential that the plants should have been well hardened off, the greenhouse-raised plants having been transferred to cold frames, and having been progressively given more air, while plants that have been raised in cold frames may have been stood outside, being afforded some protection on cold nights. Whether the plants are home-raised or bought in from a nurseryman, at the time of planting out they should be about 8 in. high, sturdy and hard. Any leggy, weakly or rogue plants should be neglected, as they will never give a good crop.

It is essential that the roots should be disturbed as little as possible on planting and that they should have a good ball of soil. When the plants are in boxes a knife should be used to cut the roots right down to the bottom of the box, after which the boxes should be well watered. It will then be found that each plant will come away with a good cube of soil.

The plants should not be put in too deeply, the best guide being that the roots should be covered with about $\frac{1}{2}$ in. of fresh soil. It is necessary to plant firmly and it is always advisable for outdoor tomatoes, except in the case of the bush or dwarf varieties, to provide immediate support. This can be done by putting in the stakes or supports either immediately before or after the planting and then tying the plants loosely to them.

There are a number of different ways of supporting tomato plants. If there are only a small quantity of plants stout 4 ft. stakes are generally used, but where there are a fair number of plants, one method is to put a good stake at each end of the row with two wires running the length of the row to which the plants can be tied. Bamboo canes are usually too light to support the weight of a fully grown tomato plant by themselves, but make a very neat form of support for each plant when steadied by a wire running the length of the row.

As far as planting distances are concerned, the general rule is not to have the rows closer than 2 ft. 6 in., with 15 in. between the plants, except in the case of dwarf tomatoes to which I shall refer separately.

Growing Tips

Hoe regularly throughout the season to keep a loose surface and the weeds down.

In order to get good-sized fruits, tomatoes are usually grown on a single stem, which means that the side-shoots have to be removed as soon as they can be handled, preferably before they are an inch long. The side-shoot can either be pinched out between the finger and thumb-nail, or it can be nicked away with a sharp knife. The fingers should not be tobacco stained, nor the knife infected—for the tobacco viruses are easily transferred to tomato plants. I cannot over-emphasize this.

The plants will grow quickly and must be kept tied to their supports as new growth is made. Green twine or 'Nutscene Twist' is very suitable for the purpose, but raffia can also be used. It must be remembered that although the plant must be made secure to the support, the tie should not be made too tight as the stem still has to grow.

Plants are best stopped, that is the growing point is pinched out, in in the first week of August. By stopping, no further growth is allowed and the energies of the plant will be directed into ripening the fruit. Stopping should be done with a sharp knife, cutting the main stem one leaf above the last truss of flowers.

It will be found that side-shoots now appear even more plentifully and care should be taken to remove them all.

There are always a number of arguments about defoliation, that is removal of the leaves from the plants. The leaves, perform a very important part in the manufacture of the plant foods which are essential in the production of the fruit, but where the plants have been put in close together a tight mass of leaves will hinder the circulation of the air and will open the way for such diseases as potato blight. If the planting is close the lower leaves can be removed as soon as the trusses below them have ripened and they are no longer performing a directly useful task, but where the spacing is wider removal of the leaves is not really necessary. Complete leaves starting from the bottom up should be removed and not just parts of leaves all over the plant. Naturally any diseased or old yellowed leaves are best off the plant.

The main trouble or disease that affects tomatoes grown outdoors is potato blight and it is well worth while to take the precaution of spraying with Bordeaux mixture in late July or early August as a preventative (see page 281). If possible it is advisable to keep tomato plants well away from the ground where potatoes are being grown, as the spores of the disease are quickly carried from one crop to the other.

Ripening

If glass square cloches are available they are most useful for ripening the fruits at the end of the season. The plants should be stripped of leaves and then laid down on a good layer of straw or sedge peat, before being covered by the cloches.

DWARF TOMATOES

Messrs. Unwins of Cambridge have recently raised a variety of bush tomato called The Amateur, which has proved to be very successful and is now extremely popular. This tomato does not require any staking, in fact it does not like to be staked, it does not need to be de-side-shooted and it does not have to be stopped. The plants can be spaced 15 in. sq. in a double row and they will spread all over the ground, not growing to more than 1 ft. high. If a layer of sedge peat is spread on the ground it will act as a mulch and keep the fruit off the soil. There is also the advantage that it can be grown under ordinary barn, continuous cloches all the summer, without pushing out of the glass.

Harvesting and Using

The fruit is picked as it becomes ripe. If it has to be picked before it is fully ripe, owing to the depredations of birds, the ripening can usually be completed indoors.

By the beginning of October any fruits that are still on the plants can be picked off and ripened in trays indoors or by hanging up complete trusses on wires.

Tomatoes are rich in food value and luckily lose but little of this value on cooking.

Varieties

Hundredfold. Heavy cropper with medium size, bright red fruit.

Open Air. Uniform and medium size fruits, vigorous plants. Early, fine flavour.

Outdoor Girl. Vigorous plants with well-set trusses of medium size fruit.

Ibbett's Seedling. Heavy cropper, with round, medium size scarlet fruit of solid texture.

Orange Sunrise. Vigorous plants, with round, regular fruits of sweet flavour. A yellow.

The Amateur. Very early, with habit already described. Dwarf.

TURNIP

Turnips have been grown in this country for many centuries. The small quick-maturing turnip is very tender and tasty, and vastly different to the great big coarse root of some of the older varieties. If a succession of varieties is chosen turnips can be had over most of the year.

Soils and Manuring

Early turnips grow best in a light but fertile loam, which retains moisture well, but is at the same time well-drained. To produce the best tender roots, ample moisture is required. Main crop turnips are not so demanding and will grow well on most soils, though they must be fertile and well cultivated. Turnips are not a good crop for light, hot, shallow soils, as they tend to go to seed and are often savagely attacked by flea-beetle.

They do well when following another crop for which the ground has been well cultivated and manured. If at all acid the soil should be well limed to discourage club root disease. Before sowing an application of balanced fish manure with a 5 per cent potash content should be forked in at the rate of 3 oz. to the sq. yd.

Sowing the Seed

The beginning of March is the time for the first outdoor sowings, which can be made in drills 8 to 9 in. apart, either sowing in stations 4 in. apart or thinning later to 4 in. between the plants.

A second sowing can be made in April in drills 1 ft. apart in stations 6 in. apart or thinning later to 6 in. between the plants. A final main sowing of early turnips is made in May to provide roots at the end of the summer.

The sowing of winter turnips is usually carried out between the middle of July and the end of August. In this case the drills should be 18 in. apart and the stations 1 ft. apart.

Turnips when grown for turnip tops should be sown in early September, the drills being 2 ft. apart. The seed is sown thinly, the plants being allowed to grow on without thinning, as they are needed for their tops and not their roots.

Protected Sowings. Earlier turnips can be produced by sowing the seeds under a number of continuous cloches in March, three rows to the single or barn cloche.

Growing Tips

It is necessary to keep a sharp watch for the turnip flea-beetle, especially with earlier sowings, and dust when necessary with Gammexane. One crucial period is when the seedlings are just showing through the ground.

Hoe regularly to keep down the weeds.

If the weather is very dry, then a good $\frac{1}{2}$ in. of artificial rain should be given, and if possible, the ground should be mulched afterwards.

Always remember that quick-grown turnips with plenty of warmth and moisture are the best.

Harvesting and Using

The early varieties should always be pulled when young and fresh and never allowed to get old and coarse.

In milder districts it is possible to leave winter turnips in the ground until they are needed, but elsewhere it is best to lift them in the autumn and clamp them in the same way as potatoes. Cut the tops off first, but leave a bit of the neck and shorten the roots a little, but do not cut them right off.

Varieties

Early:

Milan Early White. White, flat shaped root with early top. Early and good for forcing.

Strap-Leaved Early Red Top. Flat-shaped root with white, firm sweet flesh.

Early White Stone. White globe. Early, matures in six weeks.

Early Snowball. Medium-sized white globe, of good quality.

Winter:

Orange Jelly. Yellow flesh, hardy and splendid for autumn sowing.

Golden Ball Selected. Small-topped, yellow globe. Good variety for late sowing as stands winter well.

Manchester Market. Green-topped with white globe of good quality. Sweet. Hardy.

Hardy Green Round. A good variety for growing for tops.

Turnips in Frames

Mention might be made here that turnips can be sown from the end of January in frames over hot beds. The crop matures in roughly two months. Holes 4 in. sq. and 1 in. deep are made in the soil and three seeds are dropped into each. The holes are filled in after sowing and seedlings later thinned to one. The frames should be closed at first, plenty of ventilation should be given, with an occasional spray of water once the seedlings have shown through. A good warm hot bed is required with quite a high temperature. The Gem is a good variety for this purpose.

CHAPTER 14

Controlling the Insect Pests

There are, unfortunately, large numbers of insect pests that can attack vegetables. The gardener, however, who believes in using plenty of organic matter, and so ensures that the humus content of the soil is high—soon finds that his crops are not so seriously attacked as his neighbours, who uses little or no organic matter and relies on artificial fertilizers. It has been made clear that the feeding of the soil is tremendously important, because correct soil feeding results in sturdy, healthy plants. It is when humans are ill-nourished that they are more subject to troubles than when they are properly fed—and the same rule applies to plants.

See that crops have plenty of light and air. Attend to the drainage of the soil so that the excess moisture of the soil is carried away and as against this, make sure that there is sufficient moisture present, because when plants are suffering from drought, they are often attacked by pests. Don't forget lime, for this prevents acidity in the soil, and also releases plant foods.

Be ready to recognize the difference between a sucking pest and an eater. It always pays to have a hand-magnifying glass in order that the trouble may be seen more clearly. 'Suckers' like aphides and capsids have to be killed by a paralysing agent like nicotine. 'Eaters' can often be killed by a much cheaper spray which will cause a poisonous deposit on the leaves. Never mistake an attack of a fungus disease for one of an insect pest.

Sometimes it's possible to use a repellant, some substance which can be put between the rows of plants, or even on them, for the purpose of keeping pests away. Whizzed naphthalene for instance, can be applied in between the rows of carrots to prevent attacks by the carrot-fly maggots. This is used, of course, before the seed is sown. Sprays are usually more effective than dusts because they give a better covering. Some

CONTROLLING THE INSECT PESTS

gardeners prefer dust because it saves time, and of course, there's no cartage of water.

Whether one is spraying or dusting, it is necessary to have an efficient machine for the job. Very often it is necessary to apply the insecticide over a fairly large area and in the course of an hour or so, and therefore efficient machinery does save labour and time. A Rotary Fan dust gun is very useful indeed, and so is a Knapsack sprayer. But where the acreage is at all large, it's worth while having the spraying machine which can easily be attached to the Auto-Culto. Thus the tank containing the spray fluid is pulled along by the Auto-Culto through the crops, and the two operators on either side can be spraying the crops as the machine moves forward slowly.

PESTS THAT ATTACK MANY VEGETABLES

Aphids. These are sometime called greenfly, blackfly, lice, or even bugs. They usually suck the undersides of leaves of plants, or in the case of beans, the succulent parts. They may easily cause leaves to curl and this tends to make spraying difficult. Aphids increase very quickly, and so must be killed in the early stages.

Control. Spray or dust with derris because this is non-poisonous. If the leaves of plants are curled, a malathic spray may be used instead.

Chafer Beetles. It's the grubs of the cockchafer that do the damage, as a rule. They are greyish-white, and may be up to 1½ in. long. The summerchafers are only ¾ in. long, but they are similar in appearance. The larvae of grubs attack the roots of plants.

Control. The soil can be watered with a strong solution of Nicotine.

Flea-Beetles. These spend the winter as adults in any dry vegetable rubbish. They love the bottoms of hedges. They are small and generally black or dark grey, they damage plants when they are just coming through the soil as a rule, and are very fond of all members of the cabbage family, as well as the radishes and turnips. They hop quickly and hide even when the gardener's shadow falls on a garden plot. They usually start giving trouble in May, but the attack continues until well on into August.

Control. Dust the plants when the flea-beetles are present, with Derris in dust form. Four dustings may be necessary at three-day intervals.

Leather-jackets. The leather-jackets are 1½ in. long when fully grown. They are the young of the daddy-long-legs, and northerners call them 'the bot'. The skin of the grub is very tough, hence the name. The leather-jackets usually live an inch or so below the soil on the roots of plants. They sometimes attack stems below-ground. I have known them come to the surface at night and eat the leaves also. A well-grown leather-jacket will be of a greyish-brown colour and will have no legs at all.

Control. Where the attack is bad, mix ¼ lb. of dry Paris Green with 5 lb. of damp bran. Broadcast this mixture evenly over ¼ acre of ground. The leather-jackets come up to eat the bran and are killed by the arsenic.

Great care must be taken when using arsenic.

Surface Caterpillars. These crawl about the surface of the soil, or they may be just below ground level. I have found them under clods or stones during the day, for they invariably feed at night. Many of the caterpillars are only ½ in. long and are brown or grey in colour, and some may be 1½ in. long.

Control. Use the bait as advised for leather-jackets.

Slugs. There are many kinds of slugs which trouble the gardener. Small black ones, larger grey ones, giant types, and so on. All of them, however, feed above ground at night-time, as well as below the soil during day or night. During hard frost, these creatures burrow well down into the soil.

Control. Mix a teaspoonful of blue powdered Draza with a handful of bran. Put little heaps the size of an egg-cup every 2 or 3 ft. along the rows of plants and protect the heaps from rain, covering them with a little slate or tile. The slugs will go for this bait and be killed.

Mix powdered copper-sulphate with hydrated lime in equal parts and apply this at a rate of 1 oz. to the sq. yd. when the ground has been dug. This mixture will certainly kill the creatures, but there's always the danger that the continuous use of copper-sulphate will injure the soil.

Wireworms. These are the grubs of the click beetle and they may easily live in the soil for four or five years before turning into beetles again. Wireworms as their name suggests, are very wiry, and are difficult to kill even when squeezed between the fingers. They differ from the centipedes and millipedes, because they only have three pairs of legs near their heads.

Control. The BHC insecticides have given outstanding results against wireworms. They will *not* be used, however, by those like the author who are against the use of long-lasting poisons. Care must be taken because they are apt to taint tubers and roots. One must be vary careful, therefore, when growing potatoes, carrots, parsnips and the like.

CONTROLLING THE INSECT PESTS

PESTS THAT ATTACK DEFINITE VEGETABLES

ASPARAGUS

Asparagus Beetle. The beetles are pretty little creatures, having black heads, red bodies, and black and yellow wing cases. The larvae are pinkish in colour, and are found eating the tiny leaves of the asparagus fern in the summer. The eggs are clustered like tiny black needles on the main stems of the fern.

Control. Spray the fern the moment the creatures are seen with a Derris wash, or use a Derris dust instead.

BROAD BEAN

Black Aphis. The black aphides or dolphins are quite well known. They go for the tops of the broad bean plant where they cluster in large numbers. Actually they come from the Euonymus bushes.

Control. Spray the Euonymus bushes in the garden with a 5 per cent solution of a tar distillate wash in December.

Spray the plants the moment the black aphis is first seen, with a strong solution of liquid derris.

RUNNER BEAN

Red Spider. Tiny little mites, more yellowish in colour than red, attack the underneath surfaces of runner beans especially in the summer. The leaves tend to turn yellow, and after a bad attack, a browny colour.

Control. Syringe the undersurfaces of the leaves with water in the evening every two or three days. Apply this water with as much force as possible. A solo hand machine is excellent for the purpose.

In bad cases lime-sulphur can be used, dissolving 1 pint in 80 pints of water, and stirring in a little liquid detergent to cause the sulphur to be evenly deposited over the leaves.

BEETROOT

Leaf Miner of Mangold Fly. The eggs are laid by a creature rather like a small house-fly on the undersides of the leaves. The little maggots that hatch out tunnel in between the upper and lower epidermis causing blisters. There may be three generations in a year.

Control. Spray the plants with a nicotine wash, using ¼ fluid oz. of nicotine in a 3-gallon can of water. Do this work on a nice sunny day.

CABBAGE

Root Maggot. The maggots attack the stems and roots of plants. They go for cauliflowers in particular, as well as brussels sprouts. Some of the white larvae may burrow up and down the pith of plants, others may just eat off the most of the roots.

Control. Purchase tablets of mercuric chloride. Dissolve these in water in accordance with the instructions on the container. Pour some of the solution into each hole, at planting-out time. This chemical is very poisonous and thus the cans must be washed out thoroughly after use. The normal concentration is one tablet of mercuric chloride to a quart of water.

It's possible to use a 4 per cent calomel dust sprinkled around the base of plants immediately they are put out and again a fortnight later. Should not be used by those who abhor such poisons.

Aphides. The particular aphid which goes for the cabbage family is mauvy-blue in colour. It's often found in large blisters on the undersides of leaves. It certainly causes distortion to the foliage and impedes the rate of growth.

Control. Dust or spray with Derris, but be sure and go for the undersides of the leaves, and use enough to give a good covering.

When using either of these insecticides, always allow at least a fortnight before cutting the cabbages and using them.

White Fly. The white flies which attack the members of the cabbage family are not those which are so often seen in greenhouses. The flies are minute and hundreds may go for one plant.

Control. Spray with Derris or Pyrethrum on a dry day.

Caterpillars. Most people know the white butterflies which lay eggs in batches of from 25 to 100. The caterpillars which result do a tremendous amount of damage to the leaves of plants.

Control. Spray or dust with derris in the early stages, or if the trouble is not discovered until much damage is done, spray or dust with Pyrethrum. Derris is always safe to use, being non-poisonous.

N.B.—For gall-weavil see Turnips, for flea-beetle, see page 262.

CONTROLLING THE INSECT PESTS

CARROTS

Aphides. A greenfly may attack the leaves of carrots early in the summer, and in this case the leaves will turn yellow.

Control. Dust with a nicotine dust or spray with nicotine and a detergent. A ¼ oz. of liquid nicotine to a 2½-gallon bucket of water, plus a dessertspoonful of a liquid detergent.

Carrot-Fly. The commonest of troubles. Maggots burrow and tunnel into the roots. The tops will wilt, and the growth of the plant will be arrested. The fly that causes this trouble is small, shiny and of a deep bottle-green colour.

Control. Spray the bottoms of the hedgerows with a Derris wash early in May. Spray as soon as the seedlings have developed four or five leaves with a Derris-Pyrethrum wash, and repeat the spraying three times at three-weekly intervals.

If whizzed naphthalene be sprinkled down in between the rows at 2 oz. to the yard run, the smell given off will keep the flies away.

CELERY

Leaf Miner or Celery-Fly. The eggs are laid on the undersides of leaves and the tiny maggots which hatch out soon burrow into the foliage, causing blisters. There are usually three generations in a year.

Control. As the trouble starts early, it's worth while protecting the young plants in the frames by spraying with nicotine and a liquid detergent. For formula see Carrots above. Spray again early in June to kill the second generation, and if necessary, once again early in September. If, however, the second generation has been killed, there should be no further trouble.

Dusting and spraying with Derris-Pyrethrum has given good results in some gardens. Another scheme which has given good results has been by the use of a repellant made by mixing 1 part by weight of creosote with 99 parts of precipitated chalk. This dust is then scattered along the plants and the evil smell keeps away the flies. It should always be used late in May.

CUCUMBER

Red Spider. If you look at the undersides of the leaves you will find the mites spinning their minute webs. Use a magnifying glass for the job. You always notice the leaves turn yellow first, and that makes you suspicious.

Control. Keep the undersides of the leaves sprayed regularly with water, as these creatures always multiply under dry conditions. Use a liquid derris spray in the early stages, and this will give excellent results.

LETTUCE

Aphides. There are two aphides which go for lettuces, one sucks the undersides of the leaves and the plants are thus stunted, and the other goes for the roots of the plants which appear then to be white and mealy. In the latter case the trouble comes from poplars, and the control is to use a Derris-Pyrethrum wash and to water the plants thoroughly. Sometimes seedlings are attacked in trays and then these can be dipped in a Derris solution. A spray of Derris-Pyrethrum should be used to kill the creatures that are on the leaves.

ONIONS

Onion-Fly. Little maggots enter the bulbs of young plants and soon ruin them. The flies which are about the size of small houseflies lay their eggs in May on the neck of the onion or on the soil nearby.

Control. Dust with a Derris-Pyrethrum dust when the onion plants are in their 'loop stage'. Dust again with Derris-Pyrethrum when the seedlings are 4 in. high.

As the onion-fly is attracted by the smell of the onions, take care never to damage the plants when hoeing and do not leave onion seedlings lying about at thinning time.

As in the case of carrots, whizzed naphthalene can be sprinkled up in between the rows of plants when they first come through the ground, at 2 oz. to the yard run. The naphthalene smell has the effect of keeping the flies away.

PARSNIPS

These are sometimes attacked by the celery-fly and the carrot-fly, but the trouble is never very serious. Aphides will sometimes go for the leaves.

CONTROLLING THE INSECT PESTS

PEAS

Pea and Bean Weevil. The little beetles eat semi-circular holes out of the sides of the leaves. Sometimes there are thousands of them and then the damage is very serious. They are very difficult to see during the day.

Hoe regularly so as to produce a fine tilth and to remove little clods which are their hiding places. Dust with Derris, and aim at covering the plants thoroughly.

Aphis. A green aphis may attack the peas in their young stages and again when they are three-quarters grown.

Control. Spray immediately the trouble is seen with nicotine and a detergent. For formula see carrots, page 266.

Thrips. Tiny little black creatures which are not easily seen unless you tap the plants on to a white handkerchief. They do, however, do a great deal of damage, for they suck the growing points and distort them —they cause the pods to become silvered and later brown. They are particularly bad in a dry season.

Control. See that the strip along which the peas have been sown is given a dressing of carbonate of lime at 4 oz. to the yard run. Spray the plants thoroughly with nicotine and a detergent (for formula see carrots, page 266). Some gardeners prefer to use a Derris-Pyrethrum spray instead.

TURNIP

Flea-Beetle. This has been dealt with in fair detail on page 262.

Gall-Weevil. This will not only attack turnips but all members of the cabbage family as well. The trouble is noticed by the rounded galls which grow out from the roots. These when cut open will be found to be hollow and may contain a grub. It is this which distinguishes the trouble from club root. The maggot when seen is white or yellowish with a brown head and is legless. It is usually curled up inside the gall.

Control. Bash up the cabbage stems affected by these galls with the back of an axe on a chopping block and then put them on the compost heap and sprinkle them with an activator such as fish manure.

Spray the stems of the plants with Derris-Pyrethrum early in June and again about the middle of September.

General Remarks

I have taken the trouble to include the main pests which the vegetable gardener may meet with. If by chance the gardener is worried by some particular trouble which doesn't seem to have been mentioned, he should turn to the chapter on diseases, and see whether the descriptions there fit the bill. The final alternative is to send a small sample of the trouble carefully packed in damp moss or cotton wool to The International Horticultural Advisory Bureau, Arkley, Herts, who make a small charge for the advice they give.

Note. Join The Good Gardeners Association that have experts available to help you. Write to Arkley Manor, Arkley, Herts for particulars. The subscription is £2 a year. Fellows get free advice by phone or by letter; free soil analysis; purchases are made less 10 per cent and visits to the Arkley Manor gardens are free.

CHAPTER 15

Controlling the Diseases

It would be as well to read the introduction to the chapter on insect pests for, of course, what I have said there applies to diseases as well. If the plants are kept growing sturdily in soil rich in humus, they are not so liable to diseases as they are when they are in poor soil, fed largely with inorganics. It helps if you carry out regular hoeings in between the plants to control weeds, and to create a dust mulch. It's a good thing to apply lime regularly to prevent the soil from becoming acid. It's important to give the plants plenty of room for development.

Aim to see that the sowing and planting are done at the right time, very late sowings may be subject to diseases as may the plants from sowings which are made too early. Give protection when protection is needed. Use the cloches intelligently. Always see that plants in frames are ventilated whenever possible.

When the leaves of plants turn yellow, they are useless. It is a good plan then to remove them, and this is especially true in the case of members of the cabbage family. Old yellow leaves may easily be potential homes of fungus diseases.

Lastly, remember that a fungus can be described as a lowly plant growing on another plant. It has 'roots' which spread inside the leaves or stems. It has little branches which are seen as mildew or rust, and it has little seed pods which bear the spores which are soon distributed and float about in the air infecting other plants.

DISEASES THAT ATTACK MANY VEGETABLES

Club Root. This is an evil-smelling root disease which is sometimes called Finger and Toe. It will attack any member of the Cruciferae Family, that is to say the cabbages, cauliflowers, turnips, radishes and so on. The roots become swollen and knotted and distorted, and it's when they are broken open that the evil-smelling matter is seen.

270

CONTROLLING THE DISEASES

Control. Raise healthy plants free from the disease by watering the beds where the seeds are to be sown with a mercuric chloride solution. Dissolve one tablet in a quart of water. Give the seed bed a good soaking. Water it again with a similar solution fourteen days later, i.e. after the seed has been sown. You can now guarantee that you've got healthy plants, free from the disease. To prevent their being infected, where they are going to grow, pour an eighth of a pint of a similar solution into every hole at planting time.

Mercuric chloride is poisonous. It must be used with great care because it's corrosive and poisonous. Wash out the cans, therefore, that have been used for the purpose *very carefully*.

DISEASES THAT ATTACK DEFINITE VEGETABLES

ASPARAGUS

Asparagus Rust. About the middle of the summer rusty patches will be found on the stems which have a blistered looking appearance. The little leaves usually turn yellowish brown. Then later on in the autumn the spots on the stems turn a darker colour.

Control. Cut the stems in the autumn before the little leaves, which are known as needles, fall. Cut right down to soil level so that no infection areas can possibly remain. Burn all the infected cut stems immediately.

Sometimes there is a streaky discolouration of the white stems of asparagus at cutting time. This is not the disease rust, but just a blemish, and at the present nothing is known about its cause.

Violet Root Rot. Gardeners usually call this disease 'Copper web'. It's a root rot which attacks the underground portions of the plants and the crowns can become covered with a purplish-brown 'spawn'. The plants soon become exhausted and die. I have known this disease to attack potatoes, beetroot, and carrots as well.

Control. Dig up the infected roots and burn them. Apply bleaching powder to the contaminated areas at 2 oz. to the sq. yd., late in the spring and early in the summer. Fork this in lightly.

BEETROOT

Black Leg. The young seedlings seem to rot off at soil level and the stems become blackened. Large numbers may die at one time. After a very bad attack, the roots when examined appear thread-like instead of being thick and round.

271

Control. Buy one of the proprietary organo-mercury compounds and treat the seed with this before sowing. You only need a sixteenth of an oz. to $\frac{1}{4}$ lb. of seeds. After treatment spread the seed out for a time to dry before sowing.

Heart Rot. A disease which seems to be particularly bad on chalky soils, or on land that has been over-limed. The leaves and the crown turn black and die, usually in July. In very bad cases the outer leaves will die also. The roots themselves subsequently rot away. Look for the trouble in dry summers and on soils that have not been enriched with organic matter and are thus lacking in humus.

Control. Fork plenty of fine organic matter into the ground before sowing the seeds. If properly rotted compost is not available use sedge peat. Avoid using alkaline soils. The trouble appears to be due to a deficiency of boron and it helps, therefore, if Borax crystals are applied at the rate of not more than a sixteenth of an oz. to the sq. yd. You only want the slightest trace of Boron to cure the trouble. In well-made compost boron is present naturally.

BROAD BEANS

Chocolate Spot. The leaves and stems and even the pods become covered with dark brown spots or streaks. The trouble seems always far worse in wet years.

Control. Give extra potash to the ground, either in the form of wood ashes at $\frac{1}{2}$ lb. to the sq. yd. or to those who don't mind using artificials as a tonic—sulphate of potash at 1 oz. to the sq. yd.

The plants may be sprayed when the disease is first seen with one of the proprietary copper fungicides or a dusting can be carried out with copper-lime dust. Latterly I have found if the seed is treated with an organo-mercury dust before sowing, that there's less trouble from rust than in the case of plants raised from seeds which have not been so treated.

DWARF BEANS

Anthracnose. Gardeners often call this disease Blight, sometimes Rust, and occasionally Canker. Small dark spots surrounded by reddish lines will be found on the leaves as well as on the stems and pods. These spots may increase in size and eventually sunken brown patches will appear. Later still, these sunken areas will be covered with a thin whitish crust. The trouble is always more serious when the weather is cold and wet.

I have known the cankers on the stems to be so numerous and deep that the plants topple over. It's most distressing, however, to have all the pods ruined with spots.

Control. Give the plants a thorough spraying with one of the proprietary copper washes, or with a Bordeaux mixture, used at half the normal strength.

Some gardeners prefer to spray with liver-of-sulphur using 1 oz. to 4 gallons of water. It is not advisable, however, to spray once the pods are half grown.

Halo Blight. One usually notes an attack because a plant may suddenly wilt. Then when the row is examined, small angular spots will be found on the leaves, stems and pods, surrounded by a lighter coloured halo, hence its name. Very often a milky material will exude from the spots.

Control. Never sow seeds which are wrinkled or blistered, or even have yellow spots on them. Insist on clean seed. Pull up infected plants the moment they are noticed and burn them.

Sow the variety Black Wonder, which seems to be somewhat resistant.

RUNNER BEANS

These are attacked by the same diseases as French beans, though in the case of halo blight the damage is never severe.

CABBAGE

Club Root. For details of this disease and its control please see page 270.

Ring Spot. A disease which I have only found in Wales and in the south and south-west of England. Will attack cabbage, but seems to prefer broccoli. It produces circular brown spots, surrounded by a green border. These may vary in size from a tenth of an inch to half an inch. Look for the trouble on the lower leaves first.

Control. Pick off the lower leaves the moment they are attacked and put them on the compost heap, sprinkling them immediately with a fish fertilizer as an activator. Aim not to grow members of the cabbage family on that piece of ground for three years.

CARROT

Sclerotinia Rot. This is a disease which always attacks the roots in store. It can be very serious in clamps, 'burys' or 'hales'. The roots not only shrink but rot, and the trouble starts near the crown.

CONTROLLING THE DISEASES

Control. Don't store any carrots which are damaged by the fork or by the carrot-fly maggots. Any roots which show infection should be burnt, to prevent the spread of the disease. Don't make too large clamps, and always take care to see that there's efficient ventilation.

CAULIFLOWER

Damping off and Wire Stem. The fungus seems to attack the cauliflower seedlings when they are young and causes the stems to shrivel and look wiry. They are not only brown but brittle and shrunken towards the base.

Control. Water the seed bed before sowing the seed with the mercuric-chloride solution as advised for club root (see page 270). Raise your plants in the John Innes Seed Compost (see Appendix), or Alex No-Soil Compost.

BROCCOLI

Virus. When this trouble occurs, the leaves usually turn yellow and certainly appear mottled. The plants are stunted and poor heads are formed. It's always the aphides which cause this virus to spread and they must be kept down at all costs.

Control. Raise the plants in a bed as far away from other members of the cabbage family as possible. Put infected plants into the middle of the compost heap covered with a suitable activator, such as a fish fertilizer. Do not grow brassicas on the same piece of ground year after year. Spray the cauliflowers with nicotine, formula $\frac{1}{4}$ oz. to $2\frac{1}{2}$-gallon bucket of water, in order to kill the greenfly.

CELERY

Leaf Spot or Blight. A very serious celery disease, and a very common one. I have found it all over Great Britain. It must not, however, be confused with celery-fly (see page 266). The leaves first of all become discoloured and on the blotches will be found black fluted bodies. Look for them with a hand magnifying glass. Gradually the spots increase in size until finally the whole leaf withers away. The attack is usually first seen in July though it may have started a little earlier.

Control. The trouble invariably starts from infected seed and the gardener should always ask his seedsman to supply him with seed which has been treated with Formaldehyde. Some catalogues actually state that this has been done.

CONTROLLING THE DISEASES

In the garden it pays to spray the plants with Bordeaux mixture from the first week of June onwards, say three times at three-weekly intervals. In wet years, however, more applications may be necessary. Some gardeners dip the seedlings in a Bordeaux solution before planting them out.

It's important to grow celery on land which is very rich in fine organic matter and to make certain that the plants never suffer from lack of moisture.

Root Rot. Dark brown or black areas appear on the roots and on the stems just below soil level. In very bad attacks the tops of the plants break off. I have seen the disease in all parts of Great Britain.

Control. It is most important to obtain Formaldehyde-treated seed or seed which is absolutely free from disease. The trouble is undoubtedly seed-borne.

Heart or Soft Rot. The hearts of celery plants go brown and rotten and they are then quite useless. The trouble starts in December as a rule and continues throughout the winter. The bacillus which caused the trouble always get in through wounds made by insects and especially slugs.

Control. Keep down all slugs as advised on page 263. Do not grow celery on the same piece of ground year after year. Remove badly affected plants and burn them. Apply Borax crystals along the rows before planting out at a sixteenth of an ounce to the yard run. Rake this in lightly.

CUCUMBER

Anthracnose. The gardener calls this disease leaf spot. The leaves are are attacked by a fungus which causes pale green or reddish coloured spots to appear. These, when they enlarge and unite, cause the foliage to wither and die. Later on the stems may be attacked and the fruits too.

Control. The disease will live on stable manure and on paper, straw, wood or even cotton wool, if any of these substances are kept moist.

Remove the spotted leaves the moment they are seen and spray the plants with dispersable sulphur. It may be necessary to spray once a week say for a month.

If the plants are being grown in frames, it's well worth while washing down the woodwork in the winter with emulsified cresilic acid.

Canker. A rot will appear on the stem just above or just below soil level. This causes the plants to collapse, an occurrence which takes place when they are starting to fruit.

Control. The trouble is invariably brought about by water being allowed to lie at the base of the plants, therefore never pour water directly on to the stem, and keep the base of the plants as dry as possible. Water around the plants but not actually on them.

Dust the base of the plants with a mixture consisting of 10 parts of dry slaked lime, 3 parts of finely ground copper sulphate, and 3 parts of flowers of sulphur.

Mildew. Greyish spots will appear on the leaves and on the stems. In very bad cases the whole plant may appear covered with a white or mealy substance.

Control. Give the plants a good dusting with a fine sulphur dust the moment the trouble is seen. If the cucumbers are being grown in frames, see that ample ventilation is given.

LEEK

White Tip. A disease which is particularly bad in Scotland and in Worcestershire. The tips of the leaves, as its name suggests, die back and turn white. The margins of the leaves may be twisted. Water-soaked areas may develop towards the base of the plant.

Control. Cut off the tips of the leaves that tend to droop towards the ground, and burn them. Give the plants a good dusting with a copper-lime dust at the rate of 2 oz. to the sq. yd. Continue to dust once a month from, say, the middle of October to the early spring, if this appears necessary.

There is little doubt that the disease is seldom serious where the land has been plentifully enriched with fine organic matter.

Rust. A disease which is bad in the north but may occur in the south and in Wales. Yellowish spots will occur on the leaves, usually scattered, but sometimes arranged in rows. These will turn yellowish-red later.

Control. Remove all the affected leaves and put them on the compost heap, sprinkling them with an activator, such as a fish fertilizer.

Spray the remaining plants with a colloidal copper wash.

Do not plant leeks on the same piece of ground for four years.

LETTUCE

Ring Spot. Brown spots occur on the leaves starting with the outer ones. The attacked portions then drop out and holes are left, surrounded by white margins. Sometimes you get rusty-brown blotches on the undersides of the mid-ribs.

Control. Do not grow lettuce on the same piece of ground year after year. Apply wood ashes to the soil before sowing the seed at ½ lb. to the sq. yd. Do not dig into the soil decaying lettuce leaves which have not been properly composted.

Grey Mould. Gardeners often call this disease 'red leg', because the stem at soil level may be reddish in colour before it rots away. When badly attacked, the plants are covered with the grey mould before they wilt. It's a disease which affects lettuce grown in frames very badly, as well as varieties which are sown to over-winter.

Control. If lettuces are planted out, care must be taken to see that they are never put in too deeply or too shallowly. They should just, so to speak, sit on the soil. No dibble hole should be left at the side of plants.

Use one of the proprietary organo-mercury dusts. Give a fine dusting with a dust gun at monthly intervals from the end of December onwards.

MINT

Rust. This disease is known all over the country. Orange-yellow 'cushions' appear on the leaves and stems of the plants. The shoots will become distorted and abnormally thick, and the leaves will be small. In the winter, dark brown spores are formed.

Control. Put dry straw on the mint bed late in September or early in October, and set light to this. The rapid fire will burn the stems and the disease.

Some gardeners have achieved complete control by cutting down the tops about October 15th, and putting them in the compost heap, covered with a fish fertilizer at 3 oz. to the sq. yd. The beds are then watered thoroughly with a 5 per cent solution of a neutral, high-boiling tar oil wash.

Those who are lifting mint roots for forcing in the greenhouse or frame, give them a thorough washing, preferably under the tap, and certainly in two or three changes of water.

ONION

Downy Mildew. A disease which is bad in wet years and which will attack shallots as well as onions. White or grey mildew appears on the leaves, and these soon turn yellow and collapse. The keeping qualities of the bulbs are impaired because they are often over-run with the mycelium of the fungus, though they may not show any external signs.

Control. Never grow onions on badly drained land. Keep the autumn and spring sown onions as far apart from one another as possible.

Spray the plants with a colloidal copper wash when they are 4 in. high and give two further applications at ten-day intervals.

The varieties Up-to-Date, Rousham Park Hero, and Cranston's Excelsior appear to be fairly resistant.

Smut. A very serious disease indeed and one, in fact, which is scheduled under the Destructive Pests and Diseases Acts. Dark opaque spots or streaks will be seen on the leaves soon after the seedlings come up. The skin covering these dark areas will eventually split, and a black powdery mass will exude. Badly infected plants will die, but others will produce new leaves on which more blisters can appear.

Control. Water the seed drills before sowing the seed with a dilute solution of Formalin. To make this, dissolve 1 part of Formalin in 300 parts of water.

Do not grow onions on the same piece of ground for five years. Pull up the infected plants before the skins crack and the spores are released. Burn these.

White Rot. A disease which is sometimes confused with downy mildew, but actually is quite different. The onion plants will be seen to wilt at the end of May or early June, and the foliage will turn yellow. By the beginning of August the plants are usually dead. The white rot develops at the base of the bulbs and if anybody has any doubt about the cause of the trouble, black bodies like poppy seeds will be found embedded in the white 'roots' of the fungus, right on the base of the bulb. Look for badly shrivelled onions and look for these.

Control. Apply a 4 per cent calomel dust along the rows at 1 oz. to the yard run before sowing or transplanting. This will give a good measure of control, though it isn't 'a dead cert'.

Grow a resistant variety, such as Up-to-Date, Rousham Park Hero, Improved Reading and White Spanish.

Do not grow onions on infected land for eight years.

PARSNIP

Canker. A bad disease in many parts of the country and especially the north. The roots will crack, specially towards the top, and a brown rot appears, and sometimes in bad cases a black wet rot may cause complete destruction.

Some gardeners say that it pays, when the roots are half grown, to sprinkle some dry sand over the tops of the roots.

CONTROLLING THE DISEASES

The writer has found that the varieties Tender and True, and Large Guernsey are fairly resistant.

Peas

Marsh Spot. This is another common trouble, unfortunately, and particularly on the light soils or those which are lacking in humus. When the seeds of the peas are split open, a brown spot is found in the centre of the seed leaves. The seedlings produced from such seeds are always weak and queer looking. Sometimes they are branched at or below ground level.

Control. The trouble is invariably lack of magnesium in the soil, and the answer to those who do not use plenty of compost is to apply magnesium sulphate to the soil at a sixteenth of an oz. to the sq. yd. An alternative method is to dissolve a teaspoonful of magnesium sulphate in two gallons of water, and water this carefully over 10 sq. yds.

Well made powdery compost contains all the magnesium needed.

Potato

Blight. A disease which may cause trouble all over the country. The leaves are attacked first when irregular dark green blotches are seen. These may turn browny-black and soon will become covered with a delicate white mould. In the south and west the disease often starts in June, and it gradually spreads throughout the country until it reaches the north in August.

The disease is particularly bad in damp muggy weather, and under such conditions all the haulm of the potatoes may be killed. The disease spores fall to the ground and then attack the tubers. These develop sunken areas on the skin, and finally a rotting takes place. Affected tubers will not keep.

Control. Start spraying late in June in the south of England, but not till mid-July in the Midlands, and as late as the end of July in the north and in Scotland. Give a second spraying three weeks later in each case, and third sprayings yet another three weeks after that in damp seasons. Use for the purpose either a proprietary copper fungicide or Bordeaux mixture. In smoky districts near towns, a Burgundy mixture should be used instead.

The alternative is to dust the plants with a copper-lime dust once a fortnight from the time that the trouble may appear. The idea in all cases is to try and prevent the disease attacking and not to cure it only.

If a bad attack should occur, then it's advisable to cut the tops off to soil level before they start to die down, and this will prevent the spores of the blight from falling on to the tubers when they are being lifted.

Common Scab. Brown scabs appear on the skins of the potatoes. These make the tubers very unsightly and, of course, there's far more waste in cleaning. The attacks are particularly severe in dry season and on soils which are deficient in humus. The disease is also particularly virulent where lime has been used, or where the soil is alkaline. I have known scab to cause the 'eyes' of the potatoes to go blind, and thus they are useless for planting.

Control. Always use plenty of fresh grass mowings in the drills at planting time. Never apply lime, ashes or soot to land intended for potatoes.

Be very generous with organic matter. One can use composted vegetable refuse at the rate of one barrowload to 4 sq. yds., with great effect.

If the seed tubers appear to be scabby at planting time, dip them in flowers of sulphur first.

Virus. There are a number of virus diseases which may affect potatoes. Sometimes these cause the leaves to be mottled and yellow, other times the foliage is crinkled with perhaps yellow blotches, and very often the tops of the potatoes are stunted. In the south and south-east of England there is a virus which causes dots and streaks on the undersides of the leaves which in July turn dead. Eventually the leaves die and yet remain hanging on the main stems.

Control. Buy certified Scottish or Northern Ireland seed.

Never buy seed which has been saved locally.

Virus diseases are undoubtedly spread by aphides.

Dry Rot. First of all the skin of the potato turns brown and the trouble usually arises from a bruise, or even a little cut. A few weeks later the areas will become sunken and even corrugated, while the flesh of the potato will shrink. Concentric rings of the disease will be seen.

I have found that some potatoes seem more susceptible than others. Arran Pilot, for instance, Majestic and Doon Star.

Control. Don't throw potatoes about and bruise them. Always handle them carefully. Sprout the seed potatoes early. Dust the tubers at the time they are lifted with Fusarex 6 at the rate of 1 lb. per 4 lb. of potatoes. Fusarex will also prevent sprout growth.

Wart Disease. A very serious, but fortunately somewhat rare disease these days, because it is possible to plant immune varieties. The trouble first occurs around the eyes of the tubers, where warts appear, and these grow until the tubers are covered by a browny-black spongy mass.

Control. There is no method of control. The answer is to grow immune varieties and all good seedsmen's catalogues show which these are.

RHUBARB

Crown Rot. The bases of the stems become swollen and distorted. The leaves turn a 'puce' colour. The crowns of the plant usually go soft and rot. The terminal buds are usually destroyed. Spindly, useless shoots appear.

Control. Take care to puchase plants which show no sign of rot at all, especially around the crown.

Remove all infected plants and burn them, together with any refuse around.

SEAKALE

Black Rot. A trouble which usually occurs where the soil is badly drained. Black streaks appear on the roots first of all; finally these turn black and rot away completely.

Control. Drain the soil properly and be sure to double dig the land so that the subsoil is broken up.

Do not plant thongs which show black streaks in the cut tissue.

SPINACH

Downy Mildew. A disease which I have found all over Great Britain. The leaves are often covered with yellow spots and this is followed by a violet-grey mould which appears on the undersides of the leaves first of all, and then seems to creep on to the upper sides as well.

Control. As moist conditions favour the disease, drainage is important. Dust the plants the moment the trouble is first seen with a reliable sulphur-dust. Use an efficient dust gun for the purpose.

TOMATO

Blight. This is the same as the potato-blight disease for which please see page 279. Unfortunately, the trouble is far more serious on tomatoes than on potatoes.

Control. Spray the plants once a fortnight from early August to the end of September in the Midlands and north, but start spraying early in July in the south and south-west. Use Bordeaux mixture or one of the proprietary copper-base washes. Some people prefer a colloidal copper preparation.

Canker or Didymella. The trouble occurs on the main stem, generally near the base of the plants where the tissues seem to dry up and crack. I've usually seen it first when the plants are 4 in. high. Plants may die without any external symptoms, but when they are cut across a brown stain will be found in the stem. The fruits when affected show sunken patches.

Control. Remove and compost the affected plants, sprinkling them with a fish fertilizer activator. Water the spot with Sterizal, dissolving a pint of this in 100 pints of water, and *pro rata.*

Spray the stems of the plants with salicylanlide in accordance with the instructions on the container. This prevents the spread of the disease from one plant to another. Give the plants a watering with Cheshunt compound.

Stripe. The stems are seen to have brown, longitudinal stripes on them. The leaves may be mottled, and they will finally shrivel. Dark brown blotches will appear on the formed fruit.

Control. Apply wood ashes to the ground at $\frac{1}{2}$ lb. to the sq. yd. before planting, or those who don't mind using inorganics may apply sulphate of potash at 2 oz. to the sq. yd.

Trim off the affected leaves with the sharp blade of a knife, which must be disinfected first, and afterwards, in a 2 per cent of Formaldehyde. This prevents the virus being transferred to other plants.

Buck-Eye Rot. Discoloured patches appear on the tomatoes forming on the bottom trusses. These usually take the form of concentric rings which start at the blossom'end of the fruit as a rule. These 'rings' may be grey or brown.

Control. The disease is undoubtedly soil-borne and splashing, therefore, should always be avoided when watering. It pays, therefore, to mulch the ground all round the plants to the depth of an inch with sedge peat.

Do not allow the trusses of fruit to touch the soil, but loop these up with raffia, tied to a bamboo or stake.

Try spraying the soil and the lower parts of the plants with Cheshunt compound, which can be bought ready to dissolve in water from the chemist.

VEGETABLE MARROW

Mildew. First of all the leaves and then the stems become covered with what looks like a white powder. In bad cases the plants may wither and the fruiting period will be curtailed. The trouble is always worse when the soil is dry. Watering the plants well will therefore prevent this trouble.

Control. Give plenty of water.

Spray the plants in bad cases with liver of sulphur, using 1 oz. to three gallons of soft water, or dust with a fine sulphur dust early in the morning.

A VEGETABLE USED AS A FRUIT

RHUBARB

(As this is not strictly a vegetable crop it appears here.) This is extremely easy to grow. It stays 'put' for a large number of years in the same spot.

Soils and Manuring

Any soil will do. Manure the land heavily to start with. After that cover the bed with straw 1 foot deep and give a fish fertilizer at 3 oz. to the square yard each May and September. Apply this over the straw. Add more straw each December as necessary.

Planting

Buy good crowns and plant the late autumn in rows 4 foot apart, giving 3 feet between the plants. Plant firmly.

Growing Tips

Don't let the plants seed. Cover some roots up in December with upturned pots or boxes for earlier results.

Harvesting and using

Pull as desired—but don't overdo at any time.

Varieties

Timperley Early—the earliest.
Hawkes Champagne—the most delicious.
The Sutton—does not seed.

Appendix

John Innes Composts

These composts can now usually be purchased ready and correctly made up from nurserymen, but for those who wish to make up their own, the composition is as follows:

Seed Compost

This consists of 2 parts by bulk medium loam.

                    1 part by bulk sedge peat.

                    1 part by bulk coarse sand.

Add for each bushel of the above mixture, by mixing with the sand, $\frac{3}{4}$ oz. ground chalk or limestone and $1\frac{1}{2}$ oz. of superphosphate.

Potting Compost

This consists of 7 parts by bulk of medium loam.

                    3 parts by bulk of sedge peat.

                    2 parts by bulk of coarse sand.

Add for each bushel of the above mixture, by mixing with the sand, $\frac{3}{4}$ oz. ground chalk or limestone, $1\frac{1}{2}$ oz. Hoof and Horn ($\frac{1}{8}$ grist), $1\frac{1}{2}$ oz. superphosphate, and $\frac{3}{4}$ oz. of sulphate of potash.

In the correct composts the loam should be sterilized, but even with unsterilized loam the composts should be fairly satisfactory for most purposes.

No-Soil Composts

These have largely taken the place of John Innes Composts. They are bought 'ready made' and in each bag there is a sachet containing the exact plant foods that must be added. No-Soil composts are ideal for amateurs as there is no soil sterilization to be done.

Index

INDEX

INDEX

INDEX